I0672021

BEDDED BLISS

FOUND IN OBLIVION BOOK 1

CARI QUINN

TARYN ELLIOTT

Bedded Bliss
© 2016 Cari Quinn & Taryn Elliott
Rainbow Rage Publishing
978-1-940346-57-1

Cover by LateNite Designs
Photograph by Sara Eirew

First print edition: March 2019

ACKNOWLEDGMENTS

WORD WENCHES SHOUTOUT!

We love the girls in our reader group. We had a naming game for Lila & Nick Crandall's twins.

Congrats to Jennifer Beck Miller & Jeannie Huffman for coming up with **Charlotte**, *aka Charlie*. As well as Shyla R. Wright for her offering, **Avery**.

Pretty names for two of the prettiest girls to come out of fiction. Nick's already ordered their chastity belts.

FYI: *Sometimes we make up fictional places that end up having the same names as actual places. These are our fictional interpretations only. Please grant us leeway if our creative vision isn't true to reality.*

For all foolish moments that turn into wonderful pockets of forever.

Dedicating this one yet again to Michael Hutchence of INXS, as we did Seduced in our Lost in Oblivion series. To Cari, he was pretty much the epitome of a rockstar, and INXS's Wembley 1991 concert was in heavy rotation while we were writing Bedded Bliss. He'll never be forgotten (nor will the word "f$%king" said in that delicious accent of his.)

ONE

"Your Tabby has missed you. Don't you want to pet my pussy?"

Michael Shawcross rolled over in bed and flung out an arm. Instead of colliding with the mattress as it usually did, he hit soft, warm flesh.

A second later, wetness glided down his belly, stopping just above the sheet tangled around his torso. He shifted his hips against the bed, his body straining toward the slick line of liquid without thought.

"That's it, baby. Whatcha hiding under this sheet? Is he excited to see me too?"

Even still half asleep, he frowned. What the hell? It felt like someone was licking him. Pouring more liquid on his stomach, low, lower, lowest, then dragging down the sheet to where he was popping up like a damn sailor saluting his country.

Then his eyes popped open to match, and he groaned. And it wasn't because a gorgeous brunette was currently a deep breath away from sucking his cock.

"Dammit, Tabitha, how did you get in here?"

"That's how you greet an old friend?" She sighed and sat up, gripping the bottle of champagne in one hand and the towel precariously wrapped around her body with the other. Catching his glance at her obviously wet and dripping legs, she let the towel fall down

1

a bit more and smiled. "I had to wash the travel dirt off me, didn't I? It's been so long since we've seen each other, and I didn't think you'd mind if I borrowed a little water from your shower." She crawled up the bed toward him, her expression feral. "Don't worry, I have some wetness to give back."

He groaned again, and this time it wasn't entirely because the sexy witch had broken into his apartment or tried to give him a sponge bath using bubbly and her tongue.

Some stupid, ridiculous part of him just wanted to tell the world to fuck off so he could enjoy himself. She was obviously more than willing, and from the feel of things, Michael Junior didn't have the same morals as his owner.

So what if she was engaged to a senator? Sure, it was absolutely wrong on a million levels to get involved in a situation like that, and he'd told her in every variation of English that he could think of that he wasn't about to go there. Problem was, he already had, sort of, and she wouldn't let him forget it.

She wasn't the only one. Their names—along with Senator Dinkles's —were on TV and in the rags constantly lately. Then there was the elevator footage from the Squire Hotel in LA, which just happened to include him nudging her in such a way that made it appear as if he was urging her to the floor. Oh yeah, and oops, her hand was on his zipper…

No one seemed to care he hadn't even known who she was when she'd approached him that night after the concert. It hadn't been the first time. She'd gone to full-on groupie status even before that fateful evening. He'd engaged in friendly and furtive gropefests with her at a couple of meet-and-greets, because, surprise, she always seemed to have backstage passes no matter where they were. He hadn't questioned it. Even at his level of fame—which granted him a label of rising star at best and nobody at worst, depending on the day of the week—he had girls throwing themselves at him. Hell, some guys too.

He hadn't been part of a successful band for long. They were still suffering from growing pains. For some reason, they just couldn't get their lineup to gel. Members had come and gone, and Ryan had tried to fill in wherever he could, but Jesus, they needed a real drummer, someone who could kill it like Matt Sorum or Dave Grohl. So he wasn't that used to anyone seeing them as a legit entity, mainly because they didn't quite see themselves that way yet. Even with all the shows they were doing, and the EP they'd cut that had done better than expected on the Hot 100, Warning Sign was definitely still suffering from poser syndrome.

And hot, willing, adoring groupies? Well, they eased the pain.

Not that he'd gotten to enjoy *that* many of them, despite recent public theorizing otherwise. He was too worried about being a good guy. Too concerned about not being like his dad and leaving behind a trail of broken hearts—or like his mom and leaving behind a trail of broken marriages, and engagements, and embarrassing legal battles.

Tabitha was actually one of the first women he'd connected with a few times on their mini tour of the West Coast. The rest had been faceless, momentary thrills. Amazing, but brief. He'd also usually been too drunk to remember names the next day.

According to Lila Crandall, his manager—and former stepmother —he had a problem.

With the drinking and the girls? Nah. He was just having fun. No one was getting hurt, so what was the big deal?

Now there was Tabitha, who was pouring more champagne on his abs, and licking it up while her big brown eyes made love to his.

"You can't do this." His voice sounded faint, even to him.

He wasn't drunk or hungover, but he was horny. He was also a twenty-three-year-old male. Fuck, it got so tiring being the morality police all the time. That was exactly why he'd started letting loose a few months ago. He'd always been sheltered from the real world, locked away in the ivory tower created by his father's money and his mother's endless carousel of crappy relationships. When he hadn't been forcibly rejecting their bad examples, he'd been sequestered playing his guitar.

Was it any wonder he'd gone a little nuts when he'd first tasted freedom and success of his own? But he could rein it in at any time.

That meant telling Tabby sayonara. Again. This time he'd have to convince her that she was murdering both of their reputations, and he damn sure wasn't going to have sex with her anyway, so she might as well not bother.

With his background, there was no way he'd be a homewrecker or a cheater, even by proxy. Helping someone else cheat wasn't any better. If she wanted to leave her relationship, fine. Instead, she wanted her piece of "rockstar cake," as she'd once called him, while she married a senator.

Fuck that. He wasn't anyone's cake. He also needed to actually speak up and get her back into her clothes before she started eating him without benefit of a fork.

"You need to go," he managed as she dripped a few drops of champagne around his nipple and let out a husky laugh. "I'm not kidding, Tabitha. I don't know how you got in here, but it's breaking and entering. I was asleep, goddammit."

"Aw, sugar, I hate when you throw around accusations. Especially when we both know you gave me this key," she lifted a long necklace hidden by her towel, "a couple weeks ago and told me to use it. Actually, you begged me." She circled her bright pink fingernail around the sensitive peak she'd just drizzled with bubbly and he barely restrained a hiss. "You said how you get so lonely out on the road. That you hate sleeping alone on the bus but it would make you feel so much better to have a girl waiting for you in your bed. One who would keep the home fires burning." She let go of the key and reached for the knot in her towel. The terrycloth parted and her luscious body came into full, glorious view. And fuck it all, his balls clenched. "Wanna see how warm I can get for you?"

It was just a line, and a cheesy one at that. Christ, he didn't remember telling her any of that, but she had a key. She was in the apartment. He *did* get lonely on the road, especially on the nights when his bandmates had company and he didn't. Besides, sex wasn't enough. Sure, it filled the hole now and then, but he was just as hungry a couple of hours later.

The worst part was he didn't know what he wanted. He loved sex, and he had friends. He even had friends he'd had sex with, which should have been the best of both worlds. But it just wasn't. And now Lila wanted him to stop doing even that.

Not his bandmates. They had it all under control, according to her.

4

He was the tabloid bait. The one who was getting known for all the wrong reasons.

The one who had a gorgeous girl in his bed he couldn't fuck because he was thinking about his stepmom being displeased with his choices, and wasn't that frigging rich?

"I must've been drunk." He swallowed hard, allowing himself only the briefest glance at Tabitha's perfectly rounded tits and large brown nipples before he met her gaze. "I don't remember telling you any of that. I definitely don't remember giving you a key. I wouldn't have done that if I'd been in my right mind. The last thing I want is for you to—"

"To what? Get the wrong idea? To think that maybe you want me to climb on top of you and ride this big dick until we both come our brains out?"

The fact that she was practically screaming those questions near his ear in her raspy voice should've turned down the arousal factor. Instead, his cock was starting to throb. Of course the soft, warm breast pushing into his upper arm wasn't helping matters.

Jesus.

"You're almost married." He pushed himself up to a sitting position and twitched the sheet back over his jutting erection. "You shouldn't be here. Did anyone see you come in?" He shoved a hand through his spiky hair and shut his eyes at the sticky shit he couldn't move his fingers through. Damn gel. He'd meant to take a shower when he came in last night, but nope, he'd collapsed on the bed facedown and hadn't moved until morning.

He glanced at the clock on the bedside. Make that afternoon. Past two. Shit, he had rehearsal today, and they were supposed to be taking off for Vegas first thing tomorrow.

His head hurt like a bitch, too. Tension headache. Band tension, Tabitha tension, Lila tension—God, who even knew which was causing most of the pressure that had descended on his life all of a sudden?

It was all too much too fast, when this was everything he'd ever wanted.

Minus Tabitha shooting death rays at him while he tried to remember in which room he'd dropped his pants.

"You don't need to worry about my marriage. I'm not looking for a counselor."

"No, you want a sugar daddy on the side, to go with the one who gave you that ring." He inclined his chin at the huge honking rock on her left hand. A sapphire surrounded by diamonds.

His dad had given his mother a sapphire engagement ring. If that didn't prove they were bad omens, then nothing did.

She snatched back her hand. "Oh, and is that supposed to be you? You're a struggling artist. You can barely take care of yourself, never mind me." She rolled her eyes and threw out a hand to encompass his master suite. "Look at this place."

He glanced from the snowy white linens on the California king-size bed to the heavy Queen Anne-style furniture that dominated the room. The French doors led to a balcony that gave a gorgeous view of the ocean in the distance. The apartment wasn't quite up to penthouse-level, but considering rents in the area, he was doing okay.

And fuck it all, it was *his*. Paid for on his dime, not his father's. He was no longer a kept son, meant to sit down and shut up. Most of all, he'd been expected to pretend he agreed with everything his dictator of a dad had to say. He was making his own way now.

That also meant he didn't have to prove himself to anyone. If Tabitha thought his standards were below her, well, then that was just fine, since he doubted they could even be friendly after this mess.

"Yes, look at it. To you, it may not be much. Senator's wife-to-be and all. To me, it's everything. I got here on my own, and I'm going to continue to build." He threw his legs over the side of the bed and grabbed the sheet, wrapping it around himself.

She spluttered, apparently not liking being left sheet-less, although she'd been so damn intent on getting naked. "You're going to regret tossing me out. I don't give second chances."

Michael crossed his arms over his chest. The champagne was still drying on his skin. "Yeah, well, let's hope your fiancé does, after you've dragged his name through the dirt with all your chasing after me and God knows who else."

She had the decency to direct her gaze at her left hand, now clutching her towel—*his* towel—to her chest. "Is it so hard to believe I thought we had a connection?"

"Even if we did, what kind of guy would I be to get with you while you're hooked up with another man? You know what they say—how she did the last guy is how she'll do you next time."

"You know what? Forget it. If you want to pretend you're no longer into me, that's fine. I don't have to beg for scraps." She rose from the bed, still holding the champagne bottle. At least she'd brought that, since he rarely drank the stuff and definitely didn't stock it. "You'll regret treating me so harshly the next time you're on that bus and wishing you weren't all by your miserable self." She yanked off the key necklace around her neck and tossed it in the middle of his bed before flouncing out the door.

A moment later, he heard the front door slam in her wake.

He rubbed his forehead and stumbled into the bathroom. Yep, he looked as bad as he thought. He needed a piss, a shave and a shower, in that order.

His cell buzzed before he'd completed the second thing.

Heaving out a breath, he headed back into the bedroom and grabbed his phone off the nightstand. Ryan Waters, his favorite bandmate. Most of the time he was his favorite, anyway. When he wasn't pissing Michael off by being so damn together all the time.

Fuck, was he late for rehearsal? He was almost sure it wasn't until five. They'd be up late anyway, so no one wanted to start working early.

Except Ry. That guy made the early bird look like a slacker for not pulling an all-nighter.

"What's up? You mad at me because I didn't camp out in the rehearsal hall?" Michael asked, returning to the bathroom. Maybe he could finish his freaking shave. The halfway scruffy look wasn't doing him any favors.

He'd just picked up his straight razor—he was all about the old school when it came to shaving—when Ryan's desolate voice came over the line.

"Dude, I'm out. I can't play."

"What do you mean you can't play?" Michael gripped his razor so hard the handle trembled in his hand. "We have Vegas tomorrow night. Our biggest fucking show."

"I sprained my hand. I'm out. Doc says I won't be able to play the drums for weeks, depending how I heal."

Michael couldn't breathe. He couldn't think. "What the hell happened?"

"That doesn't matter right now. Man, we're fucked."

TWO

Fucked in every way but the one that included an orgasm. Yeah, that about summed it up.

"I went biking, you know, down at Shelby Ridge? Those crazy paths up through the woods, and when I came down—" Ryan broke off.

"When you jumped down, you mean. With your bike. Because you're a crazy motherfucker."

His best friend cleared his throat. "Correct on all counts."

Michael tried to relax the tension in his spine. It had been an accident. Stuff happened. He couldn't say Ryan hadn't granted him the same courtesy after his own numerous fuckups.

They'd been friends since the first day of college at Caltech, when they'd found themselves in the same engineering seminar and wondering why they'd thought that was the right career path when all they wanted to do was play music.

Michael knew why he'd been there, of course. Controlling, overbearing father, need to please, yadda yadda, pass the therapy bill. Next.

Ryan, though, had been battling his own concerns that music wasn't a viable choice. His family had a business repairing instruments, and he'd always had a skill with them, but he'd fallen into the "I should be doing something more" trap. Especially since he had a genius-level ability with math and science, which actually explained some of his ability to play just about any instrument, since math and music were way more linked than most people realized.

It had taken them a few miserable, drunken months to realize that nothing mattered more than music and friendship and family, and making something out of all three. They were still trying, still finding their way, but they'd come far from those usually hungover, often philosophizing jerks they'd once been.

That didn't mean he wouldn't kick Ryan's ass for screwing up the best opportunity they'd had yet to make their mark.

"I get that biking is a release for you. I get you're a thrill seeker. But did you really have to do that shit right before the biggest show we've ever done?"

"I know, man, I know." Ryan's voice lowered. "I was going to call Lila, but I figured maybe you could? Since you have the in."

Michael dropped his razor and hung his shoulders, laughing at the absurdity of his life. It was either that or get rip-roaring drunk, and he wasn't about to do that before rehearsal. He had standards, dammit. "Not sure you've noticed, but Lila isn't too thrilled with me lately."

"Because you've been on hardcore pussy patrol."

"I wouldn't say that, necessarily."

"Uh, Tabitha Tremaine? Does that name ring a bell?

"One girl is not hardcore pussy, hate to tell you, bro. If it is for you, then maybe you need to up your game."

"My game is on point. And all the rules go out the window when you're banging a senator's girlfriend and it's all over the news. You can't even say the band's name without someone mentioning how Senator Dickless wants to take you out."

Michael snorted. "Right. I'm a real threat to a guy like that. Old money, powerful, can have any woman he wants—"

"Except his fiancée, who is hung up on you."

Michael put his phone on speaker, set it down on the counter and picked up his razor. "That's over."

"Uh-huh. Sure it is. Just like you're going to quit partying. Isn't that what you told Lila last week?"

"I didn't say I was going to quit partying. I just said I could if I wanted to."

Ryan chuckled. "Right. You're going to give up gorgeous Tabitha who'll spread them for you anytime anywhere, and you're going to stop drinking and having fun when you've finally got something to celebrate. Absolutely. Gonna happen."

Michael nearly told Ry that he hadn't had sex with Tabitha, then decided there was no point. Whatever he said, people believed what they wanted. Lila sure was. And she was just going to love this latest piece of crap news.

News *he* had to deliver. *Thanks, bro.*

"Maybe I want something more. That ever occur to you? Partying gets old after a while."

"It sure does, but you were definitely feeling no pain when you were up on that bar, dirty dancing with Juliet the other night. You're damn lucky Lila wasn't there, or else you'd have gotten the "no band fraternizing" lecture she likes to throw around, though she knows no one gives a shit. I think she was a principal in a former life or something."

Michael had to laugh. "She's managed a lot of groups. She knows what causes strife within a band. She should, since Oblivion nearly imploded because of that."

"Yeah, and then she married one of the members of Oblivion. It's not like she can talk."

"Truth. Just saying, she doesn't want to see us do anything stupid. Jules and I were just messing around. Just dancing," he amended, because Ry would take the "messing around" thing and run with it right into a bedroom. "She's a fun girl. But not for me."

"You have fun with a lot of girls, which, you know, good for you, dude. We're all enjoying our trip on the banging bus. Just saying that you can't really claim you could clean it up in a second and get on the straight and narrow because, sorry, I don't believe you. Neither does anyone with eyes and ears who's seen one of the rags or heard a story on one of those tabloid news shows."

"Can we discuss something other than my dick for five seconds? Any more talk about it and I'll think you want a ride yourself."

"In your dreams, pal. So Lila? You gonna talk to her for me?"

Michael did a half-assed job finishing his shave before rinsing off and patting his face down with a towel. "How long did the doc say you were out?"

"Depends. At least through this leg, probably, as far as drumming goes. It's just too much strain on my wrist. I can come back in a support role onstage though."

Michael took the phone off speaker and held it to his ear. "A support role. You mean playing some of those crazy instruments you love? Fucking xylophone or some shit?"

"Can do a xylophone one-handed if need be. You'd be surprised at the richness it can add to a song. Imagine how it'd sound at the end of 'Tenacity'?"

Michael snorted. "Right. Look, I'll call Lila, but she's going to want to talk to you. So you're only putting off the inevitable."

"Thanks, man. You're the best. Good luck. Catch ya later."

Michael stared at the dead phone and tossed it on the counter. It was just a symbolic gesture, because less than a minute later, he'd pressed his speed dial to call Lila.

No use putting off misery. Might as well start the recovery process as soon as possible.

"Michael. Are you hungover again? That's not an acceptable way to show up at rehearsal, especially not today."

"What? No." He pinched the bridge of his nose. Jesus, was he really that bad or were the people in his life just excessively particular?

"Just checking."

"I've only shown up to rehearsal hungover twice." He pinched a little harder. "Okay, maybe three times, but opening for The Slayers? C'mon. That's as good as it gets. Of course I was going to get loaded."

"Right, and playing at the House of Blues tomorrow night is your biggest gig ever, even bigger than The Slayers. Logic dictates you probably trashed a hotel room last night."

"Why would I get a hotel room when my apartment is nearby?"

"You tell me. Also something you've done before. Remember that Quincy girl? Diana, was it? Cost Ripper Records ten grand to bail you out of that mess, and that's not even talking about PR."

"I'm not fucking drunk, okay? I'm not with some random chick, and I'm not in a hotel room, trashed or otherwise." He brought his fist down hard against the counter. Pain sang up his arm, but not enough to cause any real damage when he had to play the next night. Despite what everyone seemingly believed, he wasn't some colossal screwup. "Christ, can't anyone just give me a little space?"

"Sure. I can give you all the space you need when I stop caring about you. Except you're the closest thing to a son I have, so——"

"You have your own kids now, ones who actually belong to you. Stop using me as a substitute, all right? It's not necessary anymore. I'm a goddamn grown man."

The silence that came over the line made him clench his throbbing fingers. "Li, I'm sorry. You know I don't mean that. I know you mean well."

"I'm overstepping." Lila's voice sounded stiff. "I get it. Sometimes it's easy for the roles to get blurry between stepmother and manager, and I'm as guilty as anyone of losing focus. But let's get clear about one thing. As far as I'm concerned, you're my son. You were my son the day Martin introduced you and Mal to me, and you'll be my son when you're seventy-five and in the nursing home. Biology doesn't make a family. Love does. Call me back when you remember that."

For the second time in as many minutes, a line went dead in his ear. Except this time, he deserved it.

He pressed his fingers into his eyes. The day had already been a shitstorm and he hadn't even gotten on his pants yet.

A shower. He needed a freaking shower, and maybe to jerk off until he didn't remember Tabitha or Senator Dickless or anyone else.

He stripped off his sheet and got into the stall, then turned the spray to cold. He needed a good slap in the face, so until he got coffee, this would do.

Tipping back his head, he let the icy needles of water drive away the voices in his mind. Tabitha. Ryan. Lila. Especially Lila. He hated hurting her, but what she'd said had struck too close to home on the heels of Ryan's comments.

Because he had it under control. He was done being that guy. Besides, it wasn't like he'd done anything he couldn't take back.

Yet.

He ducked under the showerhead and let the spray beat on the back of his neck. It helped pulse away some of the pressure there, but grabbing his dick would take care of the rest.

Fumbling for the liquid soap, he squirted some into his hand. He did a cursory pass of the important parts, then lubed himself up in short, fast strokes. He was in no mood to take the time to build. This would have to be quick.

He squeezed his fingers, pumping, letting out a hiss as his flesh swelled in his grip. Harder and harder, he worked himself, bracing his forehead on the arm he pressed against the damp wall of the shower. His balls drew up, tighter than his hold on his cock. Just another minute more—

Dimly, he heard his front door buzzer. Probably Jehovah's Witnesses or girls selling cookies. Who the hell cared?

He was close. So damn close.

Another buzz, longer than the last. Someone was leaning on the damn thing.

They'll go away.

Except they didn't. The buzzes might as well have been someone slamming the hi-hats.

Clang, clang, you're not gonna get to come, so might as well stop prolonging the torture.

Cursing, he turned off the water and yanked open the shower door. He pulled a towel off the rack and swished it around his waist.

"Someone better be fucking dead," he muttered, slicking a hand down his dripping face and over his sopping hair.

He padded barefoot to the door, not caring that he was leaving a path of wet footprints across the floor. Probably yet another sign that he was out of control.

Shit, he was a hotel trasher, a pussy partaker, and practically an alcoholic, if his family and friends could be believed. What were a few damp spots?

Once he reached the panel beside the door, he pressed the button for the lobby. "Yes? Who is it?"

If the person had gone, he was probably going to throw something. It didn't count as trashing a place if he owned it.

Hell, it probably did.

"Mike, it's me. Let me up."

Michael frowned. Only one person called him Mike and didn't get a double barrel of snark in return. He'd always been Michael, since his days as a pretentious kid who hated nicknames. "Mal?"

"Yeah." The response was gruff, as most things were from his brother. "C'mon, buzz me in. Pretty sure they think I'm trying to break into the place."

In spite of everything, Michael laughed and released the door.

A minute later, he turned the knob and found Malachi standing on the other side of the threshold. Huge, hulking, tattooed, bald. His opposite in every way.

"Long time no see, little brother."

THREE

Malachi Shawcross, his older brother. In the flesh.

Giant flesh, but good goddamn.

"Mal," Michael managed before he was swept up into a massive bear hug. He didn't have much choice but to return it, or risk losing lung function.

Sweet hell, Malachi was one big motherfucker. Shit, it was great to see him.

Long time no see was an understatement. He hadn't been this physically close to his brother in a year or two, though they lived in the same frigging state.

Born eleven months apart, they'd gone from being best friends to practically enemies after their parents had divorced. Malachi had sided with their mother, and Michael had been closer to his father. He also hadn't had such a hard time accepting Lila in their lives. Malachi had blamed Lila for the breakup while Michael had taken it much more in stride. Somehow he'd known even at that young age that Lila wouldn't have been able to come between two people who were truly in love. His parents had fought all the time, and once they were apart, things got better. Life calmed down, minus the fact that his older brother had started pulling away.

Lila had been a fun stepmom, always taking him to cool places like the zoo and her parents' orchard back in New York. Through his dad's marriage to her, Michael had gained another parent, one who wasn't out mainly for her own interests.

And he'd repaid her for all those awesome years by making her feel bad. Yeah, he was winning all kinds of awards today.

Now his estranged brother was standing in front of him, and he'd be damned if he screwed this up too.

Maybe this would be the one thing that actually went right in a so far completely shitty day.

"Everything okay?" Michael asked as Malachi stepped back. "You okay, man?"

"Yeah, yeah, everything's fine. Me, Ma. We're both fine." The smallest glimmer of a smile twisted his mouth and disappeared just as fast. "Well, she's not fine, but she's healthy."

"Aw, Christ, now what?"

When Malachi clenched his jaw, Michael held up a hand and paced over to the wall of windows. His balcony extended the length of the apartment, and he opened one of the French doors to get some air. A lot of air.

"Okay, lay it on me."

Malachi dipped his hands in the pockets of his jeans. They were so worn that patches of skin showed through. The slashes weren't for fashion though. Mal didn't believe in such things. He just happened to be a millionaire who wore his clothes until they were rags.

Mal pulled out a folded piece of paper and walked over to join him by the French doors. Wordlessly, he pushed it into Michael's hand.

Michael opened the fancy card stock and read the first few lines. That was all he needed to shove the invitation back at his brother. "I'm not going."

"I figured you'd say that."

"Are you?"

Mal stared out the open door. "She's our mother. What the fuck can I do?"

Michael's gaze followed his brother's to the shimmer of ocean in the distance, crystal blue with a scatter of pinprick diamonds on top. Light bounced off the high-rises across the street, reflected off dozens of panes of glass. But the million-dollar view didn't occupy all of his attention. Nope, he was too fixated on how someone could take the institution of marriage so fucking lightly.

"Five times. Five goddamn times, Mal. How can we continue to support her? She's clearly lost her damn mind."

Mal crumpled the invitation in his giant fist. And said nothing.

He'd worked on cars before he could race them, then he'd turned to the illegal side of things. Michael's mother had turned her back on what Mal was up to, both the crowd he was running with and the unlawful betting and racing he was doing, but Michael hadn't been able to. That had been yet another bone of contention between them, and had driven one more wedge. Eventually, there had been too many to count them all.

They'd stopped talking to each other shortly after Mal's high school graduation. He'd moved out practically the second he turned eighteen, and in the years since, they'd rarely spoken. They had conversations now and then at family events and on holidays, along with the even more occasional text. Michael had come to terms with the fact he'd lost the older brother he'd once idolized, just as he'd dealt with the fact his parents were both batshit crazy.

But now with Mal standing beside him, looking both so fucking familiar and so different that his teeth ached, Michael realized he hadn't dealt with shit.

"Christ, you came over here for some reason. Say something, why don't you?"

"What do you expect me to say? That you were right all along?" Mal flexed his fingers around the balled-up piece of paper. "Neither of them gives a crap about us."

"What was your first clue?" Michael asked, regretting the sarcastic question as soon as it was out. He pushed a hand through his damp hair. "Look, I'm not mad at you. I'm mad at them. Both of them put way too much on our shoulders when we should've been focused on our own stuff. Their love lives are some fucked-up BS, man."

"Dad having another baby, and another on the way. Jesus, the first is barely a year old."

Michael blinked. "Say what?"

"Oh, yeah." Mal let out a dry laugh. "Didn't hear that tidbit? Guy should be getting ready to plan his upcoming retirement and instead he's having newborns."

"I haven't seen Dad since the band signed with Ripper." Michael gripped a handful of his own hair. "Guess that's a good thing."

"Ripper. Ah yeah, about that. Congratulations." Mal cleared his throat. "You guys have been doing good. Or it seems that way, from what I've seen."

"Thanks." Mal had texted him a few congrats along the way after different milestones, usually when Michael had clued him in to the latest. But hearing him say it in person, unprompted, was different—and nice. "You've seen stuff about us?"

"Here and there. Can't say I really keep up with the magazines or TV, but I catch what I can."

Classic Mal there. He cared about pop culture not at all. Celebrities? Fuck that shit. Even if the celebrity was his little brother.

Hell, at times that would've been an even bigger deterrent.

"What have you been up to?" Michael asked.

"Workin' on cars. What else do I do? Not a flashy type like you or Dad. Or fuck, like Mom, for that matter." Mal rubbed a hand over his gleaming bald head and shoved the invitation into his back pocket with the other. "Some of us aren't meant for the limelight."

"Says who? You were the one who got me into playing."

Mal raised a brow. "You call the messing around we used to do playing? We were worse than a garage band. More like a basement outfit."

"Yeah, and what we were is what led to me hooking up with Ryan and West when you weren't into it anymore."

"You always wanted more. Music's in your blood." The corner of Mal's mouth lifted. "Only thing Dad gave us worth having."

"Not true. They both gave me a kickass older brother. Even if he tried to sell me for sixteen dollars online when I was nine."

Mal shocked him by letting out a laugh. "Twenty-six dollars, bartered down from fifty. And I could only get that much because you came with your guitar. Besides, you counter-sold me for thirteen, and that included my fucking glorious Sonor drum set. Damn steal that guy would've gotten if our auctions hadn't been shut down."

"Your drums." A buzz skipped along the back of Michael's neck as he turned toward his brother. "Do you still play?"

Malachi rasped out a sound that wasn't quite a laugh. "I work at a chop shop. It'd be kind of idiotic for me to whale around on those when I get home every night, wouldn't it?"

"You still do. Holy shit."

"How you got that from what I just said, I don't know." Mal shook his head. "I play now and then. Mostly keep going over the same songs we used to play."

"What about 'In The Air Tonight'?" Michael questioned. "You still play that?"

His brother jerked a beefy shoulder. "I guess."

"You had a killer sense of rhythm. Have you ever considered joining a band? Like a real band?" *My band*, but he didn't say it. Mainly because he didn't think he could actually force the words past the rock in his throat.

"Me? Dude, are you crazy? I spend my days up to my elbows in grease and shit. I'm not meant for some pussy band. No offense," he added quickly.

"Pussy is one of the main benefits," Michael said, keeping his face sober until Mal drove his fist into Michael's arm. Hard.

Damn, that asshole never pulled a punch. Ever.

"You might need that dick prop in front of you to get girls, but some of us do just fine on our own. Anyway, I gotta go. Just wanted to tell you about the wedding. Hoped I'd convince you to go with me." That mercurial half smile flitted over his mouth. "Be my date or some shit."

"I haven't gone to the last two, so why would I go to this one?" Besides, their mother hadn't invited Michael, unless maybe his invite had gotten lost in the mail.

Small favor, that one.

"She insists it's the last time. Came to me crying last night, drunk off her ass, begging me to get you to come. Says all she wants in this world is for her boys to be with her as a family. Biff wants that too." Mal rolled his eyes. "I called her driver and sent her home with a travel mug of coffee."

"But you promised."

He shrugged. "It made her stop crying."

"Softie."

Another shrug. "It's hard to say no to a crying woman. You gotta have some experience with that."

"Nah, they usually make *me* want to cry lately." Michael shook his head and shoved Tabitha to the back of his mind. "Or more accurately, get drunk."

"Drunk for sure."

Wheels spinning, Michael cocked his head and gave his brother an easy smile. "How about we make a deal? One where we both get what we want, and everyone goes home happy?"

Mal crossed his arms in front of his barrel chest. "I didn't realize you wanted for anything. Big fancy rockstar, making good and making his own money now."

The faint tinge of pride in his big brother's voice could've bolstered him for months. Maybe years. "I'm getting there. We still haven't figured everything out yet. The band lineup is still in flux."

"You will." Mal's utter certainty just increased *his* certainty that it was no coincidence Mal had shown up when he did. Michael wasn't one to believe in woo-woo crap, but he also knew when the universe had dumped the perfect opportunity in his lap.

Whether or not Lila would agree was another question, but they'd get there when they got there. He needed to get Mal on board first.

If that meant offering a temp role until he got his brother to agree to more, then he would do just that. Whatever it took.

"We have to. We're on the way up, but we won't make it if we don't have the right people in place."

"Which people aren't right? That singer of yours is smoking hot."

"Molly? Yeah. She knows it too, but man, she fills the seats."

"You've got a couple hot ones. Gorgeous brunette and another blond, but I haven't paid much attention to her. She doesn't have the same stage presence as the other two, though she certainly goes toe-to-toe with you."

"Elle, yeah." Formally Richelle Crandall, or Ricki as she'd once been known. She'd joined the band and started using the name Elle to try to distance herself from her troubled past. Some of them called her Ricki, some called her Elle, but no one could deny her talent. Especially Michael. "She makes me work for it every night."

"And Ryan and West. I remember you introducing me to those guys back at Christmas one year. Ry, always with the plans. And West had his hair colored Kool-Aid blue."

"It's blond most of the time now. Not at the moment though. Usually it just looks like he hacked at it with pinking shears."

"Sounds about right. So what's the problem?"

"The problem is Ry's stuck on drums when he's always been more comfortable being a jack-of-all-trades. He knows a bunch of different instruments and loves changing up the arrangements of songs. Getting stuck behind the kit is like hell to him."

Mal snorted. "Some hell, being part of a band with an incredible sound."

The confidence his words instilled in Michael made him surer with every passing second that this was right. It had to be right.

In his current world of fuckery, this one good thing needed to happen.

"He sprained his wrist and he can't play tomorrow night. We have gig at the House of Blues in Vegas. Three of us on the bill, though of course Warning Sign is opening."

"For now." Mal nodded. "You do your time, then you move on."

"Yeah. But without a drummer, we can't go anywhere. Lila's gonna rip us a new one."

"So she'll nab a studio musician from somewhere. There's gotta be tons of them."

"This is our biggest gig yet. You really think now is the time to try to work with some studio type none of us have ever even met?"

"Doesn't sound like you have much choice. Sorry to say."

"That's where you're wrong." Michael took a deep breath. "You wanted to know what the deal was? I'll come to the wedding. You fill in on drums tomorrow night."

Mal stared at Michael for a minute, then dropped back his head and roared with laughter. "Jesus fuck, you've lost your mind."

"No, I think I've finally found it." Michael clapped his hand on his brother's shoulder. "So what do you say? You in or not?"

Mal said nothing, so Michael nodded, dropped his hand and moved back. "I get it. It's scary to come out on a big stage like that without any experience, or even any real practice time in years. It's fucking terrifying."

"You think I'm scared? Do you know what I used to do?"

"Yeah, I know you used to get behind the wheel and race fuckers as stupid as you, risking all your lives. Believe me, I know. That doesn't mean you're not scared to touch the sticks again."

Mal turned away. "Fuck that shit. And fuck you too."

"We'll be at the plane at nine a.m. tomorrow." Quickly, Michael rattled off the address of the airstrip where Donovan Lewis's jet would be located to take them to Vegas in the morning.

Malachi didn't respond. Just walked away and slammed the door shut behind him.

Michael locked his hands behind his neck and bent at the waist, sucking in a deep breath. Either he'd just saved their asses or they were just as fucked as before.

And his brother probably wouldn't ever speak to him again.

FOUR

"I STILL SAY WE COULD HAVE DONE THIS AS A ROAD TRIP. VEGAS ISN'T that far from LA."

"I could only get three days off, remember?" Chloe Adams glanced at one of her best friends. Her white-knuckled grip on the arms of the plush airplane seat belied the calmness of Jinx's voice. She wasn't wild about letting people know her weaknesses. Flying being one of them, of course.

Personally, Chloe wasn't worried about the massive personal jet they were on. Or keeping it in the sky. Mr. Lewis only owned the best—this ridiculous Lear jet was only one in the fleet that he owned. Seriously, who owned a fleet of planes other than an airline?

Right, a billionaire, that's who. Something that was so far out of her stratosphere it was laughable. She'd had to work three doubles, and sell off her precious weekend to Jersey Janice to get time off for this little trip. Dude, she hated Janice.

Almost as much as she hated her job. It was a toss-up, truly.

No, all her worry was at home, in her tiny duplex, with her almost two-year-old son. She pulled out her phone again.

Jinx flipped her braid over her shoulder. "If you FaceTime with the kid again, I'm going to steal your phone."

She stuffed her phone back into her hoodie pocket, resisting the urge to pout. "There's free Wi-Fi, it seems stupid not to use it." And when they got to Vegas, who knew if her little prepaid phone would have a good signal. She'd paid extra for data and minutes for this trip just so she'd be available at all times.

"He's having grandpa time. He's fine."

Her father had cleaned up his act a lot since she'd gotten pregnant. Then when Snake had died, he'd really stepped up. She was still waiting for him to backslide even two years later. It wasn't like he didn't watch Axl when she was working. She split up the babysitting between her father and her next-door neighbor with a little girl the same age. And sometimes with Nick and Lila Crandall.

God, the weirdness there.

But her son loved Nick. Sometimes it felt like he loved Nick more than *her* on the difficult days. All he had to do was bring out his guitar, or hell, even play a pretend one, and Axl was instantly enthralled.

This was how weird her life had become. Her former fiancé's bandmate was nearly a surrogate dad. She swallowed down the lump in her throat—hard. She hardly ever thought of Snake anymore—she'd been too busy being a mom, being a provider, being everything to a twenty-one-month-old little boy who was becoming a person more and more every day.

Axl would be fine.

Truly.

This was supposed to be Mommy time. The fact that two of the hottest bands in the country were sitting at the front of their jet seemed surreal.

She would be fine. Everyone would be fine.

It was just a few nights away from him. She could totally do this. She used to know how to go out and have a good time. She was only twenty-three, not forty-three. Nick had given her—and her friends—a free trip to simply have fun.

Once upon a time she'd known the definition of fun. And she was more than fine with her nights in with her son, but a tiny piece of her was looking forward to a change of pace.

"He'll be fine." Maybe if she said it out loud.

"Damn right." Jinx hummed under her breath as the plane bounced. "Fuck."

"Relax." Ivy clicked back her seat until she was nearly in her sister's lap. "I'm trying to sleep here."

"How can you sleep?" Jinx gritted her teeth and squeaked as the plane suddenly increased altitude. "God, how long do we have to be in this tin can?"

Ivy rolled onto her side. "Tin can?" She looked around. "Do you have eyes? This is a luxury jetliner with seats the size of tricked-out leather movie recliners. You know, like the theater we go to when we splurge for a movie?" The light dinged over their heads. "Oops, my cue to sit up." A humming sound came from Ivy's chair as she raised it back to a more upright position.

Chloe shook her head and folded her hands over her stomach, holding her phone to her middle. Okay, that jolt was a little more than turbulence.

The stewardess came down the aisle. "Bear with us, folks. The pilot just pulled up into higher airspace to avoid a storm. We'll level off in a few minutes."

Jinx snapped her window shade shut. "Yeah, I can't watch our fiery plummet."

Chloe rolled her eyes. "Drama llama."

"Shut up." Jinx slammed her head back as they veered a bit to the left then leveled out.

"See, there we go. Nothing to worry about."

"Miss," Jinx called to the stewardess.

She came back down the aisle. "Yes?"

"Could I get an adult beverage? Preferably one that includes vodka?"

"Absolutely. We have a fully stocked bar."

Jinx perked up. "How stocked?"

"Top shelf for everything. Is Grey Goose all right? Or would you prefer Ketel One?"

Her brown eyes bulged. "All right, now this I can get behind."

"Easy, tiger," Chloe muttered.

"Actually, I think we all need one. Time to get a little lubricated before we land. Vegas, here we come, baby."

"No thanks, I don't—"

"She needs one most of all," Jinx interrupted.

"I concur," Ivy said.

Chloe pressed her lips together. She needed to lighten up. They were in Vegas—well, currently over the Mojave, if her watch was correct. It was only an hour flight.

She deserved to go and hang with her friends. Even if Nick had to practically drag her to the airport to get her to leave the house.

"You know what? Yes. I'd like a vodka tonic with lime, please."

"That's more like it." Jinx clapped. "The same times three."

"What if I didn't want a vodka tonic?" Ivy popped her head up.

"What do you want, then?"

Ivy sighed. "Vodka tonic."

"I thought so."

The stewardess gave them an indulgent smile. "I'll be right back, ladies."

Jinx leaned into Chloe, her eyes fixed on the broad shoulders of Oblivion's bass player, Deacon McCoy. "So, which of those delicious babes are you focusing on this weekend?"

Chloe snorted. "You're on drugs. I'm so not interested in a rockstar again. Nope."

Jinx winced. "Right. But you've been off the market for ages." She tapped the ring on Chloe's hand. "Even if you keep wearing that little ice chip."

Chloe used her thumb to straighten her ring. "It's just easier." It didn't even feel like her ring anymore. More like a little guardian angel against dealing with men. Of course, some nights at Rafferty's, it was more like a neon challenge sign over her head, but mostly a deterrent.

"Well, this weekend isn't about easier. It's about fun. And it's past time you get back on the horse. Or a studly male in this case."

"I don't jump into bed with people, Jinx. You know that."

"Maybe it's time to loosen up. You have a prime twenty-three-year-old pussy that is rotting away."

Chloe crinkled her nose. "Nice." She sighed. "Besides, this girl has given birth. There's nothing prime about my…anything."

Ivy turned in her seat and peeked over the top. "Seriously, you're a hot redhead with curves that make men drool. You're prime everything."

Chloe rolled her eyes. "Also, every one of the guys in Oblivion is married."

Jinx slumped in her chair. "That's unfortunate."

The stewardess came down the aisle with a tray of drinks. Jinx perked up again. No plastic cups on this flight. No, these were tall glasses with garnishes and thin straws with perfect wedges of lime on the rims.

Not like the half-dehydrated lime scraps from the restaurant Chloe worked at. These were fat and juicy. She could tell just from the looks of them as the woman set the drinks on their tables.

Jinx took a sip before the stewardess had a chance to step back. "Oh, we need to get married."

The woman laughed. "I'm glad you like them. We'll be landing in twenty minutes. Enjoy."

"Can we have one more round then?"

The dark-haired woman winked. "You got it."

Jinx held up her glass. "To an unforgettable weekend."

Chloe clinked glasses with her two best friends. "To remembering I'm single."

"Damn right."

They all laughed, and Chloe caught Nick craning his neck to check on her. She lifted her glass in his direction. He gave her the half grin that had gotten her panties around her ankles as a teenager.

Yeah, she didn't need any lusty thoughts about a rockstar. Past or present, thank you very much.

FIVE

"Did you see this view?" Ivy screeched.

Chloe pushed her bangs out of her eyes. The trip in from the airport to the Mandalay Bay Resort had been a long one. Traffic on the Strip had been hideous, but they'd ended up drinking a bottle of champagne during the limo ride. Two drinks and champagne was already catching up to her.

She widened her eyes until everything came back into focus. Their room was ludicrous. Two huge headboards dominated the queen-size beds. She dropped her hand-me-down luggage onto the floor. She didn't dare put it on the lush white bedding.

She followed Ivy to the window and her stomach dropped. The entire Vegas strip was in front of her. The sun was still beating down on the world. It had a different feel than look at night with all the neon. Snake had brought her there once. A long bus ride and a low-end hotel on the Strip had been the highlight of their relationship.

She was pretty sure that was where Axl had been conceived, actually.

Hmm. Funny how life changed in a few short years.

Now she was in a gilded showcase of a hotel that catered to the rich and famous. Her son's godfather was a millionaire, and her fiancé… well, he was gone.

She placed her palm against the glass. Snake would have loved this kind of place. He longed for the big time, just never wanted to work for it. He was more interested in talking about being a musician than following the passion of being one. Her eyes pricked as she shut out the tangle of cars and towering buildings.

She hated to think badly of him.

Hated that he'd left her with so many questions. Just when she'd thought their lives were turning around, he went and died on her. He'd left her alone again, this time with a little person who counted on her for everything.

"Okay, we need to book time in the spas."

Chloe dabbed at her eyes and turned to Jinx. She had two brochures in each hand. Each place looked more expensive than the last. "Did you gain a sugar daddy that I'm not aware of?"

Jinx leaped onto the bed closest to the window. "Live a little."

"I have to live within a budget."

"Actually, no, you don't." Ivy waved a card propped on the six-foot-long bureau. She tucked her honey-blond hair behind her ear before clearing her throat. *"Enjoy yourselves and don't think about money. The tab is on me. Nick."*

Chloe crossed the room to snatch the note out of Ivy's hand. "No way."

Ivy cocked her hip and grinned, her dimples winking. "Yes, way."

Jinx crowed. "Yes! Salon, spa, and shopping!"

"No. We are not taking advantage of Nick's generosity."

"Hell yes, we are." Jinx bounced off the bed. "When the hell are we going to get the opportunity to be spoiled like this again?"

"This is being spoiled." Chloe whirled, arms out. "This room is us being spoiled."

Jinx came up in front of her and gripped her shoulders. "Anything we spend is a thumbnail of a fraction of what rockstars spend on their own."

Chloe's stomach flipped. "You don't know Nick. He's frugal. A penny-pincher even. There's no way he would give me an unlimited spending account."

Ivy lifted a notepad off the dresser. "Funny, that's what this says. *Charge everything to your room number, that's an order.*"

Chloe shook her head. "You're just making that up."

Jinx swiped the paper out of her sister's hand before Chloe could. "Looks like a dude's handwriting to me."

"Would you guys stop being so fucking grabby," Ivy groused.

Jinx shoved the paper at her. Sure enough, it looked like Nick's handwriting. She was used to it. He sent her a check every damn month, even after she'd asked him to stop helping them.

Even though she needed every damn penny to keep her head above water. She hated taking it. Hated cashing the check every month. She only used the money for things for Axl and socked away the extra for the future. For her not-such-a-baby's future.

She was determined to make a good life for him. A life like she'd never had as a child. Being the daughter of a crackwhore mother and an alcoholic father had not been an ideal start. Her father might have come around to begin the process of father of the year, but her mother never had. She'd split long ago, no forwarding address, no letters of remorse.

Another person who had just up and disappeared on her. Her mother could be dead for all she knew.

Fuck.

Chloe knew better than to drink. It only made her sad.

Jinx pushed her toward the bathroom. "Get cleaned up. We're finding our way down to the spa on…" She raced around to the bed she'd left the pamphlets on. "Thirty-sixth floor. If we're going all out, then we're definitely going there." She grinned. "I'm getting everything waxed. This chick is getting laid."

Chloe escaped to the bathroom. "Holy crap." The room was all marble and shine, with a tub, a separate shower, and a sink big enough to give her kid a bath in.

Even the toilet was locked away from the perfection of the room.

"Unbelievable." She dropped onto the edge of the tub and pulled out her phone. She flicked it awake and shot off a text to Nick.

Are you sure? Were you delusional when you wrote that note? It's too much.

The little bubbles on her screen came up right away.

I've been waiting for this text. Yes. Have fun. Pretend you're Princess Chloe for three days. Don't fucking argue with me. Now buzz off, I'm busy.

Chloe laughed. Only Nick could say something so sweet and so rude in the same breath. She was about to switch her phone off when she tapped on the top of her sparkly red case. "Just one call," she said quietly.

She thumbed over the FaceTime icon and her father's number. It rang three times before he answered, a harried look on his face.

"Hey, Dad. How's my kid?"

"He's currently covered in peanut butter." He panned the phone away to show her son with his russet hair sticking to the side of his face along with a smear of his snack. His cheeks were covered, and his two teeth gleamed from his bow lips.

"Pee butter, momma!" He slapped his hand on the tray of his high chair, peanut butter and jelly spraying the front of his bib.

"Wow. I see."

"Miss you!"

Chloe's belly flipped and her heart shuddered to a stop. "I miss you too, pal."

He covered his mouth and made a sucking kiss sound and blew her a kiss. "Pee butter!"

Chloe laughed and blew his kisses back.

I will not cry.

I will not cry.

"You are not using FaceTime in there, woman! You're peeing so we can go!" Jinx called through the door.

Chloe scrunched up her shoulders. "Everything okay there, Dad?"

"I'm going to go dump him and his peanut-butter-scented self into the tub. Then we're going to read a few books."

"Books!" Axl screeched.

Her dad laughed. "Yes, books. We're just fine, cupcake."

Chloe swallowed down a lump. Her boys were doing just fine without her. Was it terrible that she wished they weren't so put together?

She made herself laugh because that was what her father intended. "Okay. Call me if you need me."

"Have fun, Chloe Bear. Don't worry about us. Axlsaurus is having a blast. Right, dude?"

"Axaserres is a-okay."

Chloe laughed at Axl's bastardization of her dad's nickname for him. "I love you guys."

Her dad swung the camera around again. "Say g'night, Axl."

"Niy-nites, Mama." Again, his sticky fingers made kisses over his lips.

She blew back kisses. "Night, little man."

Her dad came back into the frame. "We're fine. Have fun. Pretend you're young and carefree for a few days."

"Come on. We're burning daylight here!" Jinx hollered again.

Chloe sniffed back a few tears. "Gotta go, Dad."

"Love you, Chloe Bear."

Man, the mushy stuff was going to kill her, but she liked it too. She blinked back tears and smiled. "Love you too, Daddy Bear," she murmured, using the old nickname she'd had for him. Every now and then, it made a reappearance, usually when she was feeling out of sorts.

This weekend qualified.

"There's my girl. See you on Sunday."

She nodded. "I'll check in tomorrow."

"Lori next door invited us to a picnic. So we'll be gone all day. But you can check in at bedtime."

"Right. Wow. Got it all planned, huh?" They didn't need her even a little bit. She tried to push aside the hurt. She wanted them to have a great time, just not *too* good a time.

So stupid.

"Yes. We'll have a full day. So text me later and I'll see if he's even still awake."

"Right." Chloe nodded. "I will."

"Bye now."

"Bye." She thumbed over the end button and rubbed her phone against her jeans. Yeah, she definitely couldn't spend the whole weekend thinking about how little her boys needed her.

She stood up and dashed the tears from her eyes. In fact, she was going to make sure she had one helluva good time this weekend. She went over to the sink and splashed cold water on her skin. Her golden-brown eyes were free of makeup, thanks to a very long day already.

She used the ultra-soft towel hanging from the ring by the sink and blotted her face. "You're going to have all of the fun, girl." She opened the door. "All right, bitches! Let's get this party started."

"Fuck yeah!" Jinx leaped off her bed. "I just made us appointments."

"Of course you did," she said with a laugh.

"So fancy." Ivy drew her fingers over the leather cushion of the creamy wingback chair in the corner of the room. "I could get used to this."

"Don't get too used to it," Chloe muttered.

"Live a little." Ivy frowned. "You used to know how to have fun."

Before the baby. Before Snake died. Before Snake…

No.

She shook her head. There were good times with Snake. Lots of them. She was just swimming in the crappy memories today. And she was tired of it. "I'm so ready to live it up this weekend. This weekend I'm not a mommy, not an ex-fiancée, or a responsible member of society."

"Now this is more like it." Jinx linked her arm with Chloe's.

They all marched toward the door. Chloe meant to stop to get her purse, but Ivy and Jinx hauled her out of the room. They linked arms, with Chloe in the middle, as they strutted down the hall, and laughter bubbled out of her chest.

God, when was the last time she'd laughed? At least when it didn't apply to Axl? He was the light of her life and made every day bearable. But she'd rarely taken time to do anything for herself. Everything was for her little boy.

Nick honestly wanted her to have some fun this weekend, and she would not feel guilty about it.

Ivy slapped the down button on the elevator. The big car was gilded and over-the-top. The back of the elevator had a huge painting that depicted the shark tanks that were part of the hotel. Everything about this hotel was over-the-top.

Hell, everything about Vegas was over-the-top.

For once, she wasn't going to feel like the little red-and-gold fish at the bottom of the picture. She was going to be the shark this time.

Ivy and Jinx pored over the pamphlet, picking out things for them to do. She tried to block out just how much the mud masks, sea wraps, and massages would cost.

The doors opened to the thirty-sixth floor. The entire floor was the spa.

Her eyes bulged as Jinx dragged her through the doors.

"Welcome, ladies. Room number?"

"Forty-one-oh-eight," Ivy said.

Jeez. She already had it memorized? Chloe wasn't even sure she had the room key in her pocket, let alone knew the number.

A very perky, very tiny blond smiled from behind the jade desk. Chloe was pretty sure it was actually jade, or at least marble of some kind. A large gold-and-red dragon covered the wall behind her. "Miss Adams, and Miss Johnson…both of you?"

Jinx smiled. "That's us. Sisters."

"Perfect. I'll just need you to scan your room key here." She pushed out a little reader.

Crap. She didn't have her purse.

Jinx pulled a spare room key out of her ass pocket. "Here we go."

Well, at least someone was prepared. The little machine beeped and the woman's smile grew wider. "Excellent. You have full access to the facilities. Janet, Suzanne, and Emily will be your technicians."

Three women seemed to materialize out of nowhere. They all wore seafoam green smocks and khakis, along with discreet gold name tags over the establishment's embroidered logo. Suzanne came forward, her smile wide in her exotically beautiful face. She had bright gray eyes that seemed to glow from her mocha skin. "We're going to fix you right up."

God, did she look that bad?

"Don't even think that thought." Suzanne clutched Chloe's fingers. "I can see it in your dark eyes. Really pretty eyes, by the way. Just need a little shaping of those brows."

She immediately smoothed the pad of her finger over her brows. She couldn't remember the last time she'd actually tweezed them.

"Stop. That's what we're here for. To pamper you and make you feel as beautiful on the outside as you do on the inside."

Chloe straightened her shoulders. "Pamper away. I'm not going to argue."

"My kind of client." Suzanne led Chloe down a hallway. The walls were a lighter color than their uniform smocks. The air was…odorless. A far cry from the small spa she'd been treated to for Mother's Day. That had been full of the smells of chemicals and an underlying blast of bleach.

She'd appreciated the bleach for the clean factor, but man, the crisp perfect air in this place was to die for.

Chloe looked over her shoulder as Jinx and Ivy were taken to separate rooms.

"Don't worry. We know that spa days are much more fun as a group. We're just going to figure out what you need and then you'll be back in the same room together."

"I look that worried?"

"A little."

She sighed. "I'm just not used to all this. Single mom."

"Oh?" Suzanne's face brightened as she opened a door at the end of the hallway. "I have a little boy. My husband is home with him right now. We work opposite shifts so he's always got someone home with him."

Chloe's chest tightened. "That was the plan for me too."

"Oh, believe me, I understand. My husband isn't my baby's father—well, not biologically. He totally is his dad though. Ty and Kevin are like two peas in a pod now. Sometimes I get a little jealous."

She couldn't imagine what that felt like. It had always been her and Axl. Even her dad, as wonderful as he'd been recently, seemed as if he could melt away any day. Relying on herself was all she'd ever known.

She followed Suzanne across the threshold and hoped to hell her jaw wasn't physically on the marble floor, because it felt like it had to be.

The room was ridiculous. Bamboo chests dominated one wall with towels stacked on them and muted candles flickered from tall glass columns. Light, tinkling music piped into the room—actually, all around the room. As if the walls had their own speakers.

A huge pie-piece-shaped chair sat in the corner, piled with pillows in soft sand and sea colors. She crossed to it before she even thought to ask permission. She smoothed her hand over the microfiber material with a sigh. Microfiber hadn't been a material in her life in a very long time. It definitely didn't hold up against baby drool, food, or any other manner of baby hazards.

No, she was all cotton and plastic these days.

"Wow."

"Curl right in there." Suzanne waved toward the chair.

"If I do, I'll be unconscious."

Suzanne laughed and pushed a beautiful robe into Chloe's hands. "Get undressed and put this on then."

"All the way undressed?"

Suzanne's lips twitched. "Right down to the skin. I've decided you need a massage and a facial to start, then once you're all malleable, we're going to sit you in one of our zero-gravity chairs and let the nail techs de-mommy your hands and feet. Time to pamper yourself, Chloe."

She didn't know what a zero-gravity chair was, but she was all for it. "Sounds awesome."

Three hours later, she was sitting in an atrium with tropical plants overflowing from every corner. Huge rocks and a lovely stone bench were set up next to a water feature as large as her entire house.

The technicians had set up Chloe and her two girls in triangle formation. Each one of them was stretched out in the special chairs, which were awesome. Some girl by the name of Heather had beat the crap out of her with a massage, followed by a steam shower. Glorious. Then another girl attacked her face with tweezers and pore reducer, ending with some soothing mask that made her feel tight and young for the first time in three years.

Well, tight that didn't have anything to do with dry skin because she forgot to put moisturizer on.

She had wine-colored toenails and fingernails which made her look a little vampy—in a good way. They'd touched up her red hair with strips of deep burgundy that made her feel like she was on trend for once. Some girl named Darla had even done her makeup.

Even better, it didn't look like she'd been attacked by a cosmetology student. Everything made her feel young and fabulous.

"I think we should go to Light tonight." Jinx held her phone over her head as she tapped carefully at her screen so she didn't smudge her purple chrome nails.

"Club?" Chloe asked.

"Yes. Wait until you see this place. It's a huge pool and outdoor concert area by day, and at night a deejay takes over. All of the screens and craziness. God, it looks so cool."

"We're from Los Angeles, it's not like we don't see cool clubs." Ivy stretched her arms over head with a sigh. "We were just at one last weekend."

"This is nothing like that hole."

Ivy opened one eye. "You loved that hole last weekend."

"Well, we are getting an upgrade." Jinx dropped her phone into her robe pocket and draped her hands over the arms of her chair. "And we're shopping to match."

"Go to the eighteenth floor. Meri will take care of you at Luxe," Suzanne said from the back of the room.

Chloe frowned. "That sounds expensive."

"Room forty-one-oh-eight, baby," Jinx said with a singsong voice.

Chloe clenched her fingers on the arms of her chair. God, she so didn't want to take advantage. "We've been saying that number way too much today already." Not to mention that she had to tip the hell out of all the people who had taken care of them.

She wanted to sink lower into her seat, and she was already practically at an incline with the crazy zero-gravity chair she was in. But she wasn't going to ruin everyone's fun.

If she told herself it would be okay enough, maybe it would be true.

She just couldn't look at the bottom of the receipt or she'd probably have a coronary.

"All right, ladies. It's time to get you back into your street clothes."

"Do we have to?" Ivy stretched her toes to the ceiling. "This robe is glorious."

"You get to take it with you."

"Oh, man. For real?" She popped up and her chair swung forward. "Whoa."

"Careful there." Ivy's technician, Janet, stepped forward to help her out of her chair. "You guys were a lot of fun. Let's not break anything before you go have some real fun for the evening."

Ivy stood up. "Shopping then food? Or food then shopping?"

"I'm not eating. I want my belly completely flat for tonight." Jinx laid her hand over her middle. "No food baby."

"I recommend a little salad and cold-pressed watermelon water from the little eatery also on the eighteenth floor. Hydrates after all the things we've done today and helps to prepare you for whatever craziness you do tonight." Suzanne winked.

"I like this girl." Jinx grinned. "I like her a lot."

"You girls are a trip." Suzanne helped Chloe out of her chair.

The checkout process was terrifyingly simple. She just had to sign a little electronic clipboard. The number was slightly nauseating, but it was whipped out of her hand so fast that she didn't have time to digest it.

Oh, she memorized it. Definitely knew that four-digit number like the last four of her social, but she was trying like hell to block it out.

They were shuffled off with huge shopping bags and a bunch of product as well as samples. Oh, and the robes. Couldn't forget those bits of lusciousness.

She would guard hers with her life, and pray that she could keep peanut butter and jelly off of it for at least one full day. Maybe a week, if she hid it in the back of her closet and only put it on after Axl was in bed for the night.

Maybe.

This time, the elevator was designed like a desert sunset. There were a mind-boggling number of elevators on every floor of the damn hotel.

So many floors. It was like a maze. And the little room card was their golden ticket to everything.

Terrifyingly awesome.

The doors opened on eighteen. She thought she'd been prepared after the luxury of The Golden Dragon, but that one had nothing on the chrome, gold, and glass of the shops that seemed to go on forever.

They followed the signs to the eatery Suzanne mentioned. The watermelon drink was ridiculous, and the salad was just enough to kill the empty feeling living in her gut. Nerves didn't allow her to eat too much, but she didn't want to be looped after one drink, so food was a necessity.

"Are you done yet?" Ivy asked again.

"Dude, what's the rush?" Chloe sat back on the dainty white wrought iron chair. They were eating next to a glass balcony that looked down over two more floors. There was a double escalator and a massive fountain below.

One of the casino entrances was flooded with people streaming from the slot machines to electronic card games. It wasn't the main casino, but there seemed to be a dozen smaller game stations all over the hotel. In between were restaurants galore and a huge archway that teased the shark attraction in another building.

It was a feast for the senses.

And made her dizzy as hell, and not because of the height. She just couldn't imagine this many people in one space. Hell, she lived in LA, but it didn't feel like this. It was claustrophobic sometimes, but at least there was space and the ocean. There were little pockets where she could actually get away with Axl and sit on a patch of grass.

This was just ostentatious and overwhelming.

A world so outside of her own.

"Earth to Chloe."

"Hmm?" She turned to Ivy. "Sorry. Just people watching."

"Anyone hot?"

She laughed. "I hadn't noticed." How sad was it that she wasn't even looking for men? The last man she'd been with was Snake. Her hormones had closed up shop sometime between her pregnancy and losing him to the accident.

They'd emerged a few times for brief moments of mayhem, but the trouble of having a man in her life outweighed the benefits of getting naked with one.

You can get in all sorts of trouble this weekend.

She pushed aside that little voice. It was pretty quiet most of the time. Actually, probably in a coma more often than not. Getting an average of four hours of sleep a night usually kept that voice dormant.

"Girl, that needs to change." Jinx slapped the table. "You're a screaming-hot ginger. You need to own that."

"Sounds like an adult beverage."

"That's awesome." Ivy pulled out her phone. "I'm totally writing that down. We'll find a bartender to create it."

"God save me."

Jinx stood up. "God has no place in Sin City, baby."

Chloe looked up at her. "I don't like that look in your eye."

Jinx crossed her arms. "The longer your butt sits in that chair, the shorter your skirt is on the dress I deem worthy for tonight's festivities."

Chloe got up. "All right, all right. No need to get so bossy."

She let them drag her across the unbelievably sparkly marble and obsidian checkered floors to Luxe's gilded doors. Chloe's stomach dropped. Yeah, that wasn't going to be a cheap place. No twenty-dollar dresses on the clearance racks for this shop.

Jinx braceleted Chloe's wrist as she began to back up. "Oh no, you don't."

"We can definitely find someplace cheaper."

Ivy and Jinx hauled her through the doors. "We have permission remember, Pollyanna?" Jinx scanned the faces in the shop. "Who's Meri?"

A woman with long, sun-kissed brown hair came forward. "I'm Meredith."

"Suzanne sent us."

Meri's polite smile widened. "I just got the text. She said you girls were a lot of fun."

"Especially since we have rockstar money to play with."

"Oh, jeez. Jinx, say it a little louder."

"We have rockstar money to play with." Jinx's voice lifted.

Chloe bowed her head.

Meri laughed. "I have a friend just like you," she said to Jinx.

"Then you have taste. And you can find us hot clothes for Light tonight."

"I think we can handle that."

"Guys, can we talk about this?"

"No," Jinx and Ivy said in unison.

Meri showed them to the back of the store. Four dressing rooms were set up in a large curve. A huge tufted circular bench sat in the center. Chloe couldn't stop herself from swiping her hand over the sumptuous fabric. Everything screamed money and luxury. Shopping at Target was splurging for her.

"You're a four or six, right?"

Chloe blinked at Meri. "I honestly have no idea. I'm an eight in Target, a medium on the clearance rack at T.J. Maxx."

"Well, we'll just figure it out."

"I'm a four," Jinx announced.

"In your dreams," Ivy muttered. "You have too much hip for a four, you liar."

Meri laughed. "All right, let's take a walk around then. You can leave your bags here. They'll be safe."

A flurry of silk, satin, rayon, and even a random cotton was piled into Chloe's arms as Meri and Jinx grabbed clothes for her. Just as many were draped over Ivy's and Jinx's arms—actually, a bit more. They were far more willing to strip the hangers than she was.

Ten minutes later, she had her serviceable black leggings around her ankles and the third dress on. None of them seemed to fit right. Too tight in the boob, too clingy in the ass, or if they did fit, the price tag gave her palpitations.

"I hate this."

"Try this." A soft gray and blue dress came over the top of the door. When she didn't take it right away, Meri wiggled it. "Try it."

"It's way too short."

"You have fabulous legs. Try it."

Chloe sighed.

"And no bra."

"Um, you do know that I had a kid, right?"

"No bra."

Chloe held up the dress and gulped. The entire back was open, with a skinny chain attached at each shoulder to keep it from falling down. It was a scrap of nothing.

"Come on, hooker. We require adult beverages."

She wiggled out of the pink monstrosity she was currently wearing, unstrapped her boobs, and put the new dress on. It floated around her like a dream. The waist was elastic, of all things, but it bloused the dress just right, making her look young and fashionable.

She hadn't been fashionable since she was sixteen-freaking-years-old.

"Get out here."

"Where's the price tag on this thing?"

"I took it off," Meri said.

"I told her to," Ivy said.

She opened the door. "You too?" Chloe's breath caught. Ivy Johnson had certainly been transformed. "Wow."

Ivy twirled. "I know, right?"

"Why does she get to wear pants?" Chloe tugged at the short length of her dress. It felt like her damn ass was on display.

Ivy fussed with her floral bustier, hoisting up her girls. "Because I have to deal with a strapless top."

"I'm braless here." Chloe crossed her arms over her chest.

Meri drew her out of the dressing room. "Nope. Come look in the full mirror."

"Don't you think the one in there was enough?"

Jinx whistled. "Where have you been hiding those legs?"

Chloe felt the heat flooding her face. She did a helluva lot of walking for work, not to mention hauling kegs around when she covered the bar. Oh, and a twenty-pound kid. Couldn't forget that part.

"Get up there," Ivy said. "I wasn't sure about my outfit until Meri made me do it too."

"Wait. Shoes."

Chloe curled her toes into the ultra-soft pile carpeting of the changing area. "I have sandals."

"You don't have these." Meri held up a pair of gold, strappy sandals with four-inch heels.

"Do you want me to kill myself?"

"You remember how to wear heels. You used to wear even taller ones to the club with—" Jinx pressed her lips together. "Sorry."

Chloe took the shoes. "No, you're right. I wore spiked heels for Snake because he loved my legs in them."

Ivy came up behind her and met her gaze in the wall-sized mirror. "Time to wear them for you, don't you think?"

Chloe chewed on her lip for a moment before nodding. "Yes. Yes, it is." She straightened her shoulders before sitting on the huge hassock to buckle the shoes. Her arches made a little scream of protest before she was rock solid.

This was supposed to be a fun weekend.

She remembered how to have fun. Sort of. *Fake it till you make it, girl.* That little voice was getting louder. She climbed onto the small dais and got a good look at herself.

Young.

Objectively pretty.

Her legs were damn good. Strong because she needed to be strong for her son, for her job. But also lean and tight because she didn't know how to *not* be on her feet all day. It had been a damn long time since she'd actually looked at herself in a full-length mirror.

"You're smoking hot, you bitch."

She smiled down at Jinx standing to her left. "Not so bad yourself, bitch."

Jinx's smile broadened. "Now that's the Chloe I know and love."

Meri put her hands on her hips. "You girls are stunning. Now go kill it at Light."

Chloe stepped off the platform. "Thank you."

"You're very welcome."

They went back up to the room with armloads of bags. She tried not to think about just how much had been charged to Nick's account. Instead, she tried to focus on having fun as the three of them freshened up their makeup and hair and explored the hotel.

Light was on the main floor. The sharp scent of chlorine and cocoa

46

butter hit her as they followed the crowd of people. A deep bass seemed to vibrate beneath their feet and a buzz started under her skin.

The music was a far cry from her days at seedy bars and clubs, but the overall feel was the same. People out to have fun. Okay, maybe not exactly the same. There was money and a little wildness running through the air like its own perfume.

And she really wanted to wear it.

The bouncer waved them through with an appreciative gaze. Jinx was wearing a little black outfit that was all movement with a trace of glitter. Instead of a skirt, she had on dressy shorts. And she was already tall enough, so she went with flat sandals that laced up her toned calves. She owned her sexuality.

The opposite sex noticed. Immediately, she had three different suitors breaking away from their friends to approach her.

Within minutes, they were seated outside by the pool with drinks on their table. And they were surrounded by men.

The party had begun.

Chloe threw herself into the moment. Because she worked at a bar, she was conscious of the drinks placed on the table. She kept her hand over the top of her vodka tonic.

There were a lot of them.

And she let herself have fun.

She danced.

She laughed.

She only checked her phone three times all night. One of those times was to add the phone number of a guy staying at the hotel through the weekend.

The edge of the pool even got some play. She splashed her feet in the water with a vapid guy named Brad—owner of the number added to her phone. He was pretty and kept flirting with her. He didn't do much else but talk about himself, but she decided to live in the moment.

The past didn't matter. Only today.

It wasn't like she'd carry any of this home with her. It was just a couple of nights to let loose, then she'd go back to her real life. Dutiful Chloe, with only memories to keep her warm.

But until then? She wasn't going to regret one single thing.

SIX

Chloe pulled the pillow over her head. "Just five more minutes, Axl."

A pillow thumped on her back. "Turn off that fucking alarm."

"Wha?" She groaned. Oh crap, her head. The buzz and bleat of her phone dented her consciousness. She had her phone set for a daily alarm to get ready for work. She slapped it off and pulled the duvet over her head. "How much did we drink?"

"All the drinks." Jinx wiggled next to her on the bed. She'd started off bunking with her sister, but somehow she'd ended up with Chloe.

Chloe peeled off the duvet and squinted at her phone. Eleven? Really?

She sat up and swallowed down the immediate and all-consuming crash of nausea. She blew out a slow breath and flicked down her messages. "Who's Brad?"

"Hot guy, dumb as a lump of platinum."

Chloe laughed and her head almost fell off her damn neck. At least it felt like it. Not good. She vaguely remembered a guy with hair better than her own. "Talked about himself. Lawyer?"

"That's the one."

"Hmm." Chloe filed that away to think about later. She found two texts from her dad and winced. They were already at the picnic and would check in later. "Crap." She hadn't even heard the phone ring or vibrate.

She scrolled back and nibbled on her lip. Because there'd been no calls.

A swirl of guilt tried to fight the high tide of nausea. Instead of thinking about that one too hard, she tossed her phone onto the bedside table and curled back down into the bed she was willing to sell an ovary for.

God, it was comfortable.

Even if she did have to share it with Jinx. Damn bony butt. She shoved her over.

Jinx grunted, but moved over and flopped onto her back. "Why is there sunlight?"

"We're in the desert."

Another pillow came for her head, but this time, she blocked it. Jinx laughed. "Ow. Stop, don't make me laugh. My head is splitting."

"Get up, lazy butts." Ivy came in wearing running shorts and a tank. "Fuck off."

"I told you to hydrate before you faceplanted, but you didn't listen." Ivy sipped from a bottle of water. "I ordered breakfast and met the waiter—hot, by the way—in the hallway. You're welcome."

Chloe hid her head under her pillow. "I can't think about eating."

Jinx stumbled out of bed. "Oh, it's all grease. Bless you."

"Definitely not eating." Chloe curled into ball.

"It's bacon," Jinx spoke around her food, "and pancakes with real syrup." She bounced onto the bed.

"Get off the bed with that."

"Shut up, Mom." Jinx flipped back the bedclothes. "Bacon."

Chloe yanked back the covers. "I don't care." But her stomach started to grumble. They hadn't really eaten anything but the damn salads the night before. Which of course was why the drinks had hit her like a freaking sledgehammer.

"Bacon," Jinx sang.

Chloe sat up and filched a piece from her plate and shoved it in her mouth. "Happy?" She groaned as the salt and deliciousness hit her tongue. "Oh, man." She rolled onto her knees and when the contents of her stomach didn't rebel, she stole half of a silver dollar pancake.

"Get your own."

Ivy crossed the room. "Here you go."

"See, one of the Johnsons loves me." She took the plate from Ivy. "Thank you." She folded her pancake around the bacon and dipped it in the little cup of syrup. "Glorious." She inched back against the huge headboard. "Please tell me you didn't go work out," she said around another bite of salt and carbs.

Ivy grinned and plopped down on the bottom of the bed. "I ran off my sins. Kills the rest of the hangover."

"Still not doing it," Jinx muttered around her food.

Chloe held out her little breakfast sandwich toward Jinx. "Hear, hear."

Jinx tapped her bacon against Chloe's food. "Damn straight."

Ivy rolled her eyes. "Well, you snooze, you lose. I get the shower first."

Jinx collapsed back against her pillows. "Well, at least I don't have to worry about her using up all the hot water for once."

Chloe curled her arms around her knees. "I obviously have to make an appearance at the show tonight, but I think we're pretty much open for anything else today."

"Good. Because I was looking on my phone last night. You know when you two were sawing off logs."

"I do not snore."

"Sure, you don't. At least you're not as loud as my sister. She barely makes a peep normally. Put tequila into her and holy crap."

"Is that why I got a bedmate this morning?" Chloe asked.

"It was either that or suffocate her." Jinx picked at the edge of her nail. "I don't look good in orange. We should do nails today. Mine are already raggedy."

Subject change. As usual with Jinx, she said whatever came off the top of her head.

Chloe slid off the bed and padded to the cart of food. She took a croissant and a big bottle of water. "Want?"

51

"Coffee?" Jinx crawled down the bed with a hopeful look. "My sister did the ordering so it might not be included. She's a sadist."

"I don't know how she survives without it, but no, there's two huge mugs on here."

"Awesome. I don't have to kill her after all." Jinx leaped off the bed.

They bumped hips as they reached for creamer and sugar on the small cart. Coffee helped with the dead animal taste in Chloe's mouth, but she desperately wanted a shower.

And her toothbrush.

Luckily, Jinx wasn't paying attention when Ivy came out, so Chloe sprinted for the bathroom and slammed the door in her face with smile. The fact that she rarely was allowed a leisurely shower made her linger a little longer than she normally would.

A twang of homesickness started to grow, but she sloughed it away with an orange blossom scrub she'd found on the counter. Talk about high-end cosmetics. Some were from the spa, but the ones offered by the hotel were just as luxurious.

Scrubbed pink as a lobster, she finally gave into the pounding from Jinx. She shrugged on her robe of glory and made a turban with her towel for her hair. A plume of steam escaped as she opened the door. "So impatient."

"Dude, you were in there for days."

"The day you have a two-year-old is the day I'll feel sorry for taking extra time."

"Bah." Jinx gathered all her toiletries and sailed through the door. "If you used all the hot water, I'm cutting off your hair and selling it on eBay."

"Is everything violence with you?"

Jinx turned around with a tight smile. "I said cut your hair, not scalp you, didn't I?" And she shut the door.

Ivy was sprawled on the bed nearest the window. She swung her crossed ankles. "She's in a surprisingly good mood this morning—well, afternoon now."

"Not sure how you guys do the living together thing."

"Eh. We just stay out of each other's way on the shitty days. Otherwise she's barely home anyway."

Jinx worked more jobs than she did, and that included motherhood.

"So, my sister mentioned nails. There's a cool mani-pedi place on the seventeenth floor we can try. Maybe change up our color for our new outfits. There's a bunch of eateries there too. Hydrate up for tonight."

Chloe sat on the edge of the bed. "Yeah, the concert will definitely require that." She was excited to see Brooklyn Dawn. They were one of her favorite bands. Oh, to be lush and blond with hair down to her ass. Not to mention having men drool over her. Lindsey York was amazing, and her voice was kickass.

There'd been a time when she'd longed for that kind of life. Dating a rockstar had been thrilling at first, then reality had splashed a bucket of cold water on that dream. She'd hated wondering where Snake was every night and had hated even more that trust was in short supply.

She'd never had proof that he was unfaithful, but she'd been too afraid to dig for answers. He'd tried desperately to get clean so many times. She'd wanted to believe in him. Longed to believe in him with each hopeful smile he'd given her.

God, she'd swallowed every one of his lies. For her own sake, and for the life that had been growing inside of her. Axl hadn't been planned, but he was the very best of both of them. Snake's charm and crooked smile, her ease with people.

Ivy rolled to a sitting position and snapped her fingers. "Earth to Chloe."

"Sorry."

"Axl's fine."

Chloe rolled her eyes and gave her friend a sheepish grin. "For once it wasn't Axl."

"Oh." Ivy nibbled on her lower lip. "Snake?"

"Yeah. Usually I'm too busy to think about him, to be honest. I'm not used to being free to do what I want."

"You deserve some fun. Sunday we can go back to being responsible people."

"You're right."

"See? I don't get to hear that one often." Ivy stood up and wiggled her hips until her shorts straightened out. "We may not be gambling types, but we are definitely exploring types. And we don't even have to leave the hotel. Which is a good thing." She picked up her phone. "It's, ummm, one-hundred-and-fourteen degrees outside."

Chloe flinched. "That's hideous."

"Yeah. So, air-conditioned hotel it is. We'll get all beautified and find some new outfits."

Chloe scrunched up her shoulders. "I brought stuff."

"Come on. When do you get spoiled? This is a once-in-a-lifetime thing."

"Nick is just being nice." And he already spoiled her son plenty.

"Our mere thousand dollars' worth of—"

"*Thousand?*" Chloe spluttered. "More like three."

"It's chump change to him. He probably spends that on guitar strings."

Chloe hauled her suitcase onto the bed and pulled out shorts and a very cute Target top. This was plenty for her. She didn't need three-hundred-dollar shirts. "That's not the point." Where the hell was her bra?

"Just check your phone, would you?"

Chloe stopped digging and looked up. "What about my phone?"

"You got a text. I didn't look at it really. Well, I looked to make sure it wasn't Axl—"

Chloe crossed to the bedside table where her phone was plugged in. She perched on the side of the bed and nibbled the edge of her nail. "It's from Nick."

"Read it."

She was afraid to swipe it up to look at it.

Just look, you idiot.

Hey C – that tab seems way too small for three babes. You aren't spending your own money, are you?

Another text had come ten minutes later, according to the stamp.

I'll kick your ass if you're spending your own money. Consider it a late Christmas present, for fuck's sake. Have fun. That's an order.

Don't make me come down there.

Chloe couldn't help but laugh. She could hear his gruff voice in her ear as she read the text. He really was the sweetest guy on the planet, with a grumpy bedside manner. Even back when they were kids fumbling in the dark, he'd been far kinder than a lot of the guys she'd been with.

We're behaving, that's all.

He replied almost immediately.

Well, stop it.

Who are you? You're usually arguing for a sale price.

Retail fuckers can give me a discount. They already marked it up 200%. This is Vegas. You don't look at the check. You just sign. Don't make me find Jinx. I know she'll spend my money.

All right. Jeez. Understood.

See you at the show. Buy all the things.

She laughed. "All right. Looks like we're spending all the money today."

"I heard that," Jinx yelled from the bathroom.

"Of course you did." Chloe quickly got dressed and put on a light touch of makeup. By the time Jinx got out of the bathroom, they were all ready to go.

Hangovers a thing of the past, they did a bit of retail therapy. Clothing, makeup, and of course a manicure killed a few hours. They refueled with coffee and frozen custard before another round of shopping. They put themselves in Meri's capable hands. By the time they walked out of Luxe, she'd been numbed to the idea of signing her name to every damn receipt that day.

She soothed herself with a walk through the shark exhibit, which they pre-gamed with a frozen drink called Shark Attack. There was much rum involved. And much more laughter as they shared an appetizer under a few thousand pounds of water with a terrifying number of predators swimming right over their heads.

Jinx dunked her deep fried mozzarella medallion in the spicy dipping sauce. "So, we have Warning Sign, Brooklyn Dawn, and Oblivion at the show tonight? How the hell are we going to survive that?"

"Earplugs?" Ivy asked.

Chloe elbowed Ivy. "I think she meant more of a triple threat of awesome."

"You know I love a good show. Are you sure I can't lure Deacon away from his wife?" Jinx chewed thoughtfully. "He seems to like blonds. I might even let him call me wifey's name. What was that again? Helen?"

"Harper," Chloe said with a laugh. She knew Deacon far too well. The girls had met him at the Christmas party at Nick and Lila's new house. He was huge, tattooed, and disgustingly devoted to his wife. "Sorry, not a chance."

"Damn. He's probably a fucking stallion. Those thighs and shoulders...ugh. That back tattoo. So wrong."

Chloe picked around the dregs of their sampler platter and found a crab fry. "It's like lusting after a brother."

"Even Nick?" Jinx grinned as she took another sip of Shark Attack number two.

Chloe coughed around the last bite of her fry. "Nick was a long time ago."

"And we've never gotten the details."

"And you never will." Chloe gulped down half a glass of water.

"That bad?"

"Teenage sex is not something I think about anymore."

Ivy sat back in her chair as she spun her drink in a puddle of condensation. "My best sexual encounter was at seventeen. Of course he was twenty-two." She waggled her eyebrows. "Unfortunately, most have been duds ever since."

Jinx blew raspberries. "That's because you pick prudish bookish types."

"Oh, I should go for the tattooed, biker assholes you go for?"

Chloe grinned behind the rim of her glass. This was a conversation they had almost weekly, and it never stopped being entertaining. And it reminded her—eternally—why she was firmly out of the dating pool these days.

"Don't go grinning over there." Jinx laced her fingers over her middle as she tipped back in her chair. "You wouldn't know an orgasm if it bit you on the boob."

Chloe frowned at her, then looked around the room. There were a lot of kids in this particular restaurant. "Really?"

"What, like they haven't heard the word 'boob' before? Some of them are still *on* the boob, for God's sake."

Okay. Time to go. Jinx a little rowdy in a bar was one thing. In a family restaurant—well, at least partially a family restaurant? Yep, time to split. Those Shark Attacks were potent enough that she signaled the waitress for the check.

Room number flashy-flashy and they were out and about again.

"Why are you being such a prude? This is Vegas."

"Look, I'm a mom too."

"Not this weekend you're not." Jinx batted Chloe's hand away as she pulled her down the huge domed hallway.

"I'm always a mom. It comes with the kid."

She didn't want to ruin anyone's fun. And okay, she was probably overreacting a little. For the most part, she didn't care about curling into bed with someone. Hell, she was barely conscious by the time she actually found her bed. Between her job and Axl's less-than-awesome nighttime habits, she was always in the negative column when it came to sleep.

So no, a guy—especially one offering up an orgasm—was not high on her list. A guy offering to get up with an almost two-year-old who wanted a glass of water at two in the morning was more of a draw.

But there were times when she missed sex.

And seeing all the couples littering the hotel had given her more than one moment of jealousy. Sure, there were a number of families, but overall, Vegas was for lovers and people looking for a hook-up. And she couldn't forget the gambling, though the three of them were more than willing to avoid the games.

She playfully ran around Jinx and pushed her toward the jewelry store that she'd been begging to go into since they'd started shopping. It was dangerous to put a woman with no self-control into that arena, but she didn't want to fight.

She didn't want to own up to wanting a little something more.

So, yeah, compromise using Nicky's wallet. She tried not to wince when Jinx squealed and ran for the gemstone cases.

Ivy and Jinx cooed over diamonds and tanzanite in various settings. Chloe ran her fingertips over the gilded edges of the display cases. Having a toddler made her cognizant of keeping her fingerprints off the glass. Rubies fired, diamonds sparkled, amethysts gave off their cool, understated luminosity.

But it was the sapphires that drew her.

Had always been the deepest of blue that she loved. The ocean, the sky at night—a perfect mix of the two that was only found in the deepest and darkest blue of a perfect sapphire.

"Would you like to see something?"

Chloe curled her fingers into her palm at the sound of the male voice. "I'm fine." She smiled at the older gentleman with silver at his temples. "You can take care of my friends. I'm sure they'll make you a really nice sale."

"I'm not worried about the sale."

She raised a skeptical brow.

"I make plenty of sales, young lady. I'm more worried about finding the perfect piece for someone."

"I'm sure."

He held out his hand. "I'm Nathan."

Manners had her accepting his handshake. "Chloe."

"Now that's a beautiful name."

"Thanks."

He pulled a key away from his belt and slid the case open.

"Oh, don't do that." Her breath came out in a whoosh as he set the tray of sapphires on the glass top. Earrings, bracelets, and a host of pendants all fired off black velvet. Spotless, lintless, perfect velvet.

She couldn't stop herself from drawing the edge of her nail across the tennis bracelet. Each sapphire was bisected by a diamond. Beyond beautiful.

"They are, aren't they?"

She hadn't realized she'd said it out loud. "Yeah. I know most people go for the flash, but I've just always loved the deep blue."

"As a personal preference, or because you know the deeper the blue, the more they're worth?"

"Really?" She'd never done her homework about gemstones. They were always so far out of reach that she barely had a hint of want. "Just reminds me of the ocean at night. When the light hits it right, it just glows."

"And that should always be the reason to love a gemstone. That's true love right there."

She shrugged. "Impossible love for me. I'm more likely to get a gumball from my son."

"Son?"

She smiled. "Light of my life." She took out her phone and flashed him the screensaver. Messy red hair and the biggest brown eyes she'd ever seen to go with the most mischievous smile ever captured on film. She saw it nearly every day, but it was rare to catch it in a photo.

"Now that tells a story."

"Yeah, you have no idea." She surreptitiously checked for a message from her father before she dropped her phone into the deep pocket of her shorts. "So, yeah. I'm definitely all about sticky peanut butter and jelly more than a pretty ring."

"What about this one?" He slid away the tray of bigger stones to reveal a slim channel of sapphires and diamond rings tucked into more black velvet.

"Oh." She immediately went for a ring at the edge of the display. A fragile line of diamonds and sapphires made up an infinity symbol on either side of the ring, with a larger sapphire in the center.

"Try it on."

She immediately pulled her hands away. "No, that's okay."

"I insist."

She shook her head. "No. Best not to tempt myself." It was how she lived her life. It was how she kept some of the disappointments at bay.

He pulled out the ring. "Chloe. Out of all the rings in this case you chose the most understated one. The least you can do is try it on."

Ivy curled her arm around Chloe's waist. "Seriously. I can hear you saying no from over there. My ears are ringing from all the pretty things. Put the frigging ring on, woman."

Chloe laughed over her shoulder. "How much of Nick's money did you spend?"

"A paltry figure."

"For who?" She arched a brow. "A millionaire?"

Ivy laughed. "No, that's Jinx. She definitely hit the four figures."

"Oh God." Chloe's chest tightened.

"Try on the ring. I know you won't buy it, but you have to see the sparkler on your finger." Ivy tucked her chin on Chloe's shoulder. "Sure you don't want to try on a bigger one?"

Nathan turned the ring under lights that were designed to make gemstones sparkle. "It's a lovely piece."

Ivy pointed to the huge sapphire in the middle of the ring case. "*That's* a lovely piece."

Chloe wrinkled her nose. "Too big. It would get caught on everything."

"First world problems."

Nathan laughed. "She's being logical. It's fine to have both sides of your personality balance out when picking out a piece."

"Vegas isn't for balance," Jinx said from across the room.

"That's the truth," Chloe mumbled. Nothing had felt balanced since she'd stepped foot off the plane. As soon as she'd stepped foot *inside* Donovan Lewis's plane, to be honest.

Ivy tugged Chloe's hand from her side and held it out to Nathan. "Ring, please."

He frowned. "Only if Chloe wants to try it on."

Chloe uncurled her fingers. "Fine."

Nathan slid it over her first knuckle and then gently over her second until it rested on her finger. "Perfect fit."

She held in a soft moan at how amazing it looked. The one thing she'd always been good at was using a lot of lotion. No matter how many trays she balanced, or glasses she cleaned, or diapers she changed, she refused to have hands that looked like an elderly woman's. Her one vanity. Her nails might be short, but they were always neat. And the wine-colored nail polish made the jewels look like they actually belonged on her.

Even if they so didn't.

She quickly pulled it off her finger. "It's gorgeous. Thanks for letting me dream for a second, Nathan."

"Man," Ivy muttered. "You put us all to shame with your Mary Sue-ness."

"I don't need it." If only they knew just how many thousands of dollars she'd actually taken from Nick over the last year. At least that had been for her baby, not for her. "Thank you."

"Anytime, Miss Chloe." He winked and put the displays back into the case. "You ladies have a good rest of the night."

"Oh, we will." Ivy dragged her away from the glass and glitter to the front of the store. "See what I got?" She lifted her chin to show off the trio of delicate gold chains. A flash of diamond glittered from each one. Small diamonds, but diamonds nonetheless.

Diamonds equaled money.

Chloe forced herself not to ask how much. "That's gorgeous."

"Wait until you see Jinx's haul."

"I can't wait."

Ivy grinned. "I almost believe that."

A dozen bangles tinkled as Jinx waved them over. "You ready to rock this concert? We have work to do."

There was a lot of flash with the gold on her arm. Nope. Not asking. No how, no way. "More than ready." There, that sounded true.

She really was excited to see the show. She didn't know much about Warning Sign besides the hit that was always on the radio. Brooklyn Dawn and Oblivion would definitely be highlights though.

She let Ivy and Jinx carry the conversation on the way up in the elevator. She checked her phone and found a text from her dad. They were having a blast at the picnic and would be staying at the campgrounds.

No goodnight call tonight.

She rubbed the phantom pain in her heart. It was good for Axl to be with his Pop Pop. Really good that they were looking out for one another. But didn't Axl miss her at all?

"Chloe!"

She blinked. "What?"

"Where are our seats?"

"VIP, first level. Second row, I think."

"Damn." Jinx whistled. "We are going to have so much fun."

Chloe nodded. "Damn right." She followed the girls off the elevator and down the hall. They had so many bags they couldn't walk side by side. That so wasn't good.

Getting ready pushed away some of the homesickness for her kid. That and Jinx cranking Brooklyn Dawn's new album at an ear-shattering decibel. She was sharing the mirror with Ivy when Jinx suddenly disappeared.

"Drinks, bitches. And our passes arrived."

Chloe peeked out with one eye done. "What the hell is that?"

Jinx looked down at the cart. "Something called Mercury." She stirred the pitcher of blue liquid. For pity's sake, Chloe could smell the alcohol from across the room. Jinx came over with oversized martini glasses filled to the brim. She took a little sip. "Oh my God. You have to try it."

Had to be sapphire blue. Seriously?

Ivy wiggled her way around Chloe. "Oh, what's that?"

"Mercury."

"That sounds interesting."

"Not the word I was going with." Chloe accepted a glass.

"A toast. To the finest bitches in this hotel tonight. May we have fun, get drunk, and if we're lucky, get royally laid."

Ivy lifted her glass. "Hell yes."

Chloe wasn't sure about the getting laid part, but she was determined to have fun. "Bottoms up."

"That's the spirit." Jinx took a gulp, her eyes bulging as she got a full taste.

Chloe was pretty sure hers were a match. "Holy shit. What's in there? Lighter fluid?"

Ivy sputtered a little. "I'm going to say some grain alcohol."

The last time she had Everclear, there had been a lot of hickeys on her neck. Chloe wasn't sure if that was her being hopeful or not, but she took another swig. This time, the alcohol burned a little less and the flavor of pineapple made her taste buds demand more.

She set her glass on the counter as she went back to her makeup. She shimmied to "House of Cards" as Lindsey sang her heart out about losing the love of her life.

She knew how that felt.

When she emptied her glass, suddenly there was another one at her elbow. She sipped as she attacked her red hair with a curling iron and hairspray. The ombré skirt floated around her legs as she tried not to think about the inches of midriff she was showing with the strappy halter top.

"Fuck, you're hot."

Chloe paused as she painted on her dark lipstick. "Thanks. Still not changing teams. Even for you."

"You couldn't handle me." Jinx put her hands on her hips. "Everything's perfect except…"

Chloe recapped her lipstick. "Except what?"

Jinx held up a finger and ran into the bedroom. She came back with palm-sized scissors.

"What the hell are those for?"

"Just need a little shortening."

Chloe tried to back up. "No. This skirt cost three hundred dollars."

"And will look like a thousand dollars when I'm done with it."

"Hell no."

"I've done this a million times."

"Oh, yeah? I don't see a sewing kit."

"If you stop moving, then I'll cut straight. Legs—perfect legs, remember?"

Chloe slammed her eyes shut and stopped breathing as Jinx went around her with the scissors. She could actually hear the snip of the cloth. When air kissed her legs well above her knees, she was terrified to open her eyes. "It was ombré, now it's just going to be blue."

"Nope. Open your eyes and look."

"If you ruined this skirt, I'll skin you and steal your pants. Why you get to wear pants and I have to go with three quarters of my legs hanging out seems beyond unfair."

"Assets. I have long legs and skirts don't fit me right. You've got a rocking body you hide under mom jeans and khakis. We are not letting you hide tonight."

"Right. No hiding." Chloe opened her eyes and lightly swayed. The skirt belled around her thighs and fell in a floaty little sigh.

"I'm right."

"Shut up."

"I'll take it." Jinx stood up and hugged her. "We're going to have fun tonight."

Chloe hugged her back. "Yes, we are."

By the time they got back down to the main level where the House of Blues was, music was pumping out of the mouth of the entrance. They showed their laminated passes and were handed off to the next checkpoint.

Black walls, a black stage, and a steel support system crammed with twirling lights offered the perfect ambience. Huge screens packed each available corner to make sure no one had a bad seat. The iconic heart was flushed with purple and red flames. House of Blues—every musician's dream, no matter how famous.

She didn't have a musical bone in her body, but the heady power of the building itself was enough to send her pulse skittering. Her blood heated and fizzed the deeper they moved into the venue.

The place was packed. Now that they were inside, voices overpowered the piped-in music. Heat from too many bodies packed together made her suddenly very thankful she was wearing practically nothing. They were passed along to another staff member, who looked over their passes and checked a clipboard.

Jinx and Ivy squealed when they moved down yet another section. The stage was right there. They'd be eye level with the series of instruments set up along the stage's edge. A gorgeous pink guitar was anchored into a stand. She recognized the Takamine, the Les Paul, the Gibson, the Jackson, the Stratocaster, and the gleaming polish of the drum set. Scarves flirted around a microphone stand, catching the breeze from the fans working overtime above.

The murmur of conversation crashed around her as they found their seats. The front row was dotted with people, but this wasn't the main event. Warning Sign was the opener and still very new to the scene with only a few hits under their belts.

The VIP section would fill up as the night wore on. Local radio winners, along with ones from Sirius XM's contest would add still more people to the section. The high rollers who forever seemed to have access to the best the hotel could offer would take over more than a few seats as well. This was Vegas. The big time that her fiancé had longed for.

He'd never quite made it.

The lights flickered. Dejá vu kicked hard.

The stage had been part of her life for so long. This was a helluva lot bigger than the dives that Snake had played in, but the feel was the same.

That sense of anticipation, the hum of energy in the audience. Everyone was waiting for those opening chords.

Including her. For the first time in a long time, she couldn't wait for the show to begin.

SEVEN

MICHAEL TUGGED AT THE VINTAGE KISS T-SHIRT HE'D PAIRED WITH worn jeans and combat boots and scanned the backstage area one last time.

It wasn't looking good. Not for Malachi showing up, and not for him making amends anytime soon with Lila.

Oh, he knew eventually she'd forgive him. Their relationship was built too strong to be blown apart by the careless words he'd thrown out when he'd still been smarting from the Tabitha situation and Ryan's injury. But she was going to make him sweat for a while.

That was the Lila he knew and loved. And occasionally growled at.

"We're going to have to do it without him." At his side, Ryan rubbed his wrapped wrist with the fingers of his other hand. "I can play one-handed. It won't be pretty, and y'all will have to carry my ass, but we can make it work." When Michael didn't reply, Ryan added, "Hey, it's just an hour, right? Barely even that."

"An hour of your biggest hits, played in front of a crowd that is excited to hear Brooklyn Dawn and Oblivion." Lila strode up to them, impeccable as always in a pale blue business suit and black pearls. "This is not the time to phone it in."

Michael pivoted toward where Elle was warming up on her beloved

Gibson. Her blond head was bent, and the flowy peasant top she wore dipped off one shoulder as she concentrated on her fingerwork. His gaze drifted to Molly, doing stretches in one corner, then to Juliet, who was pacing and texting on her phone. West was doing air keyboards to the piped-in music through the sound system. And Ryan was at Michael's side, as always.

They all had their pre-show routines, and that hadn't changed because one of them was hurt. Maybe they'd hadn't locked up tight yet as a group like Brooklyn Dawn or Oblivion, but they were making progress.

One show wouldn't make them. Nor would it break them. It was just a show.

"We won't be phoning anything in." Michael cracked his knuckles and nodded at Ryan, who looked a lot less confident than Michael would've liked. Ryan always kept his eye on the prize. He never faltered. At least he hadn't before tonight.

Michael shut his eyes. Fuck, he wasn't used to being the group's backbone. His role was to support not to lead, and that was the way he liked it. He was just a guy who played guitar.

And lines up for free booze and plentiful pussy.

Yeah, well, not tonight. He wasn't planning on getting loaded or finding a chick. He'd have to be on point to help his band through the show, and afterward, he'd be there to pick up the pieces if needed.

After all, he'd been the one who'd rejected Lila hiring a studio musician for the night to fill in for Ryan. As long of a shot as it was, Michael had held out hope that Mal would show. He might not want to, might curse his little brother mightily after, but Mal wouldn't let Michael down. Until it was actually happening, he hadn't truly believed it would.

Now they were about to go on the stage, and Mal wasn't anywhere in sight.

"We'll be fine," he said, finally opening his eyes.

Ryan and Lila were gone.

Okay then. Guess he was on his own, just like the band.

He reached under his shirt and pulled out the silver cross Lila's mother had given him on his first Christmas at the orchard. He hadn't been religious even back then, and neither were Lila's parents for the most part. But Gram had told him that as a musician, he needed to have a higher power to call on for that extra little boost at the eleventh hour. Whether he was bolstered by spirit or self, with that cross, he would never be alone.

Ever since then, he'd always gripped the cross at the times he most needed a hand. The gesture always centered him and reminded him to count his blessings, not his failures.

There would only be blessings tonight.

Feet scuffed the floor behind him and the murmur of voices turned into something else altogether. He turned and glimpsed Elle being plucked up from the bench she'd been seated upon.

By Malachi, who lifted her as if she were a rag doll and he was the Incredible Hulk.

Holy fuck.

He set her down and took the seat she'd just vacated—not by choice. While she sputtered, he opened up what appeared to be a roll of fabric on the bench. "Sorry, sweetheart, but I need this seat for a second."

"I'm not your sweetheart."

He gave her a dismissive glance over his shoulder. "No, I don't suppose you are. Too skinny for me. But cute enough in the right light. You should use more makeup on stage. Your eyes totally disappear under the glare."

Glowering, Elle lifted her guitar. Since Michael wasn't entirely sure she wouldn't have broken it over his brother's block head, he moved between them. "Hang on, Elle. No killing the talent, even if he deserves it." Still facing Elle, Michael reached back and slapped Mal against the ear. "Asshole. Don't talk to my bandmates like that."

Malachi grunted, and when Michael looked over his shoulder, he realized the roll of fabric contained a selection of drumsticks. *Casual player, hmm?* "I'm part of the band tonight. So I guess that makes little Ricki my bandmate too."

"It's Elle," she said, flexing her fist around the neck of her Gibson. "I'm not little either. You're just a freaking giant."

Having evidently chosen his preferred weapons of destruction for the night, Mal stood, drawing himself up to his full height. Michael had waited to get the same growth spurt that had sent Mal from scrawny up to mountain man, but it had never happened. Michael had made it to almost six-feet tall, but Mal was six-fucking-four. And he owned every inch.

"What kind of kit am I working with?" Mal asked Michael, though his gaze remained on Elle.

"You?" Lila walked toward them, flanked by Ryan on one side and Molly on the other. "You're not working with anything." Her accusing gaze shot to Michael. "This is who you bring on my stage?"

A muscle ticked in Mal's jaw. "Hiya, stepmommy. Did you miss me?"

Even without glancing at Elle, Michael glimpsed her hand falling slack at her side. Elle was Lila's husband Nick's twin sister, which, of course, made her Lila's sister-in-law. Evidently, she hadn't heard much about the prodigal son.

The missing Shawcross son had finally come back—temporarily at least. Assuming Lila didn't chase him away.

"He can play," Michael said defensively.

"Oh, really? Since when?" Lila glanced at Mal, but he continued tapping his sticks against his thigh and remained silent.

"He can play," Michael said again. "Trust me."

God, he hoped she could trust him. That the rest of his band could too. Right now, he just didn't know.

That Mal had a selection of sticks was a good sign, but if he asked him anything too probing, his brother was apt to split. And it wasn't like they had other options except for gimpy Ry, who would try but could only do so much.

This was as good as it got.

"Trust you," Lila murmured. "If you say so." She glanced at her iPad, then nodded at one of the stage directors who touched her elbow. "Time to get ready to go." She glanced at Mal and back to Michael. "Good luck."

She turned to wave the other members of Warning Sign closer. "You all ready to rock?"

"You know it." Molly bounced up on her toes. She was wearing one of her myriad costumes, all done in rainbow hues and filmy fabrics that hugged her sexy body. Her hair was a mass of curls, dipping over one eye.

Juliet tucked away her phone and grinned. "Vegas won't know what to do with us."

West leaned forward to shake out his crazy mop of blond and teal-streaked hair. "They won't know what to do with you, Jules, that's for sure. Or is it what you won't do?"

"That's an easy one." Juliet popped her tongue in the corner of her mouth. "Nothing."

"So I'll warm up the crowd," Ry said, cradling his sore wrist in the other hand. "Get them revved for you guys, maybe get the female sympathy vote for this." He held up his hand.

"You don't even have any signatures on it yet," West said. "Tell the girls you want someone special to come up and sign it."

"Dumbass, it's an Ace bandage, not a cast."

"People can sign those. I've seen it done," West said stubbornly. "Besides, if you get the chicks feeling bad for you, maybe they won't notice when this one flames out." He pointed at Mal, who showed no expression whatsoever. "No offense, dude."

"None taken, *dude*," Mal growled.

If *that* was Mal's unoffended voice, Michael would prefer not to hear him pissed off anytime soon.

"Children," Lila said mildly, raising her fist in the air. "Ready?"

Everyone stepped forward, forming a circle, and pumped their fists. Malachi was the last holdout, but when Lila stepped back, Elle reluctantly moved aside to make space. Finally, Mal stepped into the circle and lifted his arm too.

Outside, the crowd was stomping its feet. Already people were amped for the show, and they were just the opening act.

The back of Michael's neck prickled as his nerves and excitement took over. This was going to either be epic—or an epic failure.

Ryan ran onstage first. "How you all feeling tonight, Vegas?"

The roar of hundreds of voices melding together washed over Michael's skin. He glanced from Molly to Juliet to West to Elle, reading the anticipation and nerves in their eyes. He saved Malachi for last. He couldn't believe he was standing with his brother backstage at their concert. That Mal would occupy the same space for the first time in forever. They had a joint goal. A joint reason to kick ass.

No matter what happened from here on out, he'd have this memory to take with him.

When they got the signal to join Ryan onstage, Michael hung back. Normally he was one of the ones racing out at the front of the pack. Tonight, he waited for his brother. He nearly asked him a million questions as they walked out together. He couldn't help wondering if Mal knew any of their material, or if he'd wanted Ryan to introduce him by name instead of just "a friend who's filling in and helping out." Mal deserved name recognition, just like the rest of them.

Then again, if he sucked, maybe it was just as well he loom silently and namelessly behind the kit.

Mal leaped up and took his spot, surprising the hell out of Michael by tipping his hand to his head before dropping on to the stool behind the drums. The crowd cheered as the opening notes to "Undermine" began. It was a slow, bass-heavy build, the kind of throbbing song that would crank the energy up to fever pitch.

Michael grabbed his pink electric Takamine off a stand, then followed Elle into the song, smiling at the little licks she added to goad him into his own flourishes. They had an interesting groove during concerts, although they rarely spoke much off of it. He figured that was why they worked well together. Their focus was the music, and only the music. No messy interpersonal crap got in the way.

Molly's husky voice started off as a whisper as she lamented the lover who wouldn't cut her free, but undermined everything she did. The song wasn't one of theirs, but one they'd been given by another musician. They were still finding their songwriting legs, with Molly and Ryan and West handling a lot of the melodies and arrangements.

He and Juliet were the more lyrically-focused ones. Their collaborations were how they'd started their flirtation—onstage and occasionally offstage, like the bar interlude Ry had mentioned. Meaningless, but fun.

The audience seemed to eat up their interactions. Juliet knew that, so she was already moving into position to give the crowd another show tonight.

There was no heat between them, no sparks except the kind that came from a beautiful woman moving her perfect ass up against Michael's while she played the hell out of her Jackson. He glanced back at her as his own fingers rode the strings. Sweat dripped into his eyes, blurring everything but the sweet curve of her bare shoulder. He turned his head to the side and she turned hers until they were cheek to cheek, and they belted out the chorus together.

> Undermine me, baby.
> Take me down so deep, take it all away.
> Til you're all I've got.
> All I've fucking got.

He was so wrapped up in his byplay with Juliet, with Elle rocking out on his other side, that he only remembered it wasn't Ry behind the kit when Mal's drums crashed into the song. They were like a Humvee barreling through a wall, altering the song that had come before and reforming it into something new.

They all seemed to stutter for a moment. Michael's fingers faltered, and Juliet's tripped. West missed a note on the keyboard, then two, but Ry jumped up beside him and they started hammering on the keys together—Ry one-handed, of course—as if they'd planned on doing just that all along.

Molly's voice caressed the words, her voice more poignant than ever as she clutched the multicolored scarfs around her mic. It was part of the mystique she was crafting, just like her ethereal, slyly sexual outfit. When she bent to wail into the mic, the crowd screamed with her.

Undermine me, undermine me, undermine me.

And finally, as the drums crescendoed and then leveled out, she purred her bastardized lyrics over and over.

Under me, under me, you're always under me.

The next song was even more raucous. Their first single, "All Night Long", was about someone looking for a good time so she didn't have to face the next day. West had written that one a million years ago, and they'd been playing it since their days in their crappy rehearsal space in Encino. Molly brought a whole new feel to it, winding one of her scarves around her neck as she prowled the stage. Once again, the song didn't have a ton of drum work, since West had written it to suit his keyboard-heavy style of play and they'd adapted it to fit the band. But when Malachi's part came, he nailed it, standing up and banging on the skins and the hi-hats with a flair that belied whether or not he was keeping time. Somehow it didn't seem to matter. He had enough panache to make up for any fumbles.

And from the way the girls were screaming every time he flexed his gleaming muscles in his tank—finally whipping it off somewhere in the middle of song number three—they didn't seem to mind any hiccups.

Michael let out a deep breath at the end of the next song, "Cascade." They'd made it almost halfway through their eight-song set, and Mal was getting by. Not perfectly, not always on time, but he was blending with them in a way that even Ry hadn't quite managed. He had the skill but not as much crazy style. Mal was leaning more on the latter than the former, and damn, was it working.

By the time "Delirious" started, the crowd was right there with them, bouncing and mouthing the lyrics if they didn't have them memorized. When Molly stopped singing and held the microphone toward the crowd, they sang the words for her as best they could, amid a few enthusiastic choruses of, "We love you, Molly!"

She basked in their adulation, shedding her gauzy wrap and baring her tiny top and flowing skirt for the next song. The name "Lick" was fitting, since it was every bit as dirty as the title suggested.

Michael swapped his guitar Jimi for his battered Les Paul, letting Elle do her thing as he set it up to enter the song after her. She bent low, her blond hair streaming down her back as she made the strings sing. When he joined her, she flashed him a smile at a wattage he only ever saw from her on stage. High on it, and on the fact that his brother was playing behind him, and that somehow, somehow they were getting through the show, he let his gaze wander the crowd.

The redhead caught his eye immediately.

She was close to the front, dancing back to back with one of her girlfriends while the other gyrated against her side. They were definitely feeling the lyrics that Molly was rasping as if she were fifteen seconds away from an orgasm. Ryan and West were doing the joint thing on the keyboards again, crossing hands and all kinds of tricks that only emphasized the erotic nature of the song. They pounded on the keys like he and Elle and Juliet were shredding their guitars. Like Mal was steadily drumming the kit, slow, sinuous. Building, building, building, until the final explosion.

The redhead turned and looked up on stage, playing with the strap of her halter top. For a second, he thought she'd flashed him some damn nipple. On purpose or accidentally, he didn't frigging care. All he knew was her big eyes were on him while she nearly fondled her own breast, and her lips were wet and parted, and he couldn't stop strumming his guitar the way he wished he could play with her. He'd sit her on his lap and slip under her skirt, then push aside her panties and slide one finger between the lips he knew would be soaked for him. While she watched, open-mouthed and silently begging, he'd suck on the finger that tasted of her until she was squirming against his rock-hard erection. Bouncing back and forth while he swelled against his zipper.

Christ, like he was doing right now.

Juliet came up behind him, sliding one hand in the front pocket of his jeans as Mal's drums and West and Ryan's keyboard faded. She jerked back and quickly shot over to the other side of the stage to set up for the next song, making him smother a laugh.

Guess she thought her onstage seduction routine with him had worked a little too well.

"What's her problem?" Elle whispered, trading her Gibson for her Stratocaster.

"Almost sure she thinks I like her butt too much."

"It is a cute butt." Elle winked at him, and he laughed.

"Hers or mine?" he asked, unable to resist. Hell, he had a freaking hard-on onstage from some sexy as hell redhead in the second row, who he was trying not to look at until the next song started so he didn't tear through his jeans.

Elle pretended to think as she put the strap over her head. "Gotta say hers. Looks firmer."

"You suck."

She laughed again then dipped her head close. "He isn't really your brother, is he? Tell me he isn't."

"Afraid so."

"He's a beast."

At the dark, moody chords of "In Your Arms," heralded by Ry on the blues harp, Michael glanced back at Mal. He was tapping the skins in almost perfect time. "Hell yeah, he is."

"Men." Elle snorted and surprised him by pulling her own Juliet-type routine, going back to back with him as they slid into the song.

Elle didn't grind or dance, just challenged him to get his fingers moving as fast as hers. He kept up, rippling up and down the strings so fast that he didn't dare look at the audience. His shoulders hunched and he bent closer to his instrument, cradling it, imagining again that he had the redhead in his arms. That hot, lush body he'd scarcely glimpsed curling against his as she pressed those glossy lips to his ear and said dirty things that didn't fit such an innocent face.

Pure face, smokin' body, hair like a goddamn siren. He wanted to hear her voice to see if it matched the sexiness of the rest of her. Perhaps she'd sing to him, maybe while he was going down on her. He'd part those creamy thighs and lean in for a taste—

A crack overhead caused him to jerk, then he remembered the shower of lights that they'd scheduled for this part of the show. A million colors arced and crisscrossed across the stage while his and Elle's guitars screamed.

In the midst of the chaos, he sought the redhead again. He had to. She stood out for him like a jewel, glittering so brightly that even the dazzling array of lights that shimmered at the edges of his vision couldn't compete. There were just those eyes, and those full lips moving as she mouthed the song.

He sang the lyrics too, and he was singing with her. *To* her. Imagining she was beneath him, silently pleading.

> All I want is to be in your arms.
> Make me yours tonight.
> Every night.
> Open up, take me in.

Close your eyes, feel me there.
Inside.

Sweat popped out on every inch of his skin, and just moving in the jeans and T-shirt that stuck to him was torture. But he played on, singing for her. Making his guitar shriek so she'd laugh and jump and clutch her hands between her breasts. She was so into it, her body as electric as the instrument vibrating in his hands.

Shit, if this show didn't end soon, he was going to soak the damn front of his pants. His cock was already so rigid that his usual stage embellishments were becoming a problem. But he had to keep going, had to perform for her, even sinking to his knees as he worked the frets.

Knowing she was watching every single thing he did.

For the rest of the set, he alternated between focusing on her and his brother. But Mal was doing just fine, and the redhead dominated every brain cell, swiftly crowding out everything in his head except her. Her wild hair, her seductive movements, and the longing in her eyes were his undoing.

His fucking personal Waterloo.

He hadn't planned on hooking up with anyone tonight. Definitely hadn't expected to be riding a high like this. But the buzz in his blood and the look of her ate at him, tempting him to seek her out for real after the concert ended.

Backstage pass, hell. He'd give her a bedroom pass, then tie her to his headboard right through the next morning.

She could be taken. Possibly even married. Could be a psycho. Damn, she might even be underage. She definitely had that whole schoolgirl thing going on, even with her hot clothes and gyrations. But he didn't care. Oh, he would—later. After.

Jesus, there had to be an *after* with her or he was going to lose his mind.

To end the show, Michael changed things up and told Ry they were going to skip "Exile" and do something else. His buddy shook his head at him, but he quickly told the others. As Michael tore into the first chords of "In The Air Tonight", Mal tipped his head. The band hadn't practiced the song together, and a few of the members of the group weren't familiar with it, judging from their *what the fuck* expressions. Luckily, Molly had an almost encyclopedic knowledge of songs from the eighties onward, though she wasn't particularly thrilled at the unplanned set change. But between the two of them and Mal and Elle —who was a seventies and eighties fiend—West, Ry and Juliet soon caught up.

They ended up making the song something completely different than the original anyway. Something theirs that fit the insane energy of the night. Channeling the vibe from the audience, feeding on it. Bringing down the house even though they were just the opening act.

Fuck that. They weren't going to just be the opening act for long. Soon, they'd have their own arenas. Their own crowds to chant and cheer and cry over them.

Just like his redhead was doing. Not the cheering or crying part, or even the chanting. She was singing along, her fingers laced together as if she were praying. Swaying with them. With *him*, as he leaned toward her as if she were the moon and he was the tide. Her pull was magnetic and inexplicable. He didn't want to fight it.

He'd been waiting for this moment all his life too, just like the lyrics of the song.

They brought the house down with Mal's frenetic drumming and the slashing guitars that bled out into only Molly's voice reaching for the rafters. And the audience went wild.

Pushing forward, they all linked arms and took their bows while Molly hammed it up and blew kisses to her adoring subjects. Mal hung back, tapping his black wrapped drumsticks against his thigh. Michael gave his brother a second to decide to join them on his own. When he didn't, Michael stepped back and grabbed Mal's hand.

It was ice cold. Forget nerves. The guy must be made out of steel.

Michael lifted their joined hands and basked in the waves of applause and stomping feet. And he searched for his redhead, desperate to locate her one more time.

He found her—just in time to see her being pulled up the nearest aisle by her girlfriends. She glanced back and the strobing lights bisected her face like the Joker's. Light and dark, known and unknown.

Fuck, she wasn't just some beautiful girl at a concert.

So much for the mystery of why he'd been so drawn to her. She wasn't random at all. In the chaos his life had become, he must've been seeking something—someone—familiar.

She was the absolute worst person for him to get involved with for a million reasons.

"Chloe," he murmured.

EIGHT

Chloe Adams.

Her name followed him through a quick shower and change. He grabbed a Foo Fighters shirt and a fresh pair of jeans, stuffing his feet into a different pair of boots. These were shitkickers with steel toes, perfect for fending off the spike heels of clumsy drunk girls. He grabbed his watch, shoving it back on his wrist, and beelined for the mini bar to swig back a quarter of a bottle of the whisky he'd had specially stocked.

"Priming the pump already?" Ry walked into Michael's bedroom carting a pair of black trousers and a white button-down shirt. So far he'd spent almost as much time in Michael's room as he did his own, though their suite was so huge they barely even had to see each other. "You know they aren't going to let you into the Foundation Room like that, right?"

Michael smirked around the mouth of his bottle. "Let's see them try to stop me."

Ry shook his head. "Dude, you're feeling it tonight. Just don't get arrested, all right?"

Still carrying the bottle, Michael went to the nightstand and rooted through the top drawer. "Nah, I have something else in mind." He pulled out a strip of his preferred brand of Magnum condoms and stuffed them in his back pocket.

Ry's eyebrow climbed toward his hairline. "So much for your supposed abstinence program, huh?"

"When did I say that?"

"You didn't, but considering you claimed to be such a good boy, so misunderstood by the masses…"

"Hey, safety first. I am a good boy." He flashed a grin at his buddy and checked his phone. "Get a move on. I need to get upstairs."

"Hot date?"

"You could say that." More like he needed to find Chloe, then they'd go from there.

Obviously, he had hopes for how the night would go, and the half dozen condoms he'd just shoved in his pocket were proof. But even if things didn't progress that way, he had to find her. To hear her voice, watch her laugh, feel her rub up against him.

It was probably just the atmosphere. Something chemical that would burn off by morning. He'd definitely never felt that jolt in her direction before, although he'd pretty much steered clear of her. Understandable, since his first glimpse of Chloe had been in the photographs taken by the PI he'd hired a couple of years back.

The PI hadn't been a real one, just a former high school friend, and Michael hadn't been trying to get pix of Chloe. He'd been trying to get photos of Lila with Nick—back when she was still married to Michael's father—in the hopes of showing her how indiscreet she was being. He'd only wanted to remind her what was at risk if she got caught cheating, not cause her any trouble.

Yeah, it sounded crazy even in his own head. Which was why he'd swiftly disavowed the whole thing, including Chloe. She'd become persona non grata in his mind. Any reminders of the period when he'd been so worried about Lila had been shoved to the back of his thoughts.

And that included the cute redheaded preggo girl inadvertently captured with Nick in the PI's pictures.

Fuck, she'd been pregnant. She had a baby. So much for being just some young girl out having fun. She was somebody's *mother*.

He took another long swig off the bottle and glanced around the empty hotel room. Ry had probably gone to shower.

Chloe might be showering too right now. Getting ready for the night.

For *him*. And wasn't that a kick in the ass?

Talk about unbelievable.

He and Chloe had bumped into each other a few times on holidays and such, since she was now on the fringes of their group of friends and family. He didn't know her whole backstory, just that she'd dated one of the guys who'd started Oblivion and had his kid. The guy was dead, and he'd caused a bunch of trouble for Oblivion before he passed.

And this is who you want to have a meaningless hookup with?

He took another belt from the bottle. He didn't give a shit about what was right or wrong. Not tonight. She'd been flirting with him just as much as he'd been into her. So what if they kind of knew each other? Everyone knew what happened in Vegas stayed there.

One night. One morning after. Two satisfied people.

Hell, if she sucked in bed, or their chemistry fizzled out, well, he'd just avoid her end of the dinner table at family events. No big. Lila wasn't exactly Chloe's biggest fan anyway, since she had some past with Nick too.

He rubbed at his temple. What past, exactly? Why couldn't he remember? Shit was already getting a little fuzzy at the edges, which on one hand—fucking awesome. On the other, his lizard brain didn't have the best track record.

Especially since the serpent in his pants didn't know the meaning of the word *discriminating*.

Things were getting too serious. He'd just had the best show of his life. Mal had disappeared before he could speak to him, even to say thanks, but that was okay. The rest of Warning Sign had stuck around through Brooklyn Dawn and Oblivion's kickass sets, and the amount of excitement flowing through Michael's veins was nearly at the illegal limit. He'd be damned if thoughts about Chloe's home life lessened his buzz.

She was just a pretty girl. He'd get her over or under him, or maybe they'd just dance and flirt. If she wasn't into it, or she wasn't around, there would be someone else.

Even if he didn't want anyone else. He wanted her. Just *her*.

Fuck, he needed another drink.

He traded the first bottle of whiskey—hey, it was empty, look at that —for another. He tucked it into the inside pocket of the jacket he shrugged on just before Ry stopped by again to remind him to bring ID.

His buddy wouldn't let him open carry into a party. Even if everyone else and their cousin was tipsy, his best friend would make sure Michael kept up appearances.

Still, he managed to get more than a few sips off the bottle as Ryan finished getting ready. The alcohol was definitely doing its job. When Ry made some comment about him needing to beg Mal to come back for their next show, Michael only laughed. Mal was his brother. He wouldn't need to beg.

Damn, he loved whisky.

He'd cleared a quarter of the bottle before they passed through security at the front door of the club. They met up with the rest of Warning Sign just inside the entrance, along with a few members of Brooklyn Dawn and Oblivion. For once, no one was pregnant in the Oblivion crew, and it looked like everyone was in the mood to have a good time.

Just like him.

He'd made it about three steps before he bumped into Lila. His luck was in, however, since she was currently engaged in a conversation with her husband and didn't notice Michael behind her.

"I told you that we shouldn't have done the new single first. You just bowed to Donovan's pressure." Nick tossed back whatever he was drinking and set aside the glass. "As usual."

"I don't bow to any male's pressure, thank you very much. Including yours."

"We'll see if you say that in ten minutes."

Michael shook his head as Nick grabbed Lila's hips with the subtlety of a bear with a trout. She shoved at him, but when Michael looked back a moment later, she was whispering in his ear and he had both hands on her ass.

So much for Lila standing firm.

Michael kept going. Speaking of firm, apparently alcohol made him horny, or else he still hadn't come down from the stage. Below his waist, he had a situation going on. A serious one, just from the possibility that Chloe might be there. He had no way of knowing if she would be. She could've gone home for the night. Maybe even hopped a plane back to her kid.

Babies everywhere. He just wanted to practice. A lot.

Hell, he should get Chloe's digits from L. His stepmother would love that. Assuming she glanced away from Nick long enough to care.

Michael did a quick visual search for Ry or West, but they'd both disappeared. Likely together, since West tended to drag Ry out on the hunt. Michael preferred to do his thing solo. Fewer witnesses. Fewer people to tell him to rein it in, or throttle back. He just wanted to let loose and celebrate after pulling out an improbable win. No one would get hurt.

At the bar, he smiled at the brunette waitress and ordered—what else—a whisky. Might as well keep the theme going. Handily, he could take care of his own refills.

And shit, he was clearly feeling it already if he was laughing at his own lame jokes.

The song changed to something with an undulating club beat, the kind that made people get up and dance. He sipped his whisky and surveyed the crowd, ignoring the hopeful smiles he received from a few of the women, all dressed in their Saturday night best.

He wasn't stupid. He knew he appealed to the opposite sex, which was handy since they damn sure appealed to him.

At the moment, he only wanted one. Fiery red hair and big eyes and full lips, meant for sucking…things. He was a gentleman until he'd had a few more drinks, so she could pick the appendage she wanted to start with.

He already knew he'd go right for what was between her thighs. Why save dessert until after dinner?

"Hey, honey, you looking for some fun?"

"Yes," he admitted, glancing at the woman who'd wound her arm through his. "Just not with—" He cleared his throat as her eyes shuttered. "Sorry, I'm waiting for someone."

"You're with the band, aren't you?"

"Which one?"

"Any of them." She pinched his biceps through his jacket. "Who would keep you waiting?"

He smiled and started to answer, but a flash of red caught his eye. Those curls stood out even in a swanky place with women who had hair color of every shade. Somehow Chloe had trapped flames inside each strand.

Then again, he was pretty drunk.

Still, he recognized the waves bouncing down her back. Knew that rounded ass in a tight skirt, moving in self-conscious circles. She had nothing to be shy about. A woman that beautiful should be worshipped.

A task he'd be happy to take on for a night or a lifetime.

"Gotta go," he said to his admirer, pressing his whisky into her hand. "Here, enjoy. I didn't spike it," he tossed over his shoulder.

He wasn't going up to Chloe with a drink in his hand. Hell, he was already loaded enough. If she wanted to drink and party, he was on-board, but he had to try to collect the last of his remaining wits to bring this one all the way home.

She was dancing by herself, gripping one of the gold wrap-around bars that ringed part of the dance floor. Men kept circling close to her, but she flicked them off with a word and a smile, making those glorious curls shimmer with each movement. When one persistent guy cupped her hip, Michael grunted and stepped up behind her.

"She's mine," he said, surprised that it felt true.

They hadn't just met, but they were virtually strangers. And they hadn't met in this space, on this night. They hadn't talked or been close enough that when she glanced at him over her shoulder, he could see the fringe of eyelashes shadowing her cheek. Beneath her makeup, she had freckles. Just the barest dusting of them on her nose, and over the dark bow of her mouth.

The other guy mumbled something and vanished into the crowd.

Michael brushed closer, sliding his hand over her waist until it rested low on her belly. So low that he could stretch his fingers and feel the rise of her mound under her skirt.

But above her waistband, she was bare. Midriff exposed, revealing all that warm, silky skin.

"Keep dancing," he said against her ear.

She bristled. "This isn't a good idea."

"It feels like a great one to me." He rested his chin on her shoulder, drawing in the scent that clung to her like the night. There were a million different ones surrounding them, but the spice of hers reached him as if they were all alone. "What are you wearing?"

The corner of her mouth tugged down. "How much have you had to drink?"

He chuckled and turned his mouth against the side of her neck where her scent was strongest. Cinnamon, warmed by her skin. He flicked his tongue over the space behind her ear, not to seduce but to see if she tasted the same. She moaned and the reverberation fluttered against the hand still low on her belly. "Do you smell like cinnamon all over?" he asked, pressing his lips against her throat to gauge her reaction.

Her body said more than her mouth did by far.

"Only the places where scent should go."

Again, he chuckled. He shouldn't have been able to hear her responses considering the throb of the music around them, but they were sequestered away from everyone else. A force field seemed to box them in, cushioning them in a space where nothing was wrong and everything felt right.

Especially her, stiffly swaying in his arms.

"Do you know who I am?"

"Do you know who *I* am?" he echoed, curling his fingers into soft, giving flesh. She was a mother, and he'd always run from those, as if pregnancy was a contagious disease. He wasn't ready for kids. Wasn't ready to be a father, or to be with a woman who was a mother. But inexplicably, knowing that she'd given birth fascinated him, even made him want to trace the feathery marks on her belly with his tongue.

Shit, that was some damn potent whisky.

"Y-yes. I do now. I didn't at first." She mumbled something else and flagged down a passing waiter. She gulped some of the drink he handed her, then held the cold glass against her chest. "I never saw you play before. You're good."

"I'm amazing," Michael corrected, and glimpsed a hint of a smile curving her glossy wine-red mouth. Somehow she didn't leave a lipstick imprint on her glass.

Women were magicians, the lot of them.

"Cocky," she said, granting him a sidelong look. "I don't do cocky rockstars."

"How about modest ones?" He batted his eyelashes and she giggled. "Oh, Chloe, you shouldn't praise me. I'm really humble."

At once, her laughter subsided. "You do know."

"I know a few things. I know you're absolutely gorgeous, more beautiful than any other woman I've ever seen."

She scoffed. "Right. You've never given me a second look."

"That's because I never saw you like this." He gave her hair a light tug. "All loose and relaxed, moving your hips. By the way, you're not moving anymore." He gave her belly a light squeeze, and she stumbled into a halting dance step. "That's it. You know what to do. Just pretend we're naked."

She sucked down another gulp of her drink, but she didn't stop moving. "So I do all the work and you just stay still?"

"Oh, Red, I can guarantee you, if we were in bed, I wouldn't be still for a goddamn second." Emphasizing his words, he flexed his hips against her ass. He gripped a handful of her hair with his other hand, tugging her head back until he could speak against her ear. "You gotta tell me something."

She just kept dancing, and drinking, and occasionally darting assessing little looks at him.

"Okay then. We'll just dance. Words don't matter anyway, do they?"

She shook her head and turned toward him, arching up to wrap one arm around his neck. Her lip brushed the edge of her glass and he bent to flick his tongue along it, moaning at the hint of lime and vodka on her flesh. He grabbed the glass and tipped up her face with his other hand, waiting until her seductive sinkhole eyes settled on his. They were both more drunk than sober, so he didn't want there to be any confusion.

"I'm going to kiss you."

"Where?" she murmured, and he groaned.

"Let's start with right here." He tapped his thumb against her lips and they parted for him, dark red and slickly wet.

Reminding him of other wet places he couldn't wait to taste.

He would've sworn he lowered his head forever. She closed the distance between them, fisting a hand in his hair to bring him the rest of the way. Their mouths collided, hungry, seeking. No finesse, no artifice. Just all-consuming lust as he slipped his tongue around hers.

She trembled at the first glancing blow, and all out shuddered as he drove in deep. Something shattered, and it didn't take a genius to realize it was her glass. He'd simply let go, and now his hand was in her hair, gripping it so he could pull back her head. She opened for him, every part of her lush and welcoming. He was straining, hard, desperate.

He'd never been more urgent in his life.

She pulled back and gasped for air, and he dropped his forehead against hers. If she moved away, he'd just yank her back again. They were tethered, linked in a way that defied logic.

"Ask," she panted. "Ask your question, Michael."

The relief that she knew who he was too sang through him like a note that went on forever. He could barely speak around the tightness of his throat. "Do you have freckles all over, Chloe?"

Saying her name again felt like a form of defiance. Yeah, they weren't supposed to be doing this. Not the sweet, single mom with the difficult past and the asshole rockstar who wreaked destruction wherever he went. But she was still looking up at him with those glowing eyes, and her mouth was still swollen from his.

No one could tell them no. Apparently, not even each other.

Saying nothing, she gripped his hand and led him over to the woodgrain bar at one side of the club. The final stool was empty and she leaned back on her elbows, giving him room to slide her onto the bar. Up, up, up, until that expanse of bare belly was fully on display and she was stretched out in front of him.

It was Vegas, and it was crazy, and no one thought anything of her lying down on top of the end of the bar. If they did, they didn't say, and he didn't care in any case.

She was his entire focus.

"Why don't you find out?" she whispered.

NINE

Hours seemed to pass while she was on that bar. Lost to him and the fire he'd stoked inside of her.

Now it was raging.

The watery tones of the song seemed to infiltrate her skin. Her hips followed the silky rhythm as she lifted her arms. She closed her eyes just enough so the twirling lights became streaky trails dragging her away from reality. Her fingers brushed over crystals dripping off the overhead lighting fixtures of the bar.

She had enough vodka in her veins to ignore the fact that Michael Shawcross was at her feet. When his fingers skimmed over her calves and around to the backs of her knees, she opened her eyes and met his hooded gaze.

Silver winked from his eyebrow, and the shadow of a beard emphasized the angular lines of his face. He was absurdly handsome. Too attractive. No man should be that hot and be even remotely attainable.

Yet there she was. On the bar, with the calloused tips of his fingers dragging up the backs of her thighs.

She slid her fingers into his hair. The super short hairs sifted around her trimmed nails until she got to the denser wavy strands on top. Just enough to twist, so she did. She tugged his head back, pressing her knee to his shoulder.

He reached up for her, gripping her waist with his huge hands. His long fingers made her feel tiny. Wanted.

His eyes screamed hunger.

No. Not for her. He wasn't for her.

Rockstar.

Wrong type.

So much the wrong type.

Too bad the crackling arc of attraction between them wasn't freaking listening.

Her breath shuddered out as she slid down his body, her breasts rubbing against his firm chest. Muscles everywhere. The breadth of his shoulders wouldn't allow her to encircle all of him. She held onto what she could, her toes dangling off the floor.

His mouth was right there.

So close that she could taste the tequila shooter he'd just sipped off her flesh on his breath. The bite of lime would still be on his tongue. Her nails dug into his shoulders.

She wanted that lime.

Wanted his afterburn one more time.

She couldn't remember the last time her skin had felt so tight and responsive. She didn't want to question it. Didn't want to play it safe.

Safe made no sense tonight.

She covered his mouth. There was no teasing between them. Foreplay had been the air between them, the lights and the music that followed him around like its own forcefield.

Power and haunting charisma drenched in charm.

She felt the hint of his smile before their tongues tangled.

Slick and dominant, he brought every want into the foreground. She'd believed the lies she told herself. That she didn't need to be touched. She could live without passion.

Now she'd learned otherwise. The starvation diet never worked. As soon as she'd sampled off the forbidden tray, the craving had become all-encompassing.

Hot. Worse than any drug she could imagine.

Want eroded sense. Sense floated away the moment his taste infiltrated her body.

He demanded participation with a tempting wind of lips and tongue. Just when she thought she would need to rip herself away to breathe, he adjusted their kiss and offered a hint of oxygen.

Just enough to feed the beast building inside her chest.

In one sweeping move, he lifted her then carted her across the room. He dropped suddenly and she went free-falling into his lap. Startled, she tried to find her footing, but he pulled her astride him.

"Feel that?" He dragged his lips over her chin to her jaw and down the column of her neck. "Feel how hard I am?"

She sucked in a breath. *Please don't talk. Don't make me think.* He nipped at the strings of her halter top to move them before he wrapped his lips around her pulse.

Gone.

She was simply gone.

Thoughts slid away into the corners where mistakes didn't matter. Under the dark cover of shadows, she forgot to be the responsible Chloe. The next song urged her to roll her hips against him. Faster. The sensual words of the song emptied her brain.

His lips brushed over the material of her shirt. He scraped his teeth over her shoulder then slid down to hover over her nipple. A whisper of hot breath then a tease of teeth at the tip made her shudder. Her moans drifted out over the cacophony of voices.

He stared up at her.

Was he asking permission?

No.

It was demand.

He didn't give her time to think about saying yes.

He grinded her down on his cock.

Fuck.

The word was foreign even in her own head. But it belonged here in the relentless beat of the song with this hard, hot male under her.

He was just a body. This was just sex.

It was just a basic need that was finally coming to the surface. But no other man in three years had come close to drawing even a fraction of this out of her.

Hunger so thick and consuming it battled with the alcohol she'd fed her out of control inner bad girl all night. Except being bad felt so damn good.

She'd touched and flirted with others the night before. A pretty lawyer who was probably a better choice even for just a one-night-stand.

But no, it had to be *this* man who set off the conflagration that had lain dormant inside her.

The worst man in legions of ways.

She gripped the back of the chair as her hips undulated against him. Muscle memory crashed into something so new and different she shuddered to keep up with it.

"That's right. Fuck. You're so fucking hot. Can you come on my jeans like this? Just grinding on me. Use me. Let me feel you come on me." His turbulent sea eyes flashed in the flickering dark.

His hand slid under her skirt to cup her ass.

"This is crazy."

"Crazy is good. Crazy is hot. Right here. No one cares about us." He looked around. "See over there? That girl on the table has all the eyes on her."

Chloe craned her neck toward the statuesque blonde gyrating on a club table.

"But right here," he gripped her cheek, "look at me."

She hissed out a breath as the tips of his fingers coasted along the edge of her panties. But her attention was back on him. This man.

Michael.

Not some stranger she could forget in the morning.

"We're alone as far as they're concerned. So let go." He lifted his hips and his shaft rubbed against the front of her panties. "I need to watch you let go."

Her breath came faster as she used the rough material of his jeans for friction.

His fingers slid between them, and his thumb rubbed against her tight clit over her panties.

"So hard and sensitive. How wet are you?"

She sucked in a sharp breath. Wetter than she could remember ever being. Even during the rare instances when she had to take the edge off on her own, she'd barely been damp enough to get the job done.

She rocked against his thumb.

Suddenly, he moved and she whimpered.

No. Don't fucking move.

She was so fucking close.

He pulled down the front of her panties, tucking his thumb into her pussy. "Fuck." His breath hitched against her neck as his nail flicked over her clit.

She bucked at the sudden touch.

He held her down with his other hand, circling her clit with his thumb. "That's it. You're like liquid fire. If we were alone, I'd drag you up and over my face right now. I'd drink every bit of you down."

Chloe gasped and his features dissolved in the dark. She wasn't even aware that she'd flipped over from almost there to full detonation. With her head flung back and her breasts in her face. She didn't even care if the whole room figured out what she'd experienced.

Or what he'd been doing to her.

It had been so goddamn long since she'd actually had an orgasm like that. She could only chant "thank you," over and over as he strummed her like his instrument. As if she were the fret board and her pleasure was the vibrating strings.

He reached up and caught the back of her neck, dragging her back into the moment. Into the reality of all the people around them. He drew his thumb out of her panties and stroked up her midriff. She let out a shaky breath at the wetness—*her* wetness on her skin.

He watched her as he dragged his lips and tongue over her bare flesh, twirling his tongue on a lazy path across her shoulder. "Chloe," he said in a harsh voice just before he kissed her stupid.

She tasted herself on his tongue.

She could have been imagining it. Surely her wetness had dissolved by now, but logic didn't make her certainty any less overwhelming. Didn't lessen the riot taking place in her mind and body.

She and Snake had been fumbling fingers and grunts in the dark. She'd loved him to distraction, but he'd never taken care to seduce her.

He had been the seduction. Just being a musician. Being a man who other people wanted.

And her rose-colored glasses had made everything better in her head than the reality of their sex life.

It had been *nothing* like this.

Her nails raked through the thick thatch of hair at the top of his head. Ropey arms came around her, squeezing her breath out as if he was going to steal her very essence.

So much.

Too much.

She wiggled back until he let her go. She stood and dragged him up off the chair. "Too hot."

"Yeah, you are."

"No." She laughed. Mania bubbled out of her throat. At least that was what it sounded like to her. "Too hot in here. I can't think."

"Thinking is overrated."

Her head roared as she got her bearings. She glanced around the room, but her friends were nowhere to be found.

How long had she been with Michael?

She peered back up at him, but his face swam a little.

"Let's go outside."

She nodded. "Good idea."

He laced their fingers together and drew her through the crowd. She tried not to pay attention to how wonderful his hand felt in hers. No fumbling fingers, no re-tangling to make them sit right. First time absolutely perfect.

Her heart raced as she curled her fingers around his wrist and followed him without a qualm. Before she could wonder if it was a good idea or not, he drew her out onto the balcony.

Vegas spread out before her.

She gasped. The lights shone in the dark. As if Vegas was putting on a show only for her. Did everyone feel like this?

Was *this* the allure?

He pushed his way through the people and made a space for her at the railing. He hauled her in front of him and crowded behind her, his shaft tucked against her ass. Still hard for her. "Fuck, you fit me," he said against her neck.

She did.

It didn't make any sense.

"On your toes."

She almost did just that. It shocked her how much she wanted to follow his direction. To see what it would be like.

"I could slip inside you and ride you with that fucking view as our audience."

She gasped.

"There you are!"

Chloe groaned at Jinx's voice.

Michael growled in her ear. "Come back to my room."

She should say no. The lunacy of the club was one thing. The reality of getting naked with him was a step too far. There would be no going back from it.

She'd have to look at him across the Christmas dinner table forever.

Nick and Lila would get forever, not her. She wasn't meant to find that with anyone.

The pang of reaction blindsided her. *Forever* wasn't something she said easily. Hers had been taken away from her. She tried to ignore it— had practically deleted that particular word from her vocabulary.

She was a mother. A responsible adult.

This was just a wild weekend, nothing more.

She twisted out of his arms and toward her friend. Toward sanity.

When Michael touched her, she lost any will to listen to reality. And that was more than dangerous. She'd already had a man like that in her life and look how that had turned out.

She'd ended up alone. Just her and her baby.

Jinx shouldered her way through the crush of people with her sister holding up the rear. "You disappeared on us." She glanced up at Michael. "With good reason." Her eyes narrowed. "You're from the band."

He nodded, an easy grin sliding across his boyish face. "Michael."

Jinx glanced at Chloe then back up to Michael. "Are we interrupting?"

"Yes."

"No," Chloe said over him.

"Which is it?" Jinx hooked her arm through Ivy's "Have you met Michael?"

Ivy shook her head. "But I think that's a shame." She held out her free hand. "Ivy. This is my sister, Jinx."

Michael shook their hands instead of stepping back. Seriously, how many signals could Chloe give the guy? He didn't seem to care.

He shifted behind her, pressing his erection against her hip. As if Chloe needed the reminder of where they'd been heading.

"Looks like we need drinks." Michael nodded toward someone, then held up four fingers.

Chloe frowned. "What did you order?"

"I think I ordered four tequila shots. At least if her shirt was correct."

"Chicks are walking around with labels across their boobs. It's like the ultimate billboard for booze at this party."

Michael lifted one shoulder. "Makes it easier to order a drink. The bartenders can't keep up."

"Evidently."

When the blond came back, she had a tray of large shot glasses.

Michael grinned at her and dropped a bill on her tray. "Thanks."

He hadn't called the waitress *baby*. At least Chloe hadn't had a sexist pig's tongue in her mouth five minutes ago.

Little victories.

He passed around the glasses to everyone. "To chaperones."

Jinx sputtered out a laugh after she downed her shot. "Is that what we are?"

"Your timing is certainly suspect." He said it with an easy smile as he leaned against the railing.

Chloe swallowed hard. His cock wasn't touching her anymore. She could actually think again. Did it have some sort of super power? That really was the only thing that made sense. As soon as she'd rubbed against his dick, she'd been like a freaking cat in heat.

Not like her at all.

"We can certainly make ourselves scarce."

Chloe grabbed for Jinx's arms. "No."

Jinx's eyebrows shot up before she tipped her head and squinted up at Michael. "This guy hassling you?"

"No, it's not that."

Chloe darted a glance at him. His glass dangled from his long fingers. Fingers that had been all over her mere moments ago. Michael crossed his feet at the ankles, his huge boot resting a bare inch from her. He invaded her space in a lazy, feline way that made her nipples harden again. What the hell was wrong with her?

Jinx threw back her shot. "Then let's have a little fun, shall we?"

Michael grinned and followed suit.

As if she needed more alcohol swimming through her veins. But it was either that or face Michael's offer of a trip to his hotel room.

She wasn't quite sure she was ready for that idea yet.

For once, downing tequila was a helluva lot safer.

After the third tray of drinks had been consumed, it was easier for Chloe to laugh at Jinx's ridiculous commentary on the men in the room than to focus on the guy who had her panties still wet.

He hovered behind her. A stray touch here and there to remind her that he was there. Her arches screamed, but she couldn't sit. Sitting reminded her of his cock rubbing her off in a sea of strangers. She'd been out of control in a way she couldn't study right now.

She preferred to drift on the hazy out of focus colors and heady sexual undertones within the safety net of her friends.

The party was finally thinning out a little. The Foundation Room had been set up as a VIP room after the show. Not for the general public. People moved on to other parties, or more personal ones as the night wore on.

Michael twisted his fingers around hers, dragging her back against him. "Dance with me."

Not a question.

Again, that almost order urged her forward. If he touched her, she might not have the strength to say no. Another tray of drinks came by. She welcomed the open smile of the waiter. She frowned slightly when she didn't recognize the shirt he was wearing. A single blue teardrop on the left side of his chest, but no other logo.

Michael's lips found the back of her neck. She handed him one of the sapphire blue shooters. Blue was her color tonight. She couldn't—wouldn't—allow the jewels, so she'd drink a hint of it instead.

She turned around, clinking the plastic cylinders that reminded her of high school chemistry. Of how they'd stolen trays to make their own moonshine after hours. She laughed as she wrapped her lips around the end and tipped her head back.

The blue liquid slid down her throat easy as could be.

Michael pushed her through the room to the dance floor. Katy Perry's voice drowned out her laughter. He took the shooter from her, passing it off to another waitress. They circled each other. First him, with his calloused fingers lingering at her lower back. Almost there touches that matched the cosmic, otherworldly beat of the song.

His knee slid between hers as he suddenly dipped her. She laughed and gripped his jacket. She wasn't sure either of them were sober enough to not land on their ass with that kind of move. But he didn't drop her. He held her close and chased her laughter with his tongue.

She slid her hands under his jacket to the heat trapped along his back. Her nails dug into his T-shirt. They spun in a lazy circle and she tipped her head back to let him taste her neck again. He was so good at it. Just enough scruff to buzz, not enough to make her pull away. But the true mastery was his words.

Whispers that drew her closer.

"Mine."

She didn't want to think about being his. "You can't be my forever."

He frowned down at her. "Why not?"

Her fingers bumped against something in his pocket. Distracted, she answered honestly. "I had my chance at forever." She pulled out a bottle. "What's this?"

He shrugged. A frown line built between his silky brows.

She reached up to rub it away. "It's all right." The lights were softer now, the music further away. She uncapped the bottle and offered it to him.

He accepted the bottle from her and took a healthy swig. She went up on her tiptoes. Just like earlier, she caught his face and brought him back down to her. The sweet smoky flavor turned to a burn as her tongue tangled with his.

Chloe lowered back onto her heels and gave him a sleepy smile. She rested her cheek against his chest. "I don't expect forever. Not with someone like you," she said again on a slur.

Even as she said it, a part of her was lying. Everything was so soft and romantic. His arms around her, her cheek against his heart.

She wanted to stay in this moment for the rest of her life.

"Maybe you don't expect it," he said against her hair, tightening his grip. "But what if I do?"

TEN

CHLOE MOANED. WHY COULDN'T SHE MOVE?

Had she ended up with another Johnson sleeping with her again? Jinx wasn't usually the cuddling type, but Ivy liked to spoon sometimes. Chloe grunted and tried to wiggle free.

Was Ivy groping her boob? Okay, that might require a conversation about personal space. And seriously when had Ivy become close to two tons? She opened her eyes and immediately slammed them shut. Too bright.

Not good.

So not good.

Just how much had she guzzled last night? And her mouth tasted like death. Thank God it was Sunday. Obviously, she didn't know how to handle Vegas.

A groan dented her personal flogging. *Not* a girl groan.

"Oh, fuck."

No. No. No.

She squeezed her eyes shut so tightly that sparklers started going off behind her eyelids. She didn't. She wouldn't.

Flashes of bodies grinding in a dark room tightened her throat.

You can do it. Open your eyes. Big girl panties, goddammit.

Was she wearing panties? She wiggled her legs.

Sweet peaches, she so wasn't.

Chloe forced herself to open her eyes and look down. Definitely not the shirt she'd been wearing last night. Was that Dave Grohl? Why had her boobs grown at least two sizes?

Because a male hand was cupping each of them like she was his own personal rock wall.

She suppressed another moan when the man's hands tightened. His thumb flicked over her nipple and it responded instantly.

"Oh God."

He groaned and pushed up her shirt. "Round two?" he asked in a fuzzy mumble.

"Round none!" She kicked out and connected with something before she scrambled up against the headboard.

"Fuck me." The man curled into a fetal position.

Dark hair and naked shoulders. Was that a tattoo? Was he naked under the sheet?

She didn't wait to find out. She leaped off the bed. Not her hotel room. This one was bigger with only one bed. A lake-sized bed with tangled white sheets.

She was going to be sick. She lunged for the bathroom, slamming the door and locking it before she skidded in front of the toilet. Her stomach revolted until there was nothing but dry heaves shuddering through her.

"Are you all right?"

No, she wasn't all right. She'd awakened in a strange hotel room with a strange man. She gripped the edge of the bowl, frowning as something clicked against the porcelain.

She pulled shaking fingers away and flushed, then stumbled to the sink.

Her eyes were bloodshot, her pupils absolutely huge. Blindly, she fumbled with the faucet, causing another clink of metal against metal. She stuck her head under the spray to rinse away the sick.

She needed eight toothbrushes and a magic eraser for her brain.

Actually, not so much on the erasing because she couldn't remember a damn thing.

How had she ended up here?

Why couldn't she remember?

Where the hell was her phone?

Auto-pilot kicked in as she pumped soap on her hands. Metal clicked against metal. She still had on Snake's ring. She couldn't seem to take it off, but she'd moved it to her right hand.

That was only one hand.

Something flashed on her left hand.

On her *ring* finger.

She washed away the lather. Rubbing at the sapphire and diamond ring from yesterday. No, she hadn't bought that.

She'd said no.

She'd given it back.

She wouldn't *ever* put it on her left hand.

She slammed her elbow into the doorknob. Tears flooded her eyes as pain crashed into fear and a sob escaped. "No, no, no."

"Open the goddamn door. It's the least you can do after you dropkicked me in the balls. Are you hurt? Is there blood?"

She whirled around. Panic made the space seem smaller by the minute. Marble tile over marble countertops. Everything pristine white. She climbed into the shower and curled into the corner.

No.

No way.

"Dammit, open up. Are you okay?"

No, she wasn't okay. She pulled the shirt over her knees and tightened herself into the smallest ball she could make.

Maybe it was just her. She'd gone back to see Nathan at the jewelry store. She'd gotten crazy with the girls. She'd bought the damn ring.

But wouldn't she have put Snake's ring back on her left hand? The sapphire wasn't for left hand wear. It was too much like a—

No.

Not that.

It wasn't that.

The doorknob rattled. "If you don't open this goddamn door, I'm going to break it down."

Ask it. Talk. "What's on your left hand?" she asked in a shaky voice.

"What?" The voice was deep and hoarse. "What the hell are you talking about?"

"Your hand!" Her voice came out as a squeak. She cleared her throat. "Check your left hand."

"Have you lost your— What the fuck?"

Fear cramped her belly. *He's going to laugh. Please? Please laugh.* She was just being stupid.

"I don't fucking wear gold. Why do I have a gold ring on my hand?"

ELEVEN

H<small>E'D WOKEN UP WITH A PAIR OF GORGEOUS BREASTS IN HIS PALMS, AND</small>
now, not ten minutes later, he was pretty sure he was sterile.

Michael leaned against the jamb of the closed bathroom door and
cupped his aching dick. It matched the raging pain in his head, and the
churning in his gut.

Hangovers freaking *sucked*.

At least the hellfire in his groin had started to subside enough that
he could think. But thinking wasn't helping him to understand why he
was wearing a gold ring.

For one, he didn't wear them. His idea of jewelry was his eyebrow
piercing and his watch. He had a couple of ear piercings but he usually
didn't bother with those.

He definitely wouldn't be wearing a ring on *that* finger. Not unless—

"What the hell happened last night?" he roared, louder than he'd
intended.

His response was precisely nothing.

He rattled the doorknob, knowing it was a futile gesture. She'd
locked him out.

Chloe. He'd spent the night with Chloe Adams.

Had they had sex? Actual full penetrative sex? Normally, he could kind of tell, especially if he'd gotten especially, uh, vigorous, but his cock and sac were currently feeling so abused he wasn't even sure he could still pee.

Damn, that girl had some legs on her.

He already knew she had an incredible ass, as he'd had it in his hands several times the night before. He remembered that much. Recalled fuzzily that he'd gotten her off while she sat on his lap in the club. Dancing, drinking, talking. Her tipping her head back to laugh at him, her big eyes shimmering like brown velvet.

Obviously, the alcohol was still talking, because she was just a chick. Pretty eyes, gorgeous hair like a sunset. Or like the fireball that had swept through his crotch and left only embers behind.

But still, just a woman.

Just a woman he'd married.

No. He didn't marry people. He didn't even consider marriage. He was twenty-three, for God's sake. Added to that, he wasn't going to be like his parents. When he did the deed, it would be forever. So if that meant he never actually said vows, well, then fine. He was in no rush.

Except he had a ring on his hand, one that hadn't been there yesterday. Evidently, Chloe did too, or she wouldn't have asked him to check for one.

"Matching couples' jewelry, right?" he asked himself out loud, wincing at the throb in his head. He'd given up on her answering him.

For all he knew, she was loading up on Valium. God knows he wouldn't have minded something to take the edge off himself, except no, he would not be doing that again. His drinking had caused this clusterfuck in the first place.

Not just his. Hers too. He'd gotten drunk before with no ill effects, minus the Tabitha situation. Compared to this, though, that seemed like a minor inconvenience. So it stood to reason that since Chloe was the new element in the equation, clearly it was her fault they'd gotten mar —sprung for couples' jewelry.

"I'm not happy about this," he said through the door. "If you were looking for a commitment, you shouldn't have looked at me."

He'd barely gotten the last word out when the door swung open. Chloe stood there in his Foo Fighters T-shirt and one white sock he was pretty sure was his too. She'd painted the nails on her other foot wine-red to match her fingernails—and her mouth last night, before he'd kissed off her lipstick.

Goddamn, his shirt barely covered her thighs. She was naked under there. She had to be, since he was nude himself. And she'd definitely checked him out before she'd flung her arm over her eyes.

"Can you put on some clothes? And while you're at it, check your attitude. I'm not interested in a commitment with a *rockstar*."

Annoyed at her tone, he gripped the top of the doorframe and glared. Not that she could see him, of course, on account of her getting the vapors at the sight of his penis. "Sure, honey. Hate to tell you, but I'm not that naïve. I know full well exactly how many women want to land my kind of fish."

She shocked him by shoving past him to go back into the bedroom. "FYI, your fish is limp," she shot over her shoulder.

"That's not what you said last night," he tossed back, well aware of how juvenile he sounded. But hello, his fish was a prime specimen. He'd been told that numerous times. "And of course it's limp, because you sterilized me with your bony knee."

"You're not sterilized. Your type lives to spread their seed far and wide." She dropped to the floor on the other side of the mattress.

He came around the bed and saw her on her knees, bare ass up, digging under the bed. For what, he had no clue. But he liked her ass a lot. Shit, was that a hickey?

He'd leaned forward without thinking to trace the mark when she jerked up. Unfortunately, she was still partially under the bed at the time, and screeched as she bumped her head. He grimaced in sympathy. She had to be in as rough shape as he was.

"Did you just touch my butt, creeper?" she asked, cupping the back of her neck as she eased out from under the mattress.

"Creeper? We're wearing rings. If I'm a creeper, I'm your creeper." He nudged his toe against the arch of her foot just to piss her off. "And you're mine."

"You wish." She blew her curls out of her face and lurched to her feet, trying to hold down her—his—shirt while she gripped her head.

"I don't have to wish anything. See this?" He held up his hand and tapped the finger with the ring. "This here gives me rights."

Which ones, exactly, he didn't know, and he didn't really want to believe they were married in the first place. But for the sake of argument, he'd use whatever he could.

Including his own idiocy.

"We're not married. Why would we get married? I don't even know you."

"Now, see, you're just hurting my feelings. Of course we know each other. Didn't I ask you to pass the stuffing last Thanksgiving?"

"You aren't funny." She huffed and puffed as she yanked the sheet off the bed, then wrapped it around herself. Guess she thought he was becoming unduly aroused by her bare legs.

And what if he was? The visuals were the only good part of this mess.

So far, being married royally sucked.

"We're not married," he muttered, grinding the heels of his hands into his burning eyes. "It's just the hangover talking."

"What about the rings?" she asked him in a near shout. "What about those?"

"Couples' jewelry," he shouted back, dropping his hands. "It's a thing. Read *Vogue*."

She rolled her eyes at him. "Couples' jewelry like, say, wedding rings, jackass?" She flung herself on the bed and rolled off the other side without displacing her sheet. Then she bent to root around on the floor again.

"What the hell are you doing?"

"I'm looking for my clothes. Like my skirt. Like my top. Like my freaking panties!"

Lazily, he glanced around. "Don't see 'em. Sorry."

For that matter, he didn't see any traces of Ryan either. Their suite was pretty ginormous, and Ryan had his own bedroom and bathroom and all that, but he usually popped over onto Michael's side on the regular. Which meant his buddy had shacked up somewhere else for the night.

Hopefully he hadn't gotten married too, unless it was a pandemic.

Come to Vegas, see a hot girl, find a fake Elvis, get a marriage license and boom.

Trauma for the rest of your life, all thanks to one night of potentially incredible sex you didn't even remember.

"Marriage license," he muttered, grabbing his pants off the floor to dig out his wallet.

If he didn't have that little piece of paper, all of this would be solved. Because of course they wouldn't have gotten a marriage license. Not possible. There were waiting periods and all that, right? Maybe not in Vegas. Possibly faux Elvis got special dispensation from the Pope or something.

He sat on the edge of the bed and flipped open his wallet, then paused. Once he'd ascertained he didn't have a marriage license—as it naturally would be his job to hold on to all important papers as the male —he wouldn't have a chance to ask her more questions. So it was better to do so now while she was distracted pushing aside dust bunnies to find her panties.

"So, I was good, right? I mean, you enjoyed yourself." He cleared his throat. "I'm assuming your reaction isn't because you weren't satisfied. That's never happened, I'll have you know. Not even one time."

She straightened and pushed a hand through her hair. "I would ask you the same question, but I'm known as a goddess in bed, so no need."

"Really?" He glanced behind them at the obviously messed up sheets. Hell, they might already be married. A calamity and all to be sure, but he'd never had legally-sanctioned sex before. "Sucks I don't remember. We could always—"

"No." She held up a finger as if she was speaking to a small, possibly non-English speaking child. "You are not going to suggest we get back in bed."

"Okay. I won't. But the offer is on the table if—"

"I won't. I can assure you, if you were the last man on this planet, I wouldn't have sexual intercourse with you."

"*Again.* You mean again, because we clearly did it once. Or two or three times. What's your take on the situation?"

She was getting redder by the minute. He wasn't one to pull out

Annie jokes—and she certainly hadn't resembled the movie heroine the night before when she'd been all vamped up—but with her makeup worn off and her freckles on full display, there were some definite comparisons. There wasn't even a need to check to see if the drapes matched the curtains with this one, because even her eyebrows were pale red.

"My *take?*" she demanded. "Is that crude insinuation your way of asking if I can tell we've had sex?"

He shrugged. "Normally, I can tell too, but my dick was nearly crushed so I can't. It's not anything personal."

"You're asking me the current state of my—my—and it's not personal?"

"We're in this together, right? Might as well make the best of things. We definitely were last night." He gave in to the urge to look her over from the tips of her just fucked hair—pity he didn't know if that was a true statement—to the wine-red toenails peeking out from under the sheet. "You look good in my shirt. If you can't find your stuff, I'll let you borrow something."

She nodded quickly. "Okay. Yes. Thank you. I'll have my Dad drop them off once I'm back home."

The tickle in his throat made him swallow hard. "Your dad?"

"Yes." She was already heading toward the suitcase spread open on the small settee on the other side of the room. "We'll make sure the clothes get back to you soon."

"I'd rather you return them to me yourself. Better yet, I'd like to take them off of you in the shower before I soap you up." He rose, forgetting for a second he still hadn't put on his pants.

But she hadn't. Her gaze dipped to his slowly waking cock before lifting to his face, her pupils blowing wide. "The shower is the most dangerous place in the home," she said distantly as he eliminated the space between them.

The marriage thing? Yeah, that was a load of crap. It couldn't be real. Rings were one thing. An actual ceremony? No way he could forget that.

This, on the other hand, was coming back to him nicely. Alas, he didn't remember all the steps they'd taken in their dance last night—at least not yet. However, the sense of anticipation, the sizzle of arousal in his blood, the drumbeat in his dick…all of those things solely belonged to Chloe.

Pity she wasn't reacting the same way she had last night.

She kicked off her lone sock. "I need to get going. I can't stay. I have a family."

That word slowed him down. *Family.* Right. She had a son.

His wife had a frigging son.

Not your wife, twit. Your lover, who you happened to buy some bling. Much less hassle.

"Yeah. Okay. No problem." He gripped the back of his neck and cleared his throat. Maybe he'd wait to look in his wallet until she was out of the room. Now wasn't the time to deal with female hysteria.

His own hysteria was hard enough to contend with when he was hungover and still limping from his near de-balling.

"Thanks for the night though. We had fun. I mean, what I remember was fun." She went scarlet again, right up to her hairline. "I'm sure the rest was too."

He shouldn't tease her. What was the point? She wasn't feeling it, and he was just delaying the inevitable by not looking in his wallet or making a few phone calls to ascertain he wasn't a complete jackass.

But damn, she was beautiful, and she still smelled like cinnamon, and her breasts had been so fucking soft in his hands. Those small pink nipples were meant for his mouth, and he didn't even know if he'd had the pleasure of tasting them.

Stranger, my ass.

"Sure you don't want a reminder or two?" He trailed his finger over one of her springy curls and she sucked in a breath. "Something to help you bring it all back until you walk out of here and you know."

Her dark eyes flashed up to his. "Know?"

"Yes. You'll feel me inside you when you walk. When you're not panicked and in denial, there's no way you won't feel the imprint of this from last night." He rocked against her gently and she gasped.

He had barely an instant to rejoice in her reaction before she shoved him back. "I don't feel a damn thing, so I guess you aren't packing as much as you think."

Before he could reply, his bedroom door opened and Ryan poked his head in. "Um, Michael, hi, sorry to interrupt, but Lila is calling an emergency band meeting."

"You aren't interrupting shit." Spying her shoes, Chloe slid her feet into them before randomly grabbing something from Michael's suitcase. She plucked her phone off the nightstand and disappeared into the bathroom, slamming the door hard enough to rattle the fussy French renaissance-style paintings on the wall.

Ry whistled. "Who's that?"

Heart careening in his chest, Michael finally opened his wallet. He thumbed through the first couple of slots, finding nothing. Nothing in the billfold. And nothing in the ID window except his driver's license. The only place left to check was the slot on the other side.

The slot containing a crisp folded piece of paper that he'd never seen before.

He hesitated, his hand turning damp.

Just open it up and see. Reassure yourself. Everything is fine.

Pulling it out, he unfolded the paper. All he needed to read were the two words on top.

Marriage license.

"You okay, dude?" Ryan questioned. "I asked who the chick is."

Michael shut his eyes. "My wife."

TWELVE

CHLOE'S HAND SHOOK AS SHE TAPPED THE ELEVATOR BUTTON FOR HER floor. At least that one thing made sense. She could get to her floor.

She clutched her phone. She found two messages from her father. One voicemail.

One of the girls?

She held it up to her ear as the elevator pinged and slid open silently. Her stomach revolted at the backdrop for the freaking elevator. White lace and twining fingers. Of course there were gold bands on their damn fingers.

Like the heavy gold ring Michael wore.

She bent at the stomach as the world fuzzed again.

You will not be sick. You will not be sick. You will not be sick.

"Mama. We miss you, mama. Hurry home soon, mama. Pop Pop doesn't read Thomas right, but we had fun anyway. Miss you, Mama."

"Okay, let me have the phone, Axlsaurus."

Her little boy laughed. The laugh that forever pulled her out of a bad mood. The laugh that made everything okay. Her dad cleared his throat.

"We can't wait to see you. We had a great time at the picnic and he had his first campout with the kids. He had terrible food, but he was a riot. We'll definitely have to try that again. Okay, sorry. Just let me know what time your flight comes in and we'll come get you. Bye, honey. Say bye!"

"Bye!"

Then the line went dead.

She wasn't even aware of going all the way down to the lobby. The phone call had completely distracted her. She slapped their floor number, but not before a group of ladies got on with her. She tried to text Jinx and Ivy, but neither of the girls replied.

"Need the damn card." She curled her fingers into fists, squeaking when her borrowed shorts slid low on her hips. She was a hot mess and she needed her girls. Surely someone had to be in their room. It rang and rang, oh and rang some more. No answer. "Fuck."

Beside her, the older lady's eyebrows shot up and the younger girl at her side snorted.

"Sorry. No room key." She hauled the borrowed shorts back up to her waist, bunching the material at one hip.

She sucked in a deep breath and let it out slowly.

Relax.

She could do this. She was a capable woman. She juggled three jobs and a kid. This was cake. So much cake. She'd go back downstairs and get a new room key and go back to her room and pack. Then they'd get everything sorted and she could just chalk the whole weekend up to an indiscretion. A story for when she was old and gray.

Guess what? I actually married a stranger in Vegas for three minutes. Isn't that the funniest thing you've ever heard?

Best story ever.

All she needed to do was get out of the elevator. As they flew by the fifteenth floor, she slapped the button for eighteen. When the doors opened, she sprinted across the marble floors to the other bank of elevators on that level, still gripping the shorts.

Michael must be about five hundred sizes bigger than her. How could his pants be so freaking huge on her? He was lean, dammit.

She remembered curling her arms around his tight middle last night. So muscular and perfect.

Whoa. Where did that memory come from?

Gah. Not to mention that morning he'd been walking around the hotel room without a stitch on. Mouthwateringly tight everywhere, even if he was a complete asshole.

She hauled the cargos up again and bunched the material around her fingers. Something snagged on the oversized T-shirt she had on.

The ring.

She stopped in the middle of the shoppers rushing around her. She'd drooled over the ring on *this* level.

She twisted her hand free to stare down at her dream ring. Figures it would be the thing that brought her world crashing down. For God's sake, it might have been one of the lesser expensive rings, but it was still sapphires and diamonds. It still had a four digit price tag.

Maybe even more.

She swallowed down the flood of spit.

Five figures.

God, had she put it on Nick's tab?

Had she bought her *wedding ring* on Nick's tab?

The room tilted.

Someone would have some sort of answer for her. Even if she didn't have a hope or a prayer in figuring out this mess on her own she could at least check into the jewelry store. Her ring might not be completely one of a kind, but they would have records.

She hoped.

The shorts slipped and she hiked them up again. First, she had to find pants that fit.

She avoided Luxe. That kind of spending was completely unnecessary. She just needed plain shorts. And a shirt that didn't smell like him.

It was something to focus on.

And right now, she had to cling to something. She checked her phone again and crossed to one of the trendy stores. She winced over the price tag for a minute before giving her room number one more time.

She passed women in their teens and early twenties, cooing over clothes. She couldn't remember the last time she'd cooed over anything that didn't come in a size 3T.

Not one to linger over her lot in life, she rushed into the dressing room. She barely touched the button on Michael's shorts and they dropped around her ankles.

How was she completely without clothes? What the hell had she been doing last night?

Had she really had sex with him?

She winced a little as she wiggled into a pair of cotton panties. She much preferred to wash them before wearing, but beggars couldn't be choosers at this point. She turned in the mirror and stared. She stepped closer until the pink marks on her skin came in clear.

What the hell was that?

She brushed her fingertips over the abraded skin.

Oh, God, were those...?

She slammed her eyes shut and quickly turned away. It had been a damn long time, but she remembered whisker burn a time or two in her life.

Dammit. She just couldn't think about that. No how, no way.

Once she didn't look like a freaking hobo, she stuffed his clothes in her shopping bag and left the store.

The ring store was easy to spot.

Big and gold and sparkly.

Had it been that big the last time she'd been in?

She twisted her fingers together, and the smaller engagement ring Snake had given her clicked against Michael's—no, not *Michael's* ring. Her mistake ring. One that she should return.

She lifted her chin and walked through the large, gilded doors.

"May I help you?" The woman was young and Botox-injected. Why on earth would someone do that to themselves? Or maybe it was just one too many chemical peels?

Turn off the bitch mode.

"Is Nathan available?"

The woman's eyes cooled as her lips pursed. "Yes." She pointed to the back.

"Thanks." Chloe made her way back to the case. Déjà vu slapped her soundly as she approached it. She wasn't sure if it was from her day with the girls, or with...*no*. No, she just wouldn't have.

"Miss Chloe! I didn't expect you back so soon."

"Hi, Nathan."

"I must confess, I was surprised you came back last night. Your young man was very insistent we stay open ten more minutes so we could get your ring."

She didn't remember any of that. Not a single thing—

The quick flash of lips at her neck and a large palm at her lower back was there, then gone.

"What time was that?" she asked shakily.

Nathan's eyes turned worried. "Oh, that doesn't sound good."

"I don't quite remember what happened last night." She wiggled her ring finger. "But I woke up with this and definitely did not start out the night with it."

"You didn't seem that out of it last night. You two were very affectionate, but nothing untoward."

Untoward. Well, at least there was that.

"You two were quite charming. Even asked us to print out your license. I had no idea you were thinking about getting married when you came to see me."

Please God, she hoped her eyeballs weren't quite as cartoon alarmed as they seemed to be in her head. "That's because it wasn't in the plans." She swallowed. "In fact, would you happen to have video or something…" She looked around. "You have cameras, right?"

"Oh, Miss Chloe. There wasn't something going on with your young man, was there? He was perfectly polite, if perhaps a little…" Nathan shrugged with a little color in his cheeks. He cleared his throat. "He was very much into you is all I'm saying."

She gripped the edge of the case. So not good.

"Come with me."

She followed him to a doorway.

"We don't usually bring people back here. Well, not unless we're proving some sort of theft."

Chloe's cheeks flamed.

He turned back to her. "Not to worry, my dear." He opened his arm to bring her through another door. "Just sit there for a moment.

Shouldn't take me but a minute to cue it up since it was the end of the night."

She slowly lowered herself to the office chair. There was an entire bank of screens. All of them were flipping back and forth between different sections of the store and cases. No corner had been left unwatched.

"All right. Here we go."

Her gaze snapped to the screen in the center. The camera focused on Nathan's smiling face and a redhead—herself—leaning against a very tall, very broad-shouldered guy with a messy fauxhawk. Michael. There was no denying the man was Michael Shawcross. Their fingers were linked in a careless intimacy that made her stomach churn.

She'd never touched anyone like that. Even with Snake, she'd been a little reserved. Not really interested in public displays. Not that they were slobbering all over each other or anything. If anything, they were completely innocent, save for the proprietary hand on her back as they both peered into the case.

Michael made some comment that made her punch him in the arm, but then he was holding the ring and slipping it onto her finger. His thumb centered the ring, then he pushed something across the glass.

She shook her head, trying to take off the ring, but Michael clutched her smaller hand in his big one and stared into her eyes.

It didn't even feel like she was watching herself.

She remembered none of it.

Except his hands.

She rubbed her palm down her leg. She remembered his hands. And the careless touches. This morning, he'd been the same. As if he couldn't keep his hands off of her.

"He paid?" she questioned.

"You both kept joking about room forty-one-oh-eight, but in the end, your gentleman made sure his card was the one used. I wasn't exactly sure what the joke was, but you two seemed to have your own language."

She pulled off the ring. "Well, I'd like to return it, please. It's not mine to keep. I can't let him spend that kind of money on me."

"I'm afraid all sales are final here." Nathan colored slightly. "As you can imagine, it's Vegas. People do a lot of spending and have a lot of remorseful morning-afters, depending on how the game rooms go."

She swallowed. "Right. Of course." She had an immediate and overwhelming urge to put the ring back on her finger. So much so that she stuffed it into the deepest part of her pocket instead. "I'm sorry to have wasted your time."

Nathan paused the video. "Not a waste at all. I'm sorry you can't seem to remember what happened. At least that's what I'm gleaning from our conversation."

Chloe nodded. "Neither of us remember what happened last night. In fact, most of *that* is a complete blank." She pointed to the screen.

He was laughing, and she was dragging him away from the case with a huge smile. When was the last time she'd smiled like that? At least when Axl wasn't involved.

She cleared her throat. "And you said you printed a license?"

He nodded. "Your Michael—"

"He's not *my* anything," she said quickly. Her voice was shrill and her temples were pounding as if a dozen songs were trying to play in her head at the same time.

All of them loud and frenzied. All of them had lyrics jumbled over the other. None of the words made sense.

She desperately had to make this make sense.

But it wouldn't here. She had a plane to get on. She pulled her phone out of her pocket and saw that a message had come in while she was in the control room with Nathan.

Ivy.

She quickly squeezed Nathan's hand. "I'm sorry. I don't mean to take it out on you. I just…I don't even know what to do."

Nathan patted the top of her hand. "It may not be as easy to divorce as it is to marry in Vegas, but it's possible. Maybe even an annulment."

She nodded. "Maybe. Thank you for showing me this though."

"I'm sorry it wasn't what you wanted."

She forced herself to smile. How could she not smile at this sweet man? "Wouldn't be my life if there wasn't a hurdle."

"Easy is never an exciting life."

She snorted. "I'd prefer it to be a little less action-packed, thanks."

"Could be the best thing that ever happened to you. My Eva and I ran away after knowing each other only three days. Married forty-five years this September."

Chloe laughed. "Three days?"

"Sometimes you just know."

"The last surprise I had like this ended with a little boy."

"And?"

Chloe swallowed down a little bubble of hysteria. "Best day ever."

"So, don't discount it."

She nodded. She didn't mean it, but she nodded. There was so little romance in her life, but she couldn't take it away from someone else. That was just cruel. Impulsively she went up on her toes and kissed his cheek. "Lucky lady."

"I'll tell her you said so."

"You do that." She waited as he did something with the computer and led her out into the store. "Thanks, Nathan."

"You're very welcome, Miss Chloe. Good luck with your young man."

"I'm going to need it." She briskly walked through the store and opened the message waiting for her.

You're not going to believe what happened last night. I can't explain everything right now, but I'm OK. I'm not going back with you. I'm sorry. I just have to see this thing thru. Xoxo

Chloe quickly shot a few texts back.

Where are you?

Are you ok?

What do you mean you're not coming back? Do I need bail money?

She stared intently at the screen, but there were no little bubbles at the bottom to let her know Ivy was typing back. Nothing from any-damn-one.

What the hell was going on?

Chloe tipped her head back. No crying. There's no crying in Vegas even if you married a man who's pretty much a complete stranger.

Nope.

She squeezed her eyes shut until the burning stopped and black dots swam.

No crying.

She'd figure it out. That was what she did. Was always what she did.

Was it so wrong that she really wanted to rely on her girls? For once, she wanted someone to tell her what to do. She wasn't going to feel sorry for herself. It never helped anything. Wishing was useless anyway.

All she had to do was get home to her son. Then she could try to forget this whole Vegas mess had ever happened.

Maybe if she pretended long enough, at least one of her hopes would come true.

THIRTEEN

His trip was going awesome so far. Hell, he might as well do a blog about his adventures and share it with the world. He could summarize the events of the past couple of days in a few lines.

Day one of Vegas trip: blow the roof off the house with a kickass show.

Encore: get married to a woman who might as well be a stranger.

Day two of Vegas trip: wake up in bed beside new wife, who you might've remembered having sex with—and marrying—if only you hadn't consumed enough alcohol to kill a buffalo the night before. Performance issues, however, could not have been an issue because hashtag rockstar.

Yep, that covered things nicely.

The emergency band meeting was held in the VIP room of a restaurant called Sparkle. Naturally, he was the last one to arrive, which granted him the pleasure of the glare of death from Lila.

"Nice to see you could join us, though you appear a bit worse for wear." She glanced at his attire, the first pair of shorts and T-shirt he'd pulled out of his suitcase. The shirt happened to be the rank KISS one he'd worn onstage last night, paired with the bike shorts he'd brought for working out.

So much for grabbing a spin class to get his heart rate up and maybe meet some chicks. He'd had to fit in an impromptu marriage ceremony instead.

"Sorry, had a busy morning," he replied, dropping into the only remaining empty chair around the large circular table in the corner.

So he hadn't had time to shower or find a clean shirt. At least he was there. As for the fact his dick was packaged in Lycra, yeah, well, no fixing that at this point. The bright side was he wasn't wearing a fanny pack, unlike three of the tourists he'd passed on his walk through the hotel.

"Busy making some chick breakfast," West muttered, affixing an angelic smile on his face as Michael lifted a brow. "And when I say making her breakfast, I mean, making her *his* breakfast, because we all know that dude can't cook for shit."

"That's not true," Juliet piped in. "He made us eggs that one time after we were up rehearsing all night, and only two of us got food poisoning. Pretty decent record, all in all."

"I've improved since then." Michael ran his tongue over his teeth. He could still taste last night's whisky, and that was after brushing his teeth twice. He motioned to a waiter. "Could I get an OJ, please? Large?" Damn, he was dying of thirst. "Actually, just bring out a carafe."

Once the waiter had scurried off, Molly lifted a perfectly groomed blond brow. She looked as if she'd just stepped off a runway somewhere. "OJ? You do realize it's past noon."

Michael glanced at his watch. Well, look at that. Fighting with the brand new missus ate up plenty of time. "So? I drink OJ anytime I want. They have it on the menu, don't they?"

"Actually, we're not here for snacks and refreshments," Lila said. "I have a plane to catch shortly. As do all of you, although you get a while longer to play the slots."

"Oh, he loves certain slots." West laughed as Ry elbowed him. "Sorry, that was for Mr. Just Rolled Out of Bed. My night wasn't nearly as eventful, unfortunately."

"Didn't find anyone interesting?" Juliet asked.

"Oh, I did, but they tended to come in twos and threes, and you know, I'm an old-fashioned boy." He pretended to duck his head and Ry shoved him.

Juliet looked intrigued. "So what's wrong with that? The more the merrier."

Lila sighed. "Children, save your sex talk for your therapist. We have other things to discuss, namely Ryan's injury and how it affects the band."

"He's not that injured." West tapped his fingers on his glass of water. No alcohol or even soda most of the time for him. He espoused clean living and all that. "He was hogging my keyboard last night, wasn't he?"

"Just because I can do one-handed what it takes you two and your dick to accomplish…" Ry trailed off and shrugged.

"Playing drums is a bit different than some antics on the keyboard. He's capable of that, or playing the blues harp, or the xylophone."

"Or the bongos on 'Steal Away,'" Molly added. "We never perform that one, and it's a perfect showcase for—"

"Your tits, since you always wear a bikini for that song?" Juliet snorted.

Molly poked her in the side. "Bitch."

"Nah. Your tits are great. Might as well flaunt 'em. Hell, Mike's flashing us some dick today, right? Shake what your mama gave you is what I say." Jules flashed a smile at the returning waiter, who nearly bobbled the carafe of juice. "And what do you have," she read his tag, "Javier?"

"Ignore her," Lila said, grabbing the carafe and using it to fill her empty water glass before handing it to Michael. "Thank you."

"Er, no problem. Here's your glass, sir. Does anyone else need anything?"

"Duct tape for our resident sex maniac?" Molly asked sweetly, giving Juliet a sidelong look.

The waiter took that response as a "no" and booked away from the table.

Ryan leaned behind West to shove Michael's arm. "Damn, Mikey, someone's trying to steal your crown. Better bump it up a notch, dude."

Michael poured his orange juice and ignored him. Normally, he enjoyed messing around with his bandmates. They all knew he hated being called anything but Michael, so of course they insisted on calling him every variation in the book. Where he would typically laugh it off, today he wasn't finding anything amusing.

Especially not being called a sex maniac. He didn't dispute the assertion—it wasn't like he denied enjoying the act, and why should he? But considering he couldn't remember the last time he'd dipped his wick, the nickname stung more than a little.

Fucking alcohol. He was never drinking again. Ever. Hell, he wasn't even eating those liquor chocolates at Christmas anymore.

Done. Finito. Cold turkey.

"Let's focus on what's important, shall we?" Lila asked, sounding patently bored in a way only she could.

She wasn't that much older than the crew—something that had disgusted Malachi when he'd learned she was their new stepmother—but she had an air of sophistication and professionalism far beyond her years. She also tolerated zero bullshit.

"And what's that?" Molly tapped her long pale pink nails against her cup of coffee. She drank the stuff like it flowed in her veins. "We had a kickass show last night, everything is going great—"

"Except the drummer situation," Lila interjected. "Besides, Ryan was never comfortable behind the kit anyway."

Ryan said nothing. Michael knew it was sterling truth, but his buddy would never speak up and let down the band. They needed a drummer and he could play drums, so he did it, even if he preferred a more free-flowing role depending on what each song required.

"Perhaps his getting hurt ended up being a blessing in disguise, if he ends up getting to do more of what he wants to. Pain aside, of course," Lila said to Ryan, who only nodded.

"Okay, so Ryan doesn't play drums anymore, then what? We search for someone new again? We've seen how that went before. As in not well." West fingered the spiky blond hair that dipped over his forehead. "Can't say I think that's the best move now that we're finally starting to get some traction."

Lila glanced around the table. "We're all in agreement that last night's show was incredible? As is borne out by the tons of vids and positive press online. Everyone is talking about Warning Sign today, and that hasn't been true after your other concerts."

"We've had great press before," Juliet protested. "Our Instagram and Twitter followers and Facebook likes keeps climbing. We can't keep up with the fan mail anymore, especially the letters addressed 'Dear Molly's boobs.'"

Molly smiled serenely and sipped her coffee.

Michael just rubbed his temple. Jesus, was this ever going to be over?

He knew he needed to be concerned about the status of the band. The drummer situation had been a problem for a while now, and typically, he would've been the first one searching for a solution. Hell, his brother had disappeared last night during Brooklyn Dawn's set and he'd never even been able to properly thank—

"Wait a second." Michael sat up straighter and ignored the resulting throb in his head. "You want Mal?"

"Oh hell no." Elle, who had been quiet up until that point, braced her fists on the table. "Absolutely not. Anyone but that brute."

"He's not a brute," Michael said, feeling obligated to defend his brother.

"Did he pick you up last night as if you were a sack of oranges? No, I don't think so." Elle glanced at Lila, who just happened to be her sister-in-law. Elle and Nick were opposites in a lot of ways, except looks. As far as temperament went, however, they couldn't have been more different.

Until apparently right now.

"I don't want him in my band. He's an asshole. Li, you can't do this."

Lila exhaled. "Obviously, you've all made the connection that since Malachi is Michael's brother, he was also my stepson. The difference is we had no relationship, due to his personal preferences. That has little bearing on this situation. He doesn't have to like me. I look for talent, and when I spot it, I take steps to ascertain that talent is on our side." She glanced at Elle. "You know I value your opinion, but I'm sorry. In this arena, who fits each role best is what matters most. Not personal feelings."

"He was rude to me. He belittled me." Elle brushed a lock of long blond hair behind her ear, and if Michael wasn't mistaken, her hand shook. "I don't want a person like him in my environment."

"I understand that, and you're welcome to keep your distance. But I can't make personnel decisions based on emotion."

"Right. Like you've never done that before when it comes to covering my brother's ass." Elle nudged Juliet and Jules slid out so Elle could slip out of the booth and stalk away.

"Nick 2.0, here we go," Molly muttered, staring after Elle. "Tantrum city."

"She'll be back." Lila spoke with confidence, but Michael knew his stepmother well enough to understand she was rattled.

Michael knew Lila didn't particularly adore Mal either. She'd tried so hard with him, and his brother had been an A-1 dick to her in defense of their mother. Lila wanting Mal to join one of the bands she managed had to be a difficult choice, but she was making it anyway.

There was just one problem.

"I texted Mal last night multiple times after the show, during the other bands' sets. He didn't reply. I texted him again this morning on my way over here. They aren't even getting delivered, which means he has his phone off. He's not interested in all of this." Michael waved his hand at the table. "One night is about all you're going to get out of him."

Lila tapped the tips of her fingers together. "I was unsuccessful at reaching him myself. Not surprising, since he probably has my number blocked. But it's just a matter of time." She smiled thinly. "There's no reason to search for someone new, if we've already found the right person. So now it's just a matter of running him to ground."

"Good luck with that. When Mal doesn't want to be found, he isn't." Michael took a sip of OJ, then pressed his fingers into his aching forehead. He couldn't even drink his damn juice. His gut was a mess, and it wasn't just from the hangover from hell.

He had issues way, way bigger than his brother being MIA. And he didn't have the first clue how to begin to address them.

"I have my ways."

"Sure you do. Speaking of ways, how about you giving me Chloe Adams's phone number?"

130

He hadn't meant to ask it. He had no reason to. Surely Chloe would still be in his room when he returned, and then he'd get her information himself. But he had this fucking niggle at the back of his neck to go with his churning stomach and massive headache.

If Chloe ghosted on him, then what?

Ryan cleared his throat and reached for his own glass. Discovering it was empty, he snatched West's and tossed back the last of his water.

"Hey, dude. Get your own."

Ryan just arched a brow at Michael, who silently passed him the carafe. It wasn't alcohol, but it would have to do.

Ryan hadn't believed him about the whole marriage thing. Michael had tried halfheartedly to convince him, but he'd stopped short of showing his best friend the marriage license. Somehow that seemed private. Personal.

Ridiculous.

Ryan had just laughed and gone off to get ready in his half of the suite while Chloe hogged the bathroom.

"Why do you need Chloe Adams's phone number, Michael?"

"That's not really any of your concern. I just need it."

Lila lifted a brow. "I'm sorry, but I'm not the phone book. Next time, try information." She glanced around the table. "I'll see all of you on Wednesday before rehearsal for Friday's show. I hope to have information on Malachi by then."

"Good fucking luck," Michael muttered, circling his temple.

"Excuse me?"

"You heard me. For years, you've had no interest in Mal's whereabouts, now he's just supposed to tapdance to your tune? Not going to happen. And you know what? I don't blame him."

Lila's mouth pinched tight and she averted her gaze. Hurting her was the last thing he wanted to do, yet he kept doing it.

When all this insanity was over, he'd have one hell of a long list of things to apologize for. He just hoped she understood.

What, that you're being an insensitive jerk because you're dealing with problems of your own making? Good luck with that mansplaining, son.

What had transpired between them so far wasn't even the worst of it. He had to tell her he was married, before the press found out. He didn't even know how they figured out some of the crap they did, but the increased attention on him lately because of Tabitha and Senator Dickless—err, Dinkles—had put him in the spotlight. Who knew when they'd grab hold of the story?

Lila deserved to know first. And of course, some PR fielding would be much appreciated.

So, yeah, he was a dick. Being rude to the woman who'd been nothing but wonderful to him for half his life—along with often being overbearing and too overprotective, but hey, that was what parents did —was no bueno. Then he thought he had a right to ask her for help with spin?

Yes, he was an ass. A supreme, desperate ass.

"Can you guys leave us alone, please?" he asked his bandmates.

They'd all been in the process of rising and moving away from the table anyway, but Michael's sharp retort had rooted them in place like witnesses to a horrific accident. No way were they voluntarily looking away anytime soon.

Everyone looked at Lila. She was the one who dismissed the meetings, not Michael.

Her thin smile made another reappearance. "Go ahead. Thanks, everyone. Great job last night. See you all on Wednesday."

One by one, they all filed out of the booth. Ryan clapped his hand on Michael's shoulder as he went, as did West. At least his boys were supporting him.

What good that would do in his cyclone of shit, he didn't know.

Once they'd all taken off, Lila stared him dead in the eye. "Let's get something straight, shall we?"

He nodded miserably. Sure. Whatever. He obviously had no clue how to run his own life, so why not let her give him a colossal smackdown? Clearly, he deserved it.

"You're my son. You may not believe that, or see things the same way, but in here, you're mine." She rubbed her chest and he averted his gaze.

If she'd punched him in his sore head, he wouldn't have ached half as much.

"You know I do. I feel the same. It's just I can't deal with the guilt and the lectures and everything lately. It's all too much."

"You didn't let me finish."

Stiffly, he nodded.

"But when we're on the job, as we were two minutes ago, you will respect me. What I said to Ricki—Elle—applies to you too. Personal business has no room here."

"I get that. But you hate Chloe. If I'd asked for anyone else's number, you wouldn't have blinked. So you can't really talk about not bringing personal stuff up while we're at work."

She pursed her lips. "I don't hate her. I have no reason to. She just makes me wary, and whatever your reasons for contacting her, I'd advise you to tread carefully. The man she nearly married tried to bring down Oblivion, Michael. He made all kinds of wild claims that they'd stolen his songs and bilked him out of money he was rightfully entitled to. She had a past with Nick too and she—"

"What kind of past?" Michael asked sharply. "I mean, I know they were hugging in those stupid pictures the PI took, but I thought they were mostly just old friends." And a little more, but he didn't know the details.

Now he needed to.

"Old friends, yes." The careful tone of her voice let him know she wasn't telling him everything. As always.

"Old friends who once were involved?" he pressed.

"It doesn't matter. It was a long time ago, and she ended up with Snake. Nick feels responsible for her and the baby, because Snake wanted him to be the kid's godfather so he's been helping her out here and there."

Michael dug his thumbs into his forehead. There was a very good chance his brain was just going to explode. "Helping her out how?"

"Financially."

"So she used to hook up with Nick, and now he's bankrolling her." Michael leaned back in the booth and leveled his gaze on his stepmother. "And you're okay with this?" When she didn't immediately reply, he slowly shook his head. "Of course you're not. You're concerned there might be more there than simple friendship."

"No." Her voice lashed out. "That I'm not concerned about. Not anymore. Was I at first? Yes. The situation with your father made me suspicious, but Nick isn't like that. I trust him implicitly."

"You just don't trust her."

She huffed out a breath. "I don't know her well, and I'm probably being unfair. But it's hard to take back first impressions, and my first one of Chloe was her drug addict fiancé suing my band. Because, yes, Oblivion is my band, just like Warning Sign is. I take it personally when people come after what's mine. That includes all of you."

His lips twitched. "So much for keeping things all business, huh?"

Lila shook her head. "You've got me there. It *is* personal for me, but I fight it all the time. I try not to get wrapped up in your lives, and I try not to care more than I should. But I can't help it." She leaned forward and took his hands. "Especially with you. No matter how old you get, you'll always be that boy with the backward baseball cap and a sweet smile. And I'll always want to protect you, even if you hate me for it."

He curled his fingers into hers. "L, I married Chloe."

"You'll understand someday when you have your own children," Lila continued as if he hadn't spoken. "In the far, far off future. But it changes you when you're responsible for someone else—"

"L, did you hear me? I married Chloe." He shut his eyes and hung his head. "I didn't mean to do it, but I did."

She gripped his hands so tightly that he opened his eyes again. "What do you mean you didn't mean to marry her?" She threw back her head. "Dear God, Vegas."

"I may have been just a little...inebriated at the time." As was Chloe, but he wasn't about to cast aspersions on his new wife's character.

She'd married *him*, hadn't she? That was aspersion enough.

"You told me you didn't have a problem. You swore to me you didn't."

"Dammit, I got to play with my brother last night. My brother who's been on the fringes of my life for years. Do you know what a rush that was? And we were incredible. We were the best we've ever been, and she was in the audience, and Jesus, she was so into us, into *me*. I've never felt anything like that before." He couldn't explain it to himself, never mind his stepmother. "It was chemical. I couldn't control it. Fuck, I didn't even realize it was her at first."

Lila took several deep breaths before meeting his gaze again. "Did you have sex with her?"

"What?" His ears were heating up to go with the back of his neck. "I can't believe you'd ask me that."

"You're an adult, and I'm pretty sure you don't read the Bible with your female companions." She leaned forward, releasing his hands to lay hers flat on the table. "Did you have sex with her, Michael? It makes a difference as to how quickly and quietly we can make this go away, so answer carefully."

"What difference does it make? I said I married her. I have the marriage license, I have the ring…" He trailed off and shook his head. "Uh-uh. No. Not happening."

"An annulment is a simple dissolution. No fuss, no muss."

"No." His vehemence surprised him as much as it clearly surprised Lila. "No annulments. I don't believe in those."

"You don't believe in fixing mistakes? In making a problem go away?"

"That may be how you see marriage, but I don't. I spent my whole life vowing to myself I'd never be like my parents. I'd never treat a promise casually. If it wasn't forever, I wouldn't say the words."

Lila's cheeks paled. "What are you saying? That you're just going to stay married to her, because you made a mistake? That you're going to pay for your crime for the rest of your life?"

"It wasn't a crime. Christ, I fell so hard for her. In a couple of hours, I fucking fell."

"You knew each other before this weekend. You've been at the same family things a couple of times, surely you've spoken to each other. Yet all of a sudden, lightning bolt?"

"What happened with you and Nick? I highly doubt that you were all over his ass from day one, because he's a complete dick most of the time. I'm assuming at some point something changed and you saw him in a new light. Well, the same thing happened here. It took me being on stage and her being below me to—"

Lila braced her forehead against her hand and he decided to stop talking. He wasn't going to convince her anyway, and he was long past convincing himself.

He didn't get what had happened between him and Chloe either. It defied rational behavior. He might've said it was just beer goggles, but fuck, he hadn't had a drop of liquor in him the first time he glimpsed her in the crowd. Even stone cold sober, he'd wanted her enough to risk everything.

Now they'd just have to figure out where they were going to go from here.

"I don't know if it's just based on sex or if there might be something else there, something underneath, but fuck, I'm not going to figure it out by sitting here talking to you." He pulled out his wallet and withdrew a few bills to cover his juice and the tip.

And saw that too bright white piece of paper that had changed his entire life.

"I get that you're confused. But you don't want to do anything rash—"

"I'd say the rash bus has already left the station, wouldn't you?" He started to slide out of the booth.

"Michael, wait." Lila reached out to grasp his hand. "Just wait. We can talk this through, figure it out."

"No, we can't. Because she's my wife. Goddammit, somehow I have a wife." He swallowed down the ball of fear and confusion and frustration in his throat. "I need to talk to her. She's who I have to speak to right now. I'm sorry."

Halfway out of the booth, he turned back. "You have to promise me something though."

Still looking shell-shocked, Lila dropped her hands in her lap and nodded. "Okay."

"You can't contact her. You definitely can't mention an annulment. No matter what. I need to do this on my own, and in my own way. Promise me, L," he prompted when she shifted her gaze away.

After a moment, she glanced back at him and nodded. "All right. I promise."

"Guys? I'm sorry to interrupt. Lila, could I speak to you, please? When you have a moment."

He glanced up and smiled at Elle. She was gripping the padded leather end of the circular booth and biting her lip.

She'd probably returned to apologize. That was the Elle he knew. She was sweet and kind and rarely prone to outbursts. In fact, that one was the first he'd ever seen from her.

Must be something in the Vegas air. People were acting all kinds of crazy, including himself.

Especially himself.

"No problem. I was on my way out." He stood and turned toward Lila. "Thank you. I'll be in touch."

She nodded, pressing her lips together.

"Don't worry," he told her, knowing she would just the same. In this case, he didn't blame her. "Everything is going to be fine."

"It better be."

He squeezed Elle's shoulder and headed for the exit.

In under fifteen minutes, he was back on his floor. Between dodging tourists and the not-so-sneaky paparazzi he glimpsed hanging around—though he wasn't sure if they were stalking him or some other hapless celeb—he felt like he was moving through mud. He flipped out his keycard and opened the door, already braced.

The first thing he noticed was the absence of her particular scent.

So stupid to immediately associate cinnamon with her when he'd lived his whole life smelling it without it meaning much of anything. Now his room being devoid of it meant that she'd gone.

She'd just walked out and left him holding his balls.

Still, he went through the motions of checking the suite for a note. He looked everywhere he could think of, then gave in and sat down on his bed.

The sheets were still askew, the pillows tossed every which way. Guess he'd missed housekeeping with their late departure from the suite.

She'd just fucking left.

He pulled out his phone and just stared at it. What was he supposed to do now? Call Lila and ask for Chloe's number again? Or better yet, he'd call Nick. If he got to Nick before Lila filled him in, he'd hand over the number without realizing anything was up.

Michael's thumb slipped over the icons and he opened the photos app. Why, he didn't know. He had no reason to look at pictures. But something made him bring it up, and there she was, like a glimmer of light in the center of the murky darkness his life had become overnight.

She was smiling up at the camera, her hair glinting red in the darkened atmosphere of the club. There was no missing the blurriness of her expression. She was well and truly toasted, but cripes, the way she'd been looking at him. So seductively, so openly. As if every part of her was on display for him.

Only him.

He remembered that look. Seeing it on his screen brought so much of the night screaming back, just not the parts he needed most to remember.

Like saying "I do."

He needed to take a shower and get dressed for the flight back. And he needed a plan for winning back his wife, even if he didn't have the slightest clue what he was going to do with her.

FOURTEEN

C<small>HLOE SCROLLED BACK AND FORTH BETWEEN HER SINGULAR TEXTS FROM</small>
Ivy and Jinx.

Seriously?

Both of them.

So, I got kidnapped. In the best way ever. I'll fill you in next week. For now —adventure awaits, bitches!

Was there something in the water in Vegas? It was the marriage capital of the damn world, but honestly, this was a little ridiculous. And neither of them would reply, that was what killed her the most. In fact, the messages she sent didn't even seem like they were delivered.

Had they turned off their phones?

Should she be worried?

Had some insane stranger made them type that?

Could she be any more dramatic? Jinx pulled this kind of stunt all the time. How many times had she up and disappeared during a vacation with the three of them? She could actually count three of them off the top of her head right now.

Ivy, however—that didn't make a bit of sense.

She was the stable sister. Always had two jobs, and could be called on any time day or night for help. Chloe was actually a little worried about Ivy's message. If she didn't hear from them again today, she'd...

What?

Police report?

Oh, I got this random text from my two best friends that they...hooked up in Vegas?

She'd be laughed out of the station. Then shown the door and asked what she had to drink. And at this particular juncture, she couldn't even rely on her own judgment. So, she was sitting on the plane and praying that no one would notice her.

And she was doing a damn good job of being inconspicuous, thank you very much.

She was tucked into the last row of seats. The shades were down since everyone seemed to have had a little too much fun in Vegas on this trip.

She'd been one of the first people on the plane. She'd met the stewardess on the tarmac, for God's sake. Anxious much?

Deacon and Harper came down the aisle, laughing. He scooped his wife up and sat down with her tangled around him in the seat a few rows ahead of her. They were enjoying a rare baby-free weekend. The few times she'd seen them at the family parties they'd been preoccupied with kid stuff and cooking—mostly since Harper was everyone's favorite chef.

And honestly, she'd thought the couple had landed in that comfortable portion of married life. Chloe couldn't remember a time that Harper and Deacon had been all over each other. The rest of the Oblivion people seemed to be much more of a handsy bunch.

Nick and Lila especially.

Chloe scrunched down in her seat and averted her eyes. Any second there was going to be some skin action.

A flash of her astride Michael intruded and she slammed her eyes shut. When the hell had that happened? She pressed her lips together and willed another memory to come forward.

No.

No, dammit.

It faded away into the darkness of the plane. Had it been in a dark corner? It didn't feel like a hotel room. Too crowded?

"Didn't you get enough of the manster at the hotel, Harp?" Nick's voice boomed through the plane.

Chloe's eyes snapped open and the memory disintegrated like so much smoke.

Harper kept on kissing her husband and raised her hand in a special one fingered salute.

"Move along, Nicholas." Lila pushed him further down the aisle. "I need to get some work done. Let's go in the back."

"If we go in the back, the only work you're getting done is on my lap, Li."

"Dream on."

"Want to bet?" Nick dropped into the aisle seat and dragged her against him, his face in her chest. He grinned up at Lila, seeing nothing but her. He curled one arm around and under her smart pink business jacket. Even in Vegas, Lila dressed like the corporate shark she was.

Instead of putting him in his place, she cupped his face. "Didn't you get enough this morning?" she asked on a voice that barely traveled.

But of course since she was literally two rows behind them, Chloe heard the rare husky voice loud and clear.

The pang hit Chloe low. It wasn't like she had any lingering feelings for Nick, but he'd definitely never looked or talked to her like that. Everyone in the Oblivion family seemed to have found the perfect soulmate.

She didn't even believe in soulmates, but there was no way to deny it on this plane.

Especially when each of the couples still acted like it was Spring Break Hedonism version well into their marriages. Yeesh, all over each other didn't cover it.

Simon and Margo, followed by a laughing Gray and Jazz boarded a moment later. Lila looked over at the group of them. Nick reached up and turned her face back to him. "What's up?"

"Nothing."

He hauled her down and moved over a seat. "You are a superiorly awful liar, babe."

Lila elbowed him. "It's nothing." She seemed to be craning her neck.

"What?"

"Have you seen Chloe yet? Or her brood."

"Brood?" Nick laced their fingers. "They're not that bad."

"That tall one is really loud."

Chloe opened up her mouth to tell Lila off. Sure, Jinx was loud, but they'd been leaving to go to freaking Vegas. It wasn't like they were just going to sit stoically on this luxury airline and not get excited.

Nick snorted. "So am I."

Yeah, he was. Chloe crossed her arms. She didn't really want to listen in on this conversation any longer. It was one thing to know Lila didn't like her, but she really didn't need a play-by-play about just how much.

Lila sighed. "They're fine. I'd like to get into the air and get home."

Nick brushed an absent kiss at her temple. "Janice said that everyone was aboard."

Lila slumped back in her seat. "Good. I just want to get home and figure all this mess out."

Mess?

Did Lila know?

Chloe bit the corner of her thumbnail.

"Why, what's up? All the shows went off without a hitch. Including our noobs. According to our special unicorn of madcap media, the YouTubers have been doing whatever it is that YouTubers do."

Lila brushed the back of her knuckles over Nick's angular jawline. "It's quite endearing how clueless you are about the internet, yet I can quiz you about a Les Paul from 1967 and you'll know how many were made."

"Not many. They had a lull that year. Now '68—"

She held a finger over his mouth. "See?"

He took her hand away from his mouth and smoothed his thumb over her palm. "So what's the big deal? You're not going to make me dig it out of that hot and very confusing brain, are you?"

"Michael did something so stupid I can't even...I actually have no words."

"Should I buy a lottery ticket or something? That just doesn't happen."

Lila punched him in the arm. "I'm being serious."

Nick sighed. "I know. That's why I'm doing this husband shit. You know I don't really care what that kid does."

"You don't care what anyone does."

"Damn right. I am a house of four and sometimes when I'm feeling generous, I count the people in my band. Right now, nope. Don't give two flying fucks. I'm tired and I miss my girls."

Chloe swallowed. It felt too intimate to listen to them, but at the same time she wanted to know what the deal was. What did Lila know about Michael? Was it band stuff because she was their manager? Or was it *their* crazytown wedding?

Lila rested her head on his shoulder. "Me too. I'm not used to being away from them for this long. And I'm not going to get to relax with them."

"Why the hell not? It's Sunday. You can play Superwoman on Monday."

"Yes, well my idiot stepson got himself married last night, so I have to figure out what the hell to do about that."

"Married? To who?" She didn't answer. "Li. Who the fuck did he marry? Some tramp looking for a full ride? Is that what has your panties all in a bunch?"

"In a matter of speaking."

"He's a grown-ass man. Why do you have to do anything?"

"It's my job."

"Is it your job to shake off his dick when he pisses too? Jesus."

"You're such an asshole."

"You knew that going in, sweetheart." Lila tried to stand up and Nick blocked her path. "Stop getting all twisted about this and tell me the problem."

"Not when you're like this."

"Obviously, you need to get it off your chest. Husband 101, woman. I know my role."

She gave an exasperated laugh. "Did I mention you're an ass?"

"Daily."

143

Lila blew out a breath.

Chloe held hers. Lila really couldn't think she'd done this on freaking purpose. There was no way she could think *that* badly of her. Could she?

"Look, I just found out about this." Lila's voice was getting more agitated.

"Well, stop being a pussy about it. Spit it out."

"Honestly, Nicholas."

"What? It's not like he married someone in the band, right? Juliet gets her grind on with Michael sometimes, but I didn't see anything more than that. Besides we don't need another Reese in the damn mix, do we? Margo is the least crazy out of that family and she decided marrying Simon was a good idea. Obviously, they're a little touched in the head."

Chloe's heart stopped. Juliet? In the band?

Memories from the show came back to her and he'd definitely been familiar with the girls. Maybe a bit more than that with Juliet, but he wouldn't...

Wouldn't what? She didn't know a damn thing about Michael Shawcross. He could be playing musical beds with every one of the women in his band for all she knew. It was none of her business.

Umm, married?

No. Not married. Accidentally legally bound.

Her phone vibrated in her hand. She looked down automatically. Her dad, checking in for an arrival time. She'd forgotten to text him with all the eavesdropping. She opened the text and smiled for the first time since she'd sat down. A picture of Axl with his face covered in s'mores filled her screen.

Definitely a keeper.

She added it to her Axl folder and backed out to her main picture stream. Her thumb froze over the lock button. What the hell were those? She flicked over to the first picture from the night before. A candid shot of her and the girls at the show. A drunk selfie she'd taken of herself with the concert as her backdrop.

She never took selfies—well, her and Axl smushed together in a picture didn't count.

She was actually wild and smiling with a crazy happy look on her face in the picture. She didn't look tired for once. Actually, she was even semi-attractive.

Was that who Michael had seen last night?

She was so used to being seen as a mom, that the mere fact she'd looked like a young, carefree woman seemed more terrifying than the ring burning a hole in her pocket. *That* Chloe was trouble. She was the Chloe who stayed out all night with Snake and watched the dawn come up over the beach with an empty forty between them in the sand. She was the Chloe who lost days on a random cross country trip with Snake while he'd been on a coke-spree. And that Chloe had believed it was all right to live vicariously through him. She'd never been one to use. Instead her drug had been Snake.

Not her life anymore.

That Chloe had been replaced with a mother and a responsible member of society.

She thumbed to the next picture. A close-up of her and Michael filled the screen. A light flashed behind them, leaving them both with the hint of a halo around their heads and a pure alcohol haze swimming in their eyes. Soft, hazy gazes brimming with fun.

She pushed that picture away, only to find something even more damning.

Her fingers laced on top of another hand. A hand she barely recognized save for the glittering gold band.

She couldn't forget that—nothing else made sense from last night, but that ring was clear as a freaking bell. She closed her photos folder and quickly texted her father their arrival time.

"Who keeps texting you?"

Chloe's head popped up, but it was Lila talking to Nick again.

Nick growled as his phone buzzed again. "Not important. I don't even know why he's freaking texting me, for fuck's sake."

"Who?"

"Michael."

Lila gave an exasperated sigh. "Did you check?"

"No."

"You didn't even look to see what he wanted?" Lila turned in her seat. "It might be important."

"If it was important, he'd be texting you, not me. Unless..." Nick thumped his head against the seat. "Who did he fucking marry? I can't even believe I'm asking this question. I don't fucking care."

"Oh, you will."

"What the hell is that supposed to mean?" His voice went up another decibel.

Chloe's shoulders bunched. She so didn't want to be sitting through this. God, why hadn't she moved earlier? This was what eavesdropping got a person. All of the truth no one wanted to hear.

"She's your little pet project."

"I have one pet, and he's pain in the ass enough. Two if I have to count your cat."

"Let me see your phone."

Nick shoved it into his pocket. "No. Why is this a thing?"

"It's me." Chloe wanted to slap her hands over her mouth, but she couldn't listen anymore.

Lila swung around and peeked over the top of the oversized seats. "You were here listening the whole time?"

"The whole damn plane could hear you." Chloe stood up and dragged her purse with her into the aisle. She was used to no one noticing her. Snake had always been loud and larger than life. She never really minded blending into the background.

Until now. She was tired of no one seeing her.

Of course she really didn't want people to notice her like *this*. She could feel everyone's eyes on her.

"If you didn't want me to know you were trash talking me then maybe you shouldn't have opened your mouth." Chloe couldn't seem to get her own mouth to close as she loomed over Lila's seat.

If they wanted a show, they were going to get one.

God, Lila didn't even look embarrassed by it. She just lifted her chin. "I'm not saying anything other than the truth. Money has been a very real situation when it comes to you and my family."

"I never wanted any of it. Snake asked me to keep Nick in Axl's life, and yes, I had to ask for money to help out until I got on my feet. Do you even know how hard that was for me?" Chloe pointed to Nick. "He's the one who wouldn't take the money back."

Nick's jaw flexed, but he said nothing.

Lila's eyes went arctic. "And now you're moving on to greener pastures. At least it's a step up from your previous fiancé. But I will not have you derail my son's career."

"I don't *want* to be married to your son." Chloe's laughter sounded a little close to hysteria even to her own ears. "God, that's even ridiculous to say. You're barely a handful of years older than him."

"I watched him grow up."

"You were little more than a child when you married his father. Oh, and I do believe you married the great Martin Shawcross for his money and his status." Chloe lowered her face to Lila's. "So don't speak to me like you're better than me. At least I did whatever I've done for my child."

Lila's huge blue eyes went even wider. Both of them had their hands fisted.

Nick placed his hand on Lila's shoulder. "Not that I wouldn't like to see this play out into a fistfight—girl fights are hot—but let's step back a minute here, huh?"

Lila shook him off and stood until she and Chloe were toe-to-toe. "You are not going to ruin his life because of one stupid moment in Vegas."

Nick's phone bleated out an annoying crash of notes before he must have hit ignore to cut it off.

Chloe stepped back. "Finally, we can agree on one thing. You figure out a way to make this go away and I'll sign whatever you want me to."

"Fine." Lila's shoulders heaved. "At least you can be sensible about one thing."

Nick's phone went off again. Both women turned to him.

Chloe bunched her fists around her purse. "Are you serious right now?"

Nick shrugged. "Speak of the devil." He answered the phone. "Not a good time, buddy. I have two women here who aren't happy with you. One might even be contemplating putting a hit on you."

Lila held out her hand. "Is that Michael?"

Nick shook his head. "Yeah, he doesn't want to talk to you, Li."

"What?" Lila flipped her hair over her shoulder, visibly showing her agitation for the first time Chloe could remember.

Chloe reached across and plucked the phone out of Nick's hand.

"Hey!" Nick tried to grab it back. "That's mine."

Chloe marched down the aisle past a shocked Harper and Deacon and a smiling Simon with a bag of M&M's in his hand.

"Stop calling Nick, stop trying to call me. I don't want to talk to you, I don't want to have anything to do with you, Michael Shawcross."

"Well, that's too bad, Mrs. Shawcross. We have plenty to discuss."

His deep voice sent a thrill down her spine. The same feeling she remembered in a flash from the night before. Had he spoken the same way over her shoulder when she'd been dancing at the Foundation Room? Smoky and sultry with a hint of playfulness.

A sudden and consuming anger burned through her. "I'm going to do everything in my power to make sure that is never, ever my name."

"I do love when you snarl at me. Must be the red hair."

Her jaw literally dropped open. "This isn't funny. Stop making jokes."

"Of course it's not." His voice instantly turned serious. "That's why we need to talk."

"We don't need to talk at all unless it's across from a lawyer where I'm signing on the dotted line on annulment or divorce papers." She hit the end button before he could talk.

She couldn't even see through the rage blurring her vision.

"Okay, sweetie. Breathe."

Chloe's eyes burned as Jazz's soft voice came from behind her. Jazz laid a gentle hand on her shoulder and dislodged Nick's phone from Chloe's hand. She really couldn't handle someone being kind to her right now. She'd just burst into a million pieces and cry until she couldn't be put back together again.

"Chloe, wait."

But she couldn't. She broke free and headed to the front of the plane where the bathrooms were. She opened the door and slammed it closed, pulling over the lock lever. No way, no how could she face anyone. Not after she'd freaked out like that.

Embarrassment didn't even cover it.

She had no idea how long she stayed in there. People walked by and voices picked up after a few minutes. She turned on the water and let the tap water flow over her wrists. Being in the service industry, and the mother to a toddler, left her rattled some days. Sometimes a little cool water over a pulse point kept her from completely losing her shit.

She really, really needed that to work right now.

The hum of the engine poured into her until she was numb.

A light knock eventually broke her trance. "Miss. We have to prepare to land."

"I can't come out there," Chloe said through the door.

The attendant was quiet for a moment, then spoke again. "You can sit up with me. How's that?"

Chloe swallowed down a lump. "Are you sure?"

"Yes. Positive. I've got an extra seat away from the main cabin."

She peeked out the door. The woman's kind face held no judgment.

"Come on. Let me get you some water and we'll get you home."

"Thanks." Chloe slipped out the door and through the curtain to the small space where the drink and snack cart was tucked away. A little flip down seat flanked either side of the doorway with a lap belt tucked neatly to the side.

She could definitely handle that.

"Janice, right?"

The woman smiled. "Right." She handed Chloe a small bottle of water.

"I'm sorry if I made a scene."

Janice shrugged. "That's nothing. I've been taking care of these guys for years. You've got nothing on the antics I've seen."

Chloe's lips twitched. "I bet." She swallowed down most of the bottle. "I'm still going to stay back here if that's okay."

"More than."

"Good."

Landing was a lot different when it came to private planes. There was no real wait once they were on the tarmac. Everyone disembarked in record time. Chloe tapped her fingers on her purse and texted to make sure her father was outside while she waited.

"They're gone," Janice finally said.

Chloe slipped her strap over her shoulder. "Everyone?"

"Everyone."

She peeked around the curtain and sure enough, the plane was empty. Sun streaked in through the cabin windows and doorway. Her suitcase was waiting at the mouth of the stairs. She gave Janice a tight smile and escaped down the steps.

It was a crystal clear day—well, as much as Los Angeles could be clear. But the haze wasn't too bad that day. Along the edge of the private air strip, her father's old Toyota was parked.

Her father, who tended to be a little too thin no matter how much she fed him, stood with his fingers wrapped around her son's hand. Axl was tugging to get free and pointing at a helicopter above them.

Both of them had red hair, though her father's was definitely fading to graying goose-down fluff as he headed toward fifty. He was wearing his usual uniform of baggy khakis and a ratty sweater over a simple white T-shirt. And her kid—her sweet, perfect kid—was wearing a Cookie Monster shirt and jeans with a blob of unknown origin on the hem.

Finally, the helicopter had faded from sight enough that Axl noticed her walking across the pavement. He dragged her father behind him as they both raced to her.

Chloe dropped her purse and suitcase and crouched down for the best hug in all the world. "Hey, kiddo. Mommy missed you." She looked up at her father. "Thanks for coming to get me."

Her dad tilted his head. "Everything okay?"

"Right now, it is." She covered the whorl of red hair that never seemed to sit right at the back of her son's head and breathed him in. Fruit punch and baby shampoo. A damn fine combo as far as she was concerned.

Axl wiggled away. "Did you see the chopter, mama?"

"Chopper," she corrected.

"Chopter," Axl said again.

She laughed and dragged him back in for a hug. She buried her face in her son's sweet-smelling neck. "I did see it."

"Can I have one?"

Chloe slung her purse back over her shoulder and hauled him up to perch on her hip. "Not today, pal. We can go home and play with your Legos though."

"Deal. Home!"

"Home," she agreed.

This was what mattered. Not her stupid marriage. That would have to work itself out.

Right now, she had to worry about this little monster. He was everything.

FIFTEEN

A PLAN. RIGHT. THAT WAS ALL MICHAEL NEEDED.

Once he was conscious again.

After his failure to extract Chloe's number from Nick, Michael had conceded the field. Given up. Temporarily, of course, but a smart guy knew when to pull back and regroup.

Of course the treads on his face from Chloe's dismissal had sped up the retreating process, but he wasn't one to point fingers.

He dozed fitfully on the plane ride home, then went to his apartment and crawled into bed after taking a short, hot shower. He slept all day Monday, minus a few trips to piss and contemplate his shitty lot in life.

All in all, it was easier to sleep.

Tuesday, he woke up to discover the internet had exploded.

Apparently, the lead guitarist of Warning Sign getting unexpectedly married the same weekend as his band's triumphant concert was a big fucking deal.

The Vegas part was icing.

The fact that he'd married the fiancée of "a washed-up rocker who'd sued Oblivion before he'd either committed suicide or died by misadventure" made up the sugary roses.

He wondered how long it would take them to realize his wife had ghosted on him without leaving a forwarding address.

Forget address. He couldn't even get her digits.

The one thing in their favor was they'd been in the same circles for years. Someone might ostensibly believe they'd had some kind of meaningful interaction that could lead to marriage. Instead of, oh, not having any kind of contact other than his hiring a PI to take photos she'd inadvertently been a part of and possibly eating from the same bowl of peas at Thanksgiving.

No, scratch that. He was almost positive she didn't like peas, because there'd been a big brouhaha with her kid smearing them on the wall during the meal. See, there was one thing he knew about his wife.

Strangers, *pfft*.

He rolled out of bed and into the shower. Hard to see how he'd gotten dirty from sleeping, but his body was sheened in perspiration. Christ, the dreams he'd had. More like nightmares. Ones about his mother's wedding, where he'd given her away and turned around to see the audience was laughing at him. Pointing too.

No wonder he'd sweated through his sheets. He hated weddings as a whole, and his mother's were a special kind of hell.

No wonder he'd blocked out the memory of his own ceremony. Who could blame him?

He showered and was about to shave when he dropped his razor. He still had the cut on his hand from the other day, when he'd talked to Ryan after awakening to Tabitha in his bed. He'd thought his life was so difficult then.

Right. His life had been a candy apple forest compared to the bullshit of being accidentally married, yet having no contact information for his wife.

Fuck shaving. Fuck everything.

He rubbed a hand over his scruffy chin and went back into the bedroom to grab his phone. Enough of this holding his ass crap. He'd just contact Jerzee, his old PI friend, and have him find out where Chloe lived—

His gaze landed on his wallet. Shit, the license. He'd had a way to contact her all along, and he'd been too out of it to even realize.

Yeah, he was never drinking again.

He pulled out the piece of paper and scanned Chloe's info. Then swore and pitched it aside.

She'd listed her phone number as 1-800-Don't-Know.

"Goddammit." He grabbed the paper again to scan the address section, knowing it was likely a futile enterprise. Everything for the past few days had been other than the concert. He couldn't even remember if he'd managed to perform in bed.

Maybe Chloe had run from him because she recalled more than she was letting on. Had he sucked in the sack? Maybe he'd been selfish and demanded a BJ without going down on her. Or perhaps he hadn't done the whole clit thing during making love, because evidently, most chicks couldn't come solely from penetration. So odd. If he was penetrated by a large dick, he'd come for sure.

Yep, he was just going to leave that whole line of inquiry alone.

His gaze zeroed in on the address line and he let out a long, slow breath. Holy fuck, she'd put down an actual address. Whether it was hers, he had no idea, but at least it seemed feasible. Carson, California. Where the hell was that? He was pretty sure it was a suburb of LA, and he had a fuzzy recollection that it wasn't the most prosperous area.

He typed the address into his phone and cross-referenced it with her name. Yep. Bingo.

So she was honest sometimes and lied at others. Then again, according to what he'd put down, his phone number was 666-666-6666, so maybe they'd thought they were being funny.

Whatever they'd had to drink should be outlawed.

But hell, he had an address. Now he just needed to convince her that being married to him was not a horrible thing. That maybe it might even be beneficial to them. Okay, maybe just beneficial to *him*, as he'd worked out in between naps on the plane ride home.

His rep was in tatters, what with the senator's fiancée thing. What better way to seem like less of a homewrecker than to be happily married?

True, that wasn't giving her much out of the deal. But surely they could work out an arrangement. They had chemistry in spades. The value of good sex could never be discounted.

Next time, he might even get to remember it.

After pulling on jeans and a T-shirt, he added a hoodie and a pair of aviator glasses just in case. From the state of his email and texts, his recent joyous event had broken in the news in a big way, so it wasn't unreasonable to assume there might be a few members of the paparazzi outside.

He unlocked his door and peeked out, only to see his hallway full of people who were not the mailman or the UPS dude. No solicitors either. Just jerks with cameras and microphones and greedy expressions.

Holy shit.

He slammed the door and pressed his back to the wood. What now? And shit, was Chloe dealing with this too? If so, she must hate him.

Hate him *more*, since she hadn't really seemed too keen on him after their lovely union.

Digging out his phone, he quickly called Josh, his neighbor down the hall.

"Jesus, Michael, is this all for you? What the heck did you do? I know the heat's been up on you lately, but this is beyond."

"I got married." Michael rolled his shoulders. "Hey, is Davey home?"

"Yeah, why?"

"I need you guys to do me a favor. If you do it, I'll give you whatever you want. Not my Viper," he added. "Anything but my car."

"What do you want us to do?"

Michael outlined the plan for his friend, and luckily, Josh—and Davey—were onboard. It wasn't exactly complicated, and he wasn't even sure it would work. But luckily, Davey had a similar build to Michael's, and he'd given him a Warning Sign hoodie just last week.

Long shots at least had a chance, right?

Fifteen minutes later, after Davey had so considerately caused the paparazzi to chase after *him* in their misguided pursuit, Michael raced down the blissfully cleared out hallway. He headed for the service elevator that would allow him to exit in the alley behind his building.

Another fifteen minutes after that, he was in his Viper and programming the drive to Carson into his GPS.

If the paps were hassling him, that probably meant they were bothering her too. She didn't deserve that. So he'd just have to get to her place and try to convince her that maybe she would be better off staying with him until the furor died down.

And her son. Couldn't forget the kid. God, they'd have to babyproof his apartment. Kids liked to stick their body parts into outlets, right? Plus, they tried to drink chemicals and chew on the carpet—

"Dude, she has a baby, not a Chihuahua. Chill." He exhaled and gripped the wheel.

Yes, he'd been reduced to speaking out loud to calm himself down. Whatever it took. If he didn't practice some serious Zen and fast, he was probably going to lose his shit.

To soothe himself, he turned on his satellite radio and tuned it to one of the coffeehouse stations. Last thing he needed was his usual head-banging stuff. Today, he'd try something more mellow.

He'd gone less than a mile on his lengthy journey to find Chloe when "In Your Arms" came on. Confused, he stared at the station information and saw it was called the exclusive "House of Blues mix."

What the hell was that? Had Lila worked her magic to get a single out from the show? "All Night Long" had basically had its run, but still, they normally promoted their asses off for a new single, with radio interviews and articles online and lots of screen time at events. All the usual stuff that came with a big media push.

And his stepmother was no dummy. If the press was rabid over all things Warning Sign at the moment, she'd do whatever she had to in order to get the focus back on their music. Of course she'd had to select the song he would now forever associate with Chloe.

He tapped the side of his fist on the steering wheel and flicked screens back to his GPS. He still had roughly five hundred million miles to go.

Damn, where did his new wife live?

Turned out she did live in a suburb of LA, but it was pretty much on the opposite side from his own place in Malibu. He also might have understated the impoverished area consideration.

The more he drove, the more concerned he became. No one was

eyeing his extremely conspicuous Viper in an alarming way, or even acknowledging his presence at all. But Christ, there were numerous boarded-up homes in Chloe's neighborhood. She shouldn't be in a place like this. Of course he knew people did what they had to do to get by. He'd just never really seen this kind of struggle up close.

He knew he'd been lucky financially. His father's money had ensured his lifestyle growing up was as cushy as could be, and yes, he'd taken some of that for granted. Too much. Paying his own way while working in a rock band—even a fledgling one—didn't compare with what people in Carson did to make ends meet.

After a weekend in Vegas, Chloe had come home to *this*. She dealt with this life day in and out. So much for him having problems.

He didn't even have the right to say the word.

It was just past three when he pulled up down the block from the address she'd written on the marriage license. Way down the block, because the street directly outside her home was clogged with media trucks and cars.

Damn, he'd been too late again. As usual.

Better look fast, dude.

From what he could see at this distance, she appeared to live in a two-family house with flowers poking up around the weeds in the yard. Hers was the only place he could see that didn't have chipped paint or any broken-out windows, at least not in the front. He craned his neck, taking in the sagging porch and the mailbox hanging sideways on the wall.

Overall, the place was cute, if small. The houses on either side were as well, but they'd lost any redeeming features years before.

He drummed his fingers on the wheel and fought the urge to turn the car around and go back home. She didn't want him to bother her. Hadn't she made that clear? His presence had created all this chaos. Those reporters had to be making her life hell.

Added to that, he was so out of his depth he felt like he was drowning. He'd been given all kinds of breaks in life, ones he didn't deserve. So much had been handed to him. Sitting here in *this* particular car, staring at all the houses in decline, he felt so fucking guilty he couldn't stand himself.

How was he supposed to go see her and talk rationally about them figuring out how to proceed when all he wanted to do was grab her and take her back to his place?

Not just her. She has a little boy too.

The kid too, of course. That made it even worse.

Lila had intimated Nick was helping Chloe financially. If so, he must not have done much or on any regular basis. How could he let her live there? She was so young and beautiful, and she was on her own with a child. It couldn't be safe.

Maybe it was now, because no one could try anything with a camera crew outside her front door. But back before the paparazzi had flocked to her neighborhood, what had she done when she needed to run to the store for a quart of milk? She'd probably gone to that crappy place on the opposite corner that appeared to have bullet holes in some of the windows.

Fuck, fuck, fuck.

Michael was still sitting there, waiting for inspiration to hit about how the hell he was going to get close enough to talk to her—and also, how to get her to leave with him—when someone rapped on his window. Swallowing hard, he rolled it down. A woman with hair like steel wool and a shopping cart full of cans stood on the other side. "Um, hi. Can I help you?"

"You're parked on the wrong part of the street. Red on the curb means no stopping. You're going to get towed."

"Oh, yeah, right. Sorry. Thanks for telling me. I'll move." And go where, he had no idea.

"You'll want a spot that's unpainted or gray. The other curb colors have rules."

"Uh, okay. Thanks."

She nodded and smiled at him with a mouthful of perfect teeth. Just as she was about to turn away, he touched her arm. "Hey, can you help me?"

"Help you?" Her laughter was rich and warm. "I'd think you wouldn't need any help at all, fancy car like this one. What'd this set you back? One hundred grand?"

He averted his gaze. "About that, yeah."

"Nice ride. Better keep it moving. This neighborhood, someone might try to help themselves."

"I'm only passing through." Maybe. He honestly wasn't sure.

If Chloe refused to leave with him—which all indications seemed to point to—then what? He couldn't just take off. But he had no choice. She was a grown woman, and she had every right to make her own choices.

He was a virtual stranger, and he had no business trying to take over her life. His help was self-serving anyway, wasn't it? He wanted to save his rep, so of course he wanted his new faux missus stationed at his home to help make the story more convincing.

Except it so wasn't only about that. Not anymore.

"What did you need help with then? If it's trying to get past that tangle up there, sorry, no can do. They're here morning and night nowadays. The girl in that house? She got married over the weekend to a rockstar. It's the biggest news story around here since those three Carson boys made good."

Michael frowned. "Which Carson boys?"

"Deacon, Simon and Nick." She ticked them off on her fingers. "They were the best of friends around here, then went off to be rockstars. Guessing that's how she met her fella. I enjoy rock music myself." She patted the battered boom box-style radio in her cart and his chest lurched. "She's a regular *Pretty Woman*, our Chloe. Got herself saved by her own Richard Gere."

"I'm no Richard Gere." And Chloe was no prostitute. She did have the gorgeous red hair like Julia Roberts though.

Fuck.

"No, but you do all right." The older woman smiled at him, and he realized she'd known he was the rockstar all along.

"I'm sorry," he said, not knowing what he was apologizing for.

That she'd had to struggle so much while he sat in an expensive car? That Chloe obviously did too while she was raising a little boy? He didn't know.

All he knew was he wanted inside that little house to see Chloe again. More than anything.

"Nothing to be sorry for. You married that girl. She works herself to the bone to provide for her baby. When she is home, she's with that child." She cocked her head. "I bet you have a really nice place."

"Yes, I do, ma'am."

"So she should be there with you."

He swallowed hard. "Yes. She should."

Wanting her to live with him probably made about as much sense as any of the rest of this. She'd claim he felt sorry for her, but God, it wasn't that. He was growing more impressed with how she lived her life and who she was by the second.

He'd seen her with her kid. She loved him to pieces. If his own mother had been half as conscientious, he would have been lucky.

"I need to see her, but I can't get near her house. Do you have any ideas? I could just push my way past them and get inside, but they'd just bother her even more. I don't want that."

"You're lucky none of them have noticed your flashy car yet. Handy, you being parked this far up the street."

"Yeah, I kind of suck at subterfuge."

She laughed. "Just leave it to me to get you inside, but you'll have to move fast. Can't leave the car here though."

"Parking, right."

"Park around the block, pull up your sweatshirt and keep watch."

"Yes, ma'am. Thank you. But don't get yourself in any trouble on my account—"

She was already gone, shuffling up the street.

He reversed the car into a cracked and weedy driveway, then did a U-turn and zipped down a side street. After a quick study of the curb, he discovered he'd picked the wrong side again, so he drove down the street until he found an unmarked area.

If it wasn't valet parking, he was clueless.

He rounded the corner on foot and saw that there was a brief pause in the swell of foot traffic around Chloe's house. It looked like a random shopping cart had hit the side of one of the TV stations shiny maroon vans. Not only that, but the older woman he'd just spoken to was sitting on the ground, wailing loudly while people knelt and assisted her.

Michael shook his head and smiled. Damn, she was some actress. Forget Julia. This lady could've gotten an Oscar.

Man, he owed her big time. Before he figured out how to pay her back, he had to get into Chloe's place.

He jogged up the street, pretending he was out for a casual run. His dark glasses, scruff, and hoodie helped disguise him, and luckily, the crowd seemed to be mostly busy with the lady who'd saved his damn life.

Crossing the lawn at Chloe's, he paused on the bottom step. What if she wasn't home? Fuck, he didn't have time to worry about that.

He knocked on the door he thought—hoped—was hers. When no one answered, he pressed his face against the glass. He couldn't see through the lacy curtains in the window in the door.

Of course she wasn't going to answer even if she was home. And she might not answer him anyway.

Out of options, he knocked on her neighbor's door, praying under his breath as the voices in the street got louder and louder. The elderly lady was doing her best, but she wouldn't be able to hold the paps off for long.

When the door swung open, he pushed his way inside and slammed it shut with his foot.

The woman whose house he'd just invaded shrieked. Actually shrieked.

"Shh, shh, I'm not a burglar." He slipped off his glasses and gave her a sheepish smile. "I'm actually, well, a rockstar."

"Do you have ID?" she squealed.

Rockstar ID? That was a new one. "I can show you my driver's license, if you want to look me up."

She nodded hurriedly and he pulled out his wallet, showing her his info.

"You're Chloe's new husband. Why didn't you say so?" Her dark eyes widened and she peered up at him as if he was Jason Statham or something. "You're beautiful."

"Oh, thank you. Listen, I need to see Chloe. Like...now. Is she home? Can you let me into her apartment?"

"No, she's at work. But her baby is here." The young brunette woman smiled. "I'm Lori. So nice to meet you. You can stay here while we wait for Chloe to come home from work. She had the lunch shift today."

"Great, thanks. Nice to meet you too." He tucked his wallet and his glasses in his sweatshirt pockets and yanked back the hood. "Will Chloe be much longer?"

"About another hour. Axl's still asleep, but you're welcome to say hello to him. From the doorway, of course. He was fussy today and didn't want to take a nap."

"Axl." Now that she said it, he was pretty sure he'd heard them mention the kid's name before. "Like the guy from Guns 'n Roses?"

Shit, he was already hot for Chloe, and now this? Her baby had a rockstar name. Damn.

"Yes. Her and her fiancé were big fans."

"Nice." He scratched the back of his neck. Yeah, the kid's father had passed. Rough for him, and for Chloe too.

Neither of them had gotten many breaks from what he could tell.

"He's up in the room at the top of the stairs, if you want to take a peek." Then she bit her lip. "Maybe I should call Chloe first. We're friends, but she really didn't want to say much about you, even when I asked. Your whirlwind courtship has been all over the news, but she told me you have actually known each other for years."

Alas, *known of* and *known* were two very different things. He understood why Chloe had indicated they had prior history. The whole married in a weekend thing—not so kosher.

He wasn't even sure they knew each other in the Biblical sense, for fuck's sake. Well, he knew her pussy. He'd had his fingers inside her, and she'd been so warm and tight. Her clit had been so swollen and—

Okay, moving on.

"Yes, we're quite familiar with each other. So, top of the stairs?"

"Right. Maybe I'll just call her, make sure she's okay with this."

"No, please. Keep it secret. I want it to be a surprise I'm here." He used his winningest smile on Lori, and she nodded reluctantly.

"All right. Go on up. Holler if you need anything or if he fusses. He has his bottle, but his diaper might need a change soon."

No, no diapers. There was trial by fire and then there was being roasted alive and eaten by poo-flinging ants.

Michael nodded and went up the narrow flight of stairs, then entered the room she'd indicated.

Axl was asleep on the center of a circular rug.

He wore overalls, a blue T-shirt, and red Keds. His hair was almost as red as the shoes, and just as red as Chloe's. So she didn't dye it. He'd suspected as much.

Thinking about her pussy while in full view of her son seemed wrong. But he was definitely curious about getting a nice long look.

Ruminating on Chloe's girlscaping was much more inviting than stepping into the room. He'd started to, then paused half in and half out.

Michael glanced down at his hand and realized he was clutching the doorframe. Not that he was scared of the baby or anything.

Scratch that. He was terrified.

He took another step into the room and gave in to the urge to kneel beside Axl. Close, but not close enough to disrupt his nap.

Michael had seen him before, of course. He just hadn't paid any attention. Just like he hadn't paid much attention to Chloe.

How could that be, when their existence had rapidly begun to take over his world?

Michael must've made a noise, because Axl lost his hold on the bottle clamped firmly in his hand and started to whimper. Michael tried to tuck it back into the boy's hand, but Axl's eyes popped open and he started to cry. Loudly.

No, he was shrieking too. Okay, this was becoming a pattern.

Michael moved to the door and called down to Lori. "Help, I think I broke him." He tried to call softly but urgently.

Axl wasn't mollified by Michael's attempts to be quiet. He continued to sob.

Instead of Lori coming up a moment later, the one who appeared was Chloe. She was red-faced and winded, and immediately charged over to pick up her son. She then proceeded to shelter him in her arms and glare at Michael as if he'd caused the baby's distress. Which he had, kind of. Somehow. He'd probably breathed too hard or something. God knew he was panicked enough to be wheezing.

"Why are you here?" Chloe demanded.

"Because you're my wife," he said simply. "And I want you and Axl to come live with me."

SIXTEEN

HE'D BEEN WATCHING *MICKEY'S CHRISTMAS ADVENTURES* FOR TWO hours.

Actually, two and a half.

Michael didn't know if he was viewing a television season, a series of movies or experiencing an extended psychedelic trip minus the 'shrooms.

He hadn't even been fed yet, though Axl had eaten a sandwich—the innards at least, as he hadn't seemed overly impressed with the bread—then scarfed down a pudding cup with his fingers, and was now working on another bottle of juice.

The baby was lying on his belly in front of the TV, occasionally eyeing Michael in between slurps on his bottle. He didn't seem to be in any hurry to break the "getting to know you" tension.

Getting schooled by a baby, man. Better and better.

"Oh, you're still here?" Chloe sounded dismissive.

"I was waiting until you got done shaving or washing your hair or whatever so we could talk."

"I was cleaning the kitchen and working on my checkbook. No shaving. No washing. It may come as a surprise to you, but women do other things in a day besides ready themselves for a man."

Axl tried to push himself into a sitting position with his chubby arms. He managed to, but it took him a second. "Nicky?"

Michael inhaled deeply. Right. The baby who didn't have any interest in him was all about Michael's stepfather. His kind of stepfather. Cripes, their family relationship was complicated.

"No, Axlsaurus, Nicky can't come over today. He's busy."

Axl pouted and went back to Mickey.

"Nick spends a lot of time here, huh?" He wasn't going to be jealous about that. He'd barely known Chloe and Axl existed last week. How could he begrudge them spending personal time with her ex-lover?

Except he did. A lot. He wanted to be the one Axl turned to, which was illogical since he couldn't even figure out how to talk to the kid.

He wasn't good at the *goo-goo gaa-gaa* stuff. Just not his bag. Seemed hard to believe it was Nick's either. The guy wasn't a *coo*-er in any shape or form.

"Not that much. He stops by now and then to see how we're doing. Snake was his best friend."

"Snake, your ex-fiancé."

"His name was William, but yeah, you know. Stage name. How come you don't have one?"

"Because I'm not a persona. I'm just Michael, who happens to play guitar."

She narrowed her eyes before sitting down beside him on the rug. That was a bit of an overstatement, because she was actually seated closer to Axl. "Juliet is pretty," she said after a moment.

"Huh?"

"Juliet. Your bandmate. She's a beautiful woman. Have you…"

"God, no. Are you kidding me? Only an idiot sleeps with someone in their own band."

She cast a glance at Axl, who appeared blissed out thanks to Mickey and his playhouse. "Is that so? Funny, I know a bunch of people who have."

"Tell me if those bands are still together in five years, then we'll talk."

"Why are you even here?"

Not that again. "You really want me to spell it out? I will, if you like hearing it." He planted his hands on the carpet and leaned toward her, grinning as she leaned the exact amount of distance he covered in the opposite direction. "You. Are. My. Wife. That means we need to do something about this situation, not just sweep it under—"

"Aha!" Axl giggled in his loud, boisterous—and yes, semi-adorable —way, tipping over on his side.

Michael glanced at the kid. "Is he okay?"

"Those are sounds of enjoyment. Yes, he's fine." She rolled her eyes at him. "Have you never been around a child? Like ever?"

"No. My brother is older, and I don't date chicks who are mothers."

She reeled back from him as if he'd slapped her. In a way, he had. Fitting, since he wanted to slap himself over the stupid remark. "But marrying one is okay?"

"I'm sorry. That came out wrong."

"So you do date women with children."

"Not exactly, no. Most of the groupies don't have kids at home."

"Are you kidding me? You only date groupies?" Her distaste was palpable. Then her big brown eyes widened. "Oh my God, I need to get tested. So many times. Who knows where you've been?"

"Are you kidding me? You think I fu—"

She made a shrill noise that made him pop his finger in his ear to save his eardrum.

"B-a-b-y," she spelled out. "Keep your filthy language to yourself."

"B-a-b-whyyyy," Axl mimicked, making himself laugh so hard he had to clutch his stomach.

In spite of himself, Michael chuckled. "Guess you must spell that out a lot."

"I have guests other than you who forget to watch what they say."

"Oh, do you now? What kind of guests?"

"If you're asking if I date groupies, no. I gave them up for Lent."

"It's not Lent yet. Besides, your particular weakness is rockstars, isn't it? You're up to three now. And you know what they say about three."

She pursed her lips so hard that they went white around the edges. "How—it wasn't really three. It was only one. Snake was the one who counted. The others were wild weekends."

The pang that struck him made him catch his breath.

She was right. So right that he had no reason to even be there. He should've taken Lila up on her offer to make it all go away.

He didn't belong in a situation like this. He'd said it himself. He "dated" groupies. The last time he'd had an actual girlfriend had been so long ago he didn't remember.

Common theme with you, pal.

"It only counts as a wild weekend if both parties remember every last detail." He circled his finger on the rug and tilted his head. "We should work on that, don't you think?"

"No." Her breathing sped up audibly. "Why? What does it matter?"

"We can figure out what happened and what went wrong. You know, for next time. In my case, for the next time I see a woman in the audience and get so turned on by her that I have to marry her."

A faint smile played around her lips. "You didn't marry me because you were turned on. If we really are even married. I have my doubts it's all real."

Of course she did, because she hadn't seen the marriage license yet. Instead of showing it to her and probably ruining her night, he scooted across the rug and reached for her left hand.

She gasped as if he'd gone for a tit grab. "What are you doing?"

"I'm looking at the ring I bought my wife. My prerogative, I think." Belatedly, he realized he couldn't look at what she wasn't wearing.

He should've checked out her hand before, surreptitiously. Then maybe he wouldn't have gotten yet another short-armed punch to the chest at holding her hand and finding it bare.

So what if he still had his on? He just was the chump who'd forgotten to take it off. That was all.

"Never mind." He let her hand drop. "Guess I'm too late."

"I don't wear it. Why should I? It wasn't a real marriage." She darted a glance at his hand and made a soft noise in her throat before lifting her gaze to his. "Why? Why are you still wearing it?"

He went with the easiest reason, since trying to decipher the truth was a lot harder. "Getting married to you is the best thing that could've happened to me."

Her throat worked before she shifted her focus to her now sleeping son. He'd flopped over facedown and had his bottle tucked under his arm. "I have to put him down."

"Looks like he already did that for himself."

"He should be in bed, since Lori said he didn't get much of a nap this afternoon."

It was probably starvation and sex deprivation—if he couldn't remember doing it, it was almost as if he hadn't—that made him open his mouth. "I can do it. Probably. Where's his room?"

"Hold up. You can't put my son to sleep."

"He already is. See, exhibit A."

"That's not what I mean. I mean, carting him down the hall and tucking him in and reading him a story—"

"Which is his favorite?"

"Right now, *The Spider and The Fly*, but it changes every week. That's beside the point. We aren't playing house, Michael."

"True, since you won't move in with me, although we're virtual prisoners in here now." He jerked a thumb toward the curtains she'd made sure were drawn tightly the moment they'd entered the apartment.

"Right. Like it's not the same at The Pussy Palace."

"I don't have groupies in my home."

Of course that begged the question how he could have ever consumed enough to give Tabitha a key, but he'd also thought marriage was a fine idea while he was inebriated. Guess nothing was off the table when he started tossing them back.

Nope, he was never drinking again.

"Handy, since you want to move in me and my son," Chloe muttered.

"No, I mean they've *never* been in my home." Loosely, he grasped her wrist when she started to turn away. "I've never had a woman spend the night at my place."

He'd played it off to Lila that it didn't make sense he'd mess up a hotel room when he was in town, but that had been a misdirection. He didn't bring women to his apartment. Ever.

Except now he wanted to move a woman in. *The* woman. Somehow

Chloe had already climbed several levels in status past any woman who had come before.

She shook off his hold. "And I suppose you always use a condom too."

"Always." That was sterling truth. "I won't have sex without one."

"Am I supposed to believe you?"

He tapped the heavy gold ring on his finger. "I took a vow. That means I can't lie to you."

Her lips trembled before she firmed them. "So a wedding ring is like truth serum?"

"Suppose so." He shrugged and glanced toward Axl, who'd brought his chubby hand up to his mouth in sleep. "Let me put him to bed while you keep an eye out for your dad."

"You mean so I can usher him inside in a hurry? They're relentless out there."

"If you moved in with me—"

"I'd have to deal with the same thing and I wouldn't have Lori to help with Axl when I'm at work."

"Well, you wouldn't have to do that if you didn't want to. Work, I mean. Being my wife accords you certain privileges."

"Oh, really. Next you're going to say you want me naked, barefoot and pregnant." She slapped a hand to her forehead. "Oh, I forgot. You're against chicks with babies."

"Never said I was against them, just that I didn't date them. I know my limitations."

She rose to her feet, faintly trembling with frustration. Or anger. He was never quite sure where he stood with her, which was one of the reasons he found her so intriguing. "Yet you want to put my son to sleep."

"Look at me, trying to take things to the next level." He rose as well, and enjoyed the way her eyes flashed as he loomed over her. "C'mon, Chloe. Help a guy succeed. Be part of the solution, not part of the problem."

"You know what? Fine. Go ahead." She crossed her arms. "His room is second door on the left upstairs. Right next to the powder room."

Okay, so now he was going to have to put the baby to bed. That was great. Awesome.

He scooped up Axl and shifted him in his arms as the kid predictably started to whimper. Anytime Michael even approached him, he went into reactive mode. Chloe moved forward, but Michael held up a hand. "We'll be fine."

She clasped her hands in front of herself. "Just be glad he doesn't need a bath tonight."

Michael shot her a horrified glance and hustled out of the room before Axl's tears could really take root.

He knuckled his eyes on the way upstairs though, and nearly lost his hold on his bottle. "Want Mama. Mama. Want Mama."

"She's right behind us, pal. Probably will install a baby cam in your room if she doesn't have one in there already."

"Already have one," she said from the bottom of the stairs.

Michael sighed and stared down into Axl's streaming brown eyes. "Slugger, she's still here with us. Just taking you upstairs so you can sleep. You're tired, right? Zzz."

The baby took one long, probing look at him as Michael turned on the landing to go up the next flight. And started to howl.

"*Shh.* There, there. Nice baby. Good baby." Michael patted Axl's back and felt his little body vibrate from the force of his tears. Mucus seemed to come out of several of his orifices at once.

That couldn't be good.

Chloe's feet thundered up the stairs behind them, but Michael resolutely carried Axl into his bedroom. Carefully, he set him on the mattress in his sweet blue and yellow room, with the lighted mobile above his race car big boy bed. "There you go. See?" He pulled up the little yellow blanket over Axl's squirming body. "All nice and safe and tucked in."

Axl hiccupped and wheezed, immediately shooting out his chubby little arms upon sighting Chloe. "Mama. Mama!"

But for some reason, she hung back. She remained in Axl's view, still in the room, but she gave Michael space.

So he heaved out a breath, brushed Axl's sweat-and-tear-sticky curls off his forehead and rose to look for the book she'd mentioned he liked in the tiny yellow bookcase.

He found it on the top shelf, tucked in the first slot. His fingers shook more than a little as he pulled it out before dragging over the little rocking chair barely big enough for his bony ass. Fingers still unsteady, he flipped to page one and started to read. Axl continued to sob and flop from side to side in his bed, banging his arms for emphasis.

And Michael read aloud.

By the third or fourth page, he was into it. The illustrations were really incredible and the story was cute. Toward the end, he was turning the pages as fast as he could for himself almost as much as Axl.

When he read the words "The End", he was both relieved and disappointed. Then he glanced up and glimpsed Axl gnawing on his knuckle in his sleep and did a mental fist pump.

"I did it," he said, stunned.

"Never fails," Chloe murmured from the doorway. "By the last page, he's always unconscious. It's a magical book."

"Sure, take away my accomplishment." But Michael grinned as he glanced at her over his shoulder. Her hair had partially come out of its ponytail and was curling around her cheeks. Her eyes were so big and dark, filled with shadows and secrets he wanted nothing more than to discover.

Every part of this woman fascinated him, not the least of which how she could be such a good mother and so devoted to her home life, yet still be the woman who'd entranced him so effortlessly while he was onstage. She had a million different sides, every one of them more intriguing than the last.

He rose and returned the book and chair to their spots. After looking at Axl one last time, he walked to the door and cupped her shoulders. As expected, she stiffened.

"You may think I'm a thoughtless horndog, but even I wouldn't seduce a woman in the doorway of a child's bedroom," he said, voice low so he wouldn't wake Axl.

"You won't be seducing me anywhere."

Before he could dispute that assertion, she vanished down the hall and down the stairs.

SEVENTEEN

Michael found Chloe sitting on the couch in the living room. She was chewing on her thumbnail and worrying so hard that she had grooves in her forehead.

He didn't like knowing he was contributing to her discomfort, but he was pretty uncomfortable too. In a lot of very pressing ways.

"You hungry? Because I am, extremely."

And he was only partially referring to pussy. *Her* pussy, in all its likely sunset glory.

"I'll eat after you go."

"Tsk, tsk, trying to shoo out a guest, and after I've been so helpful." He sat down beside her on the couch and slid his arm along the back to toy with the ends of her hair. "Something has been bothering me since you took off."

"What's that?" She not so subtly moved her head away from his wandering hand and he suppressed a smile.

"I started wondering if maybe you hadn't forgotten everything about that night after all."

"Of course I didn't forget everything. That isn't how drinking works. You remember stuff until you get really loaded, then your memories get muddled. But the last time I got drunk before this weekend was a very long time ago, so my tolerance was down."

So what was his excuse? His tolerance was too high?

"Maybe you should tell me what you do remember, and I'll tell you. We'll see if we can fill in some of the holes."

Instead of looking relieved at his suggestion, her brows furrowed. "Look, Michael, I have to go to back to work soon. Someone called off, so I picked up a later shift."

He frowned. She had to go back out in that insanity? "But you already worked today."

"Right. I often work a couple of shifts. I work at the bar, and I temp through the agency whenever they need me. Right now, I'm counting on the bar because my most recent positions with the agency just finished."

He glanced toward the hall. No crying yet. "What about the baby?"

"Oh, he's old enough to stay by himself." When Michael's eyes widened, she nudged his arm. "Sucker. I told you my dad's coming over. He's going to watch him."

Right, her father was en route. If being in a kid-saturated environment didn't freak Michael out enough, she had to add in some parental unit action. He should be positively itchy to leave by this point.

So why wasn't he?

Michael swallowed and reached for her hair again. Somehow curling it around his fingers settled him. "Want me to start with what I remember?"

"No, I really don't."

He traced his fingers down her shoulder. "It started onstage. I didn't notice you at first."

"Why would you? You had Juliet."

"Nothing has ever happened between me and Juliet. Nor will it ever. We do what we do for the crowd. In fact," he brushed his nose against Chloe's hair, "she slid her hand in my pocket after you and I started eyefucking the hell out of each other, and she found me hard. And she took off." He chuckled and pulled back enough to see Chloe's eyes. "Did you see her book across the stage? She never came back to my side for the rest of the set."

A wrinkle appeared between Chloe's eyes. "She thought you were really into her."

"Yes, and it freaked her the hell out. But I wasn't. I've never been hard for Juliet Reece."

"It doesn't matter. God, we never even had a conversation before this crazy weekend, so we might as well have just met a few days ago."

He picked up her hand and grazed his fingers along her soft skin. "Where's your ring?"

"That again?"

"I just want to see it. That's fair, right?"

"Okay." She slipped her hand into her pocket and withdrew the small piece.

Because of course it had to be sapphires. Didn't that just beat all?

Two infinity symbols made up of diamonds bracketed a sapphire in the middle. The deep blue color was gorgeous, and he could only imagine how lovely it would look on her pale finger. He only had one question.

Well, two, but she didn't have an answer for when she would start wearing it, so no point in asking that one.

"It's pretty," he said at length. No reason to dump his own issues with sapphires at her doorstep. If she liked it, that was all that mattered. "But why isn't it bigger?"

"What?" She gaped at him.

"A wedding ring should be special." He rubbed her knuckles with his thumb. "I know you were already engaged before, and that probably he gave you a nice ring." Out of the corner of his eye, he glimpsed her tucking her other hand under her hip. "Nothing about this situation is normal, but if you decide you want to upgrade it, just let me know. Not that I don't like the one you picked out," he added as she gawked at him.

"Are you even real?" she asked after a moment.

"I wasn't insulting your ring. Yeah, I have my own issues with sapphires, which is my problem, but—"

"Michael. You don't even know me. We barely ever spoke. Were you even aware of my existence before this weekend?"

He slid her a glance. He was in no hurry to go there, but they needed to get their past on the table before she found out in another way and hated him even more.

If that was even possible.

"Yeah. Did you ever know about the pictures?"

"What pictures?"

"So I guess that's a no." He exhaled and rubbed her knuckles again before closing his hand around hers. She must've been distracted by his latest impending revelation, because she didn't even try to pull away. "You know Lila is my stepmother."

"Even though she's barely older than you, yeah."

"My family is weird. Sorry you married into it. Anyway." He cleared his throat. "Back when she started up with Nick, she and my father were separated. I was concerned she was going to create a big issue with her divorce. My dad isn't an understanding man. The fact that he'd had affairs for years wouldn't stop him from treating L like shit. So I thought if I hired a PI friend to take some pictures of her and Nick while they were cavorting all over town, she'd see how indiscreet she was being."

"So, wait, you hired someone to take intimate pictures of your stepmother?" Chloe's eyebrows rose. "Sure you weren't off on some Freud trip? She's a beautiful woman, and I know how teenage boys are with hot MILFs."

"She wasn't technically a mother then," he mumbled. "Just a stepmother."

"Yeah, and you didn't deny guys get turned on by having a sexy stepmom. So that's how that was." Chloe shifted to sit sideways on the couch, pushing her back against the arm. He didn't blame her for needing space, but it still stung.

"The pictures weren't intimate. I specifically told Jerzee to not photograph anything of that nature. He wasn't sneaking around outside her bedroom. The photos were all taken outside, no super long lens, no big drawn out time period." Michael rubbed a hand over his face. "And one of the pictures he got was of you and Nick."

"Of me and Nick what? We didn't do anything."

"You were hugging. Smiling at each other. In one of them, it kinda looked like you were blowing him a kiss."

"I don't blow Nick kisses. What the hell? Where are these pictures?"

"Hang on. I still have them in my email. I kept them because—"

"You wanted spank material of your stepmother?"

"No," he said sharply. "I wanted to have them available so she could see all of them. I'm glad I did so now you can too. There is no spank material or anything close to it. The most Jerzee got of Nick and Lila was them kissing outside a laundromat and him grabbing her ass—which if you know them, he does about every six seconds."

"Wow. Bitter much?"

He didn't say anything. She wouldn't hear him out now anyway.

After opening his email on his cell, he scrolled through his folders until he found the one that contained the photos. Then he slid Chloe his phone.

She scanned through the snapshots without showing any reaction at first. Then her eyes misted and she glanced up at Michael. "I was pregnant with Axl."

"Yeah. You were stunning. *Are* stunning," he amended. "Do you want me to send those to you?"

Stiffly, she nodded and handed back his phone.

He tapped a few buttons and isolated just the shots of her and Nick. There were only a couple, and they were as innocent as could be.

Only a dick would be jealous of several-year-old pictures of friends hugging. Problem was, he *was* a dick, and he knew they'd once been way more than friends back in the day. How much more, he didn't want to think about.

"Need your email address," he said.

She gave it to him and he sent the pictures, then took a chance and lifted her legs onto his lap. She made a noise in her throat and tried to scoot back, but she was in the corner of the couch and there was nowhere to go.

"Full disclosure. I had a thing for Lila for a while. Teenage boys think solely with their dicks. When the gods grant you an attractive stepmother, yes, your thoughts drift bad places. But that was years ago. After she hooked up with Nick, the last of those feelings died."

Chloe's brow arched. "You certainly have a busy social life, Michael Shawcross."

"Nah, back then most of it was up here." He tapped his head. "The

Lila thing wasn't anything at all. She never saw me as anything but a son. I saw her as a mom too, and the last few years, that's *all* I've seen her as. Often a pain-in-the-ass one too."

Chloe's legs shifted in his lap. Her little toe had a flower-shaped ring on it, which might have been the sexiest thing he'd ever seen. "I saw your hair first, from the stage. All wild and free. Swaying behind you as you danced. Definitely never saw it like that before." He gave her ponytail a pointed look. "It's always up when I see you."

"I work and I take care of my son. No time for fancy hairstyles."

"Maybe not, but I'm glad there was time for this." He tweaked her little toe. "The ring's hot as hell, by the way. Almost as hot as watching you dance with your girls and get totally loose to my music. I got off on the fantasy of you being all wet and ready just from watching me. As ready as I was for you."

"Alcohol makes people do crazy stuff," she said quietly, turning her foot into his ministrations on her arch. "Oh fuck, that feels good."

Hearing her swear was always a slice of the forbidden. "Want me to give you a massage?"

"That sounds like a pick-up line."

"No, it's an 'I want to give you an orgasm before you go to work' line, so let's pretend this is innocent until it's so not." He rubbed her ankle bone under the hem of her jeans. "Oh, and just so you know—I hadn't had a drop when I was on stage. I might be a partier—might've been," he corrected, "but I always kept the music sacrosanct. I never rehearsed drunk. Never performed that way either."

Her feet wiggled. She was nervous, and trying to act like she wasn't. Even that turned him on. "I can't say the same. We pre-gamed pretty hard."

"Your eyes were unfocused when we were dancing. I couldn't decide if I wanted to take care of you or fuck you senseless."

She inhaled audibly. "You were pretty much on the fucking track all night."

"It kills me that I don't know," he murmured, digging his thumb into her arch just to hear that sexy little give in her breathing again. "I should've been able to memorize every moment of undressing you, and touching you, and licking you. I wanted to see your breasts in the light, outside the club. See the rest of you. The little slash of your belly button, the slit between your legs. Your ass. Goddamn, I want to see your ass bare. And I might have gotten to, but I was robbed of the memory and maybe I'll never get it back."

She swallowed hard. "Outie."

Her soft, shaky voice made him whip his gaze to hers. "What?"

"I have an outie." She peeled up her shirt to give him a glimpse of her belly, and Jesus, he couldn't stop the groan.

Her stomach wasn't flat. Wasn't perfect. But he'd never wanted to worship every inch of a woman's midriff more.

"Keep going," he rasped, fully expecting her to say no.

But she rolled her shirt up higher, offering him a look at the pale peach lacy cups that guarded her tits. Between them there was a tiny bow, sweet and pure.

He bent her legs and leaned closer, reaching down to stroke her adorable navel. She flicked her gaze up to his and her lower lip trembled open. Just like before, she reached up to bring his head down to hers, sending him the message loud and clear that she was into it too.

Into *him*.

Their noses bumped and their lips mashed together before he took a quick breath and aligned them correctly. He molded his mouth against hers while he caressed her belly, learning her curves as he slipped his tongue along her seam. She opened for him, inviting him inside, and he hesitated long enough to speak against her flesh.

"What I regret most is not remembering this part. That moment before I entered you. Tongue, fingers, cock." He opened his eyes and stared into hers, so deep and dark. "Kissing you nearly killed me. Imagining I missed out on recalling this..." Easing his hand between her legs, he squeezed, eliciting her gasp. "Next time, I'm going to fucking take notes."

"You need a notepad? Maybe a pen?" Her teasing questions between their quick, hot kisses made him even more mental.

"Oh, Red, I have a canvas right here." He scraped his callused thumb under the waistband of her jeans and she whimpered. "And I can paint you too."

"You're a talented man."

"You have no idea. Maybe you need a reminder too." He moved back and crooked his finger, inviting her on his lap. "Get on me."

"Work," she said halfheartedly.

"So make it fast."

She rose and straddled him, sinking down on his lap while her fingers dug into his shoulders. He reached up to free her hair and she shook it out, smiling down at him in a way that stole his breath.

"I'm not sure I've ever seen that smile before." He touched the side of her mouth. "Dimples?"

"Dimples and freckles," she said with a sigh, and he winged up a brow.

"You forgot the outie belly button and the adorable feet."

She pulled her shirt over her head, so quickly he couldn't prepare. "But all the freckles," she said, her voice fading out.

She wasn't lying. They were sprinkled all over her pale skin, layered on top of each other in some spots. He wanted to investigate them all.

Instead, he grabbed the straps of her bra and yanked them down her arms, trapping them at her sides while he lowered his head to suck on her nipple.

"Michael," she breathed. "Don't—" He paused, looking up as her head fell forward so that her glorious curtains of flame-red hair surrounded them. "Don't stop."

"Never." He nibbled the tip of her breast, absorbing her sounds of excitement like air. He coasted his hand down her torso to open her jeans. Underneath she wore mom underwear. White cotton, nothing arousing at all. Yet he couldn't nudge the fabric aside fast enough. "On my fingers," he said and she nodded, as if she wanted the same thing.

There was no teasing, no hesitation. He stroked her scant curls, swallowing over the dryness in his throat at how soaked they were. All for him.

No alcohol for either of them, no energy from a show, no dancing or club atmosphere. Just a saggy couch and granny panties and a baby sleeping upstairs.

Nothing had ever been hotter.

He separated her swollen lips with his index finger and rubbed her clit until she dropped her head back, baring her long, freckled throat.

Nibbling his way down her skin, he slid farther inside her, entering her in a slow glide that made them moan in unison. One finger soon wasn't enough, so he used two. He pushed them deeper, gauging what she could take. What would make those rosy lips fall open on a groan.

"Gotta come quick, so help me get you there." He grazed her throat with his teeth. "Shit, I want to lay down and pull you over my mouth."

Her arms were still caught close to her sides because of her bra straps so she flexed her fingers, balling them into fists. As much as he liked her being bound at his mercy, he liked even more having her hands on him. He reached back to undo her bra, allowing her to loosen the straps and drive her hands into his hair. Holding his head against her breasts, she rode his fingers, undulating with every one of his thrusts. A flick of his thumb over her clit and she pulsed around him once, twice, before shattering and soaking his hand.

Rocking his hand deeper, he kept going, ignoring her whimpers. "Sensitive?" He bypassed her clit and just pumped in and out, nice and slow, while he sucked on her nipple. She started tensing up and her nails pressed into the back of his neck. "Don't fight it."

"I can't...no multiples for me."

He smiled against her breast. "Before."

"Michael—"

"If you keep saying my name, I'm going to keep you on your back on this couch until you scream it."

She pressed her lips together and he chuckled against her breast, slowing his strokes. Giving her a chance to gather again, to find the rhythm he was coaxing her into one more time. Then going faster and faster while she sought more of what he was offering. Bearing down, she tightened up on him. So damn tight. Her walls convulsed around his fingers as she finally found her release with his name lingering on her lips like a chant. A prayer.

A song.

When she shuddered and slid down to him, he clasped the back of her head and brought it to his shoulder. Feeling her curl against him, relaxed and boneless, made the rigid shaft in his pants jerk. This wasn't about him. He knew it, even embraced it because he'd spent too little time really focusing on someone else. But his body was a hell of a lot greedier.

"God." Her mouth brushed the side of his neck. "Is there a handbook?"

"The Guide to Chloe's O? No, but give me time and I'll write it."

Her laughter washed over him, dialing down the throb in his cock to a pulse. He wanted her—so much—but he wanted *this* even more. This connection he'd never had a taste of with anyone else.

"Usually, they're rarely seen in the wild, especially the last couple of years. I haven't even managed to—" There was a commotion on the stoop, and she raised her head just as the front door burst open and a man with graying red hair flung himself into the small living room.

"What the hell is all that out there, Chloe?"

At that point, a few things happened at once. None of them good.

Chloe screeched and fumbled for her bra and her shirt. Michael scrambled to cover her with his arms. And Chloe's father's eyes grew wide before they rolled back in his head.

Actually, that might have been Michael's. He couldn't really be sure because he was looking away and begging the universe to finally do him a karma solid.

For God's sake, his wife didn't even remember marrying him. He'd just solely focused on her pleasure without considering his own. Couldn't he catch a break, ever?

"Daddy, you're early," she panted as she struggled with unforgiving cotton.

"No, I'm obviously too late." Her father scrubbed a hand through his already disordered hair. "Chloe, who is this guy? Who are you?" he demanded, staring at Michael when Chloe was too busy putting on her shirt to reply.

Her bra ended up balled up in her pocket with the straps sticking out.

"Hi, sir, um, I'm Michael Shawcross, Chloe's—"

"Don't say it."

"Chloe's *what?* Chloe Bear, you better start talking fast. I want to know who this strange man is and why you're half naked with him. And why a red Dodge Viper getting towed away is being filmed by a camera crew on the corner."

"What?" Michael bobbled Chloe in his lap, grabbing her arm to right her as she finally got her shirt back on. "My car is getting towed?"

"That's your ride?"

"Hell yes, it is. I mean, sir." He threw a glance at Chloe. "Fuck, I gotta get out there and get my car. I parked in the right spot, dammit."

"Guess not. Chloe, start talking."

"This is Michael. He's in a band. He's friends with Nicky."

"Oh, Nicky?" Mr. Adams brightened for a second then his mouth turned down as he studied Michael. "You're not in his band. What band are you in?"

"Nick isn't my friend, he's my kind of stepfather." Yet another way his life was a *Jerry Springer* episode in the making. "Anyway, I'm in Warning Sign. I'd love to stay and chat, but my freaking car is going to end up in an impound lot somewhere." Michael glanced at Chloe's dad. "Are the paps still on the lawn too or are they all down the street?"

"I don't know what 'paps' are, but if you mean the reporters, yes, they're still on the lawn. Pushy bastards. They asked me about Chloe's husband. Imagine them dredging up that Snake business again. Did the lawsuit get brought back up in the papers or something?"

Chloe flashed Michael a pleading look as she shoved up her sleeves. "Daddy, I'll explain in a few minutes, I promise. Michael has to go now."

Okay then. Talk about a boot out the door. Yes, his car was being towed and he needed to leave, but she could at least pretend not to want to toss him out on his dick.

Not on his ear, because his ear wasn't in pain like his cock, that was for sure.

"Yeah, time for me to go. I only have one purpose it seems." Michael got stiffly to his feet and held out a hand to Mr. Adams. "Sir, nice to meet you. I'm sorry the circumstances weren't better."

"You and me both. You're just lucky you had your pants on or else I would've tried my hand at some buckshot. Chloe has a gun over there in that closet." Mr. Adams jerked a thumb over his shoulder.

"Daddy, stop it. I'm an adult. We're consenting."

"We're hell of a lot more than consenting, we're goddamn marr——"

Chloe hurtled to her feet and pushed Michael toward the door. "Go save your car. I'll talk to you soon."

A moment later, he stepped onto the stoop and stared into the glare from a dozen flashbulbs. Questions were being pelted from every direction.

Normally, he tried to play nice with the paparazzi. Not anymore. He just swung right and left to make himself a path and booked for the street.

He might not be able to save his marriage, but he could save his damn car.

EIGHTEEN

"You're late, Chloe."

Chloe scrunched up her shoulders. "I know. I called Wanda." She tossed her light jacket and purse into her locker, trading it for her apron.

Lou, the owner and her boss, slapped the doorway to the piece of shit back room they called a break room. "Yeah, well, Wanda is shit at drinks. Get behind the bar. Now."

"The tips are decent, the tips are decent, the tips are decent. Diapers are expensive, Chloe," she said under her breath as she tucked her black T-shirt into her tight black jeans. She tied her black apron around her hips and grabbed a new towel from their stash in the back. She tucked it into her back pocket as she threaded her way through the tables.

She waved to three of the half-dozen waitresses on for the night. Thursday was always a little crazy at Rafferty's. People had their paychecks and they wanted to drink. The bar was also a block down from the strip, so they got the overflow when people were out and about for concerts.

Chloe ducked under the little crawl-space at the end of the bar.

"Thank God. If one more person gave me shit for how I build a Guinness, I was going to start swinging."

Chloe took the Guinness glass from Wanda. "Yeah, it's a pain in the butt. Thanks for covering."

Wanda grabbed a bottle of whiskey and splashed some in a glass before unhooking the soda tap. "What happened with your super?" She set the Jack and Coke in front of another one of their regulars with a smile and scooped up the five for the register.

Chloe sighed and held the glass at the perfect 45 degree angle then stopped to let it settle. "He's gotten a few complaints from the other tenants."

"Your kid is the sweetest on the planet."

Chloe laughed. She wished it was just from Axl being too loud. "Not about my kid. Just some stuff I have to deal with." Oh, just a hoard of reporters shuffling in zombie packs like they were trying out for *The Walking Dead*. Her life was the suck.

"Did I see you on TV, Chloe?"

She winced. The usual programming at the bar ran to ball games of all different types, not the lifestyle channels. As far as she knew, they'd only been mentioned on *Entertainment Tonight* once today. Didn't they have anything else to report on?

"*US Weekly* had a spread on hot rockstars. I saw you in my email." Amber slapped the bar and bounced with a giddy smile. "Michael Shawcross? No way." She waggled her brows. "He's a rockstar in bed too, right? I mean, wow, he's got to be. Those jeans he wears? It's not right."

"Who?" Wanda whirled around and put her hands on her hips.

Chloe widened her eyes at Amber. "Can we not talk about it, please?"

"Hmm. Too late." Amber flipped her blond ponytail over her shoulder. "There was some guy outside asking questions. I didn't know it was a secret."

Chloe sighed. "You have got to be kidding." How the hell did they find her? She'd taken three different buses to get to work.

"Can I have my beer?" A guy at the bar drummed his fingers.

"Crap." Chloe backed up to the tap and finished off the pour. She cleaned up the glass and set it in front of one of her regulars with a distracted smile before going back to Amber. "Look, people might start asking—"

"*Start?* Girl, that's the third person that's come in here asking about you two. The first one was a reporter from *Music Life*. I mean, wow." Amber tugged on the perfect curl at the end of her ponytail. "You and *another* rockstar? Do you have a special pheromone or something?"

"No," Chloe said stiffly.

"Well, come on, that's two now. No, three. You were with that Nick guy from Oblivion too, right?"

Chloe blew her bangs out of her eyes. "No—well, yes. But that was high school. He was just Nick back then."

"Still. Man," Amber's voice lowered. "You have that magic pussy, huh?" She snapped her gum.

"Oh my God." Chloe's eyebrows snapped down. "Amber, what the hell?"

The blond shrugged. "Own it, girl. Now you're married to that guitar guy…man, smoking hot. Talk about upgrade."

"I'm not talking about this."

If only they knew just how little action her…well, that *she* got. And she'd almost gotten some earlier in the week and had been interrupted by her father.

Her cheeks heated. Her dad. She'd been having sex since she was fourteen-years-old, for God's sake and it took until she was twenty-three to get caught by her dad. The levels of unfair were creeping in on epic proportions here.

She'd acted like a teen girl getting seduced by her first boyfriend. Foot massage then all of a sudden, she was on his freaking lap. Her defenses had been somewhere south of her belt thanks to his sweet mouth. Compliments given in a way that didn't sound like a line. No, they'd been coated in wonder and a purring low voice.

Then there'd been his mouth and his hands.

Lord, his hands.

Wanda bumped her out of the way as she grabbed a beer from the cooler. "Wake up, girl."

"Right." Chloe turned to the rack of glasses that needed to go into the washer and swapped them out for the cleans. The monotonous chores that came with running the bar evened her out.

Something had to. She'd tossed and turned all night half from the insanity of her life and half from the mind-bending orgasm that was eating at the edges of her brain. She'd gone so long without and now this stupid man had jumpstarted her freaking libido with jet fuel.

"What's this about you being married?" Diane came up to the bar and set her tray down.

"Not you too."

"How could you not tell us? Tell *me* especially."

"There's nothing to tell." Chloe wiped down the bar and put out coasters automatically.

"Really? Because from what I've heard, you're now married to a cheating bastard. You're better than that."

Chloe's gaze snapped to Diane's. "What?"

"Not even a week ago, this guy was climbing out of Senator Dinkles' fiancée's bed."

Her brain literally whirled. Her hearing fuzzed for a moment before everything came back into sharp focus. Her pocket buzzed. She pulled out her phone and saw Michael's name there. Definitely not reading that one, thank you very much.

"Girls, these tables aren't going to bus themselves!" Lou growled from the back.

Chloe stuffed her phone back into her pocket. "Later, Di."

Diane clamped a hand around Chloe's wrist. "Are you sure about this?"

Of course she wasn't sure of anything. She had a wedding night she didn't remember, a couch orgasm—wait. She'd had two.

The blast of memory and Michael's voice in her head made her entire body tingle.

If we were alone, I'd drag you up and over my face right now.

Why the hell had she remembered that now?

A couch in the corner of the club. Him and those freaking fingers. In a room full of strangers? Had she truly allowed him to do that?

"Oh, honey. From the look on your face—you're in trouble."

"What?" Chloe shook her head. "What? No, I'm fine."

190

"No, that's a face of a woman in the deepest of shit." Diane tucked her tray under her arm. "I recognize that face. It's how I ended up married to my second husband."

Chloe pulled her hand away. "You hated your second husband."

"I know. But holy hell, he was a beast in bed. Why I kept going back for more."

Chloe crossed her arms over her chest. "It's not like that."

Diane's eyebrow rose.

"Okay, so some of it is that." Couch orgasms—plural—at her house. She so couldn't think about that right now. "But that's not the whole story." She snuck a look over her shoulder. Lou was staring at them. Her boss was mercurial at best and she needed this job, dammit.

Diane tapped her tray against her thigh. "I'll buy you a Diet Coke and you can tell me the rest later."

Chloe blew out a breath. She hadn't had anyone to talk to since this stupid thing had happened. Jinx and Ivy were still MIA, though Jinx had finally texted her again this morning. She'd been light on the details, of course, but at least she wasn't dead.

But she couldn't exactly text—*hey, guess what? I'm married.*

Definitely one of those face to face conversations. But hell, if either of them had actually come up for air, they probably already knew. The whole freaking *world* knew. She hadn't realized Michael's band was so famous.

Oblivion, sure. There were a half dozen number one singles in their box of tricks. Warning Sign just had the one so far. And they couldn't be past one-hit-wonder status yet. That was a rule…or something.

"Diane, quit your gossiping. Table four needs a refill of pitchers."

"Yeah, yeah. Hold your ass." Diane leaned across the bar. "We will be discussing this."

Chloe tipped her head back. How was this her life?

The next hour was a flurry of activity. She tried not to focus on the crowd growing outside. Amber kept primping as she went by the door. She was one of the tens of thousands of model wannabes in Los Angeles. She was forever throwing herself at men, hoping to find the one who would take her away from this thrilling life they were leading. The Strip would give her an STD faster than a ring on her finger.

Then again, Chloe had gone to Vegas and ended up with a sapphire and diamond ring on hers. She immediately traced the curve of the ring at the bottom of the deepest pocket of her jeans.

She didn't trust to leave it at her house. Her small neighborhood was relatively safe for Carson, but getting robbed wasn't out of the question. She'd had two different break-ins before she had Axl. After the baby, even the crackheads knew she didn't have anything worth stealing. Babies were damn expensive.

Still didn't mean she was going to leave a ring like that in her little jewelry chest.

She absently toyed with her tiny diamond on her right hand. She couldn't quite come to terms with taking that one off.

Her life was the definition of a hot mess.

"Grape soda, please."

Her heart slammed against her chest. That lazy, sexy voice was going to be the death of her yet. "What the hell are you doing here?"

Michael climbed onto the bar stool in front of her. "Well, you weren't answering my texts—for days—so here I am."

"Because I'm working."

He tucked his aviator sunglasses into the neck of his button down shirt. It was open at least two more buttons than made her comfortable. The little bit of chest hair made her fingertips tingle. "I'll wait for your break."

"Too late, already had my break." *Liar, liar, panties on fire.* Which, of course, was the problem. Her panties were forever on fire around this idiot.

He shrugged. "I'll wait for your dinner break."

A murmur started to circulate around the bar. Chloe's shoulders stiffened as Wanda came up beside her. "This guy hassling you?"

Michael grinned. "It's actually my favorite pastime. She generally likes it, even if she growls about it first." He held his hand out. "Michael."

Wanda shook his hand aggressively. Chloe had to hand it to him, he didn't wince or look away from her friend. In fact, his smile widened.

"You should meet my brother. You two could arm wrestle."

Wanda snickered briefly before dropping his hand. "You mess with my girl and we're going to have words, yeah?"

Michael shook out his fingers. "I like that she has people looking out for her."

"We do." Wanda leaned forward a little. "And I know how to hide a body."

"And that's a very handy skill. I'll remember that."

"I shouldn't like this one if the rumors are true, but I like him." Wanda bumped Chloe's shoulder. "I'm holding off judgment." Wanda tipped her head and squinted at him. "For now."

Michael's eyebrow shot up and the little green gem in his eyebrow ring winked in the low light. "Does the threat come with my drink or is it extra?"

"I don't have grape soda. Go fish."

He shrugged. "Okay, you pick for me. I hate Coke and Pepsi though."

Figures he'd be fussy. "Why are you here?"

"I'm checking in on you since you won't answer a text. I know you're getting them."

She sighed. "Look, I appreciate your situation. Actually, you know what? No, I really don't. We don't mesh. You and your fancy car can go back to Malibu where you belong, okay? Just send me the paperwork for a divorce or whatever and we'll both be happier."

He grinned at her. "You checked up on me?"

She flushed. Okay, so she may have Googled him. And she may have found pictures of his stupid apartment when she'd been browsing on her phone. Everything about him was so far out of her stratosphere, she couldn't find the two of them on the same map. "That's what you got out of that sentence?"

He spread his fingers out on the bar, taking up as much space as humanly possible. And he was still wearing his damn ring. Why?

God, this was so crazy.

Another murmur twined its way to the bar. She frowned as two men in rumpled suit jackets took a seat at the end.

"You can't deny there's something here between us." Michael covered her hand.

She tried to pull away. Her gaze strayed to the two guys at the end of the bar again. "One sec," she said to Michael.

"Chloe—fuck." He raked his fingers through his hair.

She couldn't worry about him right then. She had people to serve. And busy bodies to move along. At least if her instincts proved at all on point. She flicked two coasters at the men. "Can I get you gentlemen something?"

The one on the right had the good grace to look down, but the asshat on the left stared right at her. "You're Chloe Adams, right?" His smarmy smile widened. "Or is that Shawcross?"

"I'm just a bartender. And if you're not looking for a drink, then I need those seats for paying customers."

"Two Miller Lites."

Of course, two of the cheapest beers on the planet. "Coming right up." She moved to the cooler and popped two tops before setting the sweating bottles on the bar. "Glasses?"

"No, this is fine." Smarmy dude slid a five on the bar. "Keep the change."

"Aww, can I really? That whole no cents." She gave him her fuck-off-you-cheap-bastard smile.

"Well, if you'd answer a few questions, we'd definitely give you a tip."

"Have a good night." She passed Wanda. "Reporters. Make sure they pay for every drink."

"You got it."

She'd been dealing with them for days now. In fact, she was beginning to recognize the more obnoxious ones. Those two were new, but she wouldn't forget them.

She stopped in front of Michael. "Look, I don't know if you brought in the new reporters or they're just finding their way to the bar now too, but I'd appreciate it if you went home and left me the hell alone."

He flicked his aviators open and put them over his eyes. "Look, I'm sorry—"

"I know you're sorry. I don't care. You're trouble with a billboard sized T. I don't have any room in my life for you or your cargo plane full of problems. Got me?"

"You were there and married me too, you know."

"Obviously, I can make a mistake. But what I can't do is have this kind of upheaval in my life. Every time I turn around, there's some news story about you and some Tabitha Tremaine. The last time she was spotted in your apartment was a week ago." She lowered her voice when two people turned around from a whole table away.

Cripes. He was making her nuts. She was a very calm and together person usually.

The mirrored glasses didn't allow her to see what was going on in his eyes, but the way his jaw clenched told her enough. Not all rumors there evidently.

He clicked his ring against the bar. "Me and Tabby are over."

"Was that before or after you crawled out of her bed last week?"

"No, she was crawling out of my bed. Not me into hers."

"Oh, that's better."

"No." He made a grab for her and Chloe skipped out of reach.

She pulled her towel out of her back pocket and mopped up a puddle of condensation. "Get the hell out of my bar."

"It's not like that." He growled.

"Oh, really?" She stopped and twisted her towel so tight she heard threads pop. "What's it like then?"

"I didn't sleep with her, she—dude, she's crazy. As soon as I found out she was engaged, I cut ties. She's the one who kept thinking we should be together. I don't do married chicks."

She stared at him. There were just no words. She whirled away and caught Lou in the doorway of his office, hands on his hips. She grabbed a glass, filled it with Dr. Pepper, and set it in front of him.

"Actually, the only married chick I am going to do is you, but we've been over that."

Going? Was he high? "Do you actually hear yourself when you say stuff like that?"

He leaned on the bar, his fingertips reaching over to her side. "You pretend to be all indignant, but you like my mouth more than you let on." He smirked. "You liked it the other night."

She slapped the top of his hand and lowered her voice. "You're going to get me fired. Isn't it bad enough that my landlord wants to freaking evict me?"

"What?" He stood up to his full height, his brow furrowed.

Awesome. *You and your big mouth, Chloe.*

"It's nothing."

"I told you to come live with me."

"We are not going over this again."

"You're my wife—"

"Don't say that so loud. There are freaking reporters everywhere."

"I believe that particular cat has streaked out of the bag, Red."

"Chloe, the keg is kicked. Can you change it over?"

She swung her gaze to Wanda. "Yeah. I got it." She dragged Michael down to the other side of the bar. "You know what people think of me right now? That I'm married to a cheater. A *cheater*." Again. "I have a kid to worry about." She ducked under the pass-through to the bar.

He took a step back. She tried not to notice the very firm thighs he had going on under his board shorts. Or that he was wearing Chucks instead of stupid dress shoes like most guys in L.A.. Nope, she definitely wasn't going to notice that about him.

"Where are you going?"

"To grab a keg."

He looked around. "Don't you have guys for that?"

"You think I can't lift one?"

"No, of course not. Just you know...you shouldn't have to."

"You probably haven't lifted a keg in your entire life."

"Sure I have. For parties."

"Why doesn't that surprise me?" She glanced around. "Amber, can you cover the bar for a sec? I need to change an empty."

"Sure, sure." Amber sauntered over, making sure to put a bit more of a sway in her step. "Who's your friend?" She frowned, then looked closer. "Oh, I know who you are." She jerked her shoulders back until her boobs were pressed forward for maximum effect.

Chloe rolled her eyes and went around her. "I'm going to take my break after I change it over. I'll be back in fifteen."

"Hi. Um, I'm just going to…Yeah, with her." Michael jogged after her. "Does she do that a lot?"

"What? Make sure men check out her boobs? Yes. I'm sure you did."

He lengthened his stride until he was right beside her. "Well, I kinda had to, but I like yours better."

"Are you sure you're not high?"

"Of course not." He whipped off his sunglasses again and hung them on his shirt. "And they're perfect. Next to your hair and cute freckles, it's my favorite feature. At least until I get my face between your thighs. I need a little refresher there."

Her nipples instantly tightened. She stopped so fast that he bumped into her. "Really? Could you say it a little louder?"

"What?" He curled his arm around her waist.

"Back up, buddy."

He grinned down at her as his hand slid down to her butt. His sea-colored eyes danced as he waggled his eyebrows. "You look hot in these jeans too. Forgot to tell you."

Chloe knocked his hand away and spun away from him. She was not going to focus on the fact that she wanted to curl into his very distracting chest.

"That Amber chick knows I'm your husband, right?"

"Would you stop saying that?"

"Doesn't make it any less true. Even if you want to ignore it." He crowded her into the wall beside the door to the cooler. "Would you hold up for a second?"

"Did you notice how busy it was?" She peered up at him. "Or haven't you ever had a real job?"

"I was like any other guy and had to do crap for money."

"Really?"

He invaded her space. "Just because I've never lugged around a keg doesn't mean I don't know how to earn money."

"Dial 1-800-Daddy?"

"You don't know anything about me or my father's money. I haven't taken a dime from him since I was in college."

"Aww. Should I shine you up a medal? Was that before or after you went to a fancy school?"

The little muscle in his jaw flexed, but instead of snarling at her like she hoped, he only smiled. "You did Google me."

She pushed him away. "You're incorrigible."

"So I've been told." He reached around her and opened the cooler for her, then followed her inside. "Let me get it."

"I can do it." She reached up for the large silver keg.

He gently moved her aside. "You know just because you can do stuff, doesn't mean you have to."

She put her hands on her hips. "Yeah, well that's not usually the case for me."

Michael lifted the full keg with a grunt. "Holy shit."

"Need to go to the gym more?"

"I go enough, thanks." He hauled it to the door. "Where is this going?"

She laughed. If he wanted to carry it, she wasn't going to stop him. She definitely wasn't going to tell him that she usually used a hand truck to wheel it out either. She grinned for the first time all day as he waddled his way to the bar.

When he turned around, he absently lifted the edge of his shirt to wipe his brow. Her grin slid away and all the spit dried in her mouth. So much muscle and a perfect line of hair bisected his abs. Sweet mercy. Yeah, it had been a few days since she'd seen that view and she really didn't mind the repeat showing.

She cleared her throat and turned on her heel when he caught her looking.

"I saw that," he called.

She held up her middle finger. When she heard his footsteps behind her, she ran for the side door to the break room. He caught her around the waist and lugged her through the door and shut it behind them.

"This is an employees only area."

He turned the lock on the doorknob. "You said you were going on your break."

"I'm down to ten minutes." She backed into the arm of the old couch and fell over the side. She quickly scrambled to sit up.

He stood in front of her and slid his knee between her legs. "I'll make it work."

"Oh, that's an endorsement."

He grinned down at her and jerked her shirt out of her jeans. "I'll make you come twice in two."

"I don't think so."

Michael lifted her up and sat down with her astride him. "This is becoming my favorite position." He pulled her down over the bulge in his shorts.

She gripped his shoulder. "We can't."

He buried his scruffy jaw in her neck. "Tell me this couch hasn't gotten action before."

"And this is helping your cause?" She was saved from thinking about that when he wrapped those beautiful lips around her pulse. How did he find that perfect spot every time? And then he did that swirl thing with his tongue.

A sense memory curled through her. He'd done that to her before. At the Foundation Room. She hissed out a breath. Her heart rate kicked up and the delicious slide of lust took hold.

Jet fuel engaged.

Honestly. It had to be something that could be bottled for the general public. She could make millions. She groaned. Too bad she was already getting greedy about it.

He flipped up the cup of her bra and sucked her nipple hard. Enough that the sweet tingle went dark and hot immediately. He cupped both of her breasts and tweaked her left nipple. She swallowed a moan. Instead of stopping, he focused on her left breast. Did he have a chart in his brain about what did it for her?

No one else did, dammit.

The quick shudder betrayed her, and his eyes opened.

He tugged her nipple until she twisted her fingers into his hair. The heat between them shuffled her brain until she was was all need. She ground against him and a cry escaped her chest.

He let her go with a purring groan against her cleavage. "God, you're so fucking hot when you try so hard not to like what I do to you."

"Just shut up."

"Why? You like when I talk."

She shook her head. She didn't want to like it. It made her uncomfortable. How did he learn to talk to a woman like that? Oh, right—he had to do this a lot.

"Don't." He rolled his hips under her. "Don't go away." He scraped his teeth over her shoulder and back down to her breast. "Don't think, Chloe. It's okay to feel good. We're so good together. The minute I get my hands on you, I can't think about anything else."

"It's just sex." She strained against the threads that got tighter and bulkier each time she touched Michael. She didn't want to get attached to him. She *couldn't* get attached to him.

He slid his hand up her back and into her hair. "If you think it's ever been just sex, then you better reassess, Chloe." His mouth sealed over hers.

Her heart slammed against her chest as her arms curled around his neck. She wanted to buck against his words—every single time it seemed—but she couldn't. Because he was right. The moment he touched her, something happened between them. Something bigger than she could name.

And she hated it as much as she craved it.

Her hips rolled against him and the seam of her jeans hit her just right. She shuddered over him. No. No. No. She would not give him the satisfaction of making her come this freaking fast. But it rolled over her like a monster truck tire. Dammit, she buried her face into his neck as she hung onto him.

Why was it like this with him? Surely it would blow itself out one of these times.

He clawed at her jeans and she couldn't help him fast enough. She popped open the buttons and his fingers slid down deep past her zipper to her pulsing center.

"Off."

"Oh, yeah, I got off." She sucked in a breath and tried to calm her racing heart.

"You always do, babe." He flicked his tongue over her nipple, then sucked hard enough to make her hiss. "But if you don't get these jeans off, I'm going to rip them off."

"Yeah?"

"Unless you don't want to work the rest of your shift in anything other than your panties." He dug deeper, his fingers filling her up so good. "Then again, these are a little wet." His thumb circled her clit. "But I don't want the whole bar to know what my girl's pussy smells like."

"Jesus." The tremors started again. That freaking mouth should not get her going.

"My wife's pussy," he said against her throat. "*My* pussy."

She bowed up off of him as he increased his pace. She slapped her own hand over her mouth as the scream tried to claw itself out of her throat.

"Fuck, yes. That's it." He pulled her hand away. "I want that scream. Give it to me."

She shook her head. She was at work. There was no music loud enough in Rafferty's bar to drown out the scream living inside of her.

He pulled her hand around her back and laced their fingers together. She bowed off of him so much that she was afraid she was going to tumble to the floor. "I need to feel all this on my cock. So fucking wet." The harsh words got her moving. It should have forced sense into her stupid brain, but it only seemed to incite her further.

She scrambled off of him with a growl. "If you don't have a condom in your wallet, there might be a crime scene."

He laughed. "Jesus, I hope so. Otherwise, we're raiding every fucking locker in here." He struggled out of the hole in the couch and unearthed his wallet from his back pocket.

She ripped it out of his hands. Her fingers shook as she searched in and around the credit cards, an emergency hundred folded four times, and…a wet nap? She pulled it out and flashed it at him.

"You need one right about now, don't you?"

She flipped the wallet at him. "Yes, I do, because *you* don't have a condom."

He caught it against his chest. "You didn't look in the right spot." He dug his long finger along the center of the wallet and came out with a black and gold plastic wrapped piece of glory.

"Need a Magnum, huh?" She plucked it out of his hand. "We'll see about that."

"If you can't tell by now, then I have some work to do." He slid his hands inside the back of her loosened jeans and pushed them and her underwear over her ass. He crouched in front of her, his nose bumping along her inner thigh. "Freckles and red everywhere."

She tried not to blush, but she couldn't remember the last time when someone had been between her legs. Snake had amassed a nice arsenal of sexual moves over the years they'd been together, but he'd definitely figured out her combination and didn't look for others after awhile.

Michael drew his tongue along her seam. "Soft," he said with a groan. "So soft and delicate." He looked up at her as he swiped the tip of his tongue along her clit. "When we have time, I'll have you dripping and screaming."

Too late. At least on the first part.

She slipped her fingers into his hair until she had a handful and gripped. She toed off her shoes and pulled off her jeans. She couldn't have worn her boot cut jeans tonight. Nope. Had to be her skinny jeans that were impossible to maneuver in. "Just get inside me, would you?"

He stood up, then unhooked his shorts. "Yes, ma'am." He pulled himself free and her mouth watered.

Okay, so maybe the Magnum wasn't an overstatement. It wasn't like she hadn't seen him before, but in Vegas, they hadn't exactly been at their best.

It had been awhile—at least she was pretty sure it had been awhile. Somehow she knew *that* particular piece of him had never been inside her. Because she would have been walking a lot more gingerly the next day in Vegas.

She pushed him back onto the couch. "Time to suit up, pal." She ripped open the plastic and carefully pulled it free. She knew firsthand just how fragile these things were.

There was one out there somewhere with Axl's name on it.

His chest heaved a bit as he stared up at her. "I've never had a woman do the honors."

She curled her fingers around his shaft and couldn't stop herself from stroking every blessed inch. He was deliciously hard and his blue-green eyes fired with heat as she swiped her thumb along the tip of his cock. She swirled the pad of her thumb along the drop of pre-cum and brought it to her mouth.

He gripped her hips, his fingertips digging into her ass. "I'm literally going to die here."

She covered the tip of him with the condom and rolled it down him slowly. "You can die after." She kneeled on the couch and swung her other leg over him until the head of his shaft brushed her cleft.

He lifted his hips off the couch and the head of his cock slipped inside of her. "Please tell me you're wet enough to take me."

She rolled her hips forward and sighed as her body stretched to accommodate him. She hissed out a shuddering breath as the thickest part of him burned everywhere, then she sunk down the last few inches. "Michael."

"Chloe," he said with a reverence that made her eyes mist.

Sex. That's all it was.

Chemistry at its highest level.

But when he rose up to meet her next downward glide, she couldn't lie to herself any longer. Even in this dingy little room, he watched her with rapt attention. Wonder and lust dueled in the blues and greens of his fathomless gaze.

His arm slid around her lower back, and his other hand came up to cup the back of her head. He dragged her down to his mouth. Their bodies rode in tandem to their hungry mouths. They started off slow, but there was no way to stop the bullet train once he was inside of her.

The thump of the couch against the wall made a beat that echoed inside her chest, and doubled her heartbeat. His touch went from easy to intense. His fingers dug into her ass as his hips snapped up with every thrust.

She hung on because there was nothing else she could do. She curled her arms around his shoulders and sobbed out his name as his lips and teeth coasted over every bit of her that he could reach. Chest, nipple, neck—finally, he climbed up the column of her throat and tangled his tongue with hers.

Her nails dug into his neck and shoulders as her insides reformed around him. She would never be the same.

He shuddered against her and jerked. She felt him pulsing inside of her as she squeezed around his cock, breath lost to the insanity that was this man and how she reacted to him.

She slumped against him. Her heart rate was somewhere between heart attack and sprint. "Michael."

"Michael's died and his heaven is named Chloe. Please call back later."

The giggle broke through and dissolved the tears that threatened. She shifted on him and a crack made her pause. Suddenly they both dropped down four inches and a spring shot up next to Michael's thigh.

Her giggle became a hiccuping laugh as Michael struggled out of the couch with her in his arms. He stumbled forward and bumped into the small table, then they pinballed into the lockers. He slammed her into the wall of metal, his dick still half hard inside of her.

She gripped his sides with her knees as the laughter grew between them. "You broke the couch."

"I do believe *we* broke the couch."

She shook her head. "Your fault."

He flexed his hips against her. "I have nail marks in my back that disprove that assessment."

A fist pounded on the door. "What the fuck is going on in there?" The doorknob rattled. Lou's voice rose. "Why is this locked?"

"Be right out," she called. Her head thudded against the locker and a lock dug into her back, but she wouldn't stop the light pulsing of his hips for anything.

"Come again."

"We have to go."

"After you come again." He ground against her, the light trail of hair at the top of his cock providing friction that she hadn't quite been able to get while on top of him.

He sucked at her neck.

"Fuck."

Michael pulled his head back. "Did you just swear? Why is that so hot?"

"I swear." Almost never. Mommy training usually kicked in, but this wasn't exactly her usual afternoon. She drew in a breath as she climbed up another level. "How are you still hard?"

"Young and studly," he said with a grunt. "And making you come is my Zen place."

"Zen away," she said and dug her ankles into his butt. Her cheeks heated with every rattle of the combination locks behind her, and she was pretty sure she was going to have a grid of welts, but it was so freaking worth it.

She shuddered out a litany of moans and iterations of his name until she finally melted away into a sweet, soft cloud of nothing.

"You're so fucking hot, Mrs. Shawcross."

She stiffened. Why did he have to insist on calling her that? She dropped her foot to the floor and he slowly lowered her the rest of the way. He slid out of her and turned away to take care of the condom.

She heard the rattle of paper and saw him open a fast food wrapper to completely hide the evidence before washing his hands in the handy break room sink.

Her chest tightened as she twisted her bra back to rights under her shirt. She snapped out her jeans, and quickly squeezed over the pocket to make sure her ring was still there. She looked up as Michael stared at her.

He grabbed her left hand. "Where's your ring?"

"Safe."

"Why aren't you wearing it? Still?"

She twisted her hand out of his grip. "Didn't we go over this already? Besides, I'm working." She stepped into her jeans, hopping to get them up over her ass. She could still feel the phantom fullness from him inside her, and they were already fighting. Typical.

God, she couldn't take the look on his face.

"Where's my—" Her apron dangled over her shoulder. "Thank you." She tied it around her waist and turned to him. His eyes were blazing. "What?"

"You won't wear my ring, but *that's* cool?"

She looked down at the diamond on her right hand. "That's none of your business."

"No?"

"No, it really isn't. We may be married, but we barely know each other. This ring meant something—still means something to me."

He jerked as if she'd slapped him. He slid his sunglasses on his face, and his Adam's apple bounced as his jaw firmed. "Right. As if I could ever forget the guy who came before me."

"We all have a past, Michael. Even you."

"I don't wear mine like a shield."

"No, you just have it plastered on TV, email, and blogs."

He curled his fingers around the doorknob and he pulled the door open, slamming it behind him. She growled and slapped the wall hard enough that the zing vibrated down her arm.

"Dammit." She pressed her forehead to the door. "Good going, Chloe." She drew in a deep breath and turned the knob to follow him.

The flash of a camera followed by Lou's thunderous face from across the bar was the capper to her fucking fantastic day.

NINETEEN

FRIDAY NIGHT. THE BLUE RHINO, OBLIVION'S OLD STOMPING GROUNDS and Warning Sign's new ones. And what was Michael doing?

Texting his wife, who seemed to have no interest in replying.

Hey, in the shit that was his week—not remembering his marriage or the sex that took place in his marital bed, being chased by paparazzi, nearly losing his car to a tow truck company—he'd had one shining spot.

The one where he actually got to have sex with his wife and—gasp —he even remembered it. And it had been sensational. The angels had wept, the stars had aligned, and glittery rainbows had arched across the sky.

Too bad they'd ended their amazing encounter with yet another fight. She'd been wearing another man's ring when he was *inside* her, for fuck's sake.

She wasn't replying to his texts, which was surprising not at all. The only reason he even had her digits was because she'd added her number to his phone the other night when she typed in her email addy. He'd almost wondered if she'd filled out her info on the digital contact card by habit, because it was hard to imagine her actually wanting him to call her.

Give her a couple orgasms, oh yeah, she could handle that. But call? Not so much.

Now he was backstage at this dive bar that apparently was a big part of the local music scene, stationed in front of an old peeling Oblivion poster while Lila prodded him about his brother. Again.

"I don't know where he is. I don't even have a current address for him, all right? The last I knew was he was in Encino, but that was a while ago. I'm not about to camp on his doorstep. If you want to, go ahead."

"Can you look up from your phone for just ten seconds?"

Michael sighed and met her gaze. "Looking up."

"We have Jazz tonight, because we're damn lucky that Oblivion is off the road this week. In a couple weeks when you have your next show, that isn't going to be true, and besides, you can't count on Jazz Duffy to save your band's ass in a pinch. If we haven't located Malachi and Ryan isn't well enough to play—"

"You're jumping the gun. Why not wait to see how Ryan is then before assuming we'll need someone else?"

"You've given up," Lila accused. "I recognize that defeated tone."

"No, L, I haven't given up on my brother. I've just accepted reality that we made a deal, and he fulfilled it so I can't really demand more. Asking is one thing, and I have. But acting all butthurt because he's not in a hurry to jump on a bus he never wanted to be on? No. Not going to do that."

Lila propped her hands on her hips. Tonight she wore a black pantsuit with gold at her ears and throat, and she looked every bit the record exec shark. "Butthurt? That's what you think I am?"

Michael shrugged. "I think you're used to the universe acceding to your wishes, and Mal just isn't."

"You made a deal for him to show up at one show and take off? What did you get out of this deal? Or is this like your situation with your 'new wife'?" Lila made air quotes. "The deals you make never seem to benefit you very much."

"Don't," Michael said, voice low. "Seriously, do not. Let's keep this about the band and only the band."

"So you don't care that she told me on the plane last weekend that she'd sign anything I wanted her to in order to dissolve your marriage?"

He should have expected it. He knew Chloe wasn't exactly jumping for joy over their accidental bed-and-wed situation, and Lila had probably exacerbated Chloe's feelings by goading her when they were alone on the flight back. But it still stung.

"That was then, this is now," he said quietly, putting away his phone before he could send out another unanswered message. Whether the recipient was to Mal or Chloe, he was at his limit.

"Look, Michael, I know how you view marriage, and I understand after what you saw your parents go through. You don't want to be the same kind of guy who gives up on a relationship. But you have to admit that this isn't a real anything. Accidentally pulling the trigger doesn't give you feelings for another person."

"Did you not hear me when I told you the other day that I fell for her?"

"Sex isn't falling for someone."

"No, but it's a pretty damn good start."

He wasn't about to try to explain the complicated mess of emotions he had for Chloe, because he couldn't. He just wanted to live his damn life, not analyze it. And right now, he wanted to be with his wife, whether or not it made sense to anyone else.

Even himself.

Lila gripped her iPad to her chest. "I hope you know what you're doing."

"Me too." He picked up the pink Takamine he'd set beside him and strapped it on. The Blue Rhino didn't have an elaborate stage set-up like the House of Blues, so they were pretty much on their own for managing their instruments. Fine by him. He was glad to take it back old school. "I'll see you later."

"Break a finger," she said softly, her bastardization of the old stage adage to "break a leg" before a show.

Taking it as the small olive branch it was, he gave her a quick smile and moved toward the stage. It was almost time to start.

Ry, Juliet, and West were standing around laughing, and Molly was near the drum kit with her sister, Jazz. Though Jazz was the eldest, you never would've known it since Molly towered over her older sister. They also didn't look much like sisters. Molly was blond, Jazz dark. Until he got close enough to hear what they were saying, and yep, they were definitely waving their sibling cards.

"I know you're doing us a favor, and we all appreciate it, but you can't just come in here and change the setlist. We have a way of doing things."

"Right. I'm changing the setlist for only my selfish whims, not the fact I don't know those two songs and I don't want to screw up your show."

"Ladies," Michael said smoothly, looping an arm around Molly's shoulders. The icy look she gave him made him smirk. He loved riling her up. "So glad you're joining us tonight, Jazz. Whatever set changes you need, we can make."

Molly rolled her eyes and stalked off.

"That went awesome." Jazz sighed and tapped her glow-in-the-dark sticks on her thigh beneath her flared tutu-type skirt.

It couldn't actually be a tutu, right?

Hell, maybe it was. He understood women's fashion about as much as he got everything else that had to do with the more heartless sex.

"She's a bit type A," he said with a shrug. "Doesn't like us to alter the plan, especially if it means she might get less time behind the mic."

"Lead singers, man. They're a handful. I've got my own to deal with, and believe me, I slap Simon around as much as you probably wish you could with Mol."

"Nah. I enjoy her attitude. She brings it to every show, so eh, what are you gonna do? Freaking musicians."

"Truth. So much truth." Jazz grinned and waved as a couple of people sneaked backstage. The Blue Rhino was old-fashioned enough to have an actual curtain. "Michael, you know Harp already, right? Deacon's wife?"

"Sure." He stuck his hand out toward Harper McCoy. "Always good to see you."

"Same. Gotta say thanks for having a show tonight and needing Jazz's services. Got me a free night away from the kidlet and some girl time." She linked arms with Jazz, who nodded enthusiastically.

"Hell yeah, me too. Deacon and Gray are home watching the rugrats and we get to have some adult beverages after this. We even brought some friends." Jazz pointed at a tall, lanky guy with long blondish-brown hair pulled back in a tail. "Randy Pruitt, this is Michael Shawcross, lead guitarist with Warning Sign. Randy is Harper's younger brother. He's also on the lighting crew for Oblivion and a couple of other bands. Lila pulled him in to do his magic here too."

"Magic? In this rickety old place?" Michael slapped hands with the guy. "If you manage that, we'll beg you to come out on our tour too."

"That might be arranged." Randy smiled and stepped back as Jazz pulled forward her last two friends.

Damn, she might be small, but she traveled with an entourage.

"Michael, you already know Hunter Jordan, the lead singer of Hammered?"

"Of course. He's a legend."

Hunter held up a hand. "If you're going to make a penis joke, rest assured I've heard them all before."

Hunter was referring to the article in *Rolling Stone* that had boosted his band's profile into the stratosphere the previous year. "Nah, man, I'm hoping to dethrone you." Michael grinned and fistbumped with Hunter, who only laughed.

"And this is Tristan Eves, Hunter's best friend and the dude who is helping Harp and me to make the most incredible baby food in the history of life. He's also a chef and he tries to outdo me on the hair dye score, but it's not gonna happen." Jazz pulled on the blue tips of Tristan's hair and he chuckled.

"I couldn't possibly outdo you. You probably used up most of the dye on the west coast anyway."

Jazz poked him in the arm. "Wise ass."

"Besides, you're back to brown again. What's up with that?"

"Shh, don't remind her or she'll say it's time to get pregnant again," Harper teased.

Michael lifted a brow. "Don't you have like three babies already?"

"Just two, and two is plenty for right now. Can't a girl go au naturel? Jeez. Hey Randy," she called as the guy whipped out his phone and started walking away. "Take Eves the big mouth with you, why don't you?"

Randy glanced back with a distracted smile. "Sorry. Can't bring any newbs behind the board. Sounds like we have a situation anyway."

"Why, you afraid I'll trip on a cord or something?" Tristan elbowed Hunter. "I say we go swing from the lighting rig and get him to loosen his shorts."

"You mean crap his shorts?" Harper asked drily. "He's all about safety on a set."

Juliet let out an earsplitting whistle.

"Hey people, y'all ready to go on stage or what? Let's freaking *go* already."

Michael linked fingers with Jazz. "Guess it's time, Mrs. Duffy."

"Wow, no rude nicknames. So odd backstage before a show." Jazz grinned up at him and waved at her departing friends as they disappeared under the curtain to head back into the audience. "I think I like you."

"I like you too." He lowered his voice to a mock whisper. "Can we keep you and send back Molly?"

"I heard that," Molly said from behind him as they all walked onstage.

He laughed as the crowd started to hoot and holler. He'd come to the club tonight in absolutely the worst mood, not in the least bit ready to perform, but he was in his element now. It didn't matter if the stage was a big one like House of Blues or a relatively small one like the Rhino. Once he strapped on his guitar and his band filtered out around him, taking their spots, his mind clicked into place.

Nothing mattered except the show. The music. Everything else would fall in line or it wouldn't, but right now, he was ready to rock.

"Well, hello LA," Molly purred into the mic with Ryan at her side. She wasn't about to give up greeting the crowd twice, whether or not he was hurt. "How y'all feeling tonight?"

She got the requisite applause and catcalls, and Ryan pumped his good fist. "So did you guys notice we have someone you all might be just a little bit familiar with back there on the kit? Mrs. Jasmine Duffy, also known as Jazz, the kickass drummer from a small-time band you might've heard of once or twice named Oblivion." He grinned as the clapping morphed into a dull roar. "Give it up for Jazz!"

"Yeah, yeah, that's enough of that. Don't swell up my big sister's head." But Molly smiled over her shoulder at Jazz to let her know she was kidding.

Partially.

Molly introduced the rest of the band and then mentioned how Ryan was going to be off the drums for a while, but he was still going to be part of the show. Proving it, she let him have the spotlight to start off "In Your Arms," with the blues harp. It was risky, using their latest greatest single to kick the show into gear instead of using that one as a carrot to pull the crowd through the set. Lila's trick of bringing the House of Blues mix to radio so soon had worked wonderfully, and they were getting more press than they had in a while.

Of course a good portion of that had to do with Michael's marital status and the fact that he was only a week removed from the picture some intrepid reporter had gotten of Tabitha Tremaine sneaking out of his apartment. But whatever. Lila liked to say all press sold singles, so he'd deal.

What he didn't like dealing with was knowing Chloe was at her house alone with her baby and probably swarmed by the blood-suckers. But what could he do? He'd asked her repeatedly to move in with him and she'd said no. Their marriage wasn't real.

His dick inside of her sweet pussy had been real as fuck, but yeah. Fine. Whatever she thought was best.

He poured his frustration into his fingers racing over the strings. At his side, Elle was playing like the demon in his head was riding her back too. This club had meaning for her brother, so maybe it had meaning for her as well.

Juliet and Molly got into some kind of dance, one of them moving toward the other as the other retreated. Even through the movements, Juliet never stopped playing the bass. She might as well have been on cruise control as Molly sang about wanting to be in her lover's arms. Behind them, Jazz was slamming away on the kit, doing her thing. Ry had put down the blues harp to join West and they were playing hand over hand in an intricate choreography all their own.

Halfway through the song, Michael glanced up. The last time he'd played it, he'd been staring at Chloe in the audience. Her red hair like a damn beacon, her eyes pulling him into her story. Almost strangers or not, they'd become involved with each other in a way that transcended alcohol and sex and stupid marriage licenses.

Unconsciously, he sought her again in the audience, only realizing what he was doing when his gaze snagged on the second row. She wasn't there. Of course she wasn't. He'd asked her to come to the show, mentioned he'd left tickets for her at the door, but she hadn't replied. For all he knew, she had to work. Or had Axl. She couldn't just take off and come see him because he really needed her to be there.

And then she was.

He had to be imagining things. She hadn't said she was coming. Hadn't said anything at all. She couldn't be there. He was hallucinating her like a dude in the desert might envision a spring arising out of the hot sand. His just happened to be his gorgeous, infuriating wife, looking up at him again with those melted chocolate eyes that spurred him to play faster, harder. Anything to impress her into staying just a little while longer.

Please let it be you.

As if on cue, the crowd parted and Chloe moved closer to the stage, dragging another woman with her. She turned away to speak to her friend and he swallowed, already missing her face.

Jesus, he had it bad. And it was only getting worse with every hour and minute that passed.

Once she turned back, he was sliding into the end of the song, nearing the part where he'd fallen to his knees the other night. Almost there. He climbed the frets, dueling with Elle, letting Molly's rich, whisky-soaked voice wash over him as they approached that final pinnacle. And just as he was about to let the music suck him into the end, hell broke loose.

Over his goddamn head.

Literally.

The crack above his head reminded him of the other night, as did the shower of sparks. But there weren't supposed to be any pyrotechnics at this show. Definitely weren't supposed to be screams as a large arm of lights swung down from the rafters, seeming to hesitate in mid-air before it landed on the stage—right where Molly had been a moment before.

There was a hiss and a crackle as lightbulbs exploded, setting off more sparks, then another hiss and a snapping sound from the back near the control boards. The overhead lights in the club pulsed on and off and then went out completely an instant before a roar filled Michael's ears. Water streamed from the ceiling, and he was instantly drenched from head to toe.

Somehow he gathered his wits enough to pull the strap of his guitar over his head and set it down on a speaker. Then he grabbed Elle and shoved her toward where Molly and Juliet were trying to step around the shards of glass and still sizzling wires. "Don't touch anything," he shouted.

He was about to make sure Ry and West and Jazz were okay when one overriding thought stamped out everything else in his mind. Obliterating everything else.

Find Chloe.

He'd just reached the steps at the side of the stage when a body slammed into his. Hair whipped across his mouth and he brushed it away, squinting to see in the murky darkness lit only by the emergency lights that had popped on over the exits.

It was all he needed to glimpse the eyes he adored.

Thank God.

"Are you okay?" She touched him everywhere at once, searching for wounds. It was such a mom thing to do that even in the midst of insanity, he had to laugh—and lift her off her feet to kiss the hell out of her while water poured over them both.

"Can't—do—this—not—now," she panted between hungry, frantic kisses. Already the lush, warm shape of her in his arms was familiar to him, refilling the oxygen he'd lost from the terror of not knowing she was okay.

"Have to," he chanted back, slanting his mouth over hers. "Fucking have to."

When the fear began to subside, he cupped her face and drew back. Absolute chaos had erupted in the club, with everyone running and shouting as the water poured down. And he might as well have been glued to the floor, stuck in this moment with Chloe.

Someone tugged hard on his sleeve. "Gotta evacuate, now. Let's go," Lila commanded, reaching out for Chloe with her other hand.

He swallowed hard and grabbed his Takamine—no way was he leaving Jimi behind, even if the guitar wasn't anything but potential wall art now—and followed them down the short set of stairs to begin the arduous push to the exits.

Once they were outside, Chloe wanted to find the friend she'd come with. He knew he couldn't keep her with him any longer, and besides, he had band stuff to deal with. This was a clusterfuck, and the fire trucks were already screaming in the distance.

"I'll text you later." He framed her face in his hands. "Promise me you'll go straight home with your friend."

She nodded, her long ropes of wet hair hanging in her face. Even her lashes were starred with water. "I will. Be safe, okay?"

"I will if you will." He gave her one last hard kiss and tucked her soaked hair behind her ears. "Thanks for coming to the show. Maybe next time it won't be quite so eventful."

She smiled and squeezed his wrists. "You were amazing. So good you tore down the rafters."

Laughing, he gave her a light shove and dipped his hands in his jeans pockets as he watched her walk back to her friend.

He picked up his waterlogged guitar and returned to where Lila and the rest of his bandmates and Jazz were clustered near the smaller tour bus they used for local events at the back of the lot. Hunter and Tristan had joined them, as well as Harper and her brother, who seemed to be trying to extricate himself.

"I have to get back to the crew. We checked and rechecked everything but Jesus, something went haywire."

"Let the firemen and women figure it out. That's their job."

"Harp, it's mine to make sure equipment is up to code and that everything is ready to go. If something goes wrong, it's—"

"Not an *if* something goes wrong in this case, Sparks. Something did go wrong in a big way, and I'd suggest you not try to get a job on our crew anytime soon." Juliet marched past Randy, bumping into him as she went.

Michael cleared his throat. "She's wet and pissed. Her hair's all messed up."

This time, he was the one who got bumped—by Molly, who beelined after Juliet. "Asshole."

Women. They always stuck together.

Michael tipped back his head and stared at the slice of moon obscured by the thick dark clouds above. In the distance, more sirens were wailing.

So much for being ready to rock.

TWENTY

Chloe sent back a text to Michael. It was sweet that he worried, even if she wasn't used to it. She let him know that she'd made it home before stuffing her phone back into her pocket.

"You can stop here."

Wanda slowed and pulled over. "Are you sure?"

"Yeah. It'll be easier for you to get out of here too."

"I'm not worried about that. Fifty points if I hit a reporter."

Chloe snorted and swung her feet out. They were a full block away from her house. "Thanks for the ride, sweetie."

"Anytime, doll. Your man's band is delicious. Extra points for excitement tonight and ingenuity." She waggled her eyebrows. "Hope he brings that home too."

Chloe closed the door and leaned through the passenger window. "He's not my man." When Wanda gave her an arched brow, she rolled her eyes. "We're still figuring stuff out."

"I saw what was left of the couch. You're figuring stuff out just fine."

Chloe's cheeks burned. "That was not on purpose."

"Never is. Me and Carl have busted up a few couches in our time. *We Time* is what we called it."

"Not sure I want that in my brain."

Wanda cackled. "Just because I'm almost twice your age doesn't mean I'm dead." Wanda's husband was super tall, and she...well, Wanda was about Chloe's size with five times the boobs. The only time Chloe had been busty was when she'd been pregnant. The girls left her again as soon as she'd stopped breastfeeding.

Unfairness seemed to be a recurring theme lately.

Then again, she didn't have the aching back that most of the girls did at Rafferty's. Small favors in this life evidently.

"I'll see you in the morning."

"You got it, cupcake."

Chloe's feet were aching like the very devil and she didn't want to walk the five hundred feet up her driveway let alone another block, but her father had texted her with an update at the end of Michael's show. There were still a bunch of vans waiting outside.

Why the hell was she so popular?

Because your husband was boning a senator's fiancée. She was paying a stupidity tax for every move she made these days.

She crossed the road, then cut through her neighbor's yard and through the gap in the chainlink fence.

A rustle in the bushes pushed her into a sprint. She really didn't want to have it out with Daryl, the neighborhood mutt. He was part bulldog, part retriever, all interested in eating shoes.

She got to the top of the lawn and a spotlight blinded her.

"Oh, crap." Chloe raised a hand against the light. Four more camera lamps zeroed in on her in the middle of Mr. Zulinski's lawn. Double crap. Couldn't be her neighbor on the other side. Nope, had to be her landlord's cranky uncle.

She stumbled back, tripping over the edgers along her neighbor's garden.

"How's it feel to be married to a homewrecker?"

"Did you have a quickie wedding because you're pregnant?"

"Is your son Michael's love child?"

"How long have you known Michael Shawcross?"

"Are you getting an annulment?"

"Are you divorcing him? Is there a prenup?"

"Did you marry him for his millions?"

Chloe pushed her way out of the circle of vultures known loosely as reporters. Another pack of them were trampling through the yard.

"This is private property," she said as loudly as she could.

And shocker of all shockers, she was resolutely ignored.

"Are you still sleeping with Nick Crandall from Oblivion too?"

Her heart stopped at that question. As did her forward momentum. Which only prompted them to go at her harder with questions. They definitely smelled chum in the water.

"Keeping it all in the family? You moved onto his wife's stepson?" The voice was shrill and female.

Chloe whirled around at that question. "You people should be ashamed of yourselves."

"We'd love to hear your side of things."

"So you can twist it? I've been there before, thanks." As soon as she said it, Chloe wished she could snatch it back.

"Did you receive a settlement from Oblivion? Are you still fighting for it?"

"Did you use it for drugs?"

"Why haven't you left Carson?"

"How many people were hurt at Warning Sign's show tonight?"

Chloe hunched her shoulders at the barrage of questions. She scanned for a hole in the wall of reporters. Snake's case had been thrown out of court almost as fast as he'd started a petition. Watching him shut down after that had been hard enough. The fact that he'd died so soon after had nearly killed her.

She'd lived through the media frenzy for that as well. Suicide? Accident?

Baby on the way.

Now she was right back in the middle of it.

The first time had died down within a few days. Not this time. Everything seemed to have doubled since she'd married Michael Shawcross.

The sirens in the distance didn't have any effect on the hoard of reporters circling her, nor did the fact that they were currently trampling Mr. Zulinski's prized rose garden.

She made a circle, trying to find a way out. She could only imagine what she looked like under the harsh lights of a camera in the dead of night. The sprinklers at the show had ravaged her curls and makeup, and sweating in that tiny venue had done the rest.

Oh, and the absolute lack of sleep from tossing and turning after having sex with Michael.

Yeah, she couldn't forget about that part.

She probably looked like a bedraggled and cliched single mom from the projects right about now. And only her backbone with a truckload of pride kept her on her feet instead of curled up in the fetal position.

The questions kept coming, but now they were just a confusing jumble of words.

Finally, her name came from the distance. Her father on the front porch of their little duplex holding his shotgun.

Three cruisers, full lights blazing—no sirens by some miracle—put what was left of her neighborhood on alert. Porch lights flickered on, and people came out of their houses in their robes.

All of the curious there to see just how incredibly awful her life had become.

Awesome. She was officially in an episode of *Cops*.

Mr. Zulinski's lights were blazing in the house and two of the police officers went up to his door. Chloe was left with the rest to disperse the reporters. Her saving grace had been the invasion of private property. They were no longer on the city street across from her house.

In fact, there was probably going to be a bit of destruction of private property if she didn't miss her guess.

"Miss Adams?"

She raised her hand. "Here."

"Ma'am, I need you to come with me." Two female cops pushed through the crush of people, hands on their batons.

"Gladly." But instead of helping her make a path, one of the cops clamped a hand on her upper arm. "Hey. I'm the one being harassed here."

"You're actually the one who is trespassing. The homeowner would like you charged."

"What?!" Chloe twisted. "What about the twenty reporters who cornered me?"

"We'll be dealing with that as well. For now, we'd like to take a statement."

"You've got to be kidding me." Seriously. What the hell was she supposed to do now?

"If you could just come with me, ma'am."

"Are you arresting me? I have a child. I can't be arrested."

"You should have thought about that before you trespassed."

"Do you see all these reporters? I had no choice." Chloe felt her voice rising from anger to hysteria and forced herself to bring it back down to normal. Shrieking wasn't going to get her anywhere. "And where were you when they were camping on my lawn for the last week?"

"Were they on your lawn or across the street?"

"Across the street," Chloe said between gritted teeth.

"Then they were only a public nuisance. And we were advised, and came to take care of the situation a few times. You, Miss Adams, have been a recurring problem for your neighborhood."

"*Me?*" Chloe felt like a damn parrot.

"I've been here several times in the last few years. I'm starting to recognize your street name."

The officer's tone was dry, but Chloe still wanted to crawl right into the sewer drain. From the reporters after Snake sued Oblivion to the insane period after his death, there had been far too many reporters camping out on her street over a very short span of time.

Now this.

At this point, she needed to move to the other side of the country.

The officer and her partner brought her down the sidewalk and turned onto Chloe's property. Thankfully, her father had the intelligence to put the shotgun away. He stood on the porch, his hands on his hips.

"Thank you, Officer. I wasn't sure how I was going to get her out of there."

"And you are?" The officer held a tablet, a stylus poised over the screen.

"Oh, yes. I'm David Adams, Chloe's father."

"Do you reside here, Mr. Adams?"

"No. I'm just here to watch my grandson."

"May I come in, sir?"

"It's my house, dammit." Chloe stomped up the stairs and through the door. "Is Axl all right?"

"Sleeping."

"Small favors," she muttered. Once inside, the fatigue that she'd been battling all night dropped over her like a tarp on a ninety-degree day. "Can I get you some coffee?"

The officer's eyebrow spiked. She cleared her throat. "That would be lovely."

"Dad?"

"I'm good."

Chloe had a feeling she was going to need it.

Trying to bank her frustration, she dumped coffee into the basket of her old school Mr. Coffee and brewed a pot. "Sit down. I'm assuming this is going to take a while." She leaned on the counter in her small galley kitchen. "Or do I need to go with you?"

The officer set her tablet on the round table Chloe had shoved in the corner. Usually, it was just her and Axl eating, so they didn't need much room. The little duplex didn't afford a lot of extra space. What little they had was used for a play area for her son.

Right now, all of his toys were neatly put away thanks to her father. Otherwise her house would probably look about as close to a destruction zone as her front lawn.

"I'll do everything in my power to do this as an informal interview. If your neighbor presses charges, which I'm fairly sure he will based on my information, then there may be a court date."

Chloe closed her eyes. "I don't have a record," she said stiffly. The hiss of the last of the water steaming out from the plastic top of her machine prompted her to move. Simple things like pulling down mugs for herself and the officer evened her out. Autopilot had her gathering cream and sugar onto a tray and bringing them to the table.

The officer sat down and folded her hands over the tablet. "Can I be honest with you?"

"That would be refreshing." Chloe set the mug in front of the woman.

"A simple apology goes a long way in clearing these things up. And possibly a new rosebush."

"If only it were that easy." Chloe sat down with her own mug chock full of sugar and cream. "But if that would help, I'd be happy to do all of the above."

"Good." The officer took a sip of the black coffee with a sigh. "All right, let's start at the beginning."

Three hours later, Chloe had spewed out her entire history to the officer and signed her life away in a report. They'd been interrupted a half dozen times by the officer's partner as well as various communications with the radio on her shoulder.

They managed to get the reporters off her lawn, and even off the street thanks to a bullhorn. And while Chloe was eternally grateful for the empty street, her son didn't take too kindly to the racket.

After she ushered the officer out of her house, she got to spend the next two hours curled into a car bed with her son because he didn't want to sleep in mommy's big bed. A blink later, her alarm was bleating out of her phone.

She dragged herself to the shower in an attempt to feel human. She had the lunch shift at the bar, which meant she had to be there for ten to get the place ready. She checked on her son before she left, but Axl slept blissfully on. She found her father on the couch with Lori when she got to the bottom of the stairs.

"Dad, you're still here."

"Yeah, I wasn't sure if you'd need me today."

An unwelcome flood of guilt washed over her, along with a healthy dose of relief. She was starting to get used to relying on her father. Truly, it was the only way she'd been able to raise Axl on her own. He might not have been an incredible father to her, but he was a damn fine grandfather.

"And I came over as I usually do." Lori smiled. "Rough night last night, huh?"

"Rough doesn't even cover it."

"Well, I'm taking Shelby and Axl to the park today. Get them away from the reporters."

Chloe groaned. "No way." She crossed to the window. Sure enough, three vans were back. "How? Didn't they say they were going to patrol?"

"I couldn't tell you." Lori squeezed her hand. "So, don't worry about the kids today. I'm going to take them over to my sister's to swim too."

"You're a blessing I don't deserve, woman."

Lori gave her a quick hug. "We stick together."

"Yeah." Chloe battled back the sting of tears. "I appreciate it."

"Let me take you into work today."

Chloe turned around. "Oh, Dad. You don't need to do that. I know you have to work."

He shrugged. "A few minutes won't make a difference. And saves you a bus ride."

And today, she'd take it. She was pretty sure if she got on the bus, it might lull her to sleep.

With the extra time, she went back upstairs to get Axl up and dressed for the day. She sat him in the middle of his bed and pulled out his suit and water wings. He waved one at her with Dory showing. "Mama? Swim?"

"No, bud. I wish. Mama has to work."

He sighed as he tried to pull on the swimmie. "Work sucks."

Chloe winced. "We don't say suck."

"Sucks." Frustration laced his voice when he couldn't get it over his elbow.

She sat on the edge of his bed and pulled it off. "Later."

"Now!" His face got red.

She cupped his face and covered it in kisses before he could break out in hysterics as only an almost two-year-old could. "Sorry, kiddo. You're going to the park first. How are you supposed to ride on the swings with these on?"

He slapped his hands on his chubby knees. "Okay." His voice was sad.

She smoothed his rumpled red curls out of his face. "How about you put these in your bag?" She caught him by the back of his shirt before he tumbled face first off the bed. The kid was going to be the death of her.

The blue and white water wings went down with him. He picked them up off the floor. "Swim."

"Swim!" She made her voice sound way more excited than she was. At least he'd be tired out this afternoon. And maybe she could get a nap in before they came home. Small favors. "Put them in the bag."

He held them up and waddled across the room, his face bright with smiles again. He raced to the door and put the blue water wings into the big, yellow beach bag, then returned for her. He tugged at her hand. "Go! Go, Mama."

She laughed. "Okay, okay. Let's go." She swung him up onto her hip and the bag over her shoulder.

"Lori!" His screech as they went down the stairs cut through her brain like a laser. Her kid had a set of pipes on him for sure. He bowed out of her arms to get to Lori.

She was very lucky that Lori was so good with him, even if it made her chest hurt to see her son laugh and clutch at her friend's neck. Chloe never felt like she could enjoy time with him. On her days off, she was catching up on everything else.

Her dad cupped her shoulder. "They'll be fine."

"I know." She patted his hand. "Mama's gotta get to work."

Axl waved a chubby hand in the air, his fingers backwards as he waved at himself. "Bye."

Chloe went over to her son and kissed his fingers. "Bye, bud." She grabbed her purse, rushed out the door, and down to her dad's Toyota. Her dad came out a few minutes later.

"You okay?"

She unearthed a pair of sunglasses from her bag. "Just tired."

"Are you going to let me in on some of this?" He sighed. "I know you're very independent. And I try not to pry, but there's a lot going on."

"I know, Dad."

"But married, Chloe? It's so not like you."

"I'm trying to figure everything out. His manager was working on a solution, but I haven't heard from her."

"And a solution involves you getting naked with this boy?"

Her cheeks heated. "I don't know what's going on between me and

Michael. It's not like he's a complete stranger. I know him through Nicky." Sort of. How was she supposed to explain any of this to her dad when she didn't know how she felt about any of it?

Last night had been just as confusing. She shouldn't have gone to the show, she shouldn't have gotten caught up in his music and his stupid, perfect mouth that kissed her like she was his oxygen. She should be doing everything to get herself detangled.

Didn't the clusterfuck of reporters last night prove that?

Or the chaos at his show? What if something had happened to her? Who would be here for Axl? She knew Nick would take care of her baby—knew it with a complete certainty that kept her from losing her mind some nights—but that didn't mean she had to run headlong into stupid situations like she had lately.

She lifted her chin resolutely. She had to go to work, and she had to get herself back together for Axl. She couldn't keep subjecting him to the insanity of Michael and the ever-present paparazzi who swarmed him like he was dunked in the most delicious of bee pheromones.

You like those pheromones.

She wanted to snarl at that little voice. Mostly because it was so damn truthful. There was something about him that drew her close. His sultry voice? The effortless way he talked to her like she was the most precious thing on the planet? Or was it simply because he was paying attention to her?

No.

No, that definitely wasn't it. She'd had men pay attention to her. Being a bartender put her in the crosshairs a lot. She could easily shoot down jerks at the bar. Michael was different in so many ways. His sweet talk didn't sound forced, or like he'd used it a million times.

It scared her how much she liked it.

"Is there more to it?"

She turned to her dad. "I don't know. He's a musician, for God's sake. I don't exactly have the best track record with them."

"Is he like William?"

"No—not at all actually. Well, except for the partying."

Her father pressed his lips together.

"Not like that, Dad. Michael isn't into that stuff. I can't gauge everything since most of the time we were in Vegas. And Vegas isn't exactly soda and pretzels, you know?"

"I don't expect you to be alone for the rest of your life. And neither should you. You're still so young, Chloe. Being a mother doesn't mean you aren't interested in dating."

She laughed. "Dating. How I wish it was just dating." She rubbed her thumb along the ring in her pocket. "I can't even explain what happened in Vegas. It's just…" She trailed off.

Her dad patted her hand. "You know you don't have to explain it to me."

"I know." She twisted her fingers around his for a second before letting them go. "And I'm not like that. Maybe because you and mom were so…" She didn't want to bring up old wounds, but there was a reason she didn't do a lot of heavy drinking. Axl was a huge reason, of course, but even before she'd gotten pregnant she'd been more of the designated driver than the partier in her circle of friends.

Between her junkie mom and her dad being drunk most of the time, she didn't chase the party scene like a lot of her friends had. One of the main reasons she'd ended up with Nick for a little while. They had bonded over their crappy parents. He didn't expect her to get drunk to have a good time. He'd been more than happy to split a six-pack of soda instead of beer.

"Your mom and I had our demons, but I was glad you didn't inherit them."

"But I did drink and then I somehow married this guy. I barely know him."

"There's obviously something going on between you two."

She scrunched down in her seat, crossing her arms over her purse. "I know. That's the part I don't know what to do about. Who gets married before they get to know someone? Even drunk, I'd never do something so crazy. But I don't remember."

He pulled into the parking lot at Rafferty's, parked, and turned to her. "He didn't drug you, right?"

"No. No, I'm sure he didn't have anything to do with it, but I can't be sure we didn't get something at the party. It would explain so much because Michael doesn't remember anything either. He might be a little more out of control with his friends. Hello, rockstar, but the blackout thing seems really suspicious for us both to have."

"I wish you'd told me."

"Come on, Dad."

"I know you're embarrassed and pissed about it, but you still should have told me."

"Oh, hey, Dad, I went to Vegas with my friends and totally partied my face off then got married. Okay, thanks for watching my kid. I'm off to work now!" Her voice was shrill enough that she made herself take a breath. "God, this is so crazy."

"Is it the wild weekend that's crazy? Or the fact that you're starting to like your husband?" Her dad scrubbed his hands over his face. "Now, *I* sound crazy."

"Both," she said miserably.

He laughed. "I know you loved William. Many times I had to ask myself why, but that's not what I'm trying to get at right now. You can love more than one person in your lifetime. He's gone. It's okay to let yourself care about someone new."

"But maybe Michael is even worse for me. I mean, look at all that's happened since I met him."

"And it's all bad?"

"Well, no."

"Don't be so fired up to end things. Take some time to figure it out."

"It's not just me that I'm worried about."

"I know." Her dad patted her arm. "And that's why you're such a good mom. You always put Axl first, but you're a young woman in the prime of her life too. Not that your dad wants to think of that, of course, but I'm not blind."

No, unfortunately her father had gotten way too much information the other night. "I'll think about it." Not like she'd been able to do anything else except think about Michael lately. "Thanks for the ride into work." She leaned over and kissed his cheek. "And the talk."

"You're welcome, Chloe Bear."

She slid out of the car, shut the door, and waved. When he turned back onto the main drag, she turned around and her heart sank. More vans. Why? Was there really so little in the news right now? She knew it was an election year and they loved to push buttons for the senator thing, but wouldn't it be Michael they'd really want to go after?

She lifted her chin and squared her shoulders. All she could do was get through this. Running away never solved anything. She smoothed her fingers over her high ponytail, then swiped her bangs into some semblance of order.

Questions came at her like bullets, but she was playing Supergirl to the hilt. She walked right through them, without even holding her hand up against the crush of people. Powering through the problem was the only way she'd survived the last three years. The last two reporters pushed in on her and she used her shoulders like Snake had taught her.

General admission shows could get quite competitive for spots near the band. And she liked being up front where the action was.

Of course Rafferty's was no show. In fact, it was dim and dark compared to the blast of sunshine outside. It took her a second to get her eyes to adjust, then she rushed through the room to the break room. The couch was gone. In its place was a lopsided loveseat that looked like it had been in a war with nineteen cats.

"Chloe?"

She turned toward Lou's voice. "I'll be right up to prep the bar."

"Can you come in my office?" His eyes narrowed. "Right now."

TWENTY-ONE

CHLOE STARED AT HER FEET. "LOOK, LOU. I'M SORRY ABOUT THE reporters. It's going to die down anytime now."

"I'd rather not talk about this in the break room, Chloe."

Her chest tightened as she lifted her gaze to his. His eyes were looking at anything except her. The floor, over her shoulder, the new used loveseat—all except her. "I'm the best goddamn worker you have."

"Not if this nonsense is driving people away."

Her eyebrows snapped together. "Our sales are up because of all of this crap."

"No, I've had to give away a lot of damn beer because of this." Lou put his hands on his hips. "I can't deal with the distractions. My distributors can't even get the truck around the back. No beer, no booze, no money—get me?"

Panic bloomed and threatened to choke her. She couldn't lose her job. Not after all she'd sacrificed to keep her kid in diapers and food. She'd worked doubles and every shift someone wanted to give up.

She clenched her fists, and prayed that she'd hold back the tears. She'd beg for her job, but she wouldn't cry. She wouldn't use girl tears, dammit. "I'll take a week off. They'll die down."

"Until next time? This isn't the first time you've had trouble follow you around. You're a good worker, but I can get another bartender in this town. Everyone knows how to mix a drink."

The sting went bone deep. The unexpected ache that followed expelled all the anger and frustration she'd been stuffing down up and out like a geyser. Was she really so replaceable? She'd worked at this place for years, and he was just going to toss her out like garbage?

The anger was so overwhelming she couldn't hear anything over the blood roaring in her head. He muttered some sort of apology and handed her an envelope.

All paid up. Don't let the door slap you on the ass on your way out.

She walked stiffly to her locker and took everything out.

So very little. Some female items, a bit of makeup, a pack of gum. She reached into the back, but only found a receipt for a sandwich from a shop down the street.

Four years of her life down to things that could fit in a pencil case. She curled her fingers around the pink case with happy little cupcakes on it. The sprinkles blurred into a wash of pastel colors.

She dashed away the stray tear that escaped and shoved the case into her purse. She lifted her head, then smoothed her ponytail. No big deal. Not like she hadn't been fired before. Being a single mom included a lot of crap hours along with just as many call-ins for a sick or teething baby.

Chloe walked through the door and the overwhelming silence made her heart flutter like a trapped hummingbird again. Wanda had tears swimming in her eyes. Lou's office door slammed shut a moment later.

Wanda rushed over to her. "Oh, honey. Are you all right?"

"I'll be fine. I'll find another job. I always do."

"Can I do anything?"

"No, you've been amazing." She forced her lips up into a smile. "Just keep everyone in line, okay?"

Wanda nodded as tears dripped down her cheeks and chin. Amber nibbled on her lower lip, but didn't say anything. Jersey Janice had taken *her* place behind the bar. Evidently, Lou had already called in the reinforcements. So easily replaced—as he said.

Chloe ran through the room to the door and out past the horde of reporters. They chased her down the block and three enterprising camera guys even made it up the stairs to her bus. She ran down the back and got off, waving at them with a double middle finger salute.

There was always another bus waiting. She took that one across town and into the heart of Venice. She needed to walk. She needed sand between her toes.

How many days had she wasted in Venice over the years? Endless summer days sitting on hot cement to watch Snake beat on an old white pail while Simon and Nick played guitar for a few bucks. Using her meager money to buy them water or a six-pack on the good days.

Her first job had been on the Santa Monica Pier working at the amusement park. Her first time with Snake had been under that same pier at the end of her shift. He'd spent months trying to convince her he was into her. That no other girl would do.

How simple things had been back then. It had taken her getting pregnant to actually say yes to one of the half dozen times that Snake had asked her to marry him.

She'd married Michael in mere seconds comparatively.

Honestly, she still couldn't wrap her mind around that. She'd been walking a careful tightrope since she'd gotten the news about Snake. Since her life had changed drastically. Alone for the first time in too many years to count. Except not completely alone.

No, she'd had a baby in her belly and had been living from paycheck to paycheck ever since. And now she had no paycheck. Well, save for the two hundred and thirteen dollars in her pocket. And she had the savings from Nick.

But that wasn't her money. Never had been her money. She'd hadn't touched it for anything other than emergencies for Axl. The special formula he'd had to drink for three months, the doctor's appointments that hadn't been covered under her medical program from the state, and a few other things over the years.

Most of it was in savings. Her kid wasn't going to drop out of college like she had.

But she'd dip into it if she had to. She'd just have to find another job ASAP, that was all.

She flipped off her ballet flats as she got closer to the skate park. It wasn't exactly beach weather, but the sun was warm enough to get her toes in the sand.

Sifting sand evened her out in ways nothing else could. She was used to working with nothing and building a life. She'd just start over again. Not a huge deal.

If she told herself that enough, maybe it would be true.

And Michael?

She wished that little voice would blow out to sea. She still didn't know what to do about Michael. He pulled at her like the endless tide, but she also saw the breakers coming for her. And the storm clouds in the distance. The longer she let a man like him in her life, the less chance she had for normalcy.

Hadn't she had enough of that with Snake?

Was it just a character flaw that she was attracted to men like that?

He's not one-night stand material like Nick. And he's sure the fuck not like Snake.

She raked her fingers through her hair and pulled out her ponytail to let the sea breeze shake out the ridiculous voice that craved trouble.

Craved Michael.

Nothing about him made sense. She shouldn't feel safe in his arms. She shouldn't want to lean on him. She could only rely on herself. Hadn't today proven that over and over again?

She tipped her head up to the sun and took one last deep breath of briny, sea-soaked air before she trudged back up the beach. She wiped off her feet before slipping her shoes back on. It was time to go home. It was Saturday, so she couldn't call the temp agencies until Monday.

Until then, she'd reactivate all her profiles on the job sites.

Three busses later, she got off at her usual stop and made the four-block hike to her house. The reporters must have figured out her schedule—either that or they hadn't gotten their latest scoop.

Chloe Adams fired because she's considered a nuisance, tramp, and gold digger—news at eleven!

There was only one car across the street. The sun glinted off the telephoto lens sticking out of the driver's side window. She hoped he or she got a nice shot of her sandy backside.

Lori's car was still gone. She could have used a hug from Axl right about now, but a little time to do research before she went back into mommy mode was probably best. She slowed as she got to the top of the driveway. A letter was taped to the door.

She knew she was up to date on her utilities. There had been a time when those letters had scared the crap out of her. She'd gone to Nick because the city had threatened to turn her power off. Pride goeth before hot water for her son.

Maybe it's a letter from Lori.

Except Lori used pink sticky notes with cute little unicorns in the corner.

With shaking fingers, Chloe pulled the letter off the door. It took her three tries to get her key into the lock and open her front door. No need for some lens to read the letter over her shoulder or something.

She dropped her purse on the end table and ripped open the envelope. Three pages of words melted and jumped all over the place. She had to grab the edge of her couch and suck in a slow breath through her nose and out her mouth as the room tilted back into place.

One word had been crystal clear. In capitals and a huge block font just to be sure she saw it.

Eviction.

She slumped onto the couch and put her head between her knees.

No. No. No.

It couldn't be right.

Was there a cosmic cloud over her head full of flaming meteorites set on destruction?

Chloe slid off her couch to the floor. She wrapped her arms around her shins, then pressed her forehead to her knees. The urge to rage and scream was so close to the surface.

Closer than it had ever been.

Why? She was a good person. She paid her taxes, started a college fund for her son, donated what she could to animals.

It wasn't an astounding life, but she'd at least made her mark on the earth with a beautiful child. So, why did she keep stepping in steaming shit piles every time she turned around?

She dug out her phone and texted Ivy. Again, her text went through, but didn't show delivered. Jinx wasn't exactly her first choice on the disaster front, but beggars couldn't be choosers.

The little bubbles that signified a return text came alive on her screen. Chloe blinked to make sure she wasn't seeing things.

What's up, chica? I'm boarding a plane for Jamaica. Dr. Nerdgasm is amazing.

Chloe slumped against the couch. *Hey, I'm evicted. Can you bail me out?*

Yeah, that wasn't exactly the text she could shoot back to one of her best friends as she was having the time of her life.

Fuck.

Fuck.

Fuckity-fuck-fuck.

Have the best time! I'm so jealous.

I'm going to try. I miss you guys. I'll be home in ten days, I promise. Maybe fourteen. ;)

Chloe sighed and stared at the ceiling. She could call her dad, but his little apartment was an efficiency at best. A bed, a television, and a shower the size of a closet. No place for a child to play. And obviously, Lori was out since she was literally her neighbor in the duplex.

She raked her hands through her hair, pulling at the roots until the pain cleared her stupid head.

Michael.

No. No way was she going to ask him.

He'd help.

It wasn't his place to help, dammit. She had to help herself.

What choice do you have?

She bounced her head against the cushion of the couch. None. No choice at all without emptying out her savings. First month, last month, security, on no notice? Yeah—thousands of dollars even in the crappiest parts of town. Not to mention moving.

She forced herself to read the letter. The legal jargon was hard to wade through, but the gist was that she'd become a nuisance. Gee, there was that lovely word again. That the neighbors around her—she'd bet ten dollars it was Mr. Zulinski—had complained enough that her landlord had no choice but to evict her.

She didn't want to be a nuisance. She would love to tell the reporters to take a hike, but the more she spoke to them, the more they wanted. The only recourse had been to ignore them. Why wouldn't it blow up in her face?

Shocker.

Well, one thing was for sure. She hadn't had this problem until Michael. Sure there had been a three-ring circus after Snake died, but it had died down as quickly as it had bubbled up. Michael was a rising star, with a famous family added into the mix.

And it had taken two of them to make this mistake.

She hauled herself up off the floor and up the stairs before she could think about it. She'd talk to him. Maybe she and Axl could crash at his place until she found work. Then she could get a place. Michael kept asking her take advantage of the perks of being married.

Perks that didn't include her being naked.

Though, honestly, that was a damn good one.

She pushed that aside for practical matters. She had forty-eight hours to get her life on track. She took a minute to call Lori and update her on the mess. She agreed to take Axl for the night so she could feel out Michael.

Yeah, you'll feel him out all right.

She dragged her old hardback suitcase out of the closet, and ignored that damn voice. Okay, so maybe she listened a little when she pulled out matching underwear to toss into the mix of clothes. She only took a few days' worth. The rest would have to be packed up. She'd have to use Axl's savings, but she'd be sure to put the money back as soon as possible.

She called for a cab. She'd have to use some of her precious last paycheck, but getting a bus to Malibu would take her all night in transfers. She filled her duffel bag with paperwork she thought she might need and hoped that she wasn't making a colossal mistake.

By the time the cab arrived, four more cars and a van were out front again.

An older gentleman leaned out the window. "You some sort of famous person, lady?"

Chloe opened the door and shoved her bags in before dropping into the backseat. "No, just someone in the wrong place at the wrong time." She huffed out a laugh. "About three times now."

"Now, there's a story."

"A long and rather boring one." She looked over her shoulder as two cars started following them. She gave the driver Michael's address as she glanced at his tag. "Carl, there's an extra twenty in it if you lose them."

"Now, that's what I like to hear."

There was a small part of her that felt bad for her neighbors, but the rest of her was relieved to leave them in the rearview tonight. She was tired of being selfless today. There were only so many times she could get kicked in the face before she started slapping back.

It wasn't a short ride to her husband's house. God, just the word sounded foreign on her tongue. But if she was going to ask for help, then it was time to say the word out loud.

Even if she didn't know exactly what she was going to say when she got to his door.

They got off the highway and Laguna Point's craggy coastline came into view. The waves crashed and foamed just below them on the winding coastal road. Buildings got ritzier and more glamorous with every turn. By the time Carl pulled up to the address Michael had given her, all the spit had dried in her mouth.

"Are you sure this is it?"

"Yep." He craned his neck up at the apartment complex. "You sure are movin' on up there, lady."

She opened the door, wincing as she read the fare. It took almost half the money in her pocket, but she didn't short him on the tip. Including the extra twenty she'd promised him. "Thanks."

"Pleasure." He gave her a wink and took the money from the small window. She slung her purse and duffel bag over her shoulder, then dragged her suitcase onto the huge, circular sidewalk. Her driver pulled away right after she shut the door, and she had to stifle the urge to call him back.

This so couldn't be right. She could smell the ocean from where she stood, though she couldn't see it thanks to the monolith of a building in front of her. A huge stone garden with a steel and glass sign told her she was indeed in the right place.

Laguna Estates.

The other side of the world from Carson.

She'd never cared about the way she looked until right then. For God's sake, she hadn't even taken time to change out of her work clothes. She tucked her hair behind her ear, wishing for one of her hair ties. She should have taken a shower or made herself a little more presentable—*something*.

Gilded glass gleamed out of the shadows, drawing her closer. She crossed the sidewalk to the rocky alcove that shrouded the front door. A woman Chloe's age strolled through the huge doors, barely glancing at the doorman who held the door open for her. He gave the woman a deferential smile, his posture positively perfect.

Had Chloe dropped into an alternate reality? She was used to seeing some of this behavior thanks to working on The Strip, but this was crazy.

The woman wore white from head-to-toe with gold flashing at her ears, fingers, and even her ankles.

Realization clicked like a flashbulb. Holy shit, that was Victoria Sheer.

Chloe swung around as the actress passed her by without a hello, a smile, or even a spare look. Shock and awe faded as her suitcase twisted onto its side thanks to her oh so graceful manuever.

"Can I help you, miss?"

Chloe stumbled and made a little yelp as the doorman saved her suitcase from scraping over the flagstaff. "Um, hi. Sorry."

"That's quite all right. Are you here for a resident?"

She shoved her purse back on her shoulder and smiled at him. "Yes."

He glanced at her suitcase, but he didn't betray a single thought about the status of her battered to hell suitcase from her first year at college. He probably thought she should be asking for the service entrance. "His or her name?"

She blinked. "Right, sorry." She cleared her throat. "Michael Shawcross."

A flash of surprise crossed his features before they smoothed again. "He's my...friend."

Was her wedding ring actually burning a hole against her leg? Hmm.

He opened the door. "Shall I announce you?"

"Announce me?"

"Unless you have a code?"

"Oh." Maybe she should have texted Michael before she'd come over. What if someone was up there with him? What if he wasn't home? Cripes, she hadn't really thought this through.

"Your name, miss?"

"Chloe."

"Your last name?"

Just how pretentious were the people in this building? "Adams."

He pressed a button. "Mr. Shawcross? I have a Miss Adams here to see you."

"Chloe?"

"Yes, it's me." She leaned closer to the panel inside the door.

"Send her up."

The inside door clicked open. Chloe struggled with her suitcase over the track for the door. The wheels had been tortured with multiple bus rides over the years. They barely rolled.

"Eighteenth floor, miss."

"Thanks." Chloe spun back around. "What's your name?"

"Barney, miss."

Her grin widened. "Like Pretty Woman."

"As you like." He winked and turned back to his station.

Chloe gave a little laugh as she headed across the lobby to the bank of elevators. There were signs for various perks in the building. Dry cleaning, a gym, a pool, and even a café. Fresh coffee at their fingertips each morning?

Man, talk about living the dream.

The doors slid open silently, and Chloe stepped across the threshold. It felt like an eternity, but she was blessedly alone in the car. She didn't have to unleash her babbling on another person for at least a few minutes. The light flashed and a faint chime prompted her to get moving as the doors opened. Her suitcase clattered over the track before rolling silently onto the carpeting.

Michael stood in the hallway. He wore battered jeans, an old T-shirt, and a worried look on his handsome face.

Nerves jumped around under her skin. What the hell was she doing here? She should totally turn around. This was a mistake.

An impulsive, horrifying mistake.

He came farther down the hall. Her gaze dropped to his unreasonably sexy bare feet. That really wasn't fair. She'd always had a thing about old denim and bare feet.

Okay, grab a clue and calm down.

"Chloe? Is everything okay?"

"Yes."

No, of course, everything wasn't all right. Her entire life was spiraling into a shitstorm tornado.

Just ask him. Spit it out. You can do it.

"If it wouldn't be an imposition." She swallowed down the huge lump in her throat. "It's okay to say no or whatever, but do you think I could stay here?"

TWENTY-TWO

Either Michael was still dreaming or the universe had flipped over while he was watching a marathon of *Roadies*. No other way this could be happening.

When Chloe froze, he met her partway down the hall. She had a duffel bag over one arm and a small, brown hard shell suitcase by her feet. Even her luggage was plain, modest and without frills, because that was how she lived her life.

"You want to what?" he asked, needing her to say it again. Only way he could begin to believe she'd decided voluntarily she wanted to live with him.

"I want to stay over."

Ah, the picture was getting clearer. He propped his arm against the wall. "Stay over like what, a sleepover? Maybe we'll watch movies and do each other's hair? I know, we can make brownies and talk about boys."

She gazed down at her feet, chin trembling, and for one panicked second, he was sure she was going to cry. Then she lifted her head and nailed him with the power of those direct dark eyes.

"That sounds really fun. I can't wait to hear about your experiences with boys too. Do you spit or swallow?"

His eyebrows nearly rose right off his head before he started to laugh. Hard. Damn, this woman. She never gave him an inch.

And thank God for that. He'd had way too many people act like he was important or impressive just because his dad made tons of money and his mom got married a lot. The rockstar trip was much the same, although that was a mixture of adulation and feeling overlooked, depending on the day or his marital status.

"Come on in and we'll talk." He bent to grab her suitcase and went back up the hall to his door, holding it open so she could pass him.

"Thanks." She smoothed back her hair and strode forward, stopping on the threshold to gasp. Almost immediately, she started to retreat. "I can't stay here."

He looped his arm around her shoulders to keep her from backing into the hall. She was practically shaking. "Too late. You already asked and you know I can never say no to you. Besides, don't you want to know if I swallow?" Before she could move, he whispered against her ear, "If it's you I'm drinking down, the answer is hell fucking yes."

She shut her eyes and just sagged against him. "You didn't tell me you had a place like this. I mean, I could tell from the doorman, and the ritzy building, and I know you're in a band and doing well for yourself, but all this?"

"Take a breath before you pass out, all right?" He nudged her farther inside and closed the door behind her. "You forgot a couple of things. My dad is insanely wealthy and lined my diapers with gold thread, and my mom has married a number of rich men, if you're making a list."

Chloe covered her face with her hand. "Oh, God. I shouldn't have come."

"Never say those words. Not in reference to arriving or in reference to, you know, not coming."

She let out a soft laugh, shaking her head. "You're nuts."

"Maybe a little. I'm also really glad you're here." He eased her duffel off her shoulder and placed it and her suitcase beside the long, low, black leather sofa. "Want a drink?"

"Is that your solution to everything?"

"It used to be," he answered honestly. "But I've been dry since after we got married. I meant liquid, non-alcoholic. You know, in case you're thirsty."

"Sorry." She grasped her throat and didn't move. "I'm extra touchy today."

"Well, that sounds fun."

The slightest hint of a smile curved her mouth. "You're incorrigible."

"About the whole marriage thing. It occurs to me I never showed you this." He withdrew his wallet and flipped it open. "I was waiting for a good time, and then I forgot. But you haven't seen it, and you should." He pulled out the folded white piece of paper that had knocked his world on its ear a week ago. "Make copies if you'd like. Have them verified by Johnnie Cochran or some such."

"I think he's dead."

"Oh. Too bad."

She took the paper and read it silently, chewing on her lower lip. "That's how you found my address."

"Yeah. Phone number wasn't much help though."

Seeing her smile made all his annoyance at the fake number seem like it was insignificant. Now it was. In only a week's time, they'd come a long way.

At least they could tell their grandchildren they'd known each other for years, and it wouldn't be a lie. Exactly.

Wait, what? What grandchildren? Getting married by accident was one thing. But accidental procreation? All right, you could do that too, but it was totally a different kettle of diapers when little people were involved.

"Thank God I stopped drinking," he muttered, pushing a hand through his hair.

Chloe handed back the marriage license. "What did you say? By the way, I'd like a copy of that."

"Sure. Coming right up once I have a home office and a scanner. Or else we go to Kinko's. That name always sounded dirty to me."

She scrunched up her nose. "Are you okay?"

"Yep, fine. Never better. Let me grab you a drink." *And me a reality check.* "Be right back."

"Do you have diet Co—oh yeah, you hate Coke. Fudge."

"Fudge? If you're going to live with me, honey, I should warn you. Only actual swear words allowed."

"I'm not living with you. This is just temporary until I get my feet back under me—" She pressed her lips together as if she'd said too much. "What kind of soda you have?"

"Dr. Pepper and grape. Lots of Dr. Pepper. I have this thing for spicy flavors lately. So weird."

She flushed. "I'll take that, please. Thank you."

"Gotcha. Be right back."

In the kitchen, he poured Dr. Pepper into two glasses of ice. His mother's insistence on always serving company tea cookies on a tray had him opening the cupboard and taking out the box of Girl Scout cookies he kept for that purpose. Not that he'd actually ever served cookies to anyone. Like who? His mangy bandmates? Right. Not happening.

He blew off the layer of dust on the box and took out a couple of lemon cookies to arrange on the plate on the counter. His mother would be proud.

Taking a bite of the cookie, he cocked his head. Tasted okay. Didn't smell funny. Probably fine.

Maybe the sweets would get Chloe to start talking.

He wanted to ask questions. Lots of questions. Like why she seemed to be barely holding on to her composure, and why her fingers shook every time she fiddled with her hair. Hair she'd forgotten to tie back for once. Maybe she'd tell him what was going on if he gave her space. Demanding never seemed to get him anywhere.

Chloe was on the phone when he walked back into the living room with the two glasses and plate of cookies.

"Sure it's okay if he spends the night? I can call my dad, see if he can—"

"Or he can come here," Michael interrupted, setting down the drinks and plate. "This is his home now too."

It felt more than a little weird to have her there—and to invite her son to move in as well. But she was his wife, so that made Axl his stepson.

So freaking weird. And yet nice in a way. Especially since the kid wasn't there to remind him of all the ways he wasn't cut out to be a parent, step or otherwise.

Chloe shot him a look and rose to walk to the French doors, stopping dead as if she'd just realized how close he was to the beach. From her end of the conversation, it was either that or she'd had some kind of mental break.

"Ah, yes, um, yeah, tomorrow. Yes, I'll get him. Noon? Oh, great, right. Um, thanks. You're a lifesaver. I'll call Axl tonight in bed. I mean, before bed. Okay, bye." She clicked off and tucked her phone into her pocket, then stepped forward and pressed her palms to the glass. Almost as quickly, she dropped her hands and started buffing the glass with her shirt. "Holy shit. You're on the beach."

"Above the beach, but yeah. Is Axl okay? Where is he?"

"With my neighbor, Lori. He's fine. I can't even think with that out there."

He took the opportunity to cup her shoulders and rest his chin on her head. "You like the view?"

"Like it? Are you crazy? How do you live here every day and do anything but look out?"

He didn't tell her he forgot to even glance outside some days. He'd gotten too used to the view, too jaded.

Feeling her tremble from excitement made him see it all as if it were the first time. The strip of white sand beach, the relentless roll of water toward the shore, the sparkle of the waves under the fading sun. It was almost time for the sunset, and he couldn't wait to experience it with her.

"Wait here," he murmured.

She barely glanced back as he headed into his bedroom to grab the light blanket off the end of the bed. He barely used it even in the winter, since he was perennially hot. But she'd get chilly outside as the sun went down.

And if things progressed the way he hoped, she could use it as a cover-up.

He came back out to find her still staring through the glass. She hadn't opened the door and gone on the balcony. Did she think he'd snatch away the toys if she enjoyed herself too much?

"Let's go out," he said, stroking a hand down her hair.

The instant he opened the door, she flew across the space and right to the rail. So much for being afraid of heights.

Smiling, he watched her lean forward so that her loosened hair blew in the breeze like a banner. "I smell it," she said over the wind. "The ocean. Oh, God. Michael."

After he set the blanket on the chaise, he came up behind her and wrapped his arms around her waist. It was cheating to take advantage. So not fair. He should let her have her moment and not take something for himself.

Being near her was like standing in the path of the sun. As much as he just wanted to bask in her warmth, he needed more. Had to taste every part of her and remind himself that even if none of this made sense, even if it never did, he didn't have doubts when it was just the two of them.

Was it insane? Sure. Absolutely. An insanity he craved.

Maybe that was all he needed to know.

To try to bring himself back, he laced his fingers with hers. He'd picked the hand that still bore Snake's ring. That should've been a cold shower to his libido, but it wasn't. Not today. Logically, he knew he couldn't expect her to turn her back on her past so soon. If he wanted her to be his—and fuck, he did—he had to give her reason to want to be.

"I don't come out here enough anymore. Barely check out the view. I love it, but I've gotten too used to it."

"How could you get too used to this?" The delight in her tone could have buoyed him for weeks. "It's like a fantasy. The warm breeze, the smell of the sea, the sun starting to sink into the ocean…"

"I guess sometimes you stop seeing what's right in front of you." He toyed with her hair, turning a handful of it to study the twined colors of red and gold in every strand. "That's why I saw you but I didn't see you for all that time. I'd slotted you away as forbidden and looked right through you. My loss," he said as she turned to face him.

She studied him for a long moment with the pink and orange hues of the setting sun haloing her head. "Not just yours. I didn't see you either."

"I was the last thing you wanted to notice. You've had enough of dealing with guys in bands."

"Yeah." She lowered her gaze, her lashes fluttering against her cheeks. "Axl comes first in everything. I can't risk him." She took a deep breath. "Michael, what I do affects him. I can't make a mistake and hurt my little boy."

"I understand that. And he's so lucky to have you. My parents—" He broke off and stared into the distance at the crying seagulls. "Me and Mal weren't their priority, put it that way."

"Mal?"

"My older brother. Irish twins." Michael smiled and curled her hair around his fingers. "He was on the drums at the House of Blues. Giant bald dude. Looks like me not at all. Doesn't act like me either. Rarely says a word unless he feels like it, and most often, they're rude."

"Your brother is in your band?"

"No. He's not. He has no interest in that life. He just pinch hit for Ry when he injured his wrist. We made a deal. One night only, then he split."

"But that night, he was amazing. I mean, I wasn't really focused on anyone but you, but I could tell he was really good. I kind of pay attention to drummers, you know, after Snake."

Michael tipped up her chin, relishing the ruddy flush of her cheeks. Her feelings telegraphed onto her beautiful heart-shaped face like a projector on a wall.

No wonder he was transfixed.

"You were focused on me," he said quietly. "Just like I was focused on you. Only you. For the last week, you've been like a spotlight. You've blinded me. I can't see anything else around your glow."

"It's attraction."

"You're right. It absolutely is." He swayed closer, knowing she would be able to feel how hard he was for her. Constantly.

Wanting Chloe had become a primitive beat in his blood. He couldn't imagine living without that all-consuming need ever again.

"That's just not all it is." He traced the bow of her mouth. "I want to get to know all the things I don't know about you. All the hidden chambers and vaults you hide away to keep them safe. You can open them for me."

"Let's say I do. And you get bored. You go on tour, and that pretty Tabitha girl shows up in your dressing room. Then what? I shouldn't even have a right to get mad, because we did a crazy thing." Chloe flicked her windblown hair out of her eyes. The sun was lowering in the sky, and with it, up came the chill. "Who gets married after a couple of hours?"

"Two people who've been looking for something, and finally found it."

Her gaze shot to his and stayed. "That's not enough to build a life on. Chemistry fades. The excitement will fade. It has to."

"We don't have to build a life yet. We build a relationship, day by day."

"But we're married. We're supposed to have all of this figured out, and how can we? I had to run from reporters to even get here. My picture is everywhere. Today, I lost—" She swallowed hard. "I lost so much, and now this is what's left."

Of all the questions he needed most to ask, one roared to the fore. "Axl is okay?"

"Yes." She let out a weak laugh. "My boy is okay, and that's the most important part. But God, everything else. It's all such a mess."

"Let me reassure you on one point." He tucked her hair behind her ears. "As for Tabitha, she isn't an issue. I'd vowed never to touch her again before you. After? I barely remember what she looks like."

Her huff of breath nearly made him smile. "Sure. Right. She's a gorgeous girl, and you don't care about her because you're married to a mother who hasn't been out on a date in years. Who doesn't even recall what it means to have fun and be wild. The one weekend I tried to be the girl I used to be, I ended up with a ring."

"All right, yes, that's unfortunate."

She laughed, throwing back her head. "Unfortunate. Yeah. Except everything with you is so bright and full. *I* feel so full, like I'm going to burst with all the emotions you've unlocked inside me. And I can't. I *can't*. I'm a mother now. What I need doesn't rank."

"You can't take care of him if you're not taking care of yourself."

"I don't have the time—"

"So let me. I'm standing right here, and I'll take care of you so you can take care of him."

"Why?" she whispered. "Why would you do that?"

There were so many things he could have said. So many reasons. He went with the one he thought she'd understand most.

"My mother never put me first. My father definitely didn't. They both were too busy looking out for themselves. I see you, and I see everything that my mother should have been and wasn't. And I see you fighting to hang on by your fingernails, when I have everything available that could help you and I haven't done one meaningful thing with it. I've done nothing, except play a guitar and focus on myself." He cupped her face and stroked her damp lower lip. "Let me focus on you so you can focus on him. Let me, Chloe."

TWENTY-THREE

For about the five-thousandth time, she left him hanging.

No big deal. It only felt like his chest was in a vise. Eventually, the pressure would ease, right?

Chloe's eyes went too bright before she closed them. "There's quicksand under my feet. Everything is slipping away."

"No, it isn't. I swear it's not." Michael pressed his forehead to hers and absorbed the uneven puffs of her breath. "Lean on me for a while. Trust me to be the bedrock you need. That Axl needs."

"That's not fair."

"You're right. I don't play fair when I'm winning back my wife."

She sighed and the fight seemed to drain out of her. "You can't win back what you never had."

"Au contraire. I've had you now, and I remember every second. You wrapped around me so tight. Your pupils swallowing those beautiful browns. Those sounds of yours when you can't take any more and I make you."

"Michael…"

"And that, especially that. How you sound so exasperated when you say my name, but still with that little plea that lets me know I'm not alone in this. You feel just as chaotic and needy as I do." He brushed his thumbs over her cheeks until they met over the seam of her lips. "Tell me you do, Chloe."

"How could I not?" He moved away his thumbs so she could speak. "I saw you on that stage and you were everything I'm not. Strong. Cocky. So, so talented."

"You're all of those things and more. Let me show you."

Wordlessly, he drew her toward the chaise. He grabbed the blanket and draped it around her shoulders while her gaze roamed his face. She was uncertain and worried, and he should be soothing her with words and not actions she could dismiss. But he had to do more. Not for himself.

For her. Just for her.

He bent to pull off her sandy ballet flats and then encountered more sand on the damp hems of her jeans. "You were on the beach before you came here."

"Yeah. It's my safe spot. Always has been."

Something twisted in his chest. What he'd grown far too complacent in even noticing, she sought for comfort. "Now you can see safety from here." Watching her face, he undid the button on her jeans and drew down the zipper. "While I show you anything but."

"We're outside. All the cameras…"

On his knees, he pressed a kiss to her peach panties as he drew down her jeans. "Tell me you don't care. That you want this as much as I do."

"You know I do. I'm destroying my whole life because I can't stop wanting you."

He didn't know what that meant or if she'd ever spell it out for him. As much as he needed to demand answers, he needed this even more.

Her.

He pulled her jeans down her legs and tossed them on the chair beside them, then went back for her panties, hooking his thumbs in the sides. Above them, she wore a tight Rafferty's T-shirt that revealed the full outline of her small, pert breasts. Her nipples were already distended, and he leaned up to take one between his teeth through the cotton. She moaned and grasped his head, weaving her fingers into his hair.

Fuck, he loved those subtle little tugs as she lost control. He needed more of them.

Now.

"I'm going to recline all the way on this chaise, and you're going to climb up on my face. And if anyone is taking pictures, I want you to make sure they hear you scream."

Rather than denying him—and possibly asking if he'd lost the last of his sanity—she clasped the blanket around her shoulders. "Not going to do that through my panties," she said, making him grin.

"Oh, I could. But for the sake of argument, you win." He yanked them down her long, pale legs and tossed them on top of her jeans. Then he rose and sat on the chair, leaning back and pulling on the lever that controlled the incline. It was sturdily built, more than capable of holding both of them. He'd never been more grateful for springing for quality than that very moment.

Once he'd lowered the back, he waited, breathing so hard his lungs were starting to cramp.

She was a goddamn vision. Eyes darker than the clouds rolling in, freckled skin flushed pink, her hair nothing but a flame in the dying sun. He couldn't do anything but hope to God she quickly put him out of his misery.

She moved up the chair and straddled his chest. Biting her lip, she hesitated.

"Uh-uh, Red. All the way. Don't make me die of thirst."

Without warning, she turned around, facing the other way. He was sure she'd changed her mind and was going to go inside, maybe leave his place entirely.

Instead, she grabbed his belt.

He started to tell her no. This wasn't about him. He already knew they were taking a risk. As far as he was concerned, anyone could take pictures of them and plaster them all over the web. She wouldn't see it the same way.

The blanket over her shoulders should be enough to disguise what was happening, but he couldn't be sure. He couldn't protect her when he was on his back. Leave it to his dick to do the thinking the minute his brain vacated the premises.

And his dick always made very, very bad choices.

Shit, she'd already undone his jeans.

"Lift," she murmured, and he did, because he was only a man. Just her using her hand on him would be enough to make him go crazy. Forget anything else.

She pushed his jeans and boxers down his legs, leaving them around his lower thighs like rope. Just one flex of his hips and her mouth was on him, exploring him without any of the reticence he would've expected. They were outside, and fuck, her pussy was too far away.

They'd have some tit for damn tat here.

He grabbed her hips and pulled back to his mouth, latching onto her swollen pink slit with a longing he couldn't hold back. He'd been craving this taste for so long, since the first time he'd gotten a hint of it in the club, then again, when he'd gotten more in the break room. But that first night, drunk, half delirious, he'd been consumed with the desire to taste her. The reality had nearly killed him, but a long, slow lick from the source was enough to make his body shake from the force of his groan.

She wrapped her insanely strong fingers around his cock, squeezing until his breaths came short and he could only lick her on auto-pilot.

If he passed out between her legs, he'd be grateful for the rest of his life.

He knew she had to stretch to reach him, but greedily, he yanked her back even farther, digging his fingers into the soft flesh of her ass. If he left marks this weekend, he'd kiss every one of them.

She cried out and he buried his face deeper between her thighs, making room for himself. She'd give up every drop willingly or he'd forcibly take them from her. Whatever tricks it took, he'd spend all night in this spot if necessary.

The whole world could watch them. Hell, might as well give them a show.

Sealing his lips around her clit, he sucked hard. Around his head, her legs trembled. Once, twice. Not nearly enough. With one hand, he probed her folds, and with the other still gripping her ass, he inched his fingers toward that tight pucker between her cheeks. She wasn't expecting it. Didn't know what to do when he started to slide inside. He could feel her resistance as distinctly as if she'd verbalized it, but he didn't do anything but suck, and stroke, and slowly, slowly invade.

And when she cried out again, that long, low, hungry sound that reverberated against the mouth, he growled in response. "Mine."

Almost as soon as he said it, she lifted, raising up above him like the nirvana he would never quite be worthy of reaching. Her tongue skated over the painful head of cock before traveling lower, along the side where his veins pulsed. She grazed the length of one right to the base, bouncing her pussy above his mouth just high enough he couldn't close the distance. But she gave him her own kind of gift, one he could barely make out thanks to the disappearing sun. Tiny pearlescent drops of arousal clung to her lower lips, on the verge of falling free, and he strained toward her, finally clamping his hands around her thighs and slamming her back down on his face.

Hell yes.

This time, he didn't hold back anything. He pushed a finger deep inside her while he worked her clit, earning every bit of her moisture. She wouldn't deny him again. Even if that meant his aching cock bobbed free with only the uneven swipes of her fingers to stoke the fire in his belly higher. He didn't need even that much. Just his mouth closed around her silky cleft while she pulsed through an orgasm would be enough to get him there.

He teased her between her cheeks again, not entering her this time. When he did that the next time, he'd have lube to make it easier for him to take her there like she was taking his finger inside her pussy. One finger, two. Three. He thrust them inside her and she clenched around them, riding his face just the way he'd dreamed. She was so wet. So hot. He slid his arm around her front to rub her clit, fast and hard, while he stroked his tongue inside her, relishing every flutter of her pussy. She was going to come.

Finally, she'd soak his fucking face.

Yet again she darted forward, leaving him hanging as she gripped his erection in her hand and brought him to her mouth. He wasn't supposed to come first. Shouldn't have even been that close. But she scooped out the wetness in the little slit on the head of his cock, and that was all it took. Her fingers tightened and her tongue flicked over the swollen head, and he couldn't do anything except turn his head to bite the back of her thigh along the crease where it met her perfect ass. His hips rose, driving him between her lips, and she didn't shy away. She took him deeper, making the most seductive little noises in her throat while he emptied. Extending his orgasm almost to the point of pain.

Mindlessly, he bit her again, on the other thigh. She yelped around his still draining dick, which shouldn't have made him laugh but so freaking did.

He was still laughing and still breathless from what she'd done to him when he hauled her back on to his mouth. He buried his tongue inside her again, and he clamped his arm around her hips to make sure she wasn't getting away.

Not this time. She was going to drench his goddamn chin.

Circling her clit, he rubbed her until she bore down against him. Rocking against him and clamoring for more in high, thin cries that reached him even where he was nestled between her thighs. The roar in his ears grew louder, and it didn't even matter that the last trickles of his release had been spent on his belly. This was her moment, and he hurtled toward it with her, yearning for the release as if it were his own.

"C'mon, Red," he rasped against her folds in between lengthy swipes of his tongue. He never let up the pressure on the plump little bud under his fingers. He wouldn't settle for some mild little O.

She was going to frigging scream, or he'd be out there all night, eating her until he died from oxygen deprivation.

Her legs shook around his head and she arched, lifting up for a fraction of a moment before she grinded onto his face. He growled against her and unwound the last scrap of her control, sucking her so hard that she had no choice but to break apart. Her wetness flooded his lips and he swallowed every drop, savoring the moans that shuddered through her body.

Once she'd ridden her climax to its end, he grasped her hip to steady her trembles and threw back his head to breathe.

And smiled up at the sky where the stars had begun to emerge from the clouds.

Her blanket dipped toward his nose and mouth as she sagged to his chest. He chuckled and sat up, sliding her down so that she plopped on his lap. His arms encircled her still quivering body, and he kissed the side of her neck until she let out a weak moan.

"I didn't—I've never…" She exhaled. "Outside."

"Yeah. The free show is over for tonight." After he jockeyed her enough to pull up his boxers and jeans, he clutched her hand between her breasts. "In my bed, Red. Now."

She gave him an incredulous look. "You can't go again."

"Twenty-three, baby. I can go until you can't walk." When she scoffed, he scooped her up and stood, bobbling her in his hold. "Whoa, O legs. Good job."

Her giggle was the sweetest music he'd ever heard. Not his guitar, when he was rocking out during an incredible show. Not when he was nailing it during practice, or jamming during a Slayers' concert.

She outstripped all of them effortlessly.

Stumbling a little, he carted her down the hall to his bedroom and dumped her on the mattress. He shed his jeans and boxers and joined her on the bed, his intent clear. She squealed out a laugh as he grabbed her leg and wrapped it around his hip, already prepared to go for it when reality descended.

Bare cock. Bare pussy. Dancing eyes that flashed up to his and slowly lowered as her anticipation bled away.

He kissed her to keep from saying the obvious.

No condom, can't do it.

Of course he had some in the nightstand, but the moment had been lost. The specter of real life had blown up between them like a ticking bomb.

Her kisses tasted like him. He'd come in her mouth, and she'd taken every drop, just as he had. She whimpered and he knew she'd tasted herself too. Her tongue twined around his and he fisted his hands in her hair, loving that she was finally on his pillows. In his bed, in his apartment.

His.

Truthfully, there was no *finally* to it. A week ago, he'd barely known who she was. But lifetimes could pass in an hour with her.

"Let me go grab your clothes off the deck," he murmured in between kisses.

She started to argue, then she turned her head away. "Stupid reporters. What do they do, hang out of helicopters?"

"Sometimes." He'd seen much worse things when it came to his father and his bevy of women. Money made the paps salivate just like it did everyone else. "Just in case. If they saw us, so be it. If they didn't, well, might as well tidy up the evidence of a very good," he glanced at his alarm clock, "hour. Shit, really?"

Again that giggle, although he would've sworn it was sleepier this time. "You were thorough."

"So were you, Mrs. Shawcross. O legs, remember? A favor I intend to return."

For once, she didn't jolt at the name, just smiled up at him with unfocused eyes. "You didn't let me walk in here, but trust me, I have them. If they're still attached."

He grinned and gave her another quick kiss. "Be right back."

"'Kay."

Jogging out to the deck, he gathered up her clothes and took a quick glance at the surrounding buildings. He didn't see any telephoto lenses trained on his floor, so maybe they'd gotten lucky.

He grinned again. Oh, they so had.

On the way back to Chloe, he stopped off in the bathroom to wash up and take care of business. He'd neglected to put his jeans back on for his trip outside, but eh. He didn't have anything to hide.

After grabbing the two Dr. Peppers he'd left on the coffee table along with the hopefully not stale cookies, he returned to the bedroom. And found Chloe curled up in the center of the bed, mostly asleep.

He set down her clothes and their snack, then leaned over to kiss her shoulder. She stirred immediately. "Michael?"

"Yeah. Go ahead and rest."

"Can't." Her voice was fuzzy enough to let him know for certain that she already had been. Damn, she'd gone out quickly. Probably exhausted. "Gotta tell you. Lost—lost my job. And my...my place. I lost it all."

Swallowing hard—and more than a little certain she'd regret being so forthright once she awakened—he crawled into the sheets behind her and drew her into his arms. "Don't worry about any of that now." He pressed a kiss to her silky, cinnamon-scented hair. "Sleep, Red."

"Gotta...gotta call Axl soon. Before bed."

"I'll wake you up soon, I promise. Just a little nap."

"'Kay." Her softly slurred voice made him close his eyes too.

She filled his arms so perfectly. Just like the night they'd gotten married.

The memory of the last time he'd gone to sleep like this with her tried to tickle the back of his brain, but he couldn't quite grasp it. Too tired. His body was too warm and relaxed. She'd worn him out in the very best way.

He tightened his embrace and smiled against her hair. She was back in his arms, right where she belonged. And he wasn't letting go.

TWENTY-FOUR

CHLOE WOKE TO A FURNACE BEHIND HER AND A HAND ON HER BOOB.

Again.

The recall was swift and immediate enough that she almost kicked out just as she had done that fateful morning. Instead, she only moved suddenly enough to clip his jaw.

Michael groaned and cupped the side of his mouth. "Oh, fuck. Is this going to be a thing? *Mortal Kombat* at dawn?"

She snorted and turned in his arms. The tickle of chest hair against her nipples dissolved the giggle on her tongue.

He leaned toward her, then backed away before he kissed her. "I'm not going to get bit or something, right?"

"Depends on your level of dragon breath."

He rolled his tongue over his teeth. "Not bad." He pursed his lips. "Maybe. Guess you'll have to give it a try."

She couldn't stop the laugh this time. The kiss was soft and sweet, not the engulfing pyrotechnics of last night. She wasn't sure she could take that so early in the… "Oh, shit."

He licked his lips. "It's not that bad."

She pushed him back. "No. Oh, crap. I didn't call Axl last night."

She motioned to the window. "It's already…I don't even know what time it is." She scrambled off the bed. "And where are my clothes?"

He sat up in the middle of the lake-sized bed. "On the chair."

"No, clean clothes. My bag."

"Oh, uh…" He looked around, then hopped off the bed. All six-glorious-feet of naked male.

She shook her head. Axl was the focus, not all of…*him*.

God, she was a terrible mother. How could she have blinked out like that?

She turned a full circle and finally spotted her jeans on a chair near the window. Without curtains, because why would this man-child have curtains? He probably didn't even have matching dishes. What the hell was she thinking?

She spotted a folded T-shirt on top of a pile of laundry and quickly put it on. She did not need some crazy high powered lens taking pictures of her mom body. She'd been lucky enough that her good genes had helped her bounce back after having Axl. That and walking everywhere kept her body trim and strong. Unfortunately, she didn't have time in her day to do things like Pilates and yoga like all the women with their tight little bodies these days.

Finally, she found her jeans and got her phone out of her pocket. Two missed calls. She curled her fingers around the phone and tapped it against her forehead. Bad mom. She blew out a breathy groan as she noticed the time. Seven.

She quickly dialed Lori, who picked up on the second ring. "Oh my God, I'm so sorry."

"It's fine. He and Shelby passed out watching *Finding Nemo*. Everything's just fine."

Chloe collapsed onto the edge of the bed. "It was the worst day ever yesterday."

"I can't believe that rat bastard evicted you."

Chloe flopped back on the bed lengthwise and let her head hang off the side. It was rather nice to have so much room to stretch out. Her twin bed definitely didn't rate against this bit of indulgence. "I can."

Michael set her bag beside the bed. He gave her a look, then glanced down at his lengthening erection. "We'll try that position later."

She rolled her eyes at him. Seriously, he only thought with that thing. She ignored the fact that her body fluttered in reaction. Taking him in her mouth last night had been far more exciting than it should have been.

Honestly, she couldn't remember the last time she'd enjoyed giving a man a blow job. Then again, Michael had been very focused on her. She barely remembered if she'd managed to pleasure him. His taste flooding her mouth was proof that he'd enjoyed himself, but most men could get off easily.

More easily than she could anyway.

It wasn't like she hadn't had a satisfying sex life before Michael, but...

Yeah, well but.

Not the same. Not at all the same, which also worried her. What exactly did they have when the sex faded? Because sexual afterglow *always* faded.

"Where are you? Who's that?"

She shook off that line of thought. It sure as heck wasn't helping her right now. "I'm with Michael."

"Ohh."

"Don't get excited."

"I do believe I overheard something about a position. I expect details, because I'm living vicariously through you."

"David will be home soon."

Lori sighed. "Not soon enough. Now that you're not here, I'm thinking about going back to base housing."

"You hate the base."

"I know, but the neighborhood is getting worse. You were really the only thing keeping me here."

Chloe flipped over onto her stomach. "I don't know that this will be permanent. I could be right around the corner again in a week."

Michael tugged at her hair, then crouched in front of her. "You, me, and the kid. It's permanent. I swear it, Red."

Chloe had to blink away the quick rush of tears.

Lori laughed. "Girl, you're toast."

"Shut up."

Michael stood. "Meet me in the shower, Mrs. Shawcross."

"Toast," Lori said in a singsong voice.

Chloe firmed her voice. He wasn't going to dictate where and when she was doing anything, dammit. "I'll be there to get Axl in an hour."

"Okay, I'll see you then." Lori was still laughing when she hung up the phone.

Chloe let her arms dangle off the bed. She was not going to go have sex with Michael in the shower. Nope. She didn't have time for that.

She rolled off the bed and walked into the ridiculously huge bathroom. Her tour of his apartment had been minimal at best. She remembered stumbling in there sometime in the middle of the night to take care of business, but she'd been beyond blurry.

There was a wall of glass, multiple shower heads going, and blessed steam filling the room. She couldn't remember the last time she'd actually had a hot shower that lasted more than seven minutes. Usually, because her hot water didn't last much longer than eight, but more often than not, it was because Axl didn't allow such luxuries.

Water and mint-scented suds slid down Michael's muscular form

She did have an hour to get to Lori's.

She flipped off his shirt, letting it drop to the floor.

"Fuck it," she said and opened the door.

Michael was dipping his head back under the rain hood and shampoo was foaming off his neck and down his back. He had such wide, strong shoulders. A light dusting of freckles came into view. He rolled his neck to get rid of the rest of the soap and a simple triangle tattoo was revealed.

She stepped inside and slid her hand up his wet back. "There's quite a bit of room in here. Just one problem?"

He turned and drew her under the rain shower head. "I can't see a single one, except that you're not slick everywhere just yet."

She tipped her head back with a low groan. "That's a whole lotta wrong."

"Everything looks right to me." He dipped his head and took her nipple into his mouth.

She slid her fingers into his wet hair and let a moan sigh out of her chest. He knew just how much pressure to exert before pulling back. She'd tell him about needing a tub for Axl later.

When she could think again.

Twenty minutes later, she landed in a heap on Michael's bed. He'd wrapped her in a towel the size of a damn blanket and carried her out of the bathroom.

He had to. She couldn't feel her feet.

Between the steam and his relentless need to give her three orgasms for his one—good ratio as far as she was concerned, not that she'd tell him that—she was spent. Someday, it would be lovely if she could just sprawl out on a huge bed and sleep the day away.

She'd gotten to do that in Vegas, of course, but drunk sleep was not the good kind of sleep. Not the kind that followed an orgasm and a day of pampering.

Actually, she was pretty sure she'd never had that kind of day.

"We have to go get Axl."

Michael opened up her towel and kissed her inner thigh, then her belly. "We sure do."

"Do you mind?"

He peered up at her. "Of course not."

She pushed his hair off his forehead. "I know it's an imposition."

He caught her hand and brought it to his cheek. "It's not. I want to do things for you guys. It's my job now."

"It's not your job to take care of me—of *us.*"

"I want to."

She sighed. "I'll find a job as soon as I can, then we'll be—"

"No."

"What do you mean *no?*" She struggled to sit up, and tugged the towel closed again. Being naked with this man often put a halt to conversation. And she needed to be clear-headed just now.

"Look at this place. It's huge. I have another bedroom that we can turn into a nursery, or big boy room, or whatever. You know, for Axl."

"Michael, we're moving so fast."

"I know, and I don't want to scare you. Really, I don't, but I like being needed."

"That is not the basis of a relationship." She slid off the bed and hauled her suitcase onto the chair in the corner. She pulled out underwear and dragged them up over her damp skin.

He moved to his wardrobe and started tugging out clothes. "I said we could go slow last night. I meant it." He hopped into his jeans, tugging them up over purple boxers. He left them unzipped as he walked toward her. "But why not just chill out for a little while? You've been working your ass off since before the little man was born, right?"

She snapped her bra, and pulled her shirt over her head before turning to him. "I've been working since I hit double digits, Michael."

He shut his eyes for a second then closed the rest of the distance between them. "You're more than due for some Mom and Axl time, don't you think?"

"Of course, I'd love to stay home with him." She'd missed so much. Luckily for her, Lori had FaceTimed Axl's first steps, but there had been a hundred other milestones she'd failed to be a part of. She tried like hell not to think of them as failures, but there'd been so many, she'd lost count.

"Then do it. I can afford to do this."

"I'd be taking adv—"

He grasped her upper arms. "Don't even say that word. The mere fact that you are so worried about it negates the whole aspect of taking advantage of anyone."

"Were you a lawyer in a past life or something?"

"Mathlete, actually." He hauled her into his arms, holding her close until she curled her arms around his back. "Caltech if you want the down and dirty details. Though I prefer our kind of dirty details."

She dropped her forehead against his chest. "I knew that. I Googled you, remember?"

He laughed. "I only lasted two semesters. The guitar was way more interesting."

She peered up at him. "You still had to have the grades to get in."

"Somehow I doubt your grades sucked."

"Advanced placement for everything. Even got a scholarship, but then the funding got cut and I couldn't get enough loans to cover."

"Then go back to school."

"Michael…"

He cupped her face. "We'll take it a day at a time for now, okay?"

She blew out a breath. "Okay."

"Now, let's go get him."

"Sounds like a plan." Because she'd need the rest of the day to figure out how she was going to get everything out of her house by the end of tomorrow.

She was texting Lori and her father as they left the apartment and went down in the elevator. Michael stopped at the front desk and set her up with access to the building.

"What's your license plate?"

She blinked at him while mid-text with her dad. "What?"

He laughed. "Your license plate. You have a car, right?"

"No. It was pay for an apartment, or car and car insurance. Apartment won."

His eyebrows shot up. "Well, we'll be fixing that."

"No. We'll be fine." No way was she going to allow him to buy her a car.

"Chloe, I live in Malibu. There's no buses. At least none that come up here."

"Oh." The buses went everywhere. She'd never had to worry about it. Sure, she had to carry mace and learn a bit of self-defense, but she hadn't been hassled overmuch when using public transportation.

The guy at the desk cleared his throat. "Miss Adams has been added to the system. We'll have a key ready for her by this afternoon."

"Great." Michael smiled at the man, then eased her away from the desk and through the lobby. "You'll have access to the gym and the café, both are twenty-four hours. There's a daycare on the third floor as well. I don't know much about that part though. We'll look it up on the building's website when I get home tonight."

Her head was spinning with all the info.

Michael took her hand as they left. He smiled at Barney and Chloe gave him a distracted half wave.

"The parking garage has an elevator that goes right upstairs. That's why we went out the front. I wanted to make sure you could get in."

"Thanks."

Michael always managed to keep her off-balance with his endless kindness. Then again, it seemed like he had a whole checklist going on in his head.

"How long have you been planning this?"

"Hmm?" He was checking his phone with his free hand.

"You are way too good with the details, pal."

He stopped and slid his phone into his pocket. "I told you I wanted you to live with me." He shrugged. "I looked into it."

"And I walked right into your master plan." She narrowed her eyes. "You didn't get me evicted, right?"

"No, but that would've been pretty genius, if a bit creepy. I don't want to control your life, Red. I just want you to be in mine."

"What the hell am I supposed to say to that?"

"Thanks?" He tipped his head, giving her a grin. "I promise to pay you back in sexual favors?"

She tugged her hand out of his and crossed her arms over her chest. "I'm no whore."

"Oh, Jesus. I didn't mean it like that." He grabbed both of her hands. "I swear."

She couldn't even pretend to be upset. Michael didn't have an asshole bone in his body when it came to them as a couple. He just expected sex because he was a horny male who loved having sex with her.

And she liked having sex with him too. "Forget I said that. I'm just being sensitive."

He arched an eyebrow. "I love all your sensitive parts."

"And there's the pervert."

He clasped her hand again. "I'm your pervert."

They ducked into a side door and he crossed to a parking spot that had his apartment number carved into the cement wall. There was another spot next to his Viper just waiting for her. She wasn't quite sure how she felt about that.

Thirty-three minutes later, they pulled up her driveway. By some miracle, the reporters weren't around. She was pretty sure they'd be back in no time thanks to Michael's flashy penis-mobile. Okay, so she knew firsthand that he didn't need it because of a little dick, but it was still far too ostentatious for her taste.

She twisted to look in the back. How the hell was she going to get a car seat in this thing? "Um, Michael?"

"Yeah?"

"Where are we putting Axl?"

"In the backseat…I don't have. Fuck."

She laughed. She had to laugh or she'd cry. "I guess I will need that car, huh?"

"We'll research tonight."

Out of reasons to argue, she conceded. She opened the door and Lori came out of her door with Axl on her hip. Her son's huge smile— at least what she could see around his fist currently shoved in his mouth —was a sight for sore eyes.

Chloe ran up the grass and scooped him out of Lori's arms. "Hi, bug."

"Mama." He hooked his drooly hand around her neck and went right for a fistful of hair. Another one of the many reasons her hair was up in a ponytail usually.

Michael came up behind her. "Hey, buddy."

Axl dropped his head onto her chest and hid his face.

Lori smiled. "He just got up."

She looked down at Axl. "Did you sleep in? Mama's jealous."

"Selby fish."

Chloe glanced at Lori for a clue.

"They fell asleep watching Nemo, then demanded a reshowing at five this morning. They both fell back to sleep around eight."

Chloe winced. "Oh, you poor thing."

Lori yawned. "Mine's still napping. I win."

"No nap," Axl said before scrunching his face up.

Chloe blew raspberries and kisses into his neck before he could start the waterworks. "No. How about some breakfast instead? Oatmeal?"

"Appews."

"Apples," she corrected.

"Appews," Axl said again.

Michael smoothed one of Chloe's curls around his finger. "I hate to ask, but since my car is not yet babyfied, could you bring Chloe home today?"

"Sure. No prob." Lori smiled up at Michael. "Handy you have a young, strong back for all the lifting."

"Lori." Chloe gave her a hard look.

"Yeah, we're going to get Chloe out of here as soon as possible."

"As soon as tomorrow?"

Chloe huffed out a breath. "Thanks, Lori."

Michael frowned down at her. "Eviction notice with no time?"

"I'll take care of it."

"No." Michael dug his phone out of his pocket, flicked through a few menus then held it up to his ear. "Hi, my name is Michael Shawcross..." He walked away from them as he started asking questions to someone on the other end.

"Really?"

"Girl, if that guy can help, let him."

Chloe sighed. "He's already letting us stay with him. I don't want him to deal with this too."

"What are you going to do? Empty out your savings—if you have any left at this point."

"I was going to dip into Axl's—"

"No, you are going to let that rich, lovely guy take care of this. Pay him back with meals or something."

"I don't have that kind of talent."

Lori laughed. "Sure you do. Who's the one who had us set up with two weeks' worth of crockpot meals on your last Saturday night off?"

"That's just Pinterest."

"Yeah, well, I bet that guy hasn't had home cooked meals. He probably lives off of Taco Bell and hamburgers."

Chloe looked over her shoulder. "I don't know. We don't eat around each other much."

"Because you're too busy getting naked."

Her face heated. "Maybe."

"Did I mention I was jealous? If not, consider it said." A squall came from her pocket. "Crap."

Chloe shifted Axl to her other hip. "So much for that nap."

"Yeah, no kidding. Come on in after you get rid of Mr. Rockstar."

"Will do." Chloe headed back down the lawn. She rubbed her cheek against her son's hair. Her favorite time was right after a nap. It was the only time her crazy almost-two-year-old wanted to cuddle.

"Right. Thanks, man, I appreciate it." He rattled off her address then his own and something else that sounded an awful lot like many zeros.

When Michael hung up, she approached him. She leaned back so she could meet her son's gaze. "Do you remember Michael?"

"Spider."

"Right," she said with a laugh. "He read you *The Spider and The Fly.*"

"Nemo!"

Michael smiled down at Axl as he drew them both closer. "We can switch it up to Nemo. I think I've seen that about five times. Might even have it on my iTunes."

Her heart melted. How the hell was she supposed to hold out against a man who loved *Finding Nemo*?

"Dory!"

"Don't think I have that one yet, buddy. But we can fix that."

Chloe laughed. "You want to win the heart of my kid, keep talking cartoons."

"Deal." Michael kissed her temple. "I have a fleet of guys coming to pack you up today. They'll bring what you want to the house and put the rest in storage." Her eyes widened. "Or the dumpster, whichever you prefer."

"Today?"

He nodded. "I have to get to rehearsal. Lila's on the warpath or I'd let them know I can't make it."

"No, you have to work. That's fine. I can handle it."

"You just point. They'll do whatever you tell them to do. In fact, you don't have to lift a finger. I have a maid service coming in that works with this company. They'll clean it from top to bottom after the guys leave."

"Michael, that's too much. I can handle cleaning my own place." It wasn't that dirty. She was pretty sure. Maybe a few million dust bunnies, but the rest shouldn't be bad. Okay, she hadn't gotten around to cleaning her fridge in a while. She pushed her bangs out of her eyes and switched Axl to her other hip. The kid definitely didn't starve.

Michael plucked him out of her arms and held Axl over his head, twirling them both. Her son's delighted laugh rang through the air. She resisted the urge to snatch him back. She was pretty sure Michael wouldn't drop him.

Mostly.

After a half dozen twirls, Michael stopped suddenly and shook his head, making a goofy face. "You're no lightweight, Ax-man."

She couldn't help smiling at both Michael and her son as Axl clutched Michael's shirt. "All right, no flying off into space."

"Space," Axl parroted.

"It's not going to be a long practice." He transferred Axl back into her arms. He fished his wallet out of his pocket.

"Oh, no. Don't you hand me money. I have…some."

He rolled his eyes. "Can we not make money a thing? I know you've taken some from Nick."

She ground her teeth. "That was different. And I hated asking."

"I know. I'm your husband though. I get to spoil you and to make sure your friend is taken care of today since we're inconveniencing her. Right?"

There was no argument that she could make. "Yeah, I suppose."

"Good." He took out a wad of cash and tucked it into her front pocket. "Give the guys instructions, then take her out to lunch. You guys go…wherever kids like to go for the day. Make sure it's an awesome day for the Ax-man." He dug his fingers lightly into Axl's side until her son was laughing again. "Since we're changing his whole life today, Mama. Remember?"

"Like I could forget."

"Right. So you have a great day with your friend and we'll figure out the home stuff tonight. Okay?" He bent down until their faces lined up. "Okay?"

"Yes." She hated it with the power of a thousand suns, but it would be better to take Lori out for a fun day than to sweat over her house. She looked over her shoulder at her side of the duplex with the pansies that were dying because she didn't have time to water them. No matter how much she wanted to remember, they fell by the wayside next to double shifts and spending every spare moment with Axl.

Michael slid an arm around her hip and hauled them both into his chest. "For once, just take care of your family and let me figure out the details. The bonus? I get to be your family now too."

She hooked her arm around his neck and dragged him down for a kiss. How the hell else was she supposed to say thank you? There were no words for the emotions pinging around in her chest. Her heart was beating hummingbird-fast.

Just like it always seemed to do around this man.

Michael smiled into the kiss, then impulsively smushed one into her son's cheek. "Take care of your mama for me?"

"Mama," Axl said. He clunked his big head against her collarbone.

"Ouch, careful." Michael stroked the back of his knuckles down her face. "Do easy."

Her eyes pricked. How many times had she said "do easy" to Axl, just like her dad had said to her as a kid?

Axl patted her face. "Easy."

"There you go." Michael grinned down at her. "I'll see you guys tonight. I won't be late."

"Okay."

He backed up toward his car. "No working, just ordering your minions."

She laughed. "You really don't want me to get used to having minions."

"You're a queen. Of course, you should get used to it." He rounded the hood of his car and got in with a wave.

"You're a queen," Lori said from the porch.

"I hate you," she called back. She sighed and looked at Axl. "Want to go to the boardwalk?"

"Rides!"

She hugged him close and headed up to Lori's door. "Rides it is."

TWENTY-FIVE

CHLOE HAD LIVED WITH A MAN BEFORE. SORT OF.

Snake had needed a lot of alone time to figure out lyrics or…well, she didn't really want to think about just what kind of other things he'd been doing when he wasn't with her. There had been a lot of passing each other in the night.

Most of the time it was because she was working so much. She'd paid for much of the utilities as well as the apartment they'd lived in. Snake was always bouncing between manic highs where he was jamming with friends, and lows where she wasn't sure he would come home. And often didn't for days at a time. More than a few sessions in rehab hadn't helped matters on that end.

The good days, he'd been attentive and romantic. Forever spinning stories about what their life would be like when he made it.

Needless to say, that hadn't allowed him to keep a job for very long.

Living with Michael Shawcross was very different. For two weeks, she'd been certain she was going to kill him. Not because he snored—he did, but only when he was really tired. After rather brutal practice sessions with his band, or a stressful show, those were a few of his darker moments.

But a dark moment for Michael was a grunt when he came in the door, followed by a long, thorough kiss. He'd sigh, say her name in his dreamy grumble. Dreamy was her word. He'd die if she ever said that to his face. Then he'd take a shower and her Michael would be back.

Grins and silly noises for Axl as he sprawled on the floor to play with him before bedtime. Long, leisurely conversations on the balcony for her. He never ran out of words. Some in the flowery Michael-speak she was getting used to. More so of the dirty variety that she secretly loved.

Nights were often spent naked. At least on Michael's end. The man just didn't like clothes. Considering he was approximately the body temperature of a furnace—she knew this because she barely needed a blanket at night—she could see why.

The killing part came from the boy side of his nature. Her two-year-old was better at picking up after himself than Michael was.

She picked up a bowl from beside the couch, then found another on the bookcase, and a glass on the floor next to Axl's toy box.

She shook her head as she found two more cups on her way into the kitchen.

Axl came careening through the living room, his arms out like a plane. The plus side of that? His balance was a lot better. The minus? She had to chase after him and make sure he didn't take out all of the man-child toys Michael didn't put away.

Guitars, stands, a mini amplifier that Axl thought was an awesome rock to climb—none of it was cheap Ikea or Target end tables like she had at her apartment. It felt like everything in Michael's place was from a catalog. And an expensive one at that.

She scooped Axl up before he ran headlong into the tower of gaming consoles. "Okay, buddy. No more plane, huh?"

His face scrunched up as he arched away from her. "No."

"Let's go play with your Legos."

"Chopter."

She dumped the dishes in the dishwasher with a wriggling Axl over her shoulder. Then she tried to do the same soaring over the head angle that Michael could do. Unfortunately, Axl was twenty-five pounds as of his last check up, and she was pretty sure he was more toward thirty. He'd sprout up again soon. He always chunked up a bit before zooming up.

Which would mean new clothes again.

Nope, don't think about that right now.

She hooked her arm around his middle and spun around once. Axl shrieked. Yeah, she definitely wasn't as good at that as Michael. Hmm. She eyed the yoga mat she'd picked up at Target that morning.

She'd read an article about babies and the positive effects of yoga. She read a lot of damn articles these days. She really wasn't used to having extra time on her hands.

Chloe put him down in the largest area of the living room. The tears kept coming, fat and flowing. Great. She ran for the bag with the mat and video in it. "Want to play with Mama?"

He tipped his head to the side. "Chopter."

She pulled out the smaller kid's mat and then hers. "Let's try something."

He shoved his hand into his mouth and landed on his butt.

"All right, that's a yes in my book." She scooped him up and ran with him into Michael's bedroom. When he laughed, she tossed him into the middle of the bed. He bounced and the crocodile tears disappeared into giggles.

She wiggled out of her jeans and shirt, and swapped them for the workout clothes she'd ordered last weekend. Amazon Prime was the single best thing on the planet.

Axl clapped his hands when she put on the yoga pants. They had planes all over them. "Like these?"

"Chopter!"

"Plane."

"Chopter." He said it with so much glee that she couldn't stop laughing. "Let's go do some exercise. How's that?" She swung him onto her hip and danced her way into the living room. She plucked the video out of the bag. "*Mommy and Me Yoga*," she read aloud from the cover.

"Mama."

"Right. Mama and me?" she prompted.

"Me," he parroted.

"You got it. Now, how did we do this again?" Michael had about eight plugs set up for the television. She didn't know a television could have that many cables. Then again, he had a surround sound system that required an engineering degree to use.

She slid the disk in and hoped for the best.

"Miracle of automation." The DVD player switched the system to the right channel or whatever. An unnaturally bubbly voice came through the television. "We might have to kill her, but we'll give it a try."

She got on the floor and set Axl next to her. "Watch."

His huge dark eyes soaked up the colors of the women on the screen. He started clapping when the music started. After an initial warm up, she ended up in a few poses that she and Axl both giggled through.

She really wasn't aware that she could bend like that. And she might have lost her balance midway through some stork position, but Axl was having a good time. And freaking hell, she was sweating her ass off. When they got to floor positions, her kid was in heaven as she used her feet to hoist him up over her.

See? Now she could do the chopter, dammit.

She didn't need Michael.

The door opened when she was in the middle of lowering him close to her chest and going for another rep.

"Well, well. What do we have here?"

Axl shrieked and his arms went out for Michael immediately. Michael lifted him off her knees and started zooming him around the room. Chloe's feet dropped to the mat and she collapsed spread-eagle-style. Yoga wasn't for wimps, man. She was dripping.

Michael set Axl down a few minutes later, getting down on the floor to tickle him into howls of laughter. Then he crawled over to her. "Mama Bear is sexy."

"I'm sweaty and gross."

He caged her on the floor. "Hot."

She pushed at his chest. "Get off, sicko."

Michael inched back before he lowered his mouth to her belly. "Salty and delicious." He roamed over to her side and nipped at the little bit of flesh showing above her yoga pants. He peered at the television, and his eyebrows rose. "Yoga, huh?"

"I used to be pretty flexible."

"Any more flexible and I'll have a heart attack." He inched her flowy shirt up and kissed her ribs, then moved back over to her middle.

"Razzies," Axl said and crawled over to them.

Michael grinned at Axl. "Raspberries?"

"Razzies," he said again.

Michael blew raspberries on her stomach until she curled into herself to stop him.

"No, no," she said, giggling.

"Oh, Mama's ticklish." Michael held her down and pulled Axl into the mix until there was nothing but laughter filling the room. A helluva lot better than tears.

"Uncle," she said with a gasp.

Michael flopped onto the floor next to her, as out of breath as she was.

Axl giggled and climbed between them. He patted her stomach. "Hungy."

"Me too, pal." Michael grinned over Axl's head at her. "Hiya, wife."

"You're home early."

"Juliet tried to bean West with her bass. We decided it was probably better to call it a day than to keep practicing today."

"Oh, sorry."

He shrugged. "Everyone's just getting tense about the upcoming shows. Ryan's hand isn't healing as quickly as we'd hoped. Beating on drums certainly isn't helping it along."

She reached over to push a lock of hair away from his forehead. "What happened with that studio guy? What was his name?" There'd been a couple over the last few weeks. None of them seemed to gel with the band.

"Toby. He wasn't a bad player, but he couldn't handle our jam style." Michael sat up. "We throw all sorts of covers in with our songs."

Chloe rolled up to a crosslegged position and plopped Axl between her legs. "I saw a YouTube the other night. I liked 'My Own Worst Enemy' with 'Lick.'" Axl played with her fingers, dragging her thumb into his mouth.

"Yeah? Ryan loves Lit."

"Me too. Listened to them a lot when I was in high school."

He grinned. "Looking for my songs, woman?"

"Maybe."

"Good. I like that you're interested." Michael leaned in, hovered at her mouth, then made a quick turn to Axl's neck. He lifted Axl up and stood. "I require pizza to go with my news."

News? She arched a brow. "I require a shower."

"Then hop to it, Red." He held his hand out to her, then hauled her up. "You have two hungry men on your hands." Michael bounced Axl on his hip. "How about an episode of *Phineas and Ferb* while Mom gets ready?"

"Yeah!" Axl raised his drool-covered hand.

A real shower? She might weep. "That would be awesome."

Michael grinned. "Don't take too long. I'll take the squirt in with me for a shower."

"Man, the royal treatment all around."

They'd worked around the tub issue by making it a game with the handheld shower sprayer and lots of toys. She was pretty sure that the designer hadn't had a seascape of wall clings in mind when they'd put in the marble tile, but it was pretty awesome anyway.

She walked through the baby-fied living room full of new tables with rounded corners, instead of the endless glass Michael had owned before they'd taken over his life. Their—his—bedroom hadn't fared much better. The huge Queen Anne furniture survived, but the dresser was now cluttered with her perfumes and lotions.

Instead of complaining about it, Michael kept buying her more. Including quite a few different oils. She swiped the cinnamon after-shower oil off the tray, and brought it with her into the shower. If he had news, then she wanted to make sure she primped a little.

Just in case, of course.

Twenty minutes later, she was shaved, buffed, and squeaky clean. She wasn't in the mood to do her hair so she tied it up in her usual tail. The boys came in as she was buttoning her shirt.

Michael whistled. "Well, hello there."

She sat at her shabby chic vanity. Michael still didn't understand her need to buy and repurpose, but he'd stopped giving her grief about it.

There was no way she was spending a grand on a vanity that she sat at for approximately five minutes each day.

Not to mention she had so much time on her hands. She didn't know what to do with it all, so she kept doing home stuff.

Michael hung Axl upside down as he crossed to the bathroom. "You stink, pal."

Axl giggled. "Xersize."

She dabbed on some light makeup, and listened with half an ear as her guys splashed around in the shower. Michael's deeper voice was layered with Axl's excitable one. When she was done, she grabbed towels, Pull-Ups for Axl, and underwear for both of them. She set the pile on the counter, then used her time to tidy up their bedroom.

She unplugged her phone and tucked it into her jeans pocket. "So, what's this news? Worthy of a pepperoni pizza? Or the works?"

"You know me so well."

She grinned. She was beginning to.

"Brush your teeth. Minty fresh breath gets extra kisses from your mom."

Chloe grinned and moved to the doorway. Both of them stood in matching blue boxer briefs. Michael's hair was already fixed into his messy fauxhawk, and Axl had his hair styled the same. They were both brushing their teeth in sync.

She pulled her phone out before she thought about it and clicked a photo.

She looked down at her phone. They looked so much like father and son right then. She stuffed her phone back in her pocket and shook off the rush of emotions.

Temporary, Chloe.

But they definitely didn't feel very temporary in that picture. Or in the last few weeks. She rested her cheek against her hand on the doorjamb. "Spill the news."

Michael looked over his shoulder with his toothbrush stuck in his cheek. He grinned around it, and the look he gave her was decidedly not fatherly. It might *make* a baby though.

Axl's laughter bounced around the room, breaking the moment.

"We got nominated for a Spectrum award."

She had a vague idea that it was a big deal, but there were so many different award shows that she was a little clueless. But the huge grin on his face told her it was important, and that was all that mattered to her.

She rushed in and pulled him down for a kiss. "That's amazing."

He looped his arms around her. "Yeah. For Best New Artist. We were celebrating about it at practice before all hell broke loose."

"You'd think that kind of excitement would keep everyone in a good mood for at least twenty-four hours."

He sighed and kissed her again. He was right—minty fresh breath was pretty kiss-worthy. "Now, we're even more worried about a drummer. They want us to play during the televised portion of the show."

"That's even better." She punctuated the congratulations with another kiss.

"It should be."

She threaded her fingers through his chest hair. "When's the show?"

"March, thankfully. So, we have some time."

"Imma mint too."

Michael grinned down at their Axl interruption. "Is that right?" Axl gripped his wrist and Michael made a growling noise as he hoisted him up slowly. "So heavy." He made a production of it then tucked Axl between them.

"Big boy," Axl said.

"You sure are." She leaned down and gave Axl a smacking kiss. "Minty fresh."

"Yeah, fresh."

Michael hugged the two of them tighter. "Now, let's go ruin it with garlic."

Chloe laughed. "Sounds like a very good plan."

She found him on the balcony later that night. It had been a fun evening. Axl was completely passed out in his room, with his arm clutching the Hank plush octopus that Michael had won for him at the arcade. The long ride out to the pier gave them the perfect lullaby ride back home.

Michael still had his Viper, but took to driving her Jeep more and more. Then again, most of their outings included Axl, so it was kind of a necessity.

She curled her arms around Michael's waist and pressed her cheek to his bare back. The ocean breeze was a little brisk, but February was right around the corner. There were a scant few months of cool weather in California, and she usually had to sneak down to the pier to get a taste of winter ocean air.

Now, it was literally her backyard.

"Everything okay?"

He curled his fingers tighter over the curve of the railing. Tension radiated off of him. "My fucking brother is still MIA. Lila has been bugging me daily to see if I've talked to him."

She sighed, pressing a kiss to the dip of his spine. The topic of Mal was one of the many refrains in their evening conversations. "You don't think he changed his phone number, do you?"

"Wouldn't put it past him."

She slid a trail of kisses along his biceps and ducked under his arm. "What are you guys going to do if you can't get Mal to join?" She swirled her tongue around his nipple.

He groaned. "Like I'm supposed to pay attention when you're doing that?"

She grinned up at him and moved lower. "You're so tense. I figured I should loosen you up." She licked over his ribs to the ridges of muscle that arrowed down into his jeans. "I can let you stew out here if you'd rather." She crouched in front of him before releasing two of the buttons of her blouse. He seemed to favor the lacy demi-cups she'd bought during a rare shopping spree at Victoria's Secret during an after Christmas sale.

"Is that purple leopard print?"

She grinned up at him and released another button. "Maybe." She cupped herself, tweaking her nipple so that it showed over the top of the lace.

"Fuck. Do that again. Peel it back."

"Like this?" She swiped her thumb under the lace to flick her nipple. She groaned because he liked it. She was learning not to hold back when they had spare moments alone. He tried to pull her back up, but she shook her head. "Just you tonight."

She tucked her fingers into his fly and jerked down his jeans without mercy. He hissed out a groan when she snaked her fingers up the leg of his boxers to tease his balls. She drew her nose along his rapidly hardening shaft.

Michael made sure to see to her every need. He usually left her in a heap of melted brain cells most nights, so it was rare for her to be able to take the lead. From the heat in his eyes, she was pretty sure he didn't mind just this once.

She lightly scraped her teeth over the cotton and molded each inch until she found his flared head. She cupped his balls with the hand still in his shorts, as she used the other to free him. The lights from their bedroom gave off just enough illumination that she knew he could see every move.

Michael was very visual. There was no hiding her flaws under the cover of night with this man. Then again, he never made them feel like flaws. He made her feel beautiful.

Always.

She slowly took him deep into her mouth. Deep breaths allowed her to take him down the back of her throat until he made a low groan.

"Oh, yeah. God, just like that." He slid his fingers along the back of her head, tangling them in the heavy curls she'd left down for him.

She knew he wouldn't try to choke her. As always, he was gentle with her to a fault. She wasn't really in a gentle mood tonight. She wanted to give back as he always gave to her. She bobbed her head over his head, and licked under his shaft.

His fingers flexed, but he didn't pull her forward. Oh no, she did that on her own. She took and took until her nose brushed the crisp hair at the base of his cock. He flung his head back and her name came out with a harsh emphasis on her first initial.

She hummed around him and pulled down his boxers to get to all of him. She pulled him free and gripped his shaft. She knew he liked a firm grip. She was forever worried she was going to hurt him, but he always seemed to want it just a little harder.

Then again, she liked when he thrusted inside her a little harder.

She liked when he lost control.

And he was going to tonight.

She took care to suck his balls deep into her mouth. Releasing them, she stared up at him as she licked the underside of his shaft all the way up to the head.

"I need..."

"Me," she finished with a slow grin. "Need to come in my mouth." She licked him, paying special attention to the vein that ran along his cock. She could swear she felt it pulse on her tongue. She twisted and pulled him, sucking strongly on his length until his eyes went wild.

"Fuck."

She took him deeper and quickly flipped her breasts out of the cups of her bra. It was exactly what he wanted. She tugged at her nipples and coasted up and down the top half of his cock.

"Are you wet for me?"

She nodded. She was always wet for him. She could probably rub herself on the seam of her jeans and take off right after him if she wanted to. But she didn't.

She wanted to watch him lose it for her.

Taking him deeper left him panting. She released her stiff nipple to go back to squeezing his shaft. To lift him so she could find all the pleasure centers. He throbbed in her hand and she knew he was close.

"Drink me down."

She nodded. Yes, she wanted nothing more than to feel him coming down her throat. She wanted him to fill her up. She gripped his hip with one hand and sucked. Her other hand slid up his belly to scratch through the hair there. The muscles flexed and firmed under her fingertips.

His cum burned down the back of her tongue and down her throat. She swallowed him, then milked him for more. She didn't let up until he was wrung dry and his legs were shaking. And she still demanded more when he was swaying in front of her.

Her feet were numb and her legs screamed when she stood up, but she didn't care. All of it was worth it to see every last bit of tension dissolve out of her man.

She sighed. *Her man.*

God, it scared her to say even that, but she knew it was true. Every inch of him was hers.

At least for now.

TWENTY-SIX

"I NEED WHAT?" CHLOE SKIDDED AROUND THE KITCHEN ISLAND, HER spatula aimed at the ceiling so her enterprising toddler didn't get his mitts on the raw contents of the ganache she was not-so-successfully making.

"No cheaping out on the honey," Harper said from off-screen.

Chloe glanced at the bear's face on the honey she used for baking. She sighed and took the good stuff out of the pantry. She usually saved it for when she needed a good cup of tea.

"Lila said he likes cherries."

Chloe snorted. "I can attest that he *loves* cherries."

Jazz's face filled the iPad screen. "Oh, really?" She looked over her shoulder. "Did you hear that, Harp?"

"I did."

"You know, I FaceTimed you guys to get help on the cherry-infused ganache, not commentary."

"Comes free with purchase." Jazz smiled.

Chloe was on her third batch and the last one had tasted like something she'd scrape off her shoe, not put on top of the coconut cherry cupcakes she'd found on Pinterest. She wanted a little bit of decadence to balance out the super sweet.

Not burnt tar.

It was their first Valentine's Day. She already had a two-year-old crashing her first romance-centric holiday, she was not going to have a crap dessert.

Her dad had called to let her know he had strep. No, thank you very much. And Lori's husband was finally home for a visit. Definitely no go there.

"Make sure the honey is dissolved before you take it off the heat. If you don't, it just screws everything up." Harper's voice came from the opposite end of her kitchen in the Hollywood Hills.

Jazz's huge blue eyes came into frame. "Catch that?"

Chloe looked down at her pot, finally noticing that the honey was, in fact, not ready. "Huh. Look at that."

"You should see us figuring out recipes. The grocery bill—wowsah. I swear Deacon and Gray are ready to take away the van some days."

Chloe definitely didn't have that problem. Michael was forever giving her grief because she spent hours poring over coupons. If he had his way, they'd have no budget at all.

And because she'd been spending so much time in the kitchen, she'd been talking to Jazz and Harper a lot lately. It was nice to have moms to talk to, as well as trade recipes with. "You liked my banana-apricot oatmeal swirl?"

Jazz nodded. "It was awesome. I gave it to Dylan this morning. The kid is a bottomless pit lately, but that filled him up for two whole hours. A true blue miracle."

Chloe could feel her cheeks heating. "I didn't mean to volunteer a recipe."

Jazz grinned. "Actually, Michael volunteered it. Getting him to eat anything that doesn't come in a rainbow-colored cereal box was all the testimonial we needed."

Harper peeked around Jazz's shoulder. "Actually, if you have a few more, I think I'm going to do an oatmeal chapter."

"I have one with apples…"

Harper stopped mixing whatever was in her huge bowl. "And…" she said expectantly.

Chloe gnawed on her lower lip. She was forever figuring out ways to get healthy food into both of the men in her life. "It's not traditional, but Michael practically licks the bowl when I make it."

Harper set the bowl down on her stainless steel table. "I want it."

"Maple-bacon jam swirl."

"Ding, ding. I knew you'd have something else. Can you email me the recipe? Actually, better yet, Jazz and I will come over next week. How's that? We'll make a test batch."

Surprise and pleasure battled for control of the lump in Chloe's throat. "That'd be great."

"How's the cherry ganache?"

Chloe lifted the iPad off its stand and brought it to the pot. "What do you think?"

"Perfect. Let it cool for twenty minutes. Follow the rest of the steps and you'll be golden."

Chloe blew out a breath. "Finally. I didn't think I'd ever get this thing right. I might even have time to shave my legs above the knee."

"Then it really is a good day." Harper grinned. "I'll text you and we'll figure out a time. Happy Valentine's Day, Chloe."

"Thanks. You too."

Jazz hooked her arm around Harper's neck. "She's my date." She gave Harper a smacking kiss on the cheek. "The guys have a gig."

"Then you get to watch all the sappy movies tonight."

"Damn right. *Ever After* is already cued up."

"Man, I love Drew Barrymore."

Jazz squealed. "I knew I liked you for some reason."

Chloe's smile went so wide, she felt her dimples pop. She'd wondered if that was ever going to happen. Being the fiancée of the man who tried to sue Oblivion for songwriting rights wasn't exactly the way to ingratiate herself into the family. Nick made her feel as welcome as possible, but it had taken a long time for them to look at her as anything other than an interloper.

Now, with her crazy marriage to Michael…well, it hadn't helped her cause. At least not until lately.

Harper and Jazz waved and called goodbyes to Axl.

Chloe checked the timer on her phone and started the next phase of the ganache building.

A text message popped up on her phone.

How many flat sheets do we have clean?

Well, that was a helluva question. She licked the side of her thumb and groaned. *There* was the right taste. She took the concoction off the heat and set it aside before running to the linen closet. Why the hell did Michael have six sets of sheets?

She'd never taken the time to count them, just swapped out the sheets weekly—for a few weeks, they were changed way more than that —as part of her routine.

6 King and 3 Twin, why?

He replied with an emoji sticking his tongue out. How very Michael. She rolled her eyes and went back to work. After the baking was done, she set the cupcakes up on the top of the fridge. It was really the only place safe from both Michael and Axl.

By the time Michael got home, she was sweating her butt off and she was contemplating selling her kid.

Her romance level was minus twenty-seven, and her patience was somewhere around the sub-basement of hell.

She'd managed to make cupcakes, but the meal she'd planned had been sabotaged by a screaming toddler who had no interest in giving his mother a break. He was a good child most of the time, but when a full blown tantrum hit, she was relatively sure he was the spawn of satan.

"Wow, what's going on in here?" Michael stood in the doorway, a huge bag in one hand as he nudged a huge box into the apartment with his foot.

"Welcome to bedlam. Happy Valentine's Day." She held a flailing Axl and narrowly missed an elbow to her jaw.

"Hey, hey." Michael set his bag down and kicked the door closed.

Axl wasn't listening. He was so far gone that his sobs had hiccups and bubble snot. She tried to shift him to her other hip, but instead, she yelped and had to set him gently on the floor before he took a header.

"Hey!" Michael's voice boomed through the room and Axl went quiet.

She opened her mouth to yell at him. It was okay for her to flip out on her kid, not him.

Instead of continuing to yell, Michael crouched down in front of a hiccuping and wheezing Axl. "What's going on, Ax-Man?"

He didn't answer. Instead, Axl shoved his fist into his mouth and gnawed on his finger.

Chloe blew out a breath. "He's teething."

"Ahh." Michael sat down and crossed his long legs, then picked Axl up off the floor. "Why are you giving Mom such a hard time?"

Axl gave him a whiny grunt in answer.

"Words, pal."

"Cake."

Michael looked up at her questioningly.

"I made cupcakes for later."

"We don't get cake until after dinner. Mom's rules. Even I don't get one, right?" Michael gave her a hopeful glance.

"No. No cupcakes for anyone."

"See?"

Axl started his humming scream. Michael had about eleven seconds before he was back into screaming mode.

"So, I got Mama something for Valentine's. Think you can help me?"

Axl tipped his head to the side. "Mama."

"Right." He looked over his shoulder. "See that big box?"

Axl struggled to get up and wobbled his way over to the box. He peered over the top, then back at Michael. He lifted his arms. "Up."

"The unfairness might require that I kill you in your sleep tonight."

Michael laughed and got to his feet. "Why don't you go get cleaned up?"

She flinched.

"You look amazing as always, but I bet you'd love to get that stream of snot off your neck."

Well, that was romantic. "You seem to keep saving the day."

"Nah. He still doesn't know what to make of me." Michael kissed her forehead, then turned back to Axl. He lifted him up and set him in the box.

She frowned. "Did you bring home an empty box?"

"Many empty boxes."

"Do I want to know?" She shook her head. "You know what? He's not screaming, so I don't even care."

Michael grinned at her. "Go on."

"Dinner is ruined by the way," she said as she walked away.

"We'll have hot dogs."

That was exactly what she wanted for the most romantic night of the year. She left them to their laughter and boy antics. She took the monitor into the bathroom with her just to make sure the meltdown was truly over.

Frustration and an Axl tantrum knotted her up like nothing else. She turned the steam on in the shower and stood there for ten full minutes as every muscle unlocked. The last month had been amazing, and having help was more than she could have ever wished for.

It still smarted that Axl had taken to Michael so easily. It had just been them for so long. Sure, her dad helped out, but the two of them had a system. They'd grown together, for God's sake. But she couldn't deny how amazing Michael was with her son.

She stepped under the streaming water and let it beat down on her shoulders. She was so careful not to share him with anyone—to make sure that she was enough for Axl because she had to be. She could only rely on herself. Her father had come a long way since she'd gotten pregnant, but she remembered too many years where she'd been left alone.

When she'd had to parent herself because hers didn't know the meaning of the word.

She swore that would never happen to Axl.

And she'd kept that promise to herself. But now there was Michael. And she wanted to let him in. It terrified her how much she longed to lean on him—to let him share the load.

How many nights had she dealt with teething, tantrums, and tears all on her own?

Hundreds.

As amazing as Axl was, he was still a two-year-old. He was still a baby—*her* baby.

The screech had her ducking her head out from under the water, but delighted laughter came in on the tail end of his scream. So, she took the time to primp and shave.

She might be a mother, but she was also a woman. Maybe she could salvage something of the night when Axl went to bed. Being a single parent...

No she was currently a *co*-parent. She could call it whatever she wanted, but that was what they'd been doing for weeks now.

And parents had to do this. They made plans work, and they adapted to setbacks.

She took the time to smooth on the cinnamon blend that drove Michael wild. She blew her hair out so it was full and wavy. She even put a touch of makeup on so she didn't look like she'd been dealing with a bratty two-year-old all day.

Instead of the sexy lingerie she'd bought, she went with instinct and pulled on a see-thru cotton tank and a pair of boy shorts. She tugged on a pair of soft gray pants and a flowy sweater.

Comfort and her two boys.

It was a good way to spend Valentine's Day.

She pushed her sleeves up and her ring snagged. She stared at it for a moment. The little diamond that Snake had given her had been a talisman and a shield. It was time to stop hiding behind it. He was gone, had been gone for years.

He'd been fading away from her even before his accident.

She slid it off and tucked it into her keepsake box she kept in her bedside drawer. It felt weird not to have it on her finger, but a weight had also been lifted. She traced her finger over the black velvet box she'd put Michael's ring in.

She curled her fingers into her palm, then closed the drawer. She wasn't quite ready to put that on, but she was ready to move ahead.

Small steps. Those, she could handle.

She shut off the lights in the bathroom and their bedroom. When she walked through to the living room, she didn't even recognize the apartment. White sheets were draped up everywhere. A few in the cool grays and blues that were a hallmark of the colors that had been there when she moved in.

Now there were a few reds and golds mixed in.

In fact, their living room looked like a mystical bazaar. Tiny lights were strung up to each corner of the room. Michael had turned off all the other lights. Boxes were stacked in a haphazard house-like form. Giggles came from behind the little flap.

Her eyes misted. They'd done this for her.

Michael had done this for her.

"Knock, knock."

"Password," Michael said with authority.

She laughed. "Do I get a clue?"

"Pissa."

She pressed her lips together against a full laugh.

"Password," Michael whispered. "Piss is not a romantic word."

"Passerd."

Michael snorted. "Close enough."

She crossed her arms. "Still need a clue, guys."

Michael cleared his throat. "What's today?"

"Hmm. Tuesday?"

Axl laughed. "Nooo."

"It's not Tuesday?" she asked.

"No."

"Hmm. I'm pretty sure it's Tuesday."

"Mama!"

She peeked in and was shoved back by Axl. "Mama! Word."

"Valentine's Day?"

"Yay." Axl came out like a magician with his arms open wide. "Venentine's Day!"

She dropped to her knees and hugged him.

Axl gave her a big kiss on the cheek before wiggling free. "Dinner for you." He tugged on her arm. "For you."

"For me?"

"Yes." He extended the s and rolled his eyes. "Mika!"

"I'm ready, buddy."

Chloe crawled through the flap and found a carpet picnic set up.

Bright blue bowls were full of mac and cheese and hot dogs cut up in tiny, jagged pieces. A vase with pink roses sat in the middle of the TV tray that held their water glasses.

Michael sat cross-legged at the back of the little space. She couldn't stop grinning, probably because her guy had a huge shit-eating grin on his face.

"You did all this?"

"Nuh-uh." Michael nodded to Axl. "This one did."

"Oh, I see."

Axl crawled to her with a white cloth napkin and awkwardly set it across her lap. "Dinner." He nodded to her bowl. "Eat, Mama."

"Yes, sir."

Axl settled beside his bowl, then promptly dumped half of the contents on Michael's makeshift table. They all laughed. And it was the best macaroni and cheese and hotdogs she'd ever tasted.

The next hour was a delightfully crazy family dinner. After the dishes were cleared away, Michael swapped out the table for huge pillows and they all cuddled up for story time. She'd never laughed so much with her guys.

Actually, that wasn't completely truthful. She'd laughed more in the last month than she could remember doing for two years. Michael might have moments of child-like wonder, but they were balanced with the hot looks he gave her.

He snuck kisses in over Axl's head as they plowed through a half dozen of Axl's favorite stories. Even her little boy's excitement over his very own fort couldn't keep him awake. Eventually, his head was heavy on her shoulder and his deep breathing signaled lights out.

Michael smiled. "Why don't you tuck him in, and I'll clean up?"

"Are you sure? You already did way too much."

"Axl did it."

She shifted her not-so-light baby onto her shoulder. "Thank you, Michael. Truly. I thought this day was going to end up a complete dumpster fire."

"There's an image."

She cupped the back of Axl's head. "I will thank you properly very soon."

"Now, that's exactly the kind of thanks I was looking for."

"I just bet."

Michael leaned in to kiss Axl's cheek and paused. His eyebrows shot up as he smoothed his thumb over her right ring finger. "Chloe?"

"I'll be right back."

He swallowed thickly, but only nodded.

She ducked out of their warm little cocoon and brought Axl down to his room. She took a few minutes to get him out of his clothes and into pajamas. He almost woke up, but only enough to ask her to sit with him.

Within five minutes, he was already back in dreamland. She paused at his door, looking over his tousled red curls with the sides shaved up like Michael's. Her little man was becoming a person, not just her baby.

With a sigh, she turned on his little sea life nightlight, then closed the door.

She expected the skeleton of the fort that Michael had built. Instead, she got a fairyland with soft music. Little electric tealights were lined up along every available shelf. He'd rearranged the sheets to make a drape around the mound of pillows.

All the food had been cleared away and a newer, larger vase of flowers was tucked into a corner. Huge lilies and daisies made a spring bouquet. Not traditional—because, of course, why would it be traditional with Michael Shawcross at the helm of this fantasy?

He was setting a champagne bucket down outside the pillows. Neither of them had drank much more than a social drink since Vegas. She expected to see some bubbly since it was a special occasion, but no, he'd thought of everything. A one-liter of her Diet Coke, and one of his Dr. Pepper sat in the crushed ice.

She blinked away tears, and couldn't stop a laugh from escaping.

He spun around on his heel. "Damn, I wanted it all set up before you came out."

She shook her head. "You are a wonder, Michael."

He shrugged. "First V-Day with my girl. I had to show up, right?"

"Most guys would buy a balloon and a pair of earrings."

He poured a flute of soda for her, then one for him. "We're not most people."

"You got that right."

"To us. The first of many."

She clinked her glass to his, then took a small sip. "I like the sound of that."

He took one as well—it was bad luck not to drink after a toast after all—and set them aside on one of their end tables. He drew her into his arms and they slow danced in a semi-circle. She pressed her face into his neck, drinking in his scent and his neverending warmth.

Not just his body heat, but the truest essence of Michael.

How could she have thought he was so simple and selfish? There truly wasn't a selfish bone in his body. He liked to tell her that he'd changed for her, but she had a feeling that he'd been just as generous all his life.

"Tell me I'm not imagining it."

She smiled into his neck. She knew what he was asking about. She wasn't going to play dumb about it. He deserved so much more than that. "You made tonight magical. Even before I came out to find my Axl fort, or this beautiful set-up, you'd already made this the perfect Valentine's Day."

He pressed a kiss to her temple, then down her cheek to the corner of her lips. "It was already perfect because I had someone—two someones—to come home to. You have no idea how amazing it is to not be alone for the first time in a damn long time."

"I have a feeling you didn't spend many Valentine's Days alone, buddy."

"Actually, I spent almost all of them alone."

"On the single man's guaranteed day to get laid?" She snorted. "I doubt that."

He shrugged. "There was always too much pressure associated with the day. I never wanted to disappoint anyone."

"Or to get tied to anyone?" she asked quietly.

"No. That's very true. Not until you." He sipped at her lips as they swayed to the music.

She linked her arms around his neck and let him lift her up. He curled her legs around his waist and slowly lowered her to the makeshift bed. There were little windows for their kisses to move to a more steamy level, but neither of them seemed to want to take it there.

Long, slow kisses and touches left them both restless. He nosed aside her sweater to find the sheer tank under it. "You are the most fucking beautiful woman on the planet."

She slipped her fingers through his hair. She knew that wasn't true, but the way he said it—the way he almost snarled it sometimes—made her believe he meant it. To him, she was. And it was truly the most astounding realization to hold onto.

He teased her nipple through the shirt, taking his time to keep her in the same soft, filmy space he'd created. So often they careened through the steep incline and drop off of sexual gratification. He loved to show her just how much pleasure could be squeezed out of each moment they spent together.

Tonight, he didn't push. They drifted on soft sighs and even sweeter touches. He slid down her body, taking her clothes off with sweet, lingering touches. And for once, he allowed her to reciprocate.

She rolled him onto his back, drawing his jeans down his long legs, until they were groaning through their laughter to get each other naked. He tried to flip her onto her back again, but she didn't allow it. She wanted a little piece of control for once.

She traced the tip of her tongue along his collarbone to the tendons of his Adam's apple. She sipped over his chin to find his lush mouth. Their kiss ramped up to a desperate clash of tongues and lips. She wanted to slow it back down, but there was always a piece of chaos living inside them when they got skin-to-skin.

"Protection," she groaned into his mouth.

He nodded and reached above his head.

She grinned down at him. "Such a Boy Scout."

"I don't think I ever got to do this in the Boy Scouts."

She blinked. "No way."

"What? My mom looked for ways to get me out of her hair. Prep school couldn't hold me, so…" He shrugged. "It was fun."

"The things you learn." She rolled her hips, dragging her cleft over his shaft. He groaned and arched up against her. She rolled the condom over him and took him inside within the space of a heartbeat.

His eyes flashed wide. Normally, he took his time to make sure she was ready for him. There was no doubt that her body was prepared for him, but her heart stuttered over the complete and utter connection that happened the moment he joined with her.

She slowly took him inside her again and again. Pleasure swamped her and the sweet wash of love threatened to take her under. He was her own personal undertow full of danger and power. But he never drowned her.

No, he was the current that slowly washed away her doubts and left only bright shells and clean, perfect sand in his wake. She laced the fingers of her right hand with his left, dragging his arm above his head.

She bit her lip against the rising groans that wanted to escape. When the pleasure got too big, and her heart too full, he rose up enough to catch her mouth. He swallowed the love that she couldn't hold back and gave it back to her measure for measure.

His name was a shuddering breath as she collapsed on top of him, her body shaking in reaction. She curled her arms around his neck as he clasped her tighter, their hearts racing and syncing before they slowed.

She drifted away with his heartbeat at her ear, and his sweat-slick skin sheltering her through the night.

TWENTY-SEVEN

Damn, what a beautiful day, even though it was barely the freaking crack of dawn.

Michael stood at the little breakfast nook in the kitchen, looking out at the ocean. The sun had already started to rise, and the breeze had stirred up some foamy white caps on the water. Some intrepid soul had taken out a sailboat with brightly colored sails.

He shoveled in a mouthful of apple-cinnamon oatmeal made by his resourceful wife. He'd have to show Axl the boat. He'd love the colors. Maybe they should get their own. God knows he was in the right location for one. Could launch it right within view of the apartment. Axl loved water, and he'd probably love going for rides, assuming Chloe didn't freak out about all the dangers.

Hey, that was what lifejackets were for, right?

The slap of bare feet on the floor and high-pitched giggles made Michael stop demolishing his breakfast long enough to look up as Axl shot into the room like an unsteady bullet. The kid was as naked as the day he was born, and his wet red hair was spiked up in his version of a Mohawk. Ever since the boy had noticed how Michael styled his fauxhawk—when he even bothered to mess with it—he'd insisted on Chloe styling his hair like that too.

Fuck, it was cute as hell.

Michael set down his bowl and darted around the table to grab Axl mid-run as Chloe charged into the kitchen after him. Axl squealed with laughter and she stopped to pant.

"You know better than to run around naked, young man." She glanced at Michael and lifted a brow. "Though I know where he's getting it from."

"Imagine her blaming me, huh, kiddo? It's not my fault. Guys just gotta be free." Michael swung Axl up over his head and the baby shrieked and giggled. "Nothing wrong with getting some air on our manly parts. She just doesn't get it, does she?"

Axl flapped his arms as Michael swooped him through the air. "Nekkid! Nekkid!"

"Thank you. You've now guaranteed he won't put on pants no matter how much I beg him." Chloe sighed and crossed her arms, but there was no missing her smile.

She wore one pretty often lately, and Michael didn't think he was imagining that he might be part of the reason. No doubt about it that she was a huge portion of why he found himself grinning and laughing a hundred times more often than usual. His newfound happiness definitely had something to do with his band doing well, but it was mostly due to Chloe and the squirmy kid in his hands. Axl was beaming down at Michael as if he'd hung the moon and tossed up a few stars for good measure, like he often did since they'd moved in.

It wasn't all hearts and roses. Adjusting to living with a woman and a baby wasn't easy. Not even close. As good-natured as Axl was most of the time, he also shrieked and cried when he didn't get his way, and he woke up in the middle of the night with nightmares at least once or twice a week. Two nights ago, Michael had gotten up with him while Chloe got some desperately needed rest, and he'd resorted to a few fanciful lies so he could go back to bed himself. He'd insisted to Axl that he'd vanquished the monster in his closet with fire, and now, the monster was just a pile of ashes.

Probably not the healthiest image to put in the kid's head, but eh, he was learning as he went.

But Chloe was starting to trust him to take care of Axl too. When the baby bumped his leg on the coffee table during a movie, she'd hung back while Michael patched up the scrape and doled out kisses and a snack. It still felt kind of weird, like he was on the world's longest babysitting adventure. Eventually, he'd probably get used to her and the kid being his. He was still expecting them to vanish if he closed his eyes.

He absolutely did not want them to go anywhere. They made his place feel less like a place to crash and more like a home. He'd never really had one of those—at least not in the traditional sense—other than with Lila and her parents. Her family's orchard back in New York had always been one of his favorite spots. He couldn't wait to take Axl there once spring sprung in New York. Lila's mom and dad would get such a kick out of Axl. He was their first great-grandkid after all.

And yeah, he was getting ahead of himself, and he'd long ago stopped caring. Chloe and Axl being part of his home and his life felt good. *Right.* He didn't care if the timeline seemed crazy to some. He'd finally found what he hadn't had a clue could even exist for a guy like him.

Home. Family. Something more important than a quick fumble and bounce in the middle of the night. Romantic holidays weren't just a reason to find a chick and get laid. They actually had true meaning.

Christ, the night he'd spent with Chloe on Valentine's Day a couple of weeks ago had been a damn near religious experience. Forget sex. Forget making love. They'd laughed and they'd loved and then they'd gone to sleep in each other's arms.

When Axl woke up crying, they'd stumbled toward him in the middle of the night like any other couple. Like parents.

Good thing they'd had that night to be intimate together too. Any naked encounters they'd managed since had been between Axl feedings and Axl crappy sleep and long, irritating rehearsals and Chloe crashing after cleaning his house from ceiling to floor, in spite of his admonitions not to bother. The whole parenting thing kind of killed much more than quickies most of the time

"Chopter?" Axl asked, still winging his arms up and down as Michael swung him through the air. Doing it didn't involve much thought, since the kid would've been content to fly around that way for days.

"Chopper," Michael corrected, since it was one of Axl's favorite words but he never quite got it right. "Yes, you're just like a chopper. Not quite that high though. Someday we'll go on an airplane. Would you like that?"

Axl's big brown eyes got even bigger as Michael brought him in for a landing in his arms. "Plane?" He craned his neck comically to find Chloe. "Mama, plane?"

"Yeah, baby. Someday we'll go on a plane." She came closer to scoop her fingers through Axl's floppy hair. No matter how much gel Chloe used, he had a bit too much to pull off the same look Michael had.

"Don't even have to wait for someday. My dad has a jet. We could take it out anytime you wanted." He propped Axl on his hip. "Go up to San Fran sometime maybe, show Axl the bridges and the zoo. They have some incredible B&B's. And you're not feeling it," he said as Chloe glanced away.

"A jet, Michael? Really?"

Michael shrugged as Axl chewed on the sleeve of his Nine Inch Nails T-shirt. "It's just a plane. A large one," he acknowledged at Chloe's raised brow. "My dad won't care if we take it, as long as we schedule our plans around his business trips. He's in Venezuela right now. Has been for a few weeks actually."

Which was why he'd avoided hearing from his dear old dad thus far. Well, that wasn't entirely true. His father had left him a couple of text messages, usually with mentions of the news and needing to talk to him.

That conversation probably wouldn't consist of an educational father-son chat about the joys of marriage, so Michael had avoided him thus far. The jig would be up soon though, because his father was due back in the country anytime now—if he hadn't already arrived.

"Venswayla?" Axl asked, mangling the country name so badly that even Chloe laughed. Those worry wrinkles hadn't left her forehead yet, but at least her eyes weren't so heavy anymore.

"Venezuela, pal. We'll go there someday."

"Chopter," Axl said quite seriously, lifting his head from his gummy work on Michael's sleeve.

"Chopper." Michael laughed and handed him off to Chloe. "Go on and get dressed with your mama. Daddy's gotta get to rehearsal."

He hadn't meant to say it. He definitely hadn't intended to by design. That name was reserved for someone who had earned the title, and he hadn't, not yet. He hoped he was on his way, that one day Axl would want to call him that, but man, he hadn't wanted to force Chloe's hand.

"Sorry," he mumbled at her astonished look. "It was an accident."

"It's okay." Swiftly, she brushed back Axl's wayward hair. "C'mon, buddy. Let's go get you ready so we can go to the store. Gotta get groceries for the Ax-man."

"Chopter?"

She had to laugh. "Go fish. We're going in the car like usual." She shot Michael another glance and scurried out of the room.

Actually scurried, like a mouse fleeing a certain trap.

Well, fuck.

He went back to the other side of the table to pick up his oatmeal and resume his viewing at the window. Even though it had been only a few minutes, the mood had been broken. From jubilance to a regular family morning to the feeling that he was going to have what he wanted pulled out from underneath him, just because he wanted it a little too much.

Ry had tried to tell him a couple of times that this family thing wasn't real. You couldn't meet someone who was practically a stranger and build a life with them. Sure, that worked in movies and books, but in real life? No. He was setting himself up for a fall. Setting up Chloe too, and she had a child to think about, so really, he should know better.

But dammit, he didn't know better. He didn't want to either. What he wanted was *this*. Just this. A wife and a kid who he could love and be loved back. A real foundation for the rest of his life. His career was insane enough. The idea of screwing his way through a bevy of groupies had lost its appeal for him that night at the House of Blues.

Maybe most people didn't fall in love at first sight—or re-sight, in his case—but too bad for them. Because he had, and he was sick and tired of apologizing for it. Especially to himself.

Better yet, he'd fallen in love with Axl too. That had taken longer, probably due to the heap of fear that accompanied many of his interactions with Chloe's baby. Still, he was getting there. He could figure it out. Other guys had, and he would too. All he needed was time.

"Michael."

He pushed another spoonful of his now soggy oatmeal between his lips, chewed, and swallowed. Anything to give himself another second so everything he felt wouldn't be written in chalk paint on his face.

Hey, I love you. I love your son. Please give me a chance to get this right. Just don't go.

Forcing down the last of his oatmeal, he turned to face her. She'd changed out of her pajamas and now wore jeans and a thermal top. Her hair was in a bouncy ponytail and she wore the scantest amount of makeup.

He'd never seen anyone more beautiful.

"Hey," he said, putting his bowl on the table. The spoon clattered against the stoneware. Chloe had bought the bowls, a whole matching set of them. She thought he should have sets of things. Dishes, towels, socks. He was starting to agree.

Sets weren't half fucking bad.

"Hey." She gripped the back of one of the chairs. "Axl's playing in his room. I can't be long."

"We should get another one of those baby monitors. Sucks the other one broke."

"Yes. They're very handy. Not a good idea to turn your back on an almost two-year-old for a second. Did you mean it?"

Her rush of words nearly pushed him off-guard. She'd lulled him into a sense of complacency with the banal talk, then asked him the biggest question of his life.

"Yes." There was no hesitation. "I think of myself as his father. I know I'm not. I know you don't think of me that way either, but in my head, in here," he rubbed his fist over his chest then dropped his hand, feeling like a chump, "I do. And I can't stop it or slow it down. I don't want to."

She released a shuddery breath. "You know we're asking for trouble here."

"I know I was in trouble before you came into my world. But this?

This is the sanest I've ever been. All I'm asking for is something I never got, and never realized how much I craved it. A real home and family. Something that wasn't created out of money or convenience or social standing."

"Not created out of convenience?" She laughed, almost hysterically. "We wouldn't even be standing here if we hadn't gotten loaded and made out at a club."

"You're right. We wouldn't be, and I would've missed out the best thing in my life. So you know, go alcohol." He skirted the table and walked over to her, taking her cold hands in his. "The way we started was crazy. But the rest of us isn't. Not at the core."

"You're just trying to make up for something in your childhood," she whispered, her eyes far too bright for his liking.

"So? So what if I am? Aren't we all trying to make up for something or to create a new memory to erase the old? That doesn't mean I won't be good to you and good to him. I swear to you that I will. I'll do whatever it takes."

"I already know you'll be good for us. No one's been to us what you have been. It's like you swept into our lives and turned them into a fairytale. But what happens when the story's over? Then what?"

She pulled one of her hands free to rub at her cheek. He couldn't see any tears. Didn't want to. If she was crying and he was the cause, he'd kick his own ass.

"I don't think we can go back to where we came from," she continued brokenly. "Not after all…this."

"You've struggled so much. Emotionally, financially. Of course you wouldn't want to go back to what you knew before. I'll make sure you never do. You don't understand how much money I have, and it doesn't even matter to me. If something happens and this goes south, you and Axl will be protected. I promise you."

"No. God, no. You think I'm talking about money?" She rubbed her thumb under her eye again and he knew she had to be crying, even if the tears seemed to vanish the second they hit her skin.

More Chloe tricks. She had a million of them. That was how he'd fallen in love with her and her son so fast.

"So tell me what you mean."

"Of course the money makes life easier. I've always worked two and three jobs. I didn't love it, but working is what I'm good at. I do what is required of me and I provide for my child. He won't ever have to face what I have. Even though he doesn't have his father, he's not going to want for anything," she said fiercely.

"No. He won't." He caressed the knuckles of the hand he still held. "You've made sure of that."

"I was. I'd started to, and then there was you. You've already given him experiences he never would have had. He never had anyone who was like a father to him."

Something akin to hope surged in Michael's chest. "He had Nick."

"Nick is a friend to me, and to my son. But he was never like a father. He didn't tuck him in at night and hold him while he cried." She let out a watery laugh. "He didn't tell Axl he was going to use a flamethrower to kill the two-headed monster in his closet."

"You heard that, huh?" He had to chuckle. "That was a bit of a pop fly, but hey, it seemed to work—hey, hey," he said as she plastered herself to his chest. "What?" He stroked her hair. "What is it?"

"I could withstand you. It wouldn't be easy, and I'd probably wish I could punch myself in the face later on. But I could do it. What I can't withstand is you loving my baby. You *wanting* to love him, when I was never sure anyone would but me and my Daddy." She made a muffled sound against his throat. "Snake did. He would have, but God, he died and left us. He made another choice and picked something that was more important to him than me and his kid. I know it wasn't entirely his fault, but he still did it. And ever since, I've been trying not to blame myself for not being enough to save him."

Michael gripped her shoulders and eased her back though he wanted nothing more but to enfold her in his arms and never let go. But she needed to see his eyes. To know he was being honest. "You can't save someone else. It's not possible. You can love someone, and you can stand with them, and you can try to help. At the end of the day, it's their decision. Yours was to take care of the baby you'd made. You hadn't planned Axl."

She shook her head. "No."

"You never expected him, and he turned out to be the best thing that ever happened to you. Just like that night in Vegas for me. Except I got a two-for-one deal." He tipped up her chin as it quivered. Her eyes were swimming yet her tears never fell.

She had the biggest balls of anyone he'd ever known. Way bigger than his own.

"He chose drugs. I don't know all of the particulars of the story, but I know that much. I know he used for a long time, and he gave up the two best people he could have ever had in his life. I won't. There's nothing I would ever choose over you or Axl."

She shook her head. "You could change your mind."

"Not gonna happen. When I know, I know. You don't have to know yet, and that's fine. We have forever to—"

"Haven't you been listening at all?" Her exasperation made him grin, especially when she followed it up with a swift whack to the gut. "I know, and it scares the hell out of me. Taking a risk that could hurt him is selfish."

"He's not going to get hurt. You're not going to get hurt. Me, on the other hand..." He shook his head. "You just bruised my stomach, Red."

"You can take it."

"Probably." He gripped her hand and kissed her knuckles. "I most likely won't sue. I wouldn't mind a couple sexual favors though."

"I just bet you wouldn't." She grinned up at him and slipped her hand behind his neck. His favorite fucking thing in the world was the way she pulled him down to her for a kiss. No matter how many times she did it, every time he got as hard as a damn baton. "I suppose that could be arranged—"

The shrill cry had them breaking apart and dashing out of the kitchen toward Axl's room. They struggled to get out of the kitchen doorway at the same time, then grasped at each's other clothes to push and shove their way down the hall. Michael stepped into Axl's room first by a hair and found Axl pointing at his dresser. He wasn't even crying. "Lego."

Chloe inched past Michael and scooped up Axl. "The Lego hurt you?"

"No. Lego." He pointed at the dresser again and Michael kneeled down to look underneath the dresser.

Sure enough, a red Lego sat beneath it.

He grabbed the play piece and stood to give it to Axl, who beamed the second his chubby fingers closed around it.

"You screamed because you couldn't get your toy?" Chloe asked with a heavy sigh. "Though we shouldn't have left you alone so long anyway."

"No, we shouldn't have." Michael whipped out his phone and swiped through screens. "Ordering that baby monitor. Maybe we should spring for a camera too?"

"I think we're good for now." Still holding Axl, Chloe came closer and gave Michael an uncertain look. Then she reached up and grasped his neck, bringing him down to her mouth again. The kiss she gave him was decidedly more chaste than it would've been if they'd still been in the kitchen, but Michael had no complaints.

Axl screwed up his mouth as if he was deciding how he felt about what he'd seen. Then he stretched out his arms toward Michael. "Kiss."

Michael's stomach twisted as if he'd been pummeled by two tiny fists. He had been, for all intents and purposes.

Michael tucked his phone into his pocket, then lifted the baby out of Chloe's arms and gave him a loud smacking kiss. Axl giggled and flung his arm at his mouth to wipe it away, but he was all smiles.

So was Chloe.

Switching Axl to his hip, Michael slung his arm around Chloe's shoulders. "So you guys off to the store?" He buried his face in Axl's red hair. The smells of baby powder and Michael's minty soap clung to the kid and made him ridiculously happy.

Everything did.

"Yeah, we're low on supplies. I wanted to get a pork loin for dinner, and someone needs diapers." She poked a finger into Axl's Mickey Mouse-covered belly.

Axl scrunched up his nose. "No."

"Yes. You've got a ways to go until you're potty-trained, bucko."

Axl glanced up at Michael. "No."

Michael had to laugh. "At least his mind is made up."

At the front door, he passed the baby to Chloe and decided to test his luck by drawing her in for another kiss, equally as chaste. Axl showed his approval by pushing his face in between for a kiss of his own.

Chloe grinned and picked up the baby bag she'd left beside the door. "So rehearsal today?"

"Yeah, all day probably. Show Friday night at Vista."

"Cool. Maybe we'll stop by for a little while."

Unreasonable pride swelled Michael's chest. A music studio wasn't the typical workplace for a dad to show off to his kid—and fuck if that wasn't weird to think, but nice—but it still counted. "Really?"

"Sure. If we won't be in the way."

"Are you kidding me? You'll inspire me to new heights." He kissed her once more then planted one on Axl's forehead. "Be good for your mama at the store, all right, Ax-Man?"

Axl smiled sweetly. "No."

"Sounds about right." Chloe huffed out a breath and threw the strap of the baby bag over her shoulder. "Good luck at rehearsal. See you later."

Love you.

He nearly said the words. They were right there, but at the last second, he swallowed them. "Thanks. Have fun shopping."

She rolled her eyes. "Funny man."

He shut the door and pried his cell out of his pocket. Instead of completing the order still on his screen once he swiped the phone awake, he just stood there and grinned. Dopily, he was sure.

Being nominated for a Spectrum award hadn't made him half as frigging happy, and he'd been over the moon for that one.

He loved Chloe and Axl, and he was pretty sure Chloe loved him back. On the way anyway. Axl was harder to peg, but he'd take his chances there too.

They had time. All the time in the world.

Michael completed the baby monitor purchase and started to slip his phone back into his pocket. He needed to get his stuff together for rehearsal, and shit, he was still hungry. Maybe he'd slap together a sandwich and stick it into one of those little plastic containers Chloe left everywhere for Axl. She had enough little boxes and baggies for Axl's snacks to keep him fed for a month.

The ringtone for his father sounded and Michael sighed. So much for his good mood continuing until practice. Then again, when better to deal with his father than when he was capable of deflecting anything rude he might have to say?

Forget might. Martin Shawcross used rudeness to keep people in line as a rule. In a case like this, he'd be in super attack mode. All he'd be concerned about was Chloe not getting a chance to put a finger on his precious money. Nothing else would make a difference. Especially not his son's happiness. That was probably at the bottom of the list.

He clicked to accept the call. "Hi, Dad."

"So you finally deigned to answer me, Michael."

"Can't answer a phone call you haven't made. You're the one who chose to text."

"I was between meetings. I've been out of the country."

"Yes, so I've been told. Thanks for sharing ahead of time. I might've called to tell you about Mom if I hadn't been informed by your secretary that you and your teen bride were gone yet again."

The teen bride crack was rude and uncalled for. Petaluma or Petunia or whatever his father's new wife was named wasn't a teenager. She was at least twenty-one, he was almost sure. But since the best defense was a good offense, he was ready for the attack.

"Petula isn't a teenager, and I don't appreciate your tone. The fact that you'd take it with me after what you just did is laughable."

"What I just did? What is that exactly?"

"You know what you did. You shacked up with a junkie's ex, one who wouldn't hesitate to filch every spare nickel she could to provide for her bastard."

Shock rendered Michael speechless for a full thirty seconds. "How dare you?" he spat. "You don't even know anything about her. Hell, you don't know a damn thing about me either if you think what we did is just 'shacking up.' That's what *you* do. Not me."

"And how would I know? You're not exactly forthcoming. You're no better than Malachi nowadays."

"Malachi was a lot smarter than I was. He stopped talking to you years ago."

His father rolled over Michael as if he'd never spoken. "I called your mother, and she had no information to offer me about the situation as you hadn't bothered to fill her in. So my next step was your former stepmother, as I know you've always been cozied up nice and tight to her bosom."

The jab in his back wasn't unexpected, nor was the feeling of betrayal. Of course Lila wouldn't hesitate to badmouth Chloe. She would figure she was protecting Michael too.

Even if she gave ammunition to a complete asshole.

"And?"

"Lila wouldn't tell me much. She's spent too much time in recent years with trashy rockstar types, so I suppose she considers herself more part of that crowd now than a responsible parental figure for you. Besides, that wasn't quite what you saw her as, is it?"

Michael gripped his phone to keep from pitching it at the wall. "You have no idea about my relationship with Lila, but I can guarantee we have more of a real one than you ever did with her—or any of the other females you trot out like fancy pet poodles."

His father chuckled. "Right. Your relationship is so real that she didn't even do her due diligence to help you out of an unfortunate mess. She just stepped back and let you live your own life, as she called it. Well, son, be grateful I'm not the same kind of person as your former stepmother. You're always my first concern, not my own personal life."

The irony of that made Michael choke out a laugh. There was absolutely no humor behind it whatsoever. "Right. Your personal life never mattered to you. That's why you're having baby number two with a woman you barely know while your sons are practically strangers. And why is that? Because you've proven where your priorities lay, and it's never with your sons."

"Speaking of babies and women you barely know, I want to reassure you. You're not stuck, no matter how much you think you are."

"I'm not fucking stuck. I'm right where I want to be. Axl is going to be mine, and Chloe is my wife—"

"Wrong answer. That baby is her brat, and not your responsibility. And Chloe Adams is not your wife."

Michael barked out another laugh. "Because you say so? You

weren't fucking there. I have the marriage license and I have the rings—"

"You filed for a license, but you never married her. You got to the aisle, and you stopped it at the last minute. She never said I do, and neither did you."

Pain slashed through him so fast that he nearly doubled over. Of course he'd said "I do". He had to have said it. But of course he didn't truly know.

Because he couldn't fucking *remember*.

"You don't know that. You can't," Michael breathed.

"I have proof. I have the video from the so-called ceremony. You didn't know they did those, did you? Insurance for the ridiculous chapel that took your money and gave you nothing in return. No refunds. But they make sure to cover their own asses with video proof, in case the brand new bride and groom come back the next day and don't remember taking their vows."

Michael sucked in breath after breath, but the oxygen didn't clear away the dots forming in front of his eyes. "You don't know what you're talking about."

"You'd be surprised." His father's tone turned taunting. "That wouldn't be you though, right? After what your mother and I have done with our marriages, you would never be like us. You'd never get married on a whim. Isn't that what you always said? I'm sure you loved your bride so much that you remember every single little detail. Isn't that right, Michael?"

Michael clicked off and threw the phone against the wall just as he'd wished. When it hit the ground, he stomped on it with the heel of his boot, slamming down on it again and again until it was in pieces.

It didn't matter. He could still hear his father's sly voice echoing in his head.

"She never said I do, and neither did you."

TWENTY-EIGHT

THREE DAYS.

For three days, he'd known he wasn't married.

Might as well have been a lifetime.

First, he'd struggled with the fact that he'd married a stranger. Who does that? A drunk asshole, that was who. Then when he'd begun to come to terms with that possibility, he'd had to face the reality that Chloe came with a baby. Axl was more of a toddler now, but still. He was damn small, and he had tons of needs, and Michael had never been around kids. Had never felt a huge draw toward them either. They seemed like too much trouble.

Loud. Impatient. Demanding.

Turned out they were all of those things. At least Axl was. And it didn't seem to make a bit of difference, because they were other things too.

Sweet. Loving. Soft.

Everything about Axl was so damn soft. His skin, his hair, his tiny fingers when they curled around Michael's. Sometimes he pushed and shoved, but for the most part, he wasn't too much of a wrestler.

At night, when Chloe gave him a bath and shampooed his hair into a mini fauxhawk like Michael's, he was pretty damn cute. And he smelled so good. Now and then, he was even quiet.

Somewhere along the way he'd decided he liked having a wife and a child. Instead of feeling scared by being counted on, he'd discovered he enjoyed it. Life had more meaning when someone needed you. When you needed them right back.

And fuck, even beyond that, he *wanted* them around. He could live without them, sure. He'd gone through twenty-plus years without Chloe and Axl in his world. He could carry on if they were gone. But why should he? Chloe's smiles made him feel like Superman. Axl's laughter triggered his own every damn time, no matter what kind of a mood he came home in. And band shit ceased to be quite as important.

Like Lila's not-so-subtle concern about Malachi's whereabouts.

"Donovan's talking about a full EP. He thinks the success of the 'In Your Arms' mix is a positive sign and that if you had more room to showcase your songs, you'd do even better. He's even mentioned a real tour. Across the US, Michael. His goal is to put together a package concert with a couple of the Ripper acts to get you all more exposure."

Michael scraped his fingers through his hair and leaned forward on the leather sofa in the studio. They'd been at it for hours to prep for tomorrow's show at The Troubadour. After Guns 'n Roses had played one of their reunion shows there, artists had been clamoring to get in. Lila had managed to book them a slot, but they were still working without a healthy drummer.

Ryan was back on the drums after the latest studio dude had split, citing creative differences, but he had to take lots of breaks. His failure to heal as fast as the doctors had hoped had sent him back to be checked out again, and they'd discovered he had a partial ligament tear. It wasn't bad enough to warrant surgery—yet—but the splint he put on as soon as he was off the kit didn't seem to be doing much.

All Michael could hope for was that Ryan would make it through tomorrow's set, and then he'd try harder to reach Malachi. Even trying to find a dude who clearly didn't want to be found was better than imagining what might be occurring behind the scenes with his father.

Martin's cryptic texts certainly hadn't reassured him.

I told you the marriage hadn't gone through so you wouldn't find out on TV. People are digging into what happened besides me. It's going to come out.

Knowledge is a weapon. You can be proactive. Come up with a story now. That's one thing Lila is good at, at least.

This is the best ending for this story. In time, you'll see. You're free now.

Free. Right. That was exactly what he was. He was free to not be married, though he liked it. He was free to not be tied to Axl and Chloe, though he ached for it with a fierceness that made no sense.

He'd wanted to keep the marriage going for two reasons—to save his shaky rep and because he didn't believe in divorce. In no time, he'd stopped thinking about his rep and started thinking about the man he should be. One worthy of having a kid like Axl and a sweet, smart, beautiful wife.

Drinking wasn't a part of his life anymore. Sleeping around absolutely wasn't. His idea of trashing a place now meant building a fort of boxes with his son. In the process of becoming a decent man on paper, he'd become one in reality too.

And now he was supposed to be glad he was free. Christ.

"Maybe I can drive out to Encino tomorrow," Michael said, popping the top on his cup of takeout coffee. "See if Mal's still living in the last address I had for him. I don't want Ry to get any more hurt because of all this."

"Don't worry about me." Ry leaned across the back of the couch and jabbed a knuckle into Michael's back. "Just worry about your situation."

Michael shot his best friend a glance over his shoulder. He'd confided in Ry that morning after about the twenty-third time Michael had fumbled the bridge to "Exile," despite the fact he'd nailed it flawlessly for months. So of course Ry had to blab in front of Lila.

Why not? His life already sucked.

Lila crossed her legs and set aside her iPad. "You spoke to your father, I'm assuming." She kept her voice low, and her blue eyes were surprisingly gentle.

Michael was so used to anything involving Chloe bringing out Lila's claws that he was immediately on guard. "Yeah, so?"

"I didn't tell him anything."

Michael stared into the little hole on his cup lid. He needed a refill. His coffee had gone cold.

No, what he needed was a real drink. Why the hell was he being so careful with everything if he was just going to lose it anyway?

Just tell her. Don't let her find out from someone else. You don't know that she'll leave.

He didn't. They were making progress. The other day they hadn't said "I love you," but they'd gotten close. At least he had. Then the thing had happened with his father, and he'd locked down his emotions and shut her out. Even knowing he was doing it hadn't been enough to cause him to stop.

That morning, she'd mentioned maybe coming to rehearsal again with Axl. She'd come on Monday, and he'd been so on guard after his father's phone call that he'd scarcely been able to get through practice. Somewhere around the fourth unsuccessful run-through of "In Your Arms"—thanks to Michael bungling his part each time—Chloe had finally made some excuse and escaped with the baby.

She was no better than Michael. She blamed herself every time stuff went wrong with them. Just like he did.

But cripes, he wasn't going to lie to himself. If she wasn't married to him, she definitely wouldn't stay in his apartment. He knew that without a doubt. She'd tell him it was best if she found her own place, and she'd get a job, and both of those things would be great for her if they made her happy. But he had a sneaking suspicion if she didn't have to stay around him, she wouldn't. She'd go back to her own life, and the distance would grow between them until she convinced herself they'd been some flash in the pan based on necessity.

And he would lose the family he'd only just begun to feel like he had a chance to have.

It wasn't like he didn't know all the Oprah advice. His mother was big on all that BS.

Just let people go. If they don't come back, they weren't yours to begin with.

Stuff that sounded just awesome on paper but not nearly as great if it meant you'd end up fucking alone.

He'd practiced that with Mal. How long had he let him do his own thing and let him be? Felt like frigging forever. Sure, Mal had eventually shown up again when he needed something. He'd left again just as quickly.

Now his older brother might as well be in the witness protection program. And Chloe would saw off her own tongue before she came to him for help if they didn't have those signatures binding them together. Even with them, she'd barely managed it.

So what the hell was he supposed to say to his stepmother? Yes, he'd talked to his father, and yes, he was denial, and no, he didn't want her advice.

As the silence between him and Lila extended, Ryan cleared his throat. "Okay, so that's my cue to leave. I'm going to grab a couple of drinks from that café down the street. Need the walk to clear my head. You guys want anything?"

"Whisky would be good," Michael muttered, rubbing the back of his neck.

"You're not drinking again," Lila said. "You're never going to hold on to Chloe if you self-medicate. You know that, right?"

Michael stared at her. "Self-medicate? Is that the California term you're using now? I didn't self-medicate. I drank because I needed—"

Not to think.

"It helped me to have an even better time. Is that so wrong?"

Ryan cleared his throat again. "Guys, I'm going to take off. See ya in a few."

"No. You're an adult and you're free to make your own choices. But with Chloe's past with Snake, there is no way in hell she'd be with a man who abused any kind of drug or substance. Trust me, I know. After your father, at the first sign that Nick might be with someone else, I split. He wasn't, and I jumped the gun. My psyche was sitting on the trigger because of my past."

"No more Oprah, all right? I get enough of that in my own head."

Lila's brows knitted. "Oprah? Hardly. Try Lila Crandall. I'm just saying you're going to make happen exactly what you *don't* want to happen if you scurry back into a bottle."

"How do you know what I want to happen?"

"I've been with you these past weeks. I've seen how you've changed. Just because your father threatened you doesn't mean you have to use a grenade on your life first."

"What do you mean he threatened me?"

She gripped her iPad until her fingers went white around the knuckles. "You know how Martin operates. He was never going to let you share his money with Chloe. Even if it's your money by rights, thanks to the trust. That's just not how he operates." Briefly, she shut her eyes. "I'm sorry I ever appeared to be siding with him. I was just worried about you. I'm sure Chloe is a lovely girl. We just got off on the wrong foot because of Snake, and because of Nick." She opened her eyes and stared directly into Michael's. "Because I was jealous of her."

Michael tightened his hand around his cup. "You're admitting it?"

"She said some things to me on the plane ride back from Vegas that struck too close to home. I've had time to examine myself and my motivations. Talking to your father helped remind me of who I am—and who I'm not, and don't ever want to be out of a misguided idea that I could possibly know what's better for you than you do. I don't. And even if I still believed I did, I've seen you these last weeks, Michael." She leaned forward and squeezed his wrist. "You've been better with her. More yourself, like the boy I used to know." She sat back and sighed. "You were always too sweet. I worried about you."

He started to argue the *sweet* label. What man wanted to be labeled sweet when you could be called badass like Malachi would be called? But he wasn't badass. And drinking too much and being careless with people and possessions wouldn't make him so.

"I didn't know I'd want this." He ground the heel of his hand into the ache in his temple. "I like having a family, L. My own family. How was I supposed to know how good it would feel, when I'd never had one like this before?"

"You weren't. You couldn't." She sat forward and slid her arm around his shoulders. "You have no reason to beat yourself up for that.

Your mom and dad and me—we all gave you horrible examples. You did the best you could with what you had available."

His eyes were so dry that they burned. He'd cried after the phone call with his dad. He'd sat right on the fucking floor and buried his head in his hands, knowing full well he wasn't going to have enough balls to be honest. The idea of spelling everything out to Chloe and facing the repercussions—fuck, he wasn't man enough.

Would he *ever* be man enough to deserve them?

"I don't want to lose her," he said hoarsely. "He keeps telling me that I'm lucky to have a loophole, but it's not a loophole. He searched for a way so his money wouldn't be on the hook, and because I was drunk enough to get married to a near stranger, I was also drunk enough not to seal the deal."

Lila rubbed his back, just like she had when he was twelve and pissed about getting cut from the JV football team. "You know that statement doesn't make any sense."

"I do."

"But I still understand it."

He turned his head and smiled. "Because you're my mom."

Her eyes sheened and he held up a hand. "Don't. Do not cry, especially not because I've been a jerk to you for so long and now you think I've seen the light. I always saw it when it comes to you. You were the only good thing that came out of my father's relationships. The only thing," he repeated over the soft snick of the door opening. Ryan must be back from the café already. "Even when I hated them, I loved you."

Lila didn't respond. Probably some sort of mom sense made her turn around and drop her arm from his back. But it was too late.

Not because Chloe—and he knew it had to be Chloe, because he smelled her, for fuck's sake—had witnessed something she shouldn't. But he'd ripped the lid off his emotions, and the truth was right there, staring him in the face. He couldn't tuck it away and pretend. He loved her too much, and she deserved honesty.

She deserved for him to grow up and be the man he'd never been capable of being before this very fucking second.

"Can you leave us alone?" he asked Lila. The rest of the band had scattered before their break, so for the next few minutes, he and Chloe would have studio B to themselves.

Handy that the walls were soundproof.

"Sure. Of course." Lila rose and clasped her iPad to her chest, facing Chloe over the back of the sofa.

He still hadn't looked yet. He couldn't.

"Whatever you think you heard, you didn't." Michael shut his eyes. Chloe's expression must have been every bit as stricken as he'd feared. "He's my son."

Chloe didn't reply for so long that he pressed his fist into his forehead. If the whole Lila thing raised its head again—

"I know that." Chloe's soft, certain voice made him drop his fist. "He explained how things are between you, and I believe him."

Michael shifted to face Chloe, but she wasn't gazing his way. Her focus was solely on Lila.

"I also know you're not happy about us being together, and as a mother myself, I understand why you'd be concerned. You think I'm a gold digger."

Lila squared her shoulders. "No, I do not. I had my doubts, yes. I worried he wouldn't make a good choice. Now I see in you a maturity I didn't have at your age, and probably not even two years ago." She let out a huff of laughter. "You don't need my interference. You're both doing just fine."

Chloe didn't say anything. She'd probably been struck mute, just like Michael.

"I'll make sure the band doesn't come back in until you're through. Take your time." Lila squeezed Michael's shoulder, then left them alone.

The door closing behind her was like a starting gun going off. Both he and Chloe tried to speak at once.

And then they both fell silent.

"Where's Axl?" Michael asked.

At the root, that was most important. More than his feelings, or what he wanted or needed. That baby won every contest.

"He's with my dad." She twisted the strap of her purse between her fingers. "I wanted to watch you rehearse, but I hoped I'd get to do it sneakily."

Somehow his lips curved. "Why sneakily?"

"You've been off ever since we had our big talk the other day. I wanted to see if it had to do with me or the music. You can't be yourself when I'm around."

"You're so wrong, Red. I'm more myself with you than I've ever been any other time in my life."

She glanced down and he wanted nothing more than to go to her and brush back her hair. To tell her how much he loved her and loved Axl. But he couldn't say anything that might affect the reality of their situation. She should have every opportunity to make the best choice for her and her son.

Here we fucking go, Oprah. You better not let me down.

"You're right that I've been off since then. It doesn't have a thing to do with the band. My brother doesn't want to deal with me. Nothing new there. Before he didn't want to deal with me just by myself, now I've got a band full of baggage he's avoiding. But at some point, we're going to have it out. He can't just go into hermit mode. I've given him his space, and if he thinks I'm an asshole and wants nothing to do with me, well, he's going to say that to my face and make it stick. You know why? Because if I love someone, I'll wait an eternity for them to decide to love me back." He laughed and raked his fingers through his hair. "Christ, I sound pathetic."

"No, you sound loyal. You sound like a man who might not trust easily, but once he makes up his mind, he refuses to be dissuaded no matter what."

The corner of his mouth lifted. "That's better than pathetic."

"It has to be a weight, caring so much." She stepped forward to grip the back of the couch. "You're an insanely wealthy man, and that makes it hard to trust."

"Yeah, my hardships have been epic." He set aside the coffee he'd been holding like a prop. "You know what's hard? Seeing something you want so much, and not knowing if you're worth it. Not that you couldn't be worth it with work, but you're not there yet. And what you need to do to get there might be exactly what makes you lose your chance."

"I don't understand."

"No. You don't. I've left you in the dark. No longer. If you decide you want to be with me, that will be your choice. I won't influence you with artificial constraints."

"Michael, just spit it out before I dump that coffee over your head."

He chuckled and marveled that he could right before he told her the truth. That was one more thing she'd given him. Not just a family, not just a chance to see that sex could mean more. She'd given him laughter without expectation. Appreciation for the moment, even when it was more fucked up than he could've ever imagined.

"We aren't married, Chloe."

Before she could say anything to knock him off track, he outlined all of it for her. The phone call he got after she went to the store, the conversation with his father. He even showed her the texts.

"Considering what I know about Martin Shawcross, if the papers don't break the story soon enough, he will. He doesn't want me to be married."

Her gaze never wavered. He'd told her that he'd kept this secret for days, and her expression never changed. She listened, and she waited.

If he hadn't loved her before this, her patience in letting him spill his guts would've pushed him the rest of the way.

"To me," she said quietly. "Your father doesn't want me to be your wife."

His first inclination was to soften the blow. To make it go away entirely. She didn't deserve his father's cruel judgments. But she did deserve the truth. All of it, even the ugly parts.

"No. He takes apart pieces of a person's life, and he sees what he wants to. He did the same with Lila. He's said horrible things about her, insinuated things that were even worse. No matter what wayward thoughts I might've had toward her years ago, she never had them toward me. My father says otherwise. He perverts everything he can to suit his twisted worldview."

"So you not being married to me is basically his dream come true. You don't have to share your money with me." Her mouth twisted into a smile. "Little does he know I never would've accepted it." She looked away. "Well, any more than I already have. I've taken so much, and now we're not even married—"

"No. Don't say that. Don't even think about taking." He rose and came around the back of the couch. His ideas of keeping his distance were all well and good until he couldn't be close to her, couldn't reach out and touch her to reassure himself she was truly real. "Do you want to know what you've given me? You've given me a life I didn't think I'd ever have. Forget that, I didn't think I'd want it. I thought I was happy." He shook his head. "It took you and Axl to show me what a joke my life had become. Of course my father doesn't want me to have you. He has no clue what it is to love someone for who they are, not what they have."

Her eyes filled. "You love me?"

"Christ, yes. Why would I be so fucking mad we're not married if I didn't?" He took her hand and traced the spot that no longer held Snake's ring. It also didn't hold his, and maybe it never would. "I want you to wear my ring. I want you to be completely lucid when you say yes. Just like I want to give the same thing back to you."

She curled her fingers around his hand. "I love you too," she whispered. "I've never been more disappointed to not be married."

He laughed and pulled her into his arms, tucking his chin against her hair. "I'm not giving up on us," he said, voice low. "I'll never give up on us."

"Never is an awfully long time."

"It is. I have a feeling I'm going to feel every minute of it when I walk out of here, but that's what I'm going to do." He eased her back. "I want you to stay in the apartment."

She gripped a handful of his shirt. "You want me to stay there? Where are you going?"

"I have unfinished business with my brother. I'm going to get through the show tomorrow night, and then I'm going to go talk to the jackass. He's going to tell me he's not interested in being in a band, and I'll accept it. But if he thinks I'll accept losing him from my life again, he's got another think coming."

She smiled and blinked away the dampness in her eyes. "I'm betting on you."

"You don't know Malachi Shawcross. He's one stubborn son of a bitch. But so am I." He tucked her hair behind her ears. "I'm giving you time and space to see what you want. My being in your way just clouds the issue. The last thing I want is for you to confuse gratitude with love."

"You're telling me to stay in your palatial place yet you think I'm not grateful?"

"I think you'll be able to separate the two just fine if I'm not there to force your hand."

"It's not right for me to stay in your house without you. You've already been so generous. Too generous."

"It's not generous to provide for those you care about. The fact is, if you aren't there, I will be worried about both of you. That way I'll know you're safe and we'll both be able to take the time to make sure of what we want."

He already knew. He'd never been more certain of anything in his life.

When she didn't speak, he smoothed his fingers down the back of her hand. "I haven't given you any space to figure things out. I've been too busy insisting and prodding and pushing. You should get some time to yourself to decide what you truly want, interference-free." He tipped up her chin until their eyes were closer to level. "Either way, financially you're covered. If we end up as just friends, I'd consider it a damn good investment to help send you to culinary school and offset your expenses for your son." He blotted up the tear that slipped down her cheek. "Besides, I'm thinking I'd get delicious meals out of the bargain. And he'll probably be able to pilot the band jet when he gets older, so win-win."

"God, Michael." She arched into his arms, pulling his mouth to hers as she always did. Except this time, their rough, desperate kiss was tinged with her tears.

Maybe his too.

"Think about me," he said gruffly as he pulled back.

"I will. How can I not?" She withdrew something from her pocket and pressed it into his palm, then closed his fingers around it. He knew it was the ring without looking.

The ring he'd wanted nothing more than for her to wear.

"You should have that." Her throat bobbled. "For safekeeping."

Nodding, he fisted his hand around the sapphire and went to the door before he lost the ability to leave. "When you've made up your mind, you know where to find me, Red."

TWENTY-NINE

WELCOME TO THE JUNGLE.

Michael set off for Malachi's address in Encino after the show the next night. Lila had pulled her strings and gotten Jazz to sit in again, because Ryan needed time to heal and it was the frigging Troubadour. Mention a place with history like that and most musicians would give their left nut to perform there.

Jazz hadn't offered up any appendages, but she'd been happy to assist them. Molly had also been much sweeter toward her sister, since she'd finally realized that they were—to borrow an oft used term—up shit creek without a drummer.

The show had gone off without a hitch, and also without any unexpected fires. Ever since they'd performed at the Blue Rhino, older places made him nervous. He hadn't started having to carry Mylanta yet, but it still could happen.

At least they'd been able to salvage most of the Rhino, and they'd remodeled a significant portion of it to boot. Lila had made noises about Warning Sign booking another show once it reopened, but Juliet had been adamant about a different lighting crew overseeing things. For a former Boston blue blood, she could pull out some pretty colorful language when needed.

And when it wasn't.

Harper's brother, Randy, hadn't been to blame for the fire, but jeez, to hear Juliet talk about the guy she still called Sparks, anyone would've thought he'd been back at the board with a blowtorch or something.

Michael rued the day those two crossed paths again, if they ever did.

The drive to Encino was uneventful. Evidently, traveling after midnight was a good choice, because the freeways were emptier than he'd ever seen them.

He didn't turn on music. His only accompaniment was the hiss of the wind through the crack he'd left in the window. He was as awake as he always was after a show, amped and full of energy to burn. That usually led to him finding some cute chick to fuck, but not tonight.

Tonight, he was going to see his brother if Mal was still where he'd last lived. If he wasn't, Michael would drive to the nearest hotel and crash.

The one thing he had no intention of doing? Drinking. He might end up tossing back the contents of the water bottles stacked on his passenger seat, but that'd be all he chugged.

He pulled up at Mal's old apartment building and cut the engine. The place looked pretty snazzy from the outside. Michael remembered it had a huge pool and tons of amenities, but he also recalled that Mal had picked the cheapest apartment in the place and lived like a bachelor's miser cousin. Sparse hadn't been the half of it. In the old days, Mal had barely had a bed, some stuff on the walls—always weird crap like old bicycles or a sombrero he'd picked up in Mexico—a couch and a TV. And his drum set. He'd said that was part of the décor too.

Sure it is, brother.

Michael dug out the apartment number on his phone and went to the lobby to deal with security. He asked if Malachi Shawcross still lived there and got the stonefaced response typical at such places. They weren't swayed by Michael's ID revealing the same last name either.

What worked, however, was ringing apartment twenty-two and asking the desk to inform Mal that Phil Collins would like to come up.

Hey, Mal might not admit in public that Phil was his favorite drummer since his friends preferred Lars Ulrich or Dave Lombardo, but Michael knew the truth. And he used it.

He was buzzed upstairs, effectively answering the question if Mal still lived there. He took the stairs to the second floor and knocked on his brother's door, pushing his way inside without a hello once it opened.

And came face to face with a naked woman.

"Well, hello there. Mal asked me to get the door. Who are you?" The amply endowed brunette trailed a finger over Michael's still faintly damp T-shirt. He'd hopped right in the car without a shower.

That was him, always making a great impression.

"I'm his younger brother, Michael."

"I thought your name was Phil?" She wrinkled her nose then waved it off and shut the door. "Anyway, I'm Lucretia. Mal's in the shower. Want a snack while we wait?"

Since she appeared to be offering him her body as the platter—or at least that was the vibe he got—Michael shook his head. "I'm good, thanks."

"So tell me about yourself. Look at those biceps." She wrapped her fingers around Michael's upper arm and squeezed until he detangled himself and aimed for the couch. "You're in a band. I smell it on you."

Literally in this case, but he nodded. "Yep. Warning Sign. I'm here to convince Mal to be our drummer."

"Not gonna happen," Mal shouted down the hall.

"We'll see about that." Michael smiled at Lucretia. "So you're Mal's girlfriend?"

"Oh, darling. You're so sweet." She sat on the other end of the couch and plucked a glossy grape off the bunch sitting in a bowl on the coffee table.

Surprising for Mal to have a display of fruit, but maybe he was trying new techniques to woo the ladies. Although this one didn't seem to need much woo.

"That's me." Michael gave her a grim smile and directed his attention at the ceiling. "Like candy."

"I just bet."

Mal walked out wearing a towel and a snarl. "Didn't you get the message when I didn't answer any of yours?"

"No." Michael glanced at his brother and did a doubletake. He'd seen Mal shirtless at the show but somehow he looked even more massive tonight. "Jesus, dude, did you start doubling for Vin Diesel in the *Furious* movies or what?"

Mal ignored him. "Lu, do you mind waiting for me in the bedroom?"

"Of course not, honey." She rose and gave Mal a kiss heavy on the tongue—and under the towel groping. Then she wiggled her fingers at Michael and sashayed down the hall.

When Michael started to speak, Mal held up a hand. "Since I know you're a Boy Scout in a rockstar's clothes, I'll answer your question before you ask it. No, she's not my girlfriend. No, I didn't pay her, but that doesn't morally offend me as it might you. Yes, your timing sucks royally. Anything I missed?"

"Yeah. You got any advice for your little brother who accidentally got married in Vegas, then realized he wasn't but really wishes he actually was?"

Mal sank to the couch in the spot Lucretia had just vacated. "Okay, no. I don't. You got married? What the hell?"

"We didn't finish the ceremony, but we thought we had. It's a long story. You up for it? Nah, never mind. I don't really want to hear what you're 'up for' with Lucretia down the hall."

Mal shocked him by grinning. "She's enthusiastic. She probably has a friend or two if you're looking to get over the missus. I couldn't really tell from that crazy ass story. Married, seriously?"

"Yeah. Drank too much whisky. I don't recommend it, though damn, I got the most amazing wife and son out of the deal."

Whom he might have already lost, if Chloe changed her mind and decided he wasn't what she wanted long-term.

"Wait, son? You knocked her up too? Damn, what kind of whisky was that?"

Michael had to laugh. "No, she came with the boy. His dad was one of the dudes who used to be in Oblivion. You know Elle in my band that you manhandled? Well, Axl's dad was Snake, Elle's brother Nick's best friend."

"Hold up. Way too many names, and also, I didn't manhandle anyone. She was in my way so I helped her to move. Little Ricki." He shook his head and adjusted his towel. Good thing, since he'd been on the verge of showing off things Michael didn't want to see.

"'Little Ricki' flipped out on Lila and said she didn't want you in the band. The word *beast* was used."

"Did she now? I'd probably be hurt if I gave a shit." Mal stretched his arm along the back of the sofa. "Tell me, am I supposed to care that she doesn't like me? Or that Lila's been on my damn jock for almost two months straight when she didn't so much as send me a Christmas card for the last five years?"

"When you put it that way…" Michael shook his head to clear it.

He'd had a long drive, and he was more fucked up about Chloe than he wanted to admit. And Mal was so authoritative he could've probably convinced Michael to shave his head and join him at the chop shop.

Not that he'd bother. He much preferred Michael staying out of his lane.

"Why do you want me in the band so damn much?"

He had a number of reasons, not the least of which was that Ryan was hurt and had little interest in being their drummer full-time. But the biggest was much simpler.

"Because you're my big brother, and I fucking miss you. When we were on stage together, it felt like something special. You fit with us like you belonged there. Didn't you feel it too?"

Mal rubbed a hand over his head. "I told you, I'm not meant for the stage."

"Oh, yeah? Why the hell not?"

"Because I lost someone the last time I did the whole public performance bullshit, all right? And I don't want to sit here and pour out my heart to you, because the truth is I don't fucking have one left. So if you do, good for you. I wish you well." Mal rose. "If we're done…"

"Actually, no, we're not done. I'm camping out here for a while. My wi—Chloe has my place, so I need somewhere to crash."

Mal's brows lifted. "You gave your non-wife your apartment?"

"I'm hoping she'll still want to be my wife when this is all said and done. In the meantime, I'm giving her space." Michael grabbed one of the couch pillows and tucked it under his head as he stretched out. "Don't worry about me. I'll take the sofa."

"Don't worry, I wasn't. Did it ever occur to you that maybe you'd cramp my style?"

"No. You'll just fuck her and make me listen."

Michael turned out to be correct in his assumption. Six long hours later, he wished he'd remembered to bring in his bags from the car. Headphones would obviously be a crucial part of staying at Mal's.

One night there turned into two. Two turned into three. Three turned into more.

In no time, Michael had missed a couple of rehearsals, one for the biggest night of all—the Spectrum Awards. He hadn't formally decided not to go, but apparently, between being all stoic and shit with Chloe and moving in temporarily with the sex machine known as his brother, he'd lost some of his mojo.

They didn't need him for the telecast. His band could handle stuff just fine without him. Yes, they'd be performing, but only one song and Elle could fulfill his role. She'd be thrilled to take on lead duties for once.

He didn't want to abdicate his responsibilities. Hadn't he just given Chloe a big ass song and dance about becoming a good man for her? Too bad that only seemed to take precedence when she was actually part of his life.

"All right, asshole. You've spent enough time desecrating my sofa." Mal kicked the end of it. "Either shell out for rent or get gone."

"Where's the brotherly love?" Michael rolled over and groaned. He'd been in the middle of a particularly good dream about a naked Chloe too. She'd baked him a cake inscribed with the words "lettuce pray," which he didn't get, but dreams were weird.

"In that crater your ass created in my couch. Look, if you love her this much, why are you still here?"

Michael debated acting tough, like Mal would in the same situation. But he was not his brother, and his toughness had vanished in the face of many days of radio silence. "I'm giving her time to decide I'm the love of her life."

"Or to forget about you."

"That's a possibility too."

"While she's living in your pad and running up your utilities."

"I think I can cover her wild Wi-Fi and hot water usage," Michael said drily. "God, you are so romantic. My dick is practically quivering."

"This isn't about me. You don't see me crying in my cornflakes or skipping out on my responsibilities."

"No, you won't even take them on. Ryan can't play. He's going to go on stage at the show and he's going to be hurting when all you have to do to play drums is flex those mondo muscles and snarl."

"Wrong answer. These aren't my responsibilities. I get that you want me there, even need me there, and I'd like to help, but—"

"But you won't."

"You're talking open-ended. A life sentence. I don't even know what I'll feel like doing a month from now, and you expect me to sign on forever?"

"You'd be surprised. Sometimes even forever doesn't seem long enough." Michael forced himself up into a sitting position. "Okay, forget forever. Let's just talk a couple of months. How about that? Six months to start. If you decide by, say, mid-September that you're sick of the band, then you're free. No more phone calls, no more pressure."

"And Stepmommy Dearest is okay with that too?"

"She will be," Michael said confidently.

In truth, Michael had no idea if Lila would go for that plan. But she wanted Mal in the band, and six months of Mal was better than none.

Mal cracked his knuckles. "All right. You got yourself a deal. But now you're really coming with me to Mom's shindig next month, and I don't care if you've got your wifey back by then. I'm not dealing with that shitstorm alone."

"You got it. The way it's looking, I won't have my wife back next month or anytime, so you don't have to worry." He lifted his glass to salute Mal.

That it happened to be filled with last night's water seemed particularly cruel, but whatever. At least he'd kept his oath not to drink alcohol.

He hadn't touched a freaking drop.

His phone buzzed at his hip and he pulled it out. Lila. That was surprising not at all.

"One of these days you're going to have to answer her," Mal said.

"Why? You didn't."

"I can withstand a barrage from a woman way longer than you can, little brother. Might as well ante up and get it over with already. Maybe she'll have good news for you about the little woman."

Michael's brain was fuzzy from crappy sleep. Mal's couch sucked. "You mean Elle?"

"No, I mean your would be wife."

"She's not would be. She's my will be wife—if she ever speaks to me again."

Mal snorted. "Right."

Michael took Lila's call. "I have good news. Mal's in the band."

"Temporarily," Mal added, walking to the doorway.

"Temporarily possibly forever."

"Temporarily," Mal repeated, offering Michael a raised middle finger on his way out of the room.

"Well, that's some good news at least. Now, when are you getting your ass back to LA?"

Michael pulled at a loose thread on his jeans. Showering and changing his clothes had become optional since he'd been at Mal's. As had been taking note of how long he'd actually spent channel surfing on that crappy sofa. "I don't know yet. I need some time, L."

"What you need is Chloe back. And yes, I'm surprised I'm saying this too, but more than ever, I'm convinced you need that girl in your life. Whatever it takes, make it happen. Consider it a public service for your band and the world at large."

Michael nearly smiled. "That ball is in her court. Talk to her."

"Oh, I will be. Don't you worry. And since I'm fairly certain you have no intention of coming to the award show, I'll say this much— make sure you're watching. We're expecting some pretty big revelations."

"Big revelations, huh?" Michael fought back a yawn as he heard the shower turn on down the hall. Guess he'd have time to finish his nap, since Mal was occupied. "That sounds ominous."

"It just might be. Make sure you're watching, Michael. I mean it." She clicked off.

He rolled onto his back and tossed his phone on the coffee table. He might not have heard a word from Chloe, but at least he'd snared Mal for the time being.

Looked like he'd be glued to the TV tonight.

THIRTY

"Mika, Mama. Chopter."

"I know, sweetie. We can do yoga chopper. Finish up your oatmeal and we'll—"

"Mika!"

Axl's shriek sliced through her brain. Honestly, he'd been good for most of the last few weeks, but there were moments when he fixated on Michael. When Axl wanted his chopper rides, of course. Story time had caused a few backfires, and there had been one awful night where he'd been certain a monster was going to attack him in the hours between midnight and dawn.

It had taken staying up until daylight to prove that Michael had indeed slain the monster all those weeks ago.

Nights like that had tested her resolve not to sit in the middle of the floor and throw a hissy fit that would put her son's to shame.

She missed him.

Missed him with an ache so big that her entire chest felt carved out. She slept in their bed—when she actually slept anyway—and she washed in their shower. She even managed to stand on their balcony and soak in the ocean scent without wanting to fling herself off the edge.

Every moment felt a little more separate, a little less. The entire *place* felt less because Michael's booming laugh was missing. His shoulders didn't fill up the doorways, and his minty scent didn't infuse the sheets anymore.

She'd had a particularly bad moment in the shower as she bawled over his body wash.

So, yeah...she'd passed heartache and landed squat in the middle of pathetic. She'd nearly texted him a dozen times. Usually at two in the morning when she was at her weakest. He wanted her to take some time to figure out if forevers fit in a few short months of knowing him.

She'd known within half a heartbeat.

It seemed ridiculous to own that statement, but deep down, she knew it was true.

Her reaction to him on stage had certainly started her journey. Dancing in the club had cinched the lust factor. The only problem was that lust was easy. It was pheromones, hormones, and chemicals making the correct brew that ended in an orgasm if a person was lucky.

It was the love part that had snuck up on her.

The love part that she hadn't prepared for.

The moment she'd seen the love bloom in his eyes for her son, she'd been so very lost.

Chloe crouched in front of Axl's high chair. "I think we should go get Michael. Do you think that's a good plan?"

"Mika." He slapped the tray and crumbs and orange juice splattered both of them.

She laughed until tears started dripping from her stupid eyes. Yeah, it was well past time to go get him. She unbuckled Axl and swung him onto her hip. She was halfway out the door when she realized he wasn't wearing any pants.

Some things couldn't be corrected, no matter how hard she tried. Michael had broken her kid when it came to wearing clothes. She detoured into Axl's room and got him dressed, grabbed her purse, then opened her front door.

Juliet and Ryan stood in the hallway.

"Oh, thank God." Juliet pushed her back inside. "We need to talk, girlfriend."

"What are you doing here?" A sudden and visceral fear left her breathless. "Is Michael okay?"

"No, he's a hot mess. You guys are so fucking stupid." Her dark eyes widened. "Uh, sorry, child-like creature."

"Fuck!" Axl said with crystal clear clarity.

"Sure, you can say that word no problem." Chloe rolled her eyes. "Come on in."

"You need to fix Michael. He's broken, and I can't deal with a broken guitarist in our band." Juliet paced the length of her kitchen, then back to the fridge. She opened it and peered in. "Do you have something to drink?"

"Diet Coke or Dr. Pepper."

"Bless you." She rummaged around and pulled two out. She handed one to Ryan and cracked the top on her own.

That was fine, Chloe didn't want one anyway. Resisting the urge to kill Michael's bandmate might take a bit more than she had in her reserves.

Ryan sat at the table. "Don't mind Miss Rude here. Michael's been out of touch since you guys had your meltdown. He managed to play the show, but then he split."

"That's not like him." Chloe went to the fridge and pulled out a soda for herself, and a juice box for Axl. She plopped him back into his highchair and set the box down in front of him. She stabbed the box with the straw and took a quick sip so he wouldn't geyser it everywhere.

"Exactly." Juliet took a drink from her soda. "Michael's the responsible one. I can't be taking up that job in the band. We might as well break up now."

"No one's breaking up."

"Speak for yourself, Busted Hand Boy."

Ryan rolled his eyes. "She only has two modes, unconscious and manic. Ignore her."

Juliet set down her soda and propped her hands on her hips. "I'm standing right here."

"Could you stand over there instead? You're making the kid nervous."

Chloe held up her hand. "All right. I appreciate the whole banter thing you two have going, but you need to tell me where my husband is right now."

"See, the thing is, he's not your husband."

Before Chloe could open her mouth to give Juliet the verbal beatdown she needed, the woman flipped her long dark hair over her shoulder.

"But I have an idea about how we can change all that."

THIRTY-ONE

"THIS IS A BAD IDEA. IN FACT, I DON'T WANT TO DO THIS AT ALL."

Molly and Juliet tagteamed her on the side stage at the Spectrum Awards. "We've gone over this. You want Michael back, right?"

"Of course I want him back."

"Then this is how it needs to happen." Molly nodded as if it was all decided.

It so wasn't.

In fact, she was pretty sure she was going to hurl all over her borrowed shoes.

Chloe swallowed down the spit that was trying to flood her mouth. "I don't go on stage. That crap is all you guys. I'm perfectly happy— deliriously so—to stay on the sidelines."

"Look, Michael is a good guy."

"I know he's a good—"

"Just listen," Molly interrupted. She curled her fingers over Chloe's shoulders. "I'm giving up accepting an award on national television because I believe in you two. So you're going to walk on that stage and you're going to tell the world that you love him."

"Can't I just hold a sign above your heads while you're doing your speeches?"

"No," they both shouted.

Chloe's shoulders sagged. She nibbled the side of her thumbnail as one award after another was accepted. She'd rather hunt Michael down than do *this*.

Molly started bouncing. "Okay, we gotta go do the thing."

Chloe was pretty sure even her freckles went pale.

"Sing. We're going to sing, Chloe. You need to breathe or we're going to end up scraping you up off the floor. And seriously, you don't want to think about what's on this floor."

Yeah, that wasn't helping at all.

"Don't even think about escaping."

Chloe turned to Lila. "Oh, awesome."

Lila folded her arms. "I'm just here to make sure you don't flee into the night like your...well, like Michael."

"My husband. Because that's what he's supposed to be."

Lila held up a hand. "Agreed."

"Well, that's something." Chloe smoothed down the icy blue dress that was supposed to double as her wedding dress.

Wedding dress.

God, how dumb was she to do this? She banded her arms across her middle and bent at the waist. "Panic attacks are fine, right? Little dots aren't terrible."

"All right, calm down." Lila came up beside her. "Just forget the crowd of people out there and pretend you're talking into your phone."

"Sure. Really big selfie stick."

Lila let out a half laugh. "It's all about control. You need to own it. This is nothing compared to getting that man back in your life."

Chloe straightened slowly. "You know how I feel, don't you?"

"I almost lost Nick because I was afraid. Don't do the same thing. You were right, Chloe. We're not so different."

Chloe swallowed hard. "I love him madly. I hope you know that."

"I do." Lila smiled. "Now."

The panic subsided and Chloe could hear the applause from the crowd. Evidently, her insane freak-out had only lasted three minutes and some change. Good to know. It felt like it was about five times longer. "Big girl panties activated."

"Damn right," Lila said. "Now go on and get out there."

Chloe shook her hair back, then straightened her shoulders. *Own it.* Yep, she was probably going to own a front page spread thanks to her projectile vomiting on the front row.

She took a deep breath and walked across the stage as Warning Sign's name was called.

They'd been nominated, but as with a lot of award shows, they wanted to make sure the winners were actually at the telecast, so it wasn't exactly a secret.

Molly, Elle, Ryan, Juliet, and West crowded around the podium. All of them hopped up and down for a second. Molly waved madly. "Thank you guys so much. We really appreciate it. And if you don't mind we kinda want to do something really special for our lead guitarist."

Don't trip.

Don't fall.

Don't throw up.

Chloe got to the glass podium. "Hi. I'm Chloe Adams. Actually, it's supposed to be Chloe Shawcross. And this is a proposal going out from me to Michael Shawcross. You see, we did a crazy thing a few months ago. We got married after only knowing each other a few hours. Well, we thought we got married. Turns out we weren't quite as insane as people thought and at the last minute, we didn't go through with it. Mistake. Big one. I should have said yes, and now, I want to do the 'I do's' for real."

The crowd went nuts.

Chloe's heart was going to explode out of her chest.

She held up her hands. "Wait. Wait a second, guys. Michael, meet me at the Little Elvis Chapel at one in the morning and let's make it official." The crowd became a wash of flashbulbs and watery faces. She blinked back her tears and smiled. "I love you. More than I could have ever imagined." She stepped back and Molly and Juliet held onto her.

Good thing. She was pretty sure her ankles had dissolved.

The next few minutes were absolute chaos. Between the reporters and the people running the awards show, she was inundated with questions.

Lila handled them like a pro. Chloe was swept along between Ryan and West. A limo was waiting at the side door. They all piled in and headed to the private air strip where Donovan's plane was waiting.

Donovan Lewis came through again.

Just how much was jet fuel? Did she have to give him her second-born kid to cover the fact that they'd done this a second time?

Where was her kid? "Did my dad make it to the plane?"

"Dad and kid already on the plane. Even found a few stragglers with your dad."

"Nick?" Chloe threw herself into Nick's arms. "What are you doing here?"

He patted her back. "Li and I wanted to be at the nuptials this time."

Chloe slid into her seat. "I just hope there's a wedding to see."

"My magic 8 ball says 'you may rely on it.'"

Chloe blew out a breath. "I hope so."

"No histrionics. I can see the tears from here. Put 'em back in the box."

Chloe laughed. "I'm glad you're here."

"Well, my godson is getting a new stepdad. For real this time. So you know," he shrugged, "I'm going to be there."

She hid a smile behind her hand. Nick was a big softie. He just didn't want anyone to know it. And she was okay with that. The support meant everything to her. So many people had come out to help her make this happen, now she just had to trust that Michael would come for her—come for *them*. Since she and Axl were a package deal.

The ride was eternal. Traffic was a nightmare. When they finally arrived at the airport, she was the first one out of the limo. She ran up the steps to the jet, breathless when she got inside.

"What's up, whore?"

Her heart stopped. "Jinx?"

"Damn right. What's this you're getting married? *Got* married already? Why do I not know these things?" The blond Amazon enveloped her in a tight hug. "I'm sorry you dealt with all this stuff alone. Dr. Nerdgasm kept sweeping me off my feet."

"That's okay." Chloe laughed. "I wasn't sure if he was actually real. Do I get to meet him?"

"Yes. I've got one helluva story to tell you. But I'll hold it until we get home. I require all the details."

"Me too." Ivy waved from her seat. She rushed to Chloe and the three women hugged. "How the hell did you get married?"

"It's a long story. I missed you guys so much."

Ivy sighed. "Sounds like Vegas was quite the trip for all of us."

"You got that right. I supposed you're not going to give me the details on your covert action either?"

Ivy grinned. "You wouldn't believe me if I told you."

"Mama!"

Chloe turned toward her son's voice and caught him mid-flight.

"Chopter," he said with a gleeful shout.

She hugged him close. "Where's Pop Pop?"

"We flied the chopter."

"You did?"

He nodded. "Chopter."

She collapsed into a chair with him. "That sounds super exciting."

There was so much talking that the hour flight to Vegas went by in a blink. She tried to get the details of the mysterious Vegas trip out of her two best friends, but they were determined to hear her story first.

There were far too many people on the plane with them to get the full story out, but she caught up her girls as best she could. By the time they got to the chapel, the entire band and her family had a plan for what she should do.

All she wanted was to see Michael at the end of that aisle waiting for her.

It was positively unreasonable to believe that Michael would make it by one o'clock in the morning. All their rushing only resulted in her being at least two hours early for her own wedding. Axl fell asleep in one of the wingback chairs and she was threatened at least four times to stop pacing.

Supposedly, she was making people nervous.

Shocking revelation. Guess what? *She* was nervous. She pulled her phone out again. Twelve-fifty-nine.

Disappointment coursed through her bloodstream as the dial flipped over to one in the morning. Her cell rang in her hand.

She was afraid to answer it. There was no way she could get a Dear Jane phone call while she was wearing her wedding dress. Just no way.

It stopped, then started ringing again immediately.

"Big girl panties," she muttered. "Hello?"

"Red?" He sounded like he was in a wind tunnel.

Her eyes blurred. "Michael?"

"Out—" The connection cut in and out. "Outside."

She plugged her other ear to hear him. "Outside?"

"Axl—come outside."

Right now, she wasn't going to question anything. She went over to Axl and scooped him up.

He rubbed his eye with his fist. "Mama?"

"We're going outside."

He gave a great sigh and collapsed against her shoulder. She moved down the aisle and rushed out the front door. The whomp-whomp of helicopter blades made her heart race. "Michael?"

"It's me. I'm coming, Red. Don't you leave. I'm coming."

She pointed up at the helicopter. "Look, Axl. It's Michael." She hugged Axl closer.

"Chopter."

She gave a watery laugh. "Yeah, chopter." This time, she didn't even care if she said the wrong thing. It was so very much a chopter.

She rushed back inside. "He's here." She dashed away tears. "I'm pretty sure he just landed on the roof of Mandalay Bay."

Chaos erupted as plans were finalized and the license had to be verified. Of course they couldn't do that until Michael arrived with the license in his wallet.

When a door slammed in the distance, her heart stalled. Everyone stood up as feet thundered down the hallway. Malachi came through the door first. All shoulders, bald head, and growly disposition. Heading up the back was Michael.

He wore a black blazer over a white shirt and jeans. And he was the single most beautiful man in the room.

She stalled in the aisle, her heart galloping. "Way to make an impression, pal."

"Go big, or go home."

She rushed down the aisle and into his arms. She dragged him down to her mouth. "I was so afraid you weren't going to come."

"If you didn't do something," he said between kisses, "I would have." He set her on her feet. "You're so damn beautiful."

"You clean up pretty nice yourself."

"You ready to do this thing?"

She nodded. "So ready."

There might have been wedding music, she wasn't sure. She couldn't hear anything over the happiness buzzing through her bloodstream. She got to Elvis with his swirl of black hair and oversized sunglasses and laughed so hard she had tears.

Axl came careening down the aisle in his drunken toddler walk and clasped his arms around Michael's legs.

Michael squatted down to his height. "So, you think it's okay to marry your mom? I love her very much. Just as much as I love you."

"Chopter!"

Chloe choked back tears. No crying, dammit.

Michael laughed. "I'm going with it." He stood, holding Axl close to his side. "After you, Elvis."

Chloe said her vows.

Michael said his.

She held out her hand. It was rock steady. This was exactly what she wanted. And finally, he slipped her sapphire and diamond ring on her finger where it belonged.

"No chance I'll forget this time, Mrs. Shawcross." He grinned. "Now let's go have us a honeymoon." He glanced down at Axl and his expression softened. "Or at least rent a honeymoon suite."

EPILOGUE

This definitely ranked as one of the most interesting shows Michael had ever performed.

Rather than a front row of fans rocking out, this first row was full of kids and their parents. The second and third rows too. The rest of the people were standing, clustered in groups at the back of the newly built tasting room at Happy Acres Orchard—and now Winery. His grandparents had decided to open up their brand new winery with some entertainment, and who better than Warning Sign?

They weren't exactly the kind of musical act one would expect to find at an orchard filled with kids and families, but the band had enjoyed coming up with a child-friendly set. Between his own experience with Axl, and Molly's with her nephew, Dylan, and niece, Brianna, plus Elle's with her nieces, Charlotte and Avery, the band was full up on kid time and knew what might work for a younger crowd.

Of course Juliet, West, and Ryan hadn't been as excited until they'd started jamming out to some *Sesame Street* classics, and hell, who didn't enjoy those? Add a rock flair and everyone had a good time.

Plus, Nick had allowed them to play his song, "Lullaby". The tune only occasionally came out at Oblivion's acoustic sets, on account of the fact it was a song he'd written for his twins. Oddly enough, most hard rock crowds didn't appreciate being lulled into unconsciousness at the end of a show.

This bunch though? They were lapping it up. Literally, since at least a fourth of the audience had apple juice boxes or applesauce cups.

Michael strummed through the end notes of "Lullaby" on his well-loved Gibson, which had stickers all over the back from his travels. As a teenager, he'd been stupid enough to slap stickers on the wood casing rather than his travel case. Now he liked the vintage, distressed look of the guitar, and especially loved the way the instrument purred under his touch like a well-satisfied woman. As the song came to a close, he eased back and let Elle take over, using the moment to finish up with some percussion with his hand gently thumping the guitar.

They had their own full-time percussion now though, and it wasn't Ryan, currently working his magic on a triangle. At the beginning of the song, he'd played a piccolo. The kids had stared up at Ry as if he were the Pied freaking Piper.

But on the drums was Malachi fucking Shawcross. He seemed more than a little shell-shocked at playing for a bunch of rugrats and their parents, but he appeared to be having a good time. Even Michael's gruff, often sullen older brother loved Lila's parents. Back when he'd had no use for Lila, he'd still been won over by Gram and Pop. Who wouldn't be? For two boys from sun-drenched California who'd never seen snow, Happy Acres had been like an oasis. Crisp leaves, juicy apples, a real family. They'd been as starstruck as some of these kids were now at seeing their instruments and amps.

Family, man, was a beautiful thing.

Michael smiled at his own sitting off to the side of the first row. Axl danced between Chloe's legs, clapping with the rest of the kids as the song ended. He couldn't get enough of the orchard. Lila's dad had taken him out apple picking the day before, and since then, he'd been begging Chloe and Michael to do it again.

They'd be going out tomorrow bright and early, before the Sunday crowd swamped the place in earnest. Axl was almost two-and-a-half now and getting into everything. He seemed to be teething constantly, and he had tantrums on a nightly basis. But he liked picking apples and eating applesauce and jumping in Pop's ginormous piles of leaves, so

Michael was all for it. They'd be coming back out to the orchard for Thanksgiving, and maybe Christmas too. All depended on how the rest of the year's band schedule shook out. Lila was booking them for basically anything she could get. Now that Warning Sign wasn't in the tabloids because of Michael's partying, or love life issues, or sudden weddings by Elvis, they were focusing on promoting their music.

As far as Michael was concerned, that was just freaking fine. He'd be good with never being caught in a media maelstrom again.

"How do you guys feel about doing something a little different?" Molly asked, clapping her hands and playing the peppy cheerleader routine to the hilt. She genuinely loved kids and she had a way with them. She was also as pretty as a fairytale princess so they all squealed and bounced in their tiny sneakers. "Let's play 'What time is it, Mr. Fox?' Do you guys know that game?"

There was a range of answers, most of them an enthusiastic "Yes!"

Axl definitely knew it, since the pre-pre K he'd started going to two afternoons a week while Chloe was taking culinary classes at the Institute taught the counting game like a religion. It also had the bonus of wearing out the kids, and anytime a rambunctious child went to sleep voluntarily was a good time.

Molly briefly outlined the game for those who didn't know how to play, and the kids ran to one side of the tasting room. Their smiling parents and some of the people who worked at the orchard moved the chairs to the back to give them room to run. Molly moved off the band's raised dais and into the center of the room to begin, and the kids dutifully asked her what time it was.

Michael glanced at Elle as the kids took the requisite steps forward, Axl, of course, leading the pack.

"That one's mine," he told her.

Smiling faintly, she shook her head. "No kidding. I must've missed the banner you draped over the Hollywood sign announcing that fact."

Michael grinned. He hadn't put up any signs—yet—but he just might.

Being married was pretty frigging awesome. From the instant he'd heard Chloe's proposal until he met her at the altar and slipped the sapphire ring on her finger, he'd been in a state of shock. Seeing her in her wedding gown and knowing she'd willingly chosen to marry him still stood out as the most incredible moment of his life.

She was his wife. Forever and ever, a-freaking-men.

Of course, there were squabbles about petty shit. Like when he left his socks on the floor, or fed Axl too much candy, or when he hid Chloe's panties because…well, that one was obvious.

Occasionally, the fights were bigger. Sometimes the paparazzi still swarmed too close. Once or twice, they'd snapped a picture of Chloe and Axl at the doctor's office, or at the mall, and Chloe had gone into protective lockdown mode. She'd dealt with so much after Snake's death regarding the media that she was still gun-shy. Add in the Tabitha thing and how she and Michael had gotten together, and Michael doubted she'd ever truly come to terms with their interference in their lives.

Warning Sign wasn't super huge yet. If that changed, things could get way worse. Michael had no desire to hide his family away, but if he had to, he would. He and Chloe had started talking tentatively about having more kids over the summer, sort of feeling each other out. It was obviously very early days in their relationship, but their accelerated timeline had made them both start thinking they were ready earlier than usual.

On Axl's good days, being a parent was fun. They had it all under control. Why not add another one while Axl was still little? He'd like a sibling, right? Having Mal be so close in age had been a great experience for Michael, and if they wanted something similar for Axl, they had to get on the stick.

Or Chloe had to get on the stick, early and often. Something she did pretty damn often anyway.

They'd even gone the route of ditching the condoms and the birth control a couple of months ago, during a particularly great period with Axl. His teething agony had slowed down, and he was generally a happy baby, and hey, the monster in the closet was nothing more than scorched earth, so why not?

Almost immediately after that momentous decision, Axl had gotten a double ear infection and decided he was deathly afraid of clowns. Naturally, Lila had just bought him a little miniature clown, and hiding it in a steel box under Axl's bed had not been enough. They'd had to move the doll to the master bedroom closet and finally back to Lila's place, where her daughter, Avery, had fallen in mad, fiendish love with the creepy thing.

But Axl was still traumatized, crying every time he saw anyone in too much makeup. Even Michael's occasional use of guyliner at a concert made him break into sobs.

So maybe they should wait on the baby, if she could even get pregnant that fast. She'd indicated some inconsistency with birth control back when she'd been with Snake, which absolutely had not been a factor with them. They'd been meticulous about it until they hadn't been. Now they were living wild and free, but he might just pull back the reins a little—if she agreed. They had time. Axl was still so little. They could enjoy him on his own, then figure out when to add on once life settled down.

He was almost sure it had to settle down eventually.

Molly's game included lots of children running and shrieking and making all manner of kiddie mayhem. From what Michael could tell, Molly's rules were fast and loose. Unsurprising, really.

He and the rest of the band decided to do a melodic accompaniment from the stage, which made their lead singer send them an arch look just in case any of them got ideas about wanting to sing. None of them did, and so peace reigned across the orchard.

Refreshments followed Molly's shenanigans. Children descended on the overloaded snack table and grabbed warm cider donuts and apple fritters, cups of cider, and apples and grapes out of bowls with the zest of a missionary fresh out of bible school. Soon, the excited yelps and laughter of a ton of kids high on sugar bounced around the room.

Michael unstrapped his guitar and tucked it into its case, then went to pick up his sugar monster from where he was sticking his face into a wooden cutout with a donkey's body on the other side. Chloe was standing behind him laughing, but she looked tired. Lines fanned out from her dark eyes and bracketed her mouth and she was bracing her back as if she'd been roughhousing with Axl again. The kid loved being in the air so much that Michael was pretty sure they'd have a pilot on their hands one day.

Maybe he'd just figure out how to turn into a bird.

"You okay?" Michael asked Chloe, snagging them both cups of cider. Axl had already worked his way through one, judging from the sticky ring around his mouth.

"Sure. It's been a terrific day. Gram mentioned doing a hayride after dark. I guess they do one on weekend nights in October at a nearby farm with Jason and Freddy and a lot of those gory dudes." Chloe shuddered. "The September hayride is much tamer. Just a couple glowing pumpkins and scarecrows under spotlights. Kid-friendly, I already checked."

"Sure, that sounds fun. Want to go upstairs and take a nap first?" Michael glanced at Axl, who'd moved on to stick his head in the hole with a cow body on the other side. He'd definitely have to get some shots of that.

Chloe stepped forward and laced her fingers with his. "Depends. Are you coming up to nap with me?" She waggled her eyebrows and he had to laugh.

"I'd love to, but Ax-Man isn't quite able to watch himself yet."

"No, but your grandparents would love to. As a matter of fact…" Chloe waved to Michael's grandmother and she hurried over, her arms full of decorations. "Mrs. Ronson, would you mind watching Axl for a little—"

"Oh dear, yes. Please. Can I? I want to just eat him right up. Take as long as you like." Gram pinched Michael's cheek as she passed, then moved on to Axl. He clapped his hands at the sight of the goodies she carried, and they wandered off to explore whatever treasures she'd unearthed.

"So as you were saying about that nap," Michael began, sliding his arms around Chloe's waist. "I'm suddenly so sleepy."

"I just bet." She poked him in the chest. "Let's go. We don't have long."

"I'm a magician with small windows of time."

"Sure you are." She shot him a smile over her shoulder and led him through the pocket doors that led into the front of the winery.

They meandered back over to the main house and through the general store, then up the stairs to the second level where family and close friends stayed when in town. They also had a lodge on the property with spacious rooms for those who wanted to stay overnight, but of course, Michael and Chloe had been given red carpet treatment. The rest of the band was at the lodge, which wasn't exactly a hardship. That place was huge and gorgeous and rustic in a way the cabins in California wished they could replicate.

Not that he loved the orchard or anything. Nope.

"Did you know we were given the babymaking room?" Chloe asked nonchalantly as they entered their suite.

He shut the door. "The what?"

"The babymaking room. Apparently, there's like a whole legend that goes with it. Everyone who stays in this room ends up pregnant shortly afterward."

If that was the case—and not saying that he believed in any such nonsense—he guessed they'd be shelving the whole "putting the baby on hold" plan.

He probably shouldn't be excited. Wasn't he supposed to be nervous about impending fatherhood? Well, double fatherhood, since he already was one. But he'd never been around for the whole cycle before. The conception part they had down pat. The rest would be all new for him, and he couldn't wait.

Except he'd just told himself they should. So, right, waiting. Waiting was good.

"Hmm. Even the guys get knocked up in here?" he teased. "If so, that's some special room."

Chloe sat on the bed and kicked out at him as he approached. "Wiseass."

He grabbed her feet and pried off her shoes. "Do you believe in crazy shit like that?"

She leaned back on her elbows and shrugged. "I don't believe, but I don't *not* believe. Lila found out she was pregnant when she was staying here."

"How do you know that?"

"She told me after she heard we were visiting the orchard. We've kind of talking now. A little. We're not besties or anything, but things are better. Lord, what are you doing to me?"

"Right this second? Taking off your jeans."

"No, I meant a minute ago when you were massaging my calves. Do that again."

"The plan was to massage all of you."

"God, I love you."

He glanced up at the words, his heart kicking as it always did. They were still so rare and precious, although she said them fairly often. He'd never get tired of hearing them. "Because I give a killer massage?"

"That doesn't hurt." She grinned. "Neither does the gorgeous blue eyes or the gorgeous body or the wicked skills on the guitar. But no, that's not why I love you. I'd just crush on you—hard—for those things."

He pulled her jeans the rest of the way down and off her legs. Beneath she wore a scrap of white lace. He removed that from her too and wasted no time in burying his face between her thighs.

She was so responsive. A few brushes of his thumb, a couple of long, slow licks, and she came undone around his fingers. Shivering, gasping, and already eager for the next round with his mouth.

Once was never enough when it came to his wife. Not for her, and definitely not for him.

But when he gripped her legs to tug her to the edge of the bed, she stopped him with her hands on his shoulders. "See, this is one reason right there. Our oral sex ratio is way, way off."

He was already lowering to finish his very enjoyable task. "You're right. I need to spend more time on my knees. I promise to rectify that in the near future."

Clasping his lips around her clit, he slid his fingers inside her to find that secret spot that always made her legs quake and her ass come right off the bed. He wasn't disappointed. Within a couple of minutes, she was biting a pillow to muffle her cries and saturating his chin with her release.

He rose and undid his jeans, looming over her as her pupils flared wide and she trembled. "Do you know it's been twelve hours since I've fucked you? How am I still standing?"

"Shouldn't I be asking that question?" She pretended to look around. "Oh, lookie. I'm not. Flat on my back as usual."

His laughter caught him off-guard. "Suppose that means we're tempting the baby fates." He'd said it as a test, to give her a chance to mention waiting. She seemed to read his mind more often than not, and maybe she'd had a few misgivings of her own lately.

Truthfully, he hadn't. His only misgiving was that he didn't want to shortchange Axl, and perhaps they weren't prepared yet to juggle two. But he'd been sure he wasn't ready for a wife and baby, and they'd been the best things to ever happen to him.

Sometimes you just had to leap off the cliff like a deranged motherfucker to see if you could fly.

"We've tempted many fates already." She reached up to grab his hand where it rested on his belt. "Michael, I'm scared."

He started to tease her, because that was what he did. Then he glimpsed her pinched lips and noticed her knuckles were white where they gripped his hand on his buckle. "About what?"

"Everything." She blew out a breath and sat up to press her head to his chest. "Can you explode from happiness? Because I think I just might, and that terrifies me."

Now he did laugh, and he didn't feel the least bit ashamed. "You realize that's silly, right?"

"Yes. Of course, I do. But what if this changes? What if one day you wake up, and seeing me on the other side of the bed just makes you want to bury your head under the pillow?"

"It won't. Besides, you know I wake up between your legs most of the time anyway."

"I'm being serious."

"I know, and so am I." He cupped her cheek. "If I ever give you a reason to doubt me, just kick me in the nuts and that'll get my head back on straight. And if I ever doubt you, I'll just flip your legs over my shoulders and remind you why it's good to be my woman."

Her mouth quivered into a smile. "As if I'd ever forget."

"Mom brain, maybe?"

She socked him in the gut and he chuckled, clutching her hand. Then he brought it to his mouth. "I love you and I love Axl. That's not going to change. Ever."

Swallowing hard, she nodded. "I'm trying to trust in this, in us, but it's hard. I just never expected to have so much. And now, I'll have even more." When he frowned, she nudged him again. "So, about that massage. Were you serious?"

He might be male and about as subtle as a bulldozer, but even he noticed that topic change. "Sure. Let me grab your oil stuff from the bathroom."

"Thanks. I'm all tense." She smiled up at him and pulled her top over her head.

No bra.

Glorious breasts with taut little pink nipples.

Concerns about interpersonal problems—vamoose.

A little dazed, he wandered into the next room and dug out Chloe's after shower crap. She loved when he worked it into her skin. Though maybe he should give himself a hand too, in case she fell asleep before he was finished like she sometimes did.

Her breasts, man. So fucking full and perfect.

He sighed and relegated his needs to the background. Later. She never left him wanting for long, that was for sure. He'd just wait until—

The first snore hit him before he even made it out of the bathroom.

He smothered a laugh in his fist. Damn, he adored her. Even if she did conk out before he could massage her into incredible sex.

Then again, he couldn't deny the restorative power of a nap.

After setting the alarm on his phone for a half hour, he curled up with her in bed. She snuggled up against him without even waking up.

Closing his eyes, he let sleep take him. And let the alarm rip it away half an hour later.

"Axl," he muttered, sitting straight up. "Gotta get the baby."

From beside him, Chloe laughed. "The baby can wait another five minutes. Sorry, I forgot to finish something." She yawned and reached across his lap to jerk down his zipper the rest of the way. His belt was still undone. "Time to fix that."

He fell back against the mattress. "This might be the best dream I've ever had."

"Not yet. But it will be." She pulled his waking cock out of his boxers and slid her warm mouth over the tip. She smiled around him and slipped her hand between his legs to cup his balls.

Fuck. He was a lucky man.

Half an hour later, they stumbled into the bathroom for the quickest shower in the history of life. When he started to grab her under the spray, she giggled and shoved him back.

"Babymaking bathroom," he mumbled into her mouth, boosting her up against the wall.

"All right. If you insist." She gave a long-suffering sigh. "Bring it on home."

By the time they made it back to the tasting room of the winery, the rambunctious kids were gone and most of the concert debris had been cleared away. Axl and Gram were out back pulling up mini pumpkins from a smaller patch next to the house. The real pumpkin patch was out back.

"Look, Mama!" Axl tried to jump to his feet, but his foot got caught in a vine and down he went. Yet he never lost his grip on the mini pumpkin he held over his head. "Punkin!"

"Aww, you got one. Look at that." Chloe scooped him up and smiled at Mrs. Ronson, who was sitting contentedly in the dirt. "Thank you for watching him. We were a bit longer than we intended to be."

"No problem at all. Newlyweds have to catch their moments of privacy when they can." Lila's mother winked and reached over to pat Michael's leg.

He flushed. "Jeez, Gram."

She hooted out a laugh and exchanged a look with Chloe. "You guys ready for the hayride tonight?"

"Yes, I think so." Chloe glanced at Michael and heaved out a breath. "I hope so."

Michael frowned. It was only a hayride. He was about to say just that when Axl stuck out his pumpkin in Michael's direction.

"Look, Dada! Punkin."

He tried to find his voice. He cleared his throat and blinked half a dozen times. The wind must've kicked up dust into his eyes. Maybe he was allergic to something.

"Thank you, Ax-Man," he rasped, accepting the pumpkin. When that wasn't nearly close enough, he wrapped Chloe and Axl in a tight hug and buried his face in his son's brown corduroy jacket. "Thank you."

He still hadn't recovered when it came time for the hayride. Somehow they ended up at the front of the line and were able to get seats on the perfectly shaped bales of hay at the front. Axl was so excited he couldn't stop jumping.

"Go, go!" he yelled to the driver.

"Gotta wait for everyone else, buddy." Michael laughed and ruffled the boy's hair. Axl ducked away and moved to Chloe's other side to jump.

He might've called Michael "Dada" for the first time, but he wasn't going to let the dude mess up his hair. A guy had boundaries, even if he was only two-and-a-half.

The wagon filled up fairly quickly, considering almost half of the passengers were children. They set off on the ride on a winding route through the forest, jolting and bumping over every ridge on the path.

Chloe clutched Axl with one hand and her stomach with the other. "Maybe this wasn't the best idea."

"Who says? It's a gorgeous night. Smell that woodsmoke. That crisp air. Fall's coming." He slid his arm around Chloe's shoulders. "Can you feel it?"

She moaned. "I feel something."

"You okay?" He frowned and picked up Axl, setting him beside him on the large hay bale he was sharing with Chloe. "You're not getting motion sick, are you?"

"It's only a few minutes more. I'm fine."

"Just throw up over the side if you have to."

Chloe shook her head. "Really?"

"I'm just saying, if you have to, you're in nature's bathroom. Aw, hey, pal, look at that." Michael pointed at a display of lit-up pumpkins. "Like yours, Ax-man."

Axl bounced and clapped, already wiggling to get down. "Nope, you gotta stay here. Can't run around on this thing. Hey, look, scarecrows."

"Scarecows." Axl grabbed Chloe's knee and shook it forcibly enough to make her groan. "Look."

"Oh, I'm looking." She poked Michael in the side. "Those are for you."

"What's for me?"

"The scarecrows. Count them."

"Huh?" He narrowed his eyes as the wagon rumbled past the large display. "There's one. The other two are baby ones, which are cute but don't really count."

"Tell that to my belly." Chloe rested her head on Michael's shoulder. "So, it turns out we don't need the babymaking room after all."

Michael was too busy trying to restrain Axl to hear her at first. The kid had turned into a rocket determined to launch off the hay. "Easy, kid. Stop jumping around. You're what?"

"Three scarecrows. Think about it."

Chloe's testy voice broke into his consciousness just as they lurched over another bump and she went flying into his side. He stared at her incredulously while he shifted Axl onto his belly on his lap. His little arms and legs pumped as he flailed to get free, but he was just going to have to wait a second.

"No," Axl howled. "Nooooo."

"You're—" Michael's gaze dropped to where her stomach was hidden by her jacket and the darkness. "No."

"Yes."

"No."

Chloe let out an exasperated laugh. "Okay, Axl Senior."

"You're not kidding?"

"You just told me to puke in nature's bathroom because I have all day sickness. Do you think I'm kidding?"

"Oh. Oh, wow. Holy shit." He let out a whoop and pressed a hard kiss to Chloe's mouth before jerking unsteadily to his feet. He used to surf in the Pacific. This was kind of like that—

if you were delirious. "Guess what? I'm going to be a father —again."

While the rest of the surprised riders clapped and cheered for him, Michael hoisted Axl high.

Then he toppled onto his ass on the floor of the wagon, and Axl landed securely in his lap. And they both started to laugh.

Chloe covered her face with her hands. "What have I done?"

Once he'd gotten his wind back, Michael leaned over to kiss her knee. "Made me the happiest father on the planet. Hey, can we call her Rose if it's a girl? It'd be perfect, don't you think?"

"Rose is a nice name—" Then she glared at her husband. "I'm too nauseous to get your obnoxious jokes."

"Come on, Axl and Rose. If they both have red hair, it'll be even better."

"Is it too late to divorce you, Shawcross?"

"Yes." From the seat of the wagon, he leaned up to bring her mouth to his for once. "Way too late, Mrs. Shawcross."

Thanks for reading BEDDED BLISS. Next up...Jules isn't looking for forever... but she might get twice as much as she's looking for.

Now...turn the page for a special sneak peek of TRIPLE TROUBLE, **Found in Oblivion Book 2.**

TRIPLE TROUBLE

His best friend was dancing with his girl.

Actually, since they were attending the Halloween wedding of Owen Blackwell and Callie Templeton, Superman and Wonder Woman were actually the ones getting their grind on. But their costumes didn't disguise the long rippling dark hair that flowed down Juliet Reece's back or the way Tristan Eves flashed that smile meant to detonate panties.

Randy Pruitt gripped the neck of his beer that much tighter. Besides, Juliet wasn't his girl, whether she was in the persona of Wonder Woman or just herself. Juliet didn't even like him. Tolerating him was a big step on most days. But in his head, he'd claimed her.

Now, evidently, Tristan was claiming her in reality. Or he would soon.

It wasn't as if Randy had missed the vibe between Juliet and Tristan every time they'd been in each other's orbits recently. They were both huge flirts, the types to smile as easily as they breathed, but theirs was more than a casual seduction. They weren't just dancing. What Randy was witnessing was the prelude to a fuck, and he was no goddamn voyeur.

The time had come for him to get some air. Away from this room. Away from them.

Randy had made it halfway down the hall, pushing through crowds of scantily dressed fairies and way too many pseudo presidential candidates, when he stopped and threw back the rest of his beer. Stupid. What was he running from? So what if Juliet and Tris hooked up?

They were both single, as he was. It wasn't as if Randy had ever verbalized his interest in Juliet to his buddy. Tris wasn't a mind reader.

As for Juliet, she didn't give him the time of day, night or any time, period. When she bothered to acknowledge him, it was usually something work-related and as brief as possible. Rockstars didn't mingle with the crew. At least one as perfect as Juliet wouldn't. Not that she'd ever indicated that to him, he'd just been a roadie long enough to know.

Sure, there were the occasional fumbles in the dark when the talent grabbed whomever was handy, but in the sunshine, nope. They kept to their assigned areas and that was that.

He liked rules and delineations. Normally, he even preferred them. But everything was starting to feel itchy lately, including the boxes he'd drawn around his life. His older sister, Harper, was happily settled in her life with her own rockstar husband, Deacon McCoy of Oblivion. Between their young daughter Alexa, her catering business, and feeding her hungry menagerie of rockers as Oblivion's resident chef, she never had a spare moment to think—and that seemed to be exactly what she wanted.

She'd grown up in that vagabond lifestyle just as he had, thanks to their roadie parents. The senior Pruitts were currently on tour with the Raging Eleanors, and not the least bit concerned about hanging it up and retiring. Why would they? They were as happy as could be.

Just as Harper was. She'd been as aware as Randy was of the unspoken boundaries between the crew and the musicians, and yet she hadn't let it hold her back from falling for her husband. Deacon sure hadn't seen her as anything less either.

Randy traded his empty beer bottle for a new one off a passing tray and slipped back into the crowd. Not that he had any reason to be thinking about the differences between his brethren and those in the spotlight. His role was to support, to give them room to shine—literally, since he was the head lighting tech on the abbreviated West Coast leg of Warning Sign's "Spark It Off" tour.

Fitting, since Juliet had called him "Sparks" with no small amount of derision since the night they'd met, just before the lighting disaster during Warning Sign's concert at the Blue Rhino. It just happened to be a disaster he'd been indirectly responsible for. He'd rushed through some of his usual checks, and he'd paid the price afterward.

The club and the record company hadn't bruised his ass. No, he'd done that himself, over and over again in the months since. Closing in on a year later, and he still hadn't decreased his pre-show checks back to pre-Rhino levels. He'd gone from precise to militant. Almost obsessive.

Just like he was obsessive over one Juliet Reece, and her stupidly huge dark eyes and smart mouth.

He had a smart mouth too, but he just never managed to use it when she was aiming her zingers at him. Somehow he went mute whenever she glanced his way, whether it was to make a request or to gripe.

"Can you lessen the blue light tonight during 'Carried Away'? It's blinding me when I turn toward Michael."

"Is there any way that the pink and the yellow lights can be aimed away from me during the bridge of 'All Night Long'? I get so hot and they only make it worse."

He'd simply nod and work on whatever she asked. She never made unreasonable demands, and she almost always said "please" and "thank you". If anything, she was pleasant to a fault. But every now and then, something would go wrong, and she'd blow up—always at him, as if he held the universe in his hands.

"Goddammit, Sparks, if that beam swung any lower, I'd be decapitated. There has to be a way to fix that."

Her reaction was so over the top sometimes that he'd been tempted to ask her if she was just a diva or if there was more to it. If something had happened in her past to put that fear in her eyes when the lights came too close or something sparked into flame. Granted, anyone with any sense was cautious around fire. But Juliet was always polite until those moments, and he suspected there was a reason.

Would he ever find out? Probably not. He couldn't ask, and she wouldn't confide in him. She didn't confide in anyone, from what he'd seen.

Maybe Tristan. Perhaps he would be the one to unlock her secrets.

"Fuck," Randy said under his breath, tossing back some of his beer before diverting left and up the winding staircase to the second level. On the way, he pulled off the mask that had made him hot all damn night.

Freaking Batman. As if he was a superhero of any sort. Unfortunately, "geek in a corner" had sold out before he arrived at the masquerade shop.

It was probably breaking Halloween wedding protocol to remove part of his costume before the end of the night, but he needed space. Room to breathe. There was a reason he'd gravitated toward the crew, particularly working as a light engineer. While others were illuminated, he was left in shadow. The way he preferred to be.

Taking the steps two at a time, he found himself in a darkened hallway. Voices were sparser up there, the crowd thinner. He might even get a chance to shed the cape and actually work the kinks out of his shoulders for the first time that night.

At one end of the hallway, a door stood open. As he approached, he glimpsed the balcony beyond a pair of French doors. Wavering, watery blue stripes of light bisected the far side of the room. Pool outside, probably. He could hear the splashing and laughter.

If anyone else had come to the wedding stag, he hadn't seen them.

Technically, he hadn't either. He and Tristan had driven together. In Tris's case, it hadn't been because of a lack of female company. More like he preferred to arrive single, so he could meet and mingle without impunity.

"Weddings are the best place to meet a babe, Rand. All the singletons are lonely and looking, wondering if their true love is out there somewhere. Ripe for the plucking, and we swoop in."

Right. Tris had swooped, or Juliet had swooped. Mutual swooping, from what he could tell when they'd been up against each other on the dance floor. Even with Tristan's Superman cape blocking some of the view, Randy hadn't had a problem making out Juliet's flirty smile or the way she kept slipping so naturally into Tris's space, angling those corseted breasts so they brushed his buddy's chest with every movement. Her Wonder Woman costume left little to Randy's unfortunately vivid imagination, and neither did the intent in her large dark eyes. Every emotion she felt was mirrored there, and hers for Tristan was pure want.

Not your problem, dude.

Randy sucked down another gulp of beer and moved toward the balcony. Fresh air, finally. It felt like he'd been in this house—gorgeous as it might've been—for a lifetime. Houdini's estate was a popular place for events, and the happily married couple had apparently met there the previous year at yet another shindig. Since the place was special for them, it made sense they'd get married there.

As for him, he wasn't feeling too special about any-damn-thing at the moment.

The guitar on a chair in the corner caught his eye as he reached for the handle of the balcony door. He didn't know who it belonged to, or if it was a prop. He just had to feel that smooth black wood under his hands.

Setting aside his barely touched beer, he reached for another kind of mood booster, one he rarely turned to because he didn't want the lines to blur. Looking for more than he was meant for led to problems. Discontent.

He wasn't that guy. He was happy for the most part. Brooding wasn't part of his MO under normal circumstances.

At least until his best friend moved in on the girl he'd never had the courage to admit he had a thing for.

Right in front of his goddamn face.

The song flowed out of him, traveling from his head to his fingertips before he knew which one he intended to play. "Best of You" by the Foo Fighters fit the night somehow.

He was good at his job, and he loved it. He had family and friends, and a decent place to live with his best friend until he moved on to the next place. For now, Tris's spacious loft worked.

Imagining whom his buddy might bring home at the end of the night wasn't productive. There were always other places to go. Another bed to crash in.

Surely there had to be an escape from the shitstorm his thoughts had become.

Swallowing hard, Randy strummed through the opening chords

while he fought to let his mind empty. It was beyond ridiculous to be focused on Tristan and Juliet when neither one knew he'd even so much as given Jules a second look.

Or a fiftieth.

Tristan probably wouldn't have ever guessed that when Randy dreamed, she was there. Always ghosting around the edges of his consciousness, like a whisper of lyrics he could never quite catch. In reality, the woman was a vibrant red. Almost virulent. In his mind, she was a wisp of scent, a flash of dark eyes, a caress of soft, silky hair.

"So this is where you're hiding away?"

Randy's shoulders stiffened at the familiar deep voice behind him but his fingers continued on their predestined path. He'd reached the point where he didn't have to think about the correct chord progression. Now, it had become a matter of setting the train on its figure-eight loop and standing back as it charged over the tracks.

"Huh?" Heavy footsteps thudded over the tiled floor. Something Italian and expensive no doubt, like so much of the architecture in that area. "Can't speak?"

Randy forced his shoulders to relax. Better, easier, to have something in his hands so he didn't have to turn and face his friend. He wasn't entirely sure he could stomach Tristan's slow grin right now.

Tristan was the head chef at Ace Hotel's restaurant, The Hollow, and he was every inch the cocky, talented wizard with food—and women—that he seemed. If Tris ever doubted himself, Randy had never borne witness to it. His friend was self-assured in every damn way.

Randy only envied that about a third of the time.

He also needed to speak the hell up before his silence said more than his words ever could.

"Not hiding," he replied, and he didn't even sound gruff. He was just focused on the music he usually only sought when he was pissed or happy, but rarely in between.

"No? Is that why your phone's off?"

Shit, was it? He forgot the damn thing existed as often as he remembered to turn it on. More, because he wanted to be tethered to technology about as much as he wanted to be having this conversation with Tris.

So he played. Like the musicians on the goddamn Titanic, he'd just keep on keeping on while the ship tipped onto its axis and water crept over the sides.

"Forgot," he said, jerking up his head when Tris laid his hand over the strings and rendered them silent. "What the fuck, man?"

"Yeah, what the fuck, man? Good question. Answer mine and I'll answer yours."

Before Randy could respond, Tristan stepped back with a swish of his stupid Superman cape. Intentional or not, the movement made Randy's lips twitch with amusement in spite of everything.

He really wasn't built to have temper tantrums. His mom would've skinned his hide if she'd known how he was acting, and especially over what. The Pruitt family made a habit of going after what they wanted. For that matter, so did he. He'd worked his way up from the backend of the crew, doing whatever shit jobs were dumped on his plate, to become the head lighting engineer on what just might end up a tour across the United States. Eventually, maybe even the world.

The moon was the limit for Warning Sign. And for Juliet.

"I didn't hear a question. Just some general grumbling about my etiquette. Here's my opinion on that." He flipped off Tristan and set the guitar between his feet.

Tristan grunted and shook his head. "Asshole. Here I was being all considerate and shit by even coming to find you."

Randy's ears pricked at the same time as the rest of his body hunched. He didn't even need to hear the rest. Didn't want to.

Apparently, however, his tongue worked independently of his brain.

"Considerate? You? C'mon, man, it's Halloween, but we both know costumes only run skin deep."

Even in the low light coming from the strobe lights near the pool and the sconces in the hallway, Randy saw Tris's eyes flash. "You have a problem with me? One that only showed up after we walked in the doors of this frigging wedding?"

He didn't have anything to say. Anything that didn't make him sound like a whiny asshole.

And yeah, he was being one right now. He could own that. Tomorrow he'd probably feel bad for it and offer to do Tristan's side of the chore chart Randy had put up on the fridge door shortly after moving in.

Hey, stuff had to get done. Might as well make certain they didn't live in a typical bachelor pad, bachelors or not. Tristan made sure the fridge stayed stocked. Randy handled a lot of the rest.

Right now? He was going to split before he said more and made things worse.

"Look, I've just decided weddings aren't my scene. Not to mention this fucking costume." Randy ran a finger along the collar of the damn near wet suit that clung to his body. Batman must be a fucking masochist. "I'll just take the car back and you can get a ride with her."

He tried to keep his voice even on the last word. He nearly succeeded.

Minus that little telling hitch at the end. The hitch that betrayed him as a horny idiot without the sense to get out of his own way.

"I knew it." The steely glint in Tris's eyes only intensified as his best friend got in his face. "You fucking want Juliet Reece."

Would you like to read more?
Visit quinnandelliott.com for purchasing info!

OBLIVION WORLD CHARACTER CHART

BEWARE...SPOILERS APLENTY IN THIS CHARACTER
CHART. READ AT YOUR OWN RISK!

Simon Kagan: Oblivion lead singer
Brother to Ian Kagan, married to Margo Reece, daughter Raine, co-founder of Oblivion

Nick Crandall: Oblivion lead guitarist
Twin brother to Elle/Ricki, married to Lila Shawcross, daughters Charlie and Avery, co-founder of Oblivion

Deacon McCoy: Oblivion bass guitarist
Married to Harper Pruitt, daughter Alexa Grace, co-founder of Oblivion

William 'Snake' Scotsman*: Oblivion ex-drummer
Son Axl with Chloe Adams, co-founder of Oblivion

Jazz Edwards: Oblivion drummer
Sister Molly McIntire, married to Gray Duffy, son Dylan and daughter Briana

Gray Duffy: Oblivion rhythm guitarist
Married to Jazz Edwards, son Dylan Edward and daughter Briana

Margo Reece: Oblivion violinist
Sister Juliet Reece, married to Simon Kagan, daughter Raine Kagan

Harper Pruitt: Tour Chef
Brother Randy Pruitt*, married to Deacon McCoy, daughter Alexa Grace

Lila Shawcross: Ripper Records executive and Oblivion's manager
Cousin Zoe Manning, married to Nick Crandall, daughters Charlie and Avery, stepmother to Michael and Malachi Shawcross

Donovan Lewis: Ripper Records CEO
Uncle to Denver Casey

Chloe Adams: Waitress
Married to Michael Shawcross, son Axl (Bio-father Snake Scotsman) and daughter Hope

Michael Shawcross: Warning Sign guitarist
Brother Malachi Shawcross, married to Chloe Adams, daughter Hope

Juliet Reece: Warning Sign guitarist
Sister Margo Reece, in a relationship with Randy Pruitt* and Tristan Eves, son Joshua Randall

Randy Pruitt*: Warning Sign roadie/lighting tech
Sister Harper Pruitt, in a relationship with Juliet Reece and Tristan Eves, son Joshua Randall

Tristan Eves: Head chef at The Hollow
In a relationship with Juliet Reece & Randy Pruitt*, son Joshua Randal, best friends with Hunter Jordan from Hammered

West Reynolds: Warning Sign keyboardist
In a relationship with Lauren Bryant, daughter Chloe (isn't in her life)

Lauren 'Lo' Bryant: Author

In a relationship with West Reynolds, best friends with Ethan Haywood

Denver Casey (nee: Casey Lewis): Tour bus driver for Rebel Rage and Warning Sign
Donovan Lewis's niece, married to Ryan Waters

Ryan Waters: Warning Sign jack-of-all-trades
Married to Denver Casey

Ethan Haywood: Professor at UCLA
In a relationship with Molly McIntire & Luc Moreau, best friends with Lauren Bryant

Luc Moreau: Warning Sign co-lead singer
In a relationship with Molly McIntire & Ethan Haywood, former lead singer for The Grunge

Molly McIntire: Warning Sign lead singer
Sister Jazz Edwards, in a relationship with Ethan Haywood & Luc Moreau

Malachi Shawcross: Warning Sign drummer, former race car driver
Brother Michael Shawcross, married to Elle 'Ricki' Crandall

Ricki 'Elle' Crandall: Warning Sign guitarist
Twin sister to Nick Crandall, married to Malachi Shawcross

Hunter Jordan: Hammered lead singer
Brother Noah Jordan, married to Kennedy McManus

Kennedy McManus: Publicist for Hammered
Married to Hunter Jordan

Reed 'Bats' Mason: Hammered lead guitarist

Zachary Kane: Hammered rhythm guitarist

Indiana West: Hammered band manager

Victoria Sheer: Actress/Model
invloved with Reed Mason, ex-girlfriend of Hunter Jordan

Faith 'Keys' Keystone: Hammered keyboardist
Married to Quinn Alexander

Quinn Alexander: Roth Defense specialist, former Navy Seal
Married to Faith Keystone, best friends with Noah Jordan

Callie Templeton: Photographer
Sister Ava Templeton, married to Owen Blackwell, daughter Lily

Owen Blackwell: Hammered bass guitarist
Married to Callie Templeton, daughter Lily

Hudson Wyatt: Hammered drummer, former Formula 1 race car driver
In a relationship with Piper Lockwood

Piper Lockwood: Owns Rosie & Hank's Pussy Palace Café
In a relationship with Hudson Wyatt

Dex Munroe: Ripper Records Executive, manager for Hammered and Warning Sign

Ava Templeton: Blogger, runs Hammered website and blog, writing book on Hammered
Sister Callie Templeton

Ian Kagan: Solo artist
Brother Simon Kagan, involved with Zoe Manning

Zoe Manning: Artist/photographer
Brothers, Beckett Manning, Hayes Manning, Justin Manning, cousin

Lila Shawcross Crandall, involved with Ian Kagan

Beckett Manning:
Sister Zoe Manning, brothers Hayes Manning, Justin Manning

Hayes Manning:
Brothers, Beckett Manning, Justin Manning, sister Zoe Manning

Justin Manning:
Sister Zoe Manning, brothers Beckett Manning, Hayes Manning

Bent: security for J Town, JoEllen Foundation

Rory Ferguson: Producer/Rhythm Guitarist
Friends with Ian Kagan, friends with Flynn Sheppard, friends with Kellan McGuire

Lindsey York: Brooklyn Dawn lead singer
Best friends with Jamison DuCaine, friends with Evie Pierce

Jamison DuCaine: Brooklyn Dawn lead guitarist
Best friends with Lindsey York, friends with Evie Pierce

Teagan Daly: Brooklyn Dawn keyboards/sax
High school friends with Ricki 'Elle' Crandall

Cooper Dallas: Brooklyn Dawn drummer

Zane Landry: Brooklyn Dawn rhythm guitarist

Oz Taylor: Brooklyn Dawn bass guitarist

Alexander Nash: Record producer
Friends with Logan King

Roman: Clothing Designer

Noah Jordan: Roth Defense specialist
Brother Hunter Jordan, best friends with Quinn Alexander

Flynn Sheppard: Solo country rock artist
Friends with Luc Moreau, friends with Ian Kagan, friends with Rory Ferguson

Sabrina Price: Ripper Records executive who manages Ian Kagan

Johnny Cage: Rebel Rage lead singer and solo artist
Involved with Evie Pierce

Evie Pierce: MMA fighter
Brother Sutton Pierce, friends with Lindsey York and Jamison DuCaine, involved with Johnny Cage

Logan King: All the King's Men lead singer
Married to Isabella Grace, daughter Nichole, son Jared, friends with Alexander Nash

Isabella Grace: Bookstore owner in Winchester Falls
Married to Logan King, daughter Nichole, son Jared

Aidan Roth: Roth Defense CEO and head security detail for Warning Sign
Brother Marcus Roth

Marcus Roth: Roth Defense CEO
Brother Aidan Roth

QUINN AND ELLIOTT

Lost in Oblivion Series

Winchester Falls Trilogy

Found in Oblivion Series

Hammered Series

Rock Revenge Trilogy

Made in Oblivion Series

———⟨∞⟩———

The Boss

Tapped Out

Love Required

Boys of Fall

ABOUT THE AUTHORS

USA Today bestselling author **Cari Quinn** likes music and men, so she figured why not write about both? When she's not writing, she's screaming at men's college basketball games on TV, playing her music too loud or causing trouble. Sometimes simultaneously.

USA Today bestselling author **Taryn Elliott** is obsessed with rock stars, men, and her unending playlists—maximizing these things seemed like a very good idea. When she's not writing, you can probably find her surrounded by planner supplies trying to organize her life.

They decided to combine forces and found that hey...this writing deal is even more awesome when you collaborate with your best friend.

And so the Oblivion World was born.

For more information please visit our website:
www.quinnandelliott.com

www.ingramcontent.com/pod-product-compliance
Lightning Source LLC
Chambersburg PA
CBHW060346260626
47160CB00006B/2216